Air

M.M. Reynolds

Air

Copyright © 2025 by M.M. Reynolds

Cover Design: Sweet 15 Designs

For information contact :

contact@purplerealmpublishing.com

ISBN: 978-1-922604-55-2 (ebook)

ISBN : 978-1-922604-56-9 (paperback)

ISBN : 978-1-922604-57-6 (audio)

First Edition: September 2025

Purple Realm Publishing

Purple
Realm
PUBLISHING

If you are concerned about content, please check M.M.Reyno
ld's website for a list of warnings for all of her books.
It can be found under the 'Books' tab.

mmreynoldsauthor.com

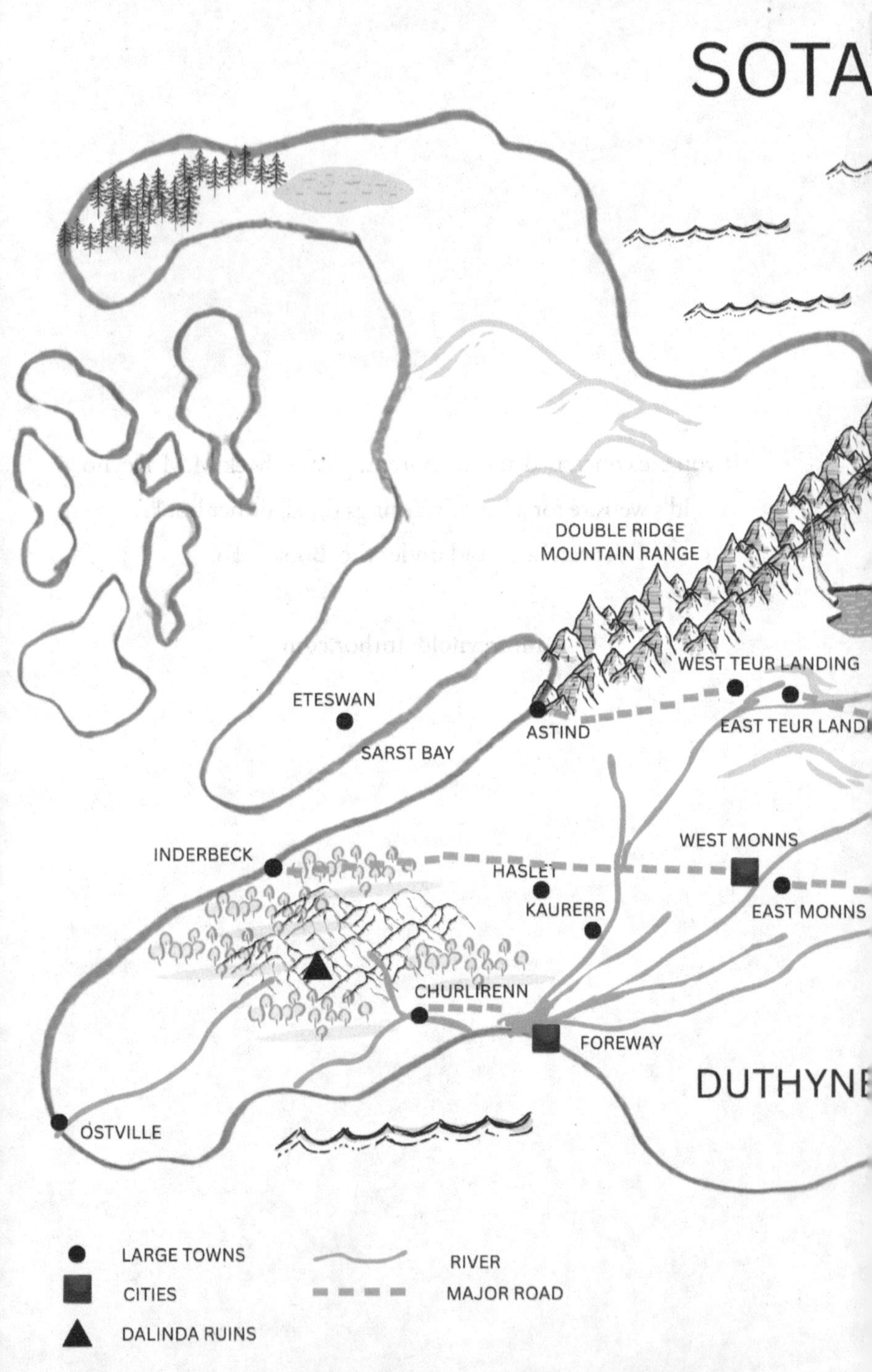

SOTA
DOUBLE RIDGE
MOUNTAIN RANGE
WEST TEUR LANDING
EAST TEUR LAND
ASTIND
ETESWAN
SARST BAY
WEST MONNS
INDERBECK
HASLET
EAST MONNS
KAURERR
CHURLIRENN
FOREWAY
DUTHYNE
ÖSTVILLE
LARGE TOWNS
CITIES
DALINDA RUINS
RIVER
MAJOR ROAD

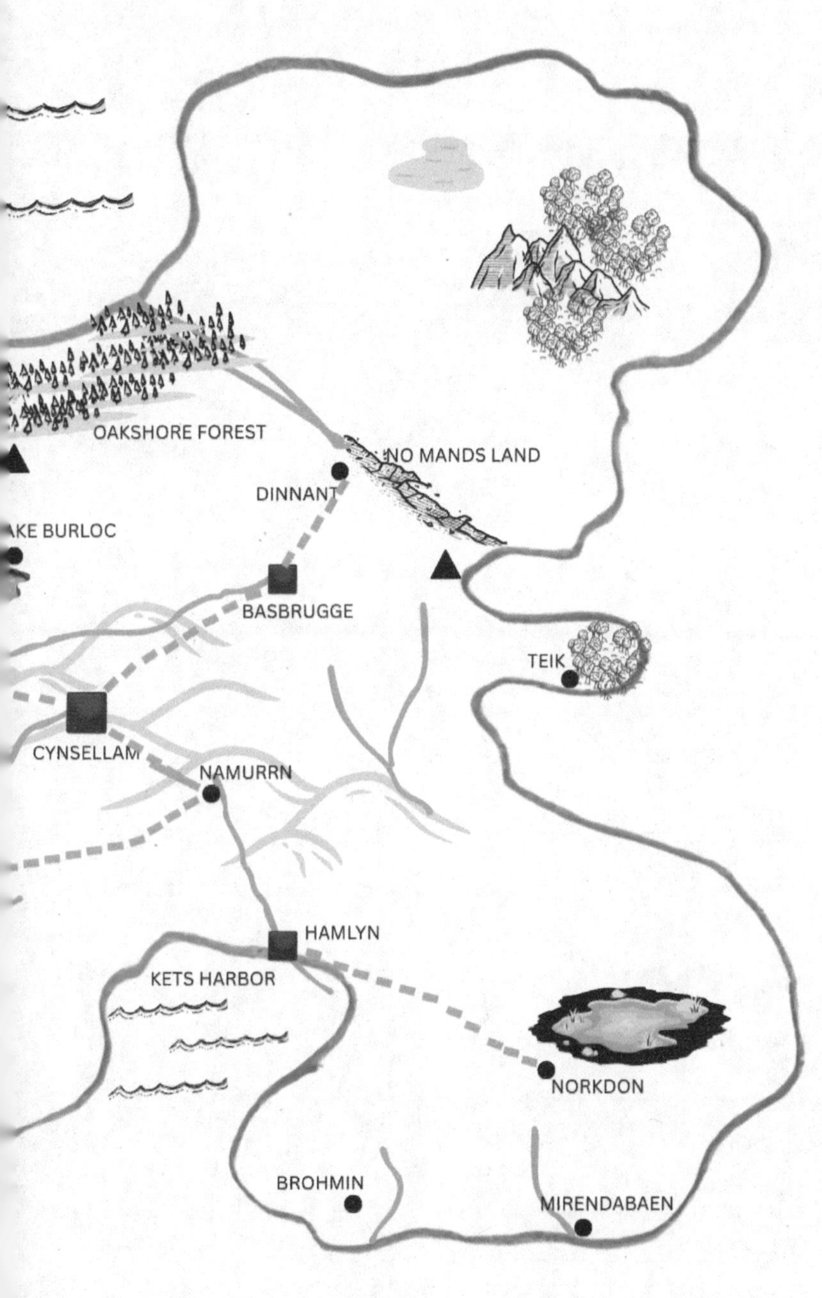
OAKSHORE FOREST
NO MANDS LAND
DINNANT
KE BURLOC
BASBRUGGE
TEIK
CYNSELLAM
NAMURRN
HAMLYN
KETS HARBOR
NORKDON
BROHMIN
MIRENDABAEN

For Kyle,
Follow your heart and dream big.
Love you.

Chapter 1
Sylvan

Sylvan drained the intricately carved pewter goblet of its unpalatable blue contents, grimacing as he swallowed the dregs before handing it over to his manservant. Jorge didn't bother to hide his smirk in answer to Sylvan's silent protest before offering his arm to the Master Shaymmi, to help him lay down as the liquid took hold immediately and started to create a film over Sylvan's normally brown eyes. Without haste, Sylvan settled his heavy frame onto the plush upholstered chaise in his private work room.

"Is there anything else, Sir?" queried Jorge as he draped a light mohair blanket over Sylvan.

"No, thank you, Jorge," answered Sylvan in a surprisingly light lilt.

Jorge bowed, even though Sylvan could no longer see him, and moved to his designated chair in the corner of the opulently decorated room. He would remain there until his master required his services.

Sylvan closed his now milky eyes and began his process of settling into a trance. He slowly tensed and released each muscle, beginning with his toes and working up his legs and through his torso. He then focused on his fingertips, again moving up his arms and finishing with his shoulders and neck. He gradually deepened his breathing so his large barrel chest rose slowly but powerfully. He stilled his thoughts, and in his mind's eye, began the process of assembling a shimmering translucent veil before him. Incrementally, he began to roll his presence out of his body and through the veil. In what he could only describe as a loud pop, his consciousness separated itself from his land-bound body and emerged fully on the other side of the veil and onto the elemental plane.

Nothing changed and everything changed simultaneously. Sylvan always savored this moment when again his sight returned, but now it was overlaid with his own unique way of experiencing the world. He could clearly see Jorge waiting and watching patiently. He could see his richly decorated room, with its deep blue and gold brocade furnishings and the well stuffed chaise surrounding his tall, overweight, slack-jawed body.

Without further reflection, Sylvan focused on moving his consciousness out of the capital city he resided in and turned his mind toward the east and his assigned province for the year. Within two beats of a heart, his consciousness found the coastal city of Hamlyn and he was very satisfied, if not a tad smug, to feel whatever it was that made him the most gifted of his peers.

When questioned, he could never explain quite how he knew when he was nearing what he was charged to find, only that it was instinct.

He took in the brilliant view of the sun clearing the horizon, casting orange rays of light across the sparkling impressive bay. Fishing boats were heading out for their daily catch while others were returning. Larger merchant ships bobbed on the gentle waves, anchored, while waiting for permission to dock at the busy city port.

Sylvan hovered effortlessly above the city walls and refined his thoughts to concentrate on the vibrations of the Elemental Plane. It was his task to find the remnants of the Ancient Ones that radiated the tainted powers of the past. Sylvan prided himself on being the most accomplished of his peers. It took incredible mental control and strength to attune oneself to the lower vibrations that the ancient artefact's emanated in the Elemental Plane when everything else gave off a much higher vibration rate. To sift your thoughts throughout the interference to find a minuscule variation was something only a score of people could do. He had been meticulously searching his new sector for two seasons and had not found an ancient artifact yet, which was frustrating and annoying as his main rival, Hadrian, had found an artifact only a season ago and was enjoying the gratitude of The First Elder.

Hovering above the residents, his consciousness swept toward the last place he had searched in the merchant area and began the tiring task of sifting through the vibrations of the elements that emanated from everything. He could distinguish from the metal of a serving plate to the wood of the closest door, or the air that ruffled hair of the citizens of Hamlyn, the packed earth in a nearby stable and the fire roaring in the nearest hearth. None of these were what he sought, nor did he acknowledge in his search. He effortlessly ignored the same five elements that mildly emanated from the human and animal population that resided here. What he, as a Shaymmi for the The First Elder, sought emitted an elemental quality that he had never been able to quantify.

Sylvan abruptly felt a distinctly different and fascinatingly strong variation coming from the wharf area of the overcrowded city. He had never encountered a vibration like it—he always compared the vibrations of people, animals, and ordinary objects as a high-pitched soprano voice and the ancient artifacts he sought as a mid-range baritone lost in the sea of voices. The depth of pitch from the unusual vibration was almost a pull on Sylvan's consciousness. Typically, the Shaymmis found minor artifacts that still gave off the tarnished impure energy of the Ancient Ones. And once a Shaymmi found the offending artifact, they would return to their body and report its exact location to their personal manservant, who would then inform those necessary to send out a patrol of monastic warriors to retrieve the object before it contaminated anyone further. Artifacts were becoming extremely rare with only a couple being found each year.

The tone of the vibration coming from the wharf area was alluring. It was a deep bass and it roughly throbbed in a much lower variation. Slowly, as if almost savoring the power of the variation, Sylvan glided above the buildings of each sector of the city. He passed over the nobles' abodes and over the merchant quarters, flying without noticing the market square below or the poorer region to his right.

As he soared above the masses, he speculated on what he might find, on what artifact from the past could possibly be giving off such strong and unusual vibrations. Typically, he and his fellow Shaymmi found jewelery items or household objects that carried a weak taint of the past. The strongest item he had ever discovered had been a metal staff buried under several lifetimes of debris in a cellar of an abandoned house at the edge of the Double Ridge Mountains and the very boundary of his sprawling country. Could this be another weapon? Had something been uncovered while excavating an old building?

He triumphantly pinpointed the throbbing vibration and swept his consciousness down into the streets to find fetid squalor as he encountered the lowest drudges of society inter-mingling with the sailors and fishermen as they disembarked their ships. The sensation and the deep thump were almost overpowering as he slowed his approach and dimmed his focus allowing some respite from the ache that was developing in his head.

A group of children played nearby, and he turned his atten-tion to them as the energy emanating from the group was al-most palpable. Gradually, he glided forward, feeling the need to be cautious but not understanding why. The typical slight pull of tainted energy when he drew near was almost overwhelming as he concentrated on one thin little girl in a dirty, tattered blue skirt. Perhaps she carried what he sought.

At that moment, the waif spun around, flailing her arms in his direction as her brown eyes widened in terror and she let out a terrified silent scream and tripped forward onto her knee.

Sylvan experienced the backlash of her fear hit him like a wall of flame and felt as if he would be engulfed in the terror that seemed to vibrate through the child as she knelt transfixed before him. His consciousness was assaulted, and he was confounded by what he had discovered. All he could do was turn and flee as he felt his body pulling him back to safety.

Chapter 2
Treena

Children gathered around her as she moved down the cobblestone street. Some walked quietly beside her, whilst others shouted their latest exploits at her to hear a word of encouragement. Others jostled for prime position of holding one of her hands, while two of the smaller ones clung to her full skirt. She looked fondly around at what she silently called "her brood" and smiled gently at one young girl who trailed along slightly behind the rest, she noticed that the diminutive girl had a slight limp. Treena had not seen the child before and briefly wondered what her story might be. Each of these children had a tale to tell… and rarely a happy one.

Collectively these children were dressed in faded, patched, worn clothes; most didn't wear shoes though the day was cool for the hot season. Collars and cuffs were frayed, dresses were torn, and the hems were either too long or too short. These children had never worn a new piece of clothing—everything was handed down.

It was nearing the fourth strike after the midday bell and Treena knew the children would be expected home soon and she needed to return to the shop, so began to give them hints that it was time to go home. Some of the more boisterous and enthusiastic children didn't take the gentle suggestions so she had to be a little more pointed.

"Okay, children, your mothers will be needing you home now. I am certain you have chores to do... now run along." Treena made a shooing motion with her now free hands to emphasize the point.

She noted that the newest addition to her brood was still trailing behind, obviously wanting something. Treena really needed to get to work, but concern and a touch of curiosity won out and she slowed until she was level with the little girl. They were now alone as the last of the rowdy older boys ran off.

"Would you like to hold my hand?" she offered in a kind voice. Usually the newcomers were too timid, having learnt harsh lessons on the streets about trusting strangers to take the proffered hand the first time but surprisingly the little girl nodded, smiled tentatively, and shyly took Treena's hand.

They walked a few feet more before she asked another question. "Won't your mother want you home to help with the chores?"

The young girl slowly shook her head. After several more steps she spoke in a sweet, soft voice. "Me Ma died."

Instantly, Treena stopped walking and bent down to the girl's level, knowing that she was definitely going to be late to help close the florist shop she owned. The girl was patient, she just stood there looking at her with big brown eyes and straggly brown hair that stuck up around her grimy face. She was too thin, as all the poor children were. There was never enough food to go round. Her filthy shirt was so faded that the original color could not be discerned, and her blue skirt was tattered at the hem and slightly too large for her. She wore no shoes, making her feet grubby and toenails dirty and torn.

"Who takes care of you?"

"Me Pa, when e's not drunk," was the sad reply.

"What is your name?"

"Aven," she replied quietly.

"Do you know my name, Aven?"

Aven nodded bashfully. "Ya Treena. The others told me ya nice and listen to em..." Aven stopped, opened her mouth to continue, looked like she thought better of it, and closed her mouth.

Treena was impressed—this one was bright. Children had a want to prattle, to feel heard, but Aven answered the questions yet didn't give away anything that could get her in trouble.

"Are you hurt, Aven? You limp, and I am wondering why."

Aven shrugged her skinny shoulders as if to imply it wasn't important and why would that matter to Treena, but she slowly lifted her skirt to reveal her left knee, bloodied and swollen.

"You are a brave girl. That must hurt a lot."

Aven nodded but remained silent.

"Would you like something to eat? You can come with me to my shop? I can give you some broth and clean your knee for you." Treena spoke gently and lightly. She didn't want to frighten the child and have her scamper off. This was one tough little girl and Treena's heart was already captivated by her earnest heart shaped face and clear warm eyes.

Slowly, as if considering her options, Aven nodded. "Food please."

Treena straightened up and offered her hand, which Aven silently took. Treena steered her down the rough dirt street and out of the poor quarter and into the sector where the area was roughly cobblestoned and the establishments slightly less shabby. It took them a further quarter strike before they reached Treena's shop on the edge of the more affluent shopping district. Treena felt a gentle tugging on her hand as Aven slowed her limping gait as they approached the shop with its shutters still open and a lady with medium brown braided hair leaning out to grab a bucket with two colorful posies from the window box.

"It's okay. No one will hurt you here and you can leave whenever you like," reassured Treena as she opened the door and ushered Aven inside. "Go, sit over there by the window while I gather a few things to clean your knee."

Before Aven could do more than nod, Treena had walked briskly through a door, muttering something quietly to the lady collecting buckets from the flower box type windowsills.

Quickly Treena gathered a few things from the open shelves in her storeroom and went back out into the store. She didn't want to give Aven a chance to change her mind and leave.

"Here we go," she announced brightly as she came through the door. Treena tried not to notice Aven jump and wondered why the girl reacted that way. Placing the items on a foot stool beside Aven, Treena looked at the older woman in the room. "Thedra, this is Aven. Could you please find her some broth and bread while I clean her knee?"

Thedra turned from her task and Treena noticed Aven attempt to sit a little straighter—Thedra had that effect on people. With her high cheekbones and slender brows, she managed to tilt her chin up in just the right way to give her a slightly superior air without ever saying anything. She was stunning with few wrinkles to give away her age of forty-five and a body that had never seen the ravages of carrying a child or giving birth could still turn the eye of most men.

"Nice to meet you, Aven. I'll go fetch your broth. I'm sure you are hungry—all children seem to always be hungry." The last was said in a slightly puzzled tone.

Aven finally found her voice and said quietly, "Thank you."

Treena sat on the clean swept wooden floor and put Aven's foot in her lap.

"Show me that knee."

Aven tried to pull her foot away. "Ma'am, me foot will get ye dirty."

"It's just dirt, it will wash out. I'm more concerned about cleaning that knee. Now, lift that skirt out the way please."

In very short order, Treena managed to clean the knee, put a healing salve on, and wrap it. At no time did Aven complain about pain as the wound was cleaned.

"How did you do this?"

"I got a fright and tripped."

Again, Treena noticed Aven's reluctance to elaborate or tell a full story, she would ust give the bare details. *What would make this lass behave this way?* she wondered. Treena had heard some of the horrific tales and seen the aftermath of what could happen to children of the poor quarter but this reticence to speak was unusual. It did not sit well with Treena. She had an almost overwhelming need to protect this child. Most children wanted a shoulder to cry on or someone to listen to their woes and give them reassurance and understanding, especially when home life was difficult.

"I still have quite a few tasks to do to close up the shop. Would you like to help me while we wait for your broth?"

Aven hesitated but eventually nodded her agreeance.

"Any time you need to go home, just say so, and I will walk you back," Treena assured her as she stood up and began to clean up.

"What would ye want me to do?"

"There should still be a few empty buckets in the window boxes to be collected. There is a grate in the road at the corner two shops down that you can tip the water from the buckets down. There is no rush, so don't do anything to strain that knee. There is still a good strike of sunlight left." Treena deliberately walked out the front of the shop and removed the lid from a low large barrel, giving Aven no time to protest.

As Treena went about her closing routine, while keeping an eye on Aven, Thedra arrived with a large wooden bowl of broth and a substantial chunk of white bread.

"Come, child, and eat."

Aven nodded. "I am almost finished." She lifted the two final buckets in her hands and headed toward the corner grate.

Treena barely concealed her smile as she waited for Thedra to start. She wasn't disappointed.

"Why do you have to bring them all home?" the older woman began with exasperation etched on her face. "Not every hurt or lonely child is your problem."

"This one is different," Treena began. "I can't explain it, but there is something there. She is too reserved, like she doesn't want to make a noise so she is noticed. She walks softly and almost barely breathes as if even that may be noticed. She startles too easily."

Thedra frowned. "Fine, have it your way. Rescue them all. It's your money and it is a worthy thing to do with your time. Just don't get side tracked from the bigger picture."

Treena smiled. "You didn't hear me. There is something different about this one."

They both watched Aven limp slowly back with the buckets. "It's been seventeen years," Treena said.

"She is too young," Thedra answered.

All Treena could do was shrug.

They both followed Aven into the shop and watched her stack the remaining buckets.

"Come, we shall wash our hands before we eat. Thedra, could you please get us two more bowls of broth? I think we should join Aven for her meal."

Aven meekly followed Treena into the storeroom, and again, Treena watched the slight hesitation before stepping over the threshold. They quickly washed their hands and came back into the shop to see Thedra setting down a tray with two more bowls of broth and the remaining bread. Aven took her bowl of broth and sat on the foot stool, leaving the chair for Thedra and the work stool behind the counter for Treena.

After a few quiet mouthfuls Treena asked, "Aven, how old are you?"

"Eleven."

Treena was surprised to hear that as she would have guessed her to be eight. By the raised eyebrows on Thedra, she was astonished too.

Thedra nodded to Treena. "Eleven," she repeated. "Younger than most but not unheard of."

Chapter 3
Sylvan

Sylvan waited impatiently for his eyes to return to their full normal vision. He still felt out of sorts with his mind having almost ungracefully raced back across the elemental plane to re-enter his body. Sylvan had never rushed the process before and wasn't sure it had been such a good idea. It was like his consciousness hadn't settled into its normal space and he felt nauseated.

"Jorge, run a bath and set out an outfit. I need to see The First Elder promptly. Have it arranged while I bathe." He knew his encounter was important, but he still needed to keep up appearances; after all, he was the Master Shaymmi.

As Sylvan continued to rest on the chaise lounge and watch his manservant, his vision had cleared enough to make out his rosy cheeks in his round face as he efficiently moved around the work room while he could hear the bath running he turned his thoughts to what he had just experienced. *How was it possible that a small female child could hold such potent tainted power of an ancient artifact? Who was she? How was it even conceivable? It didn't make sense, but it was the only explanation as she hadn't appeared to be holding anything that emanated such power.*

"Sir, your bath is ready." Jorge came forward and helped Sylvan to stand. He walked him into the adjoining bedroom and helped him disrobe before continuing on to the bathroom.

As they walked past the burnished, framed sheet of gold that was Sylvan's beautiful mirror, he absently sucked in his pale paunch. Jorge arched an eyebrow at him but refrained from commenting. Sylvan glared at Jorge but also chose not to speak.

With Jorge's aid, Sylvan was soon settled into the welcoming hot water of his over-sized gold, claw foot tub that sat in the center of the wood paneled bathroom. As his muscles relaxed and his eyesight completely cleared, he concentrated on nothing more than watching the steam creep over the bath edge and the water surface swirl with multi-colored circular patterns of essential oils. His consciousness finally felt like it had settled back into his body properly, and he was savoring the moment. As his mind wandered, and his eyes slowly touched on the gold ornaments in the room, a slow smile spread across his face. The beautiful trinkets and exotic ornaments in this room and the suite beyond had been gifts from The First Elder for finding ancient artifacts and from patrons who sought Sylvan's favor because he was the Master Shaymmi and was thought to hold sway with. His smile grew into a smirk as he began to imagine the gifts he would receive once news spread of his latest find! The thought of Hadrian's face crumbling with frustration was enough to make him break into a self-satisfied grin.

The next half strike was spent fantasizing about the expensive gifts and favors he could request once the girl had been found and verified. Jorge interrupted Sylvan's musings by announcing, "You are expected at the end of afternoon services, which is a strike away. Would you like me to wash your hair?"

"Yes, and I have quite a knot in my right shoulder that needs working on."

Sylvan lounged in the antechamber of The First Elder's outer office and nibbled on a piece of fruit. Making certain that all the juices landed on the ornate silver plate rather than his perfect ensemble. Indigo loose fitting silk shirt with cuffs and collar in elaborate brocaded silver, black loose pants in the best silk and a sleeveless black over robe in the finest goat hair money could buy with the same patterned silver brocade along the edges, black leather house slippers completed the meticulous look. Sylvan handed back the plate and accepted the proffered napkin by the serving monk who silently stood in the corner when not required.

Swiftly the heavy double doors were swung outward and The First Elder's favored servant monk beckoned for Sylvan to enter. Without fuss, Sylvan followed the monk into the sumptuously furnished office of the ruler of Duthyne and silently cursed as he noticed the twin teenage boys that sat quietly on one of the many plush olive-green lounges that were clumped in seating areas around the large office. He stopped and looked at them expectantly.

One boy stood swiftly and bowed deeply and respectfully, the other was a fraction later in his standing and almost insolent in his bow. Sylvan inclined his head in response.

"Matteo, Mathias."

Both responded, "Master Shaymmi."

Without further interaction, Sylvan turned and strode further into the office and toward the large white oak desk that dominated the back of the room. He bowed deeply to The First Elder who sat behind his desk in his afternoon service vestments. The only thing missing was the white mitre with its deep gold and olive-green embroidery that usually covered his bald head. Sylvan noted as he straightened that the mitre sat on a small table in the back corner.

The First Elder stood, his six-foot frame matching Sylvan's own taller than average height, and inclined his head.

"Master Shaymmi, you asked to see me? Please come and join us for refreshments." He indicated to where the twins reclined.

Sylvan did his best to hide his irritation at having to deal with the teens.

"I have very interesting news from my planing this morning that I believe you should know about personally."

"Yes, I'm told Jorge intimated as much." The First Elder sat and nodded to his servant monk who efficiently poured drinks for everyone before retiring back to his corner.

They sipped in silence for a while, and Sylvan took a moment to study the twins—he had difficulty telling them apart and was assured by Jorge that so did everyone else. They were about 5'7", the average height of a Duthynian, and had all the common features of the race: brown eyes and brown hair and a square face. They wore their hair long, below the shoulder, but not braided as was the fashion but hanging free and continually falling across their face. Typical teenagers, always trying to be that little bit different to their elders.

"How do your studies go?" enquired The First Elder of the teens.

"Slowly," one replied in a slightly raspy voice. "There seems to be not much time for us."

"First Elder, what he meant was that we have seemed to have progressed as far as we can without further instruction and now wait for the Shaymmi to find time in their busy schedules of service to you to continue our studies." The boy went on enthusiastically, adding, "I have been spending my spare time in the library, and Matteo has been out learning about the care of your hounds."

The First Elder turned to look at Sylvan and raised a manicured brown eyebrow in the way of asking for an explanation.

Typical teenagers, it's all about them. I've told them often enough that I am too busy to take on their basic training and that only if one shows the level of skill to be a Master Shaymmi will I take over. Sylvan placed his beautifully crafted goblet on the white oak low table and cleared his throat. *I may be able to turn this to my advantage if I play this right.*

"I will admit that I do not have the time, and have told them as much, to take on the role as tutor. However, as Master Shaymmi, I take my responsibilities seriously and the competent instruction of our trainee Shaymmi is essential to our ongoing success in serving you. To this end I asked Hadrian, a most adept Shaymmi and only a step below me in power and skill, to take on the role as mentor. I am aghast to discover that she has not taken on this vital task and that my choice has been an error in judgement on my behalf. I seek to beg your forgiveness on this account."

The First Elder steepled his fingertips, resting them on his lips, just below his large hooked nose and said nothing for several minutes. Sylvan sat still, but relaxed while Matteo and Mathias fidgeted in their seats. Finally, The First Elder spoke.

"That is disappointing to hear. You honor the Church of the One with your commitment and dedication to your task, Sylvan, but we must always remember we were young and eager to learn once and must provide guidance to those that seek it. Please speak to Hadrian again regarding the continued training of these boys and take it upon yourself to provide adequate supervision that all is progressing accordingly."

"I am honored to serve in any way you deem worthy."

"Excellent." The First Elder turned to the twins. "Would you two please excuse us? We have other matters to discuss."

Both young men promptly stood and bowed deeply, first to The First Elder then to Sylvan before hurrying out of the room.

"Now, what did you need to see me about that I put off an appointment with Cardinal Illyius?"

Sylvan could barely contain his pride as he straightened in his seat. "I have found a most surprising artifact. One with more depth of power than ever previously discovered."

Leaning eagerly forward, The First Elder let his mask of calm slip for a brief time.

"Where?"

"In Hamlyn, in the wharf sector."

"The wharf sector? How has this not been detected before? What type of artifact would give off such tainted power?"

"This artifact is unique." For some reason that he could not ascertain, Sylvan was enjoying the sense of suspense he was creating by drawing out the most astonishing detail. Maybe it was ego. That for once he had control of the conversation with the ultimate ruler of The Church of the One?

"How?" The First Elder was sitting at the edge of his seat.

"It is a little girl!"

"What?" exploded The First Elder. "How is that possible?"

"I don't know, but it was an experience unlike any other I have had on the Elemental Plane. Her vibrating power was immense. We must find her immediately before she contaminates anyone."

"Yes. For the good of all living in the wharf sector of Hamlyn, she must be detained. They must also ascertain where she lives to make certain she does not have a hidden artifact that's power has infected her. Sylvan, write down a detailed description of her and the surrounding area so I can pass it onto Arch Deacon Ulrick of Hamlyn." The First Elder stood. "While you do that, I will prepare the Spirit Mirror."

Chapter 4

Treena

Treena opened the door to the shop to discover Aven waiting patiently on the other side.

"Why did you not knock? Have you been waiting long?"

"Nah, just got ere."

"So, you have decided to agree to my offer that you help me today in payment for me tending your knee and feeding you yesterday?"

Aven simply nodded.

"Good. First thing I do everyday is go to the flower market. Would you like to join me? It is not too far a walk so it shouldn't bother your knee, but you must tell me if it becomes too sore to walk," Treena warned.

For the first time since meeting the young girl, Aven gave Treena a genuine smile.

"Ya, I would like to go to the flower market."

"Have you eaten this morning?"

Aven shook her head.

"Would you like an apple?"

"Ya, please."

Treena went back into the shop and came out a few moments later with two shiny green apples and handed one to Aven.

"Let's go."

They spent the next strike in the first rays of the glorious morning surrounded by the subtle scents of just blooming flowers. Treena loved these small moments in her life. The flower market was a spectacular sight as it sat just inside one of the gates that allowed entrance into the city. It was the second largest gate as it was designed for the farmers to bring in their harvests. In the center of the circular market was a huge ornamental water fountain with a statue of the One God with his five faces encircling his head. Treena pointed out how to pick the best flowers that were only just beginning to blossom, what were about to go out of season, and what were popular at the moment. One of her bigger clients was the monastery, where she provided bouquets for the daily services, plus several bouquets that went to each of the four larger chapels that serviced the sectors. She explained that she needed specific flowers and foliage for those bouquets. After a lively haggle with the cartman, who would deliver all her purchases to the shop once they were loaded, Treena suggested that they stop and try a breakfast pastry from a street cart that sat near the fountain.

They sat in silence on the edge of the fountain, Treena with her back resolutely facing away from the statue in her own personal protest for the lies the Church now taught. Treena watched Aven slowly nibble away at her berry pastry with a wide smile.

"Are you enjoying that?"

Aven smiled through the flakes of pastry and nodded enthusiastically.

"First time," she explained.

"We shall have to make sure you have it again then." Treena watched the hustle and bustle as the flower and herb vendors began to pack up to make way for the fresh fruit and vegetable traders that now brought their wares in through the gate for their time to sell. The grain merchants had been in before dawn, before the flower and herbs, and the live animals would be brought in after the fruit and vegetables. This way the grain could be ground in the mills ready for bread preparation the following day and the animals would be slaughtered and carved overnight. Having the livestock last in also gave the cleaners time to sweep the area before the process started again the following predawn.

"Is your knee rested? Are you ready for the walk back?" enquired Treena.

"Ya."

"Let's go then." Treena stood and brushed the last little pieces of gorgeous flaky pastry off her deep blue skirt and white lace bodice, that was just a hint too revealing of her assets.

The remainder of the morning was spent with Treena showing Aven how the church bouquets were made first as the delivery men would be by soon to pick them up and distribute them for the afternoon services. More small and large bouquets were made to go in the buckets in the special window boxes and then finally the leftover flowers from the previous day were pulled apart and put into tiny posies that were bought by the street vendors to sell out in the city. All the while, customers came in and ordered bouquets for special events or purchased the ones already made in the buckets. Treena found Aven to be very helpful and eager to learn, like most poor sector children they knew what hard work was and never complained because they could have been doing something far less appealing.

"Well, I'm off," announced Thedra at the midday strike, walking out of the storeroom with a large white and grey tapestry shoulder bag with swirls of silver thread on it. "Let's hope her Ladyship is a little less demanding this time."

"Have fun." Treena smiled.

"Bye," Aven replied softly.

She looked at Treena but didn't ask. Instead, she returned to her current job of stripping white roses of their thorns.

Treena volunteered the information. "Oh, Thedra doesn't actually work here, she is just helping me out until I find a new assistant. My former assistant married one of the flower vendors so now she works for him selecting the flowers from the farmers. It worked out well for them. Thedra is a talented seamstress who lives in Namurrn but comes here once or twice a cycle to create clothes for the wealthy citizens of Hamlyn for the festivals and celebrations. Her skills are very much in demand but some of her clients can be temperamental."

Aven nodded her understanding. "Has she ever made you somefing?"

"A few things. Now, finish up there. I want to look at your knee to make sure no infection has set in."

Aven quickly tidied up while Treena found her first aid supplies and washed her hands before sitting on the floor and again putting Aven's dirty foot in her lap. Treena removed the bandage and re-cleaned the wound. It was looking like it wouldn't scar too badly and there was no heat of inflammation to indicate an infection. She spread salve over the cut and wrapped it in a clean bandage.

"Aven, how did you trip?" she asked.

Aven looked anywhere but at Treena.

"It's okay, you can tell me."

"You won't believe me," Aven whispered.

"I know many things that people wouldn't believe are true. You must trust me that I will believe you." Treena tried to fill her voice with warmth and understanding.

"I saw somefing, and it scared me."

Treena noticed Aven's trembling hands and reached out to hold them.

"It's okay, just take it slowly."

Instead of Aven grabbing Treena's hands, she flung herself into Treena's crossed-legged lap, wrapping her arms around her neck. Treena could feel the young girl's too thin body shake uncontrollably. *What could possibly have done this to her?*

"Aven, trust me, please. I will believe you."

Aven spoke hesitantly but the trembling didn't stop. "I was playing in the street wif the other young uns when a—" She stopped and gulped before going on. "When a ghost came out of the air above me head." She buried her head in Treena's shoulder and shook but did not make a sound.

This child is used to doing everything quietly, I wonder why? Treena thought while she patted Aven's short-cropped hair.

"I believe you, but I want to ask you some questions. Is that okay?"

Aven nodded into Treena's shoulder.

"Why do you think it was a ghost?"

"It was a man that ye could see through and he was over-ing over me head." She swallowed and lifted her head to look earnestly at Treena. "He made me feel funny too."

"How did he make you feel funny?"

"Hard to say. Made somefing inside feel funny. In ere—" She pointed to her lower rib cage. "No one else saw it. They fink I made it up. Do you fink it's a ghost?"

"I'm not sure, but I know you saw something. Has anything happened since then?"

"Nah."

Treena noticed that Aven had finally stopped shaking. "Do you feel better?"

"Yes, fank you." She climbed out of Treena's lap and flattened her tattered skirt down.

"You hungry? It's lunch time."

Aven smiled and nodded.

Treena laughed. "Thedra's right. You young ones are always hungry."

Chapter 5

Hadrian

Hadrian flung a cushion at Cyrus, who ducked easily.

"Can you believe he said that?" she shouted.

Cyrus put up his hands in defense of more cushion hurling.

"No, but why are you throwing stuff at me?"

She grabbed another offending plush cushion off the main lounge in her private sitting room and threw it at him.

"Because it makes me feel better." She let out a growl. "That pompous know-it-all is so damn obnoxious. Who does he think he is?" She stalked around the lounge and threw herself down on a chair opposite Cyrus. "The First Elder has asked me to enquire as to why the Trainee Shaymmi are not being tutored correctly. You were instructed to see to their study, and nothing has been done." Hadrian did a fair imitation of Sylvan's light lilt. Her brown, almond-shaped eyes blazed as she recalled the scene. "Sylvan knows there has been no such discussion of me training anyone, but I can't go to The First Elder and call his favorite and most prolific Shaymmi a liar."

Cyrus ducked another flying cushion and laughed.

Hadrian's eyes narrowed. "You are laughing at me."

"Well, yes. I know you are angry, but you are adorable when you are annoyed."

"Don't try to charm me. That man is the bane of my existence. If he was not here, I would be the strongest Shaymmi. I would be the Master and not have to take orders from anyone but The First Elder."

Cyrus stood and went to a sideboard where he poured himself a wine. He felt uncomfortable asking Hadrian's manservant, Garm, who stood waiting to serve in the corner to do it.

"Do you want one?" He waved the carafe.

"Yes."

He poured her one and handed it to her before settling back on the now denuded lounge.

"Have you heard the newest rumor?" she went on.

"No, what is the latest gossip and how accurate do you think it is?"

"Garm overheard one of The First Elder's servants whispering about it when he went into the kitchen earlier today."

Cyrus turned his face to Garm. "How accurate?"

"Fairly accurate. The source is not prone to exaggerate too much," the manservant confirmed.

Hadrian flicked what she knew to be her greatest asset: her thick, soft, waist length auburn hair to regain Cyrus attention.

"I hate to admit it, but it would appear that Sylvan has again outperformed us all and found the most powerful tainted artifact yet."

"Really? Where?" Cyrus lent forward.

"Somewhere in Hamlyn. But that is not the juiciest part of the story..." She left him hanging.

"Hadrian," growled Cyrus.

"Cyrus," she growled back.

He stood and stalked toward her. She stood to match his advance. She was a few inches taller than him normally but in her private rooms she always went barefoot and he with his healed boots on became about the same height. Without warning, he crushed his lips to hers and she felt the same thrill she always did when he took control. He held her with one arm around her waist while his other hand grabbed a handful of her luxurious hair at the back of her head. His tongue fought to enter her mouth and join with his hers. She eventually gave in and opened her mouth to his advances. Her own hands moved down his muscled back to grab his buttocks firmly. She gently pushed her hips forward while she held him firm and moaned into his mouth.

Without pulling his body away he moved his head back to look at her and grinned, "What is the best bit?"

She looked at him and felt a pull in her lower tummy as she admired his handsome face, even with his slightly receding hairline at such an early age, he was achingly desirable to her. Laughing she circled her hips into his groin.

"Isn't that the best bit?"

Cyrus pulled gently on the handful of hair he held and tugged her head back, exposing her throat. He began to nibble under her ear and slowly moved across her neck to the lobe of her other ear. Cyrus stopped and breathed in her ear, "That's a great bit too, but not what I want to know."

She giggled and moved her hands to untie the cord in his trousers, but he was quicker and took a step back leaving her body wanting him. She stamped her foot in protest.

"That's not playing fair."

"The sooner you talk, the quicker we get back to the good stuff. And I have some great stuff in mind." He leered at her before moving further away.

"Really? That does sound inviting. Oh, very well," she pouted and gave in. "If what Garm heard is to be believed, the artifact is actually a young girl!" she explained triumphantly.

"But everything you have ever told me is about objects from the past, tarnished by the corroded power of the forbidden." Cyrus was incredulous.

"I know what I have told you, and you know to keep that to yourself or there will be trouble for you and me." She hoped he realized that her threat was serious. She had told him many secrets only the Shaymmi and the inner circle of the Church of the One God knew because he had flattered her and was handsome and seemed to want her even though she was several years older than him. There had been a pull, a connection that she couldn't explain. Then it had eventually turned to sex, and she had revealed more of her true nature and lust for power, and instead of being repulsed, he was turned on and insatiable.

Cyrus stepped forward and picked her up. Even though she had a firm strong body, his was more muscular and moved to carry her to the bedroom. "I know what you have risked, and I would never betray you."

A knock on the door stopped him in his march to the bed chamber. He gently put her down. Hadrian pouted but didn't resist.

"Garm, see what they want," she told him while she took a step away from Cyrus, making certain whoever was at the door didn't get the wrong idea about the two of them. She didn't need the gossip.

Garm opened the door to reveal a monk who handed over a sheet of paper.

"For Shaymmi Hadrian." He spoke formally before bowing and leaving.

Hadrian took the letter from Garm and looked at the handwriting of her name on the front. It was from her father. She opened the letter warily and read it quickly. Her annoyance at being interrupted changed into anger as she read her father's praise of the new exceptional student he had this year and how promising they were. She would never live up to his expectations. Hadrian blew out her breath and glared at both Garm and Cyrus.

"I need to find a way to beat Sylvan." She didn't add that maybe then her father would see just how special she was.

Chapter 6

Treena

Thedra sat sipping her cup of sweetened tea, with her feet resting on the stool in the florist shop, enjoying a break before starting the process of closing the shop for the evening. Treena sat on the stool behind the serving counter with her elbows resting on the bench and her chin resting in her hands.

"Maybe we should ask Elldean Stiann?" suggested Thedra.

"Yes, the Lore Keeper might know what other signs we should be looking for. But I tell you that she is special. Unique. One of us or not, there is something different about her."

"Fine, I will trust your instincts and believe you are not just being overprotective and mother-henning her."

Treena snorted. "I may have been at the start, but her description of the ghost man and her gut response made me assess my responses to her, and whilst I am the first to help others, this need for me to protect her is stronger."

"Send for Reza and arrange to see Elldean Stiann sooner rather than later, as well as start seriously looking for a new assistant, please. I need to get back to Namurrn."

"Why do you need to get back so quickly?" Treena asked slyly. "You don't usually need to be back at a certain time."

Before Thedra could reply, there was a pounding on the door.

"Treena! Treena! Help!" a young male voice yelled.

Treena jumped off the stool and stood but Thedra was closer and she yanked open the door to find a young boy, no more than ten, standing there panting with a slowly bleeding gash on his forehead.

"What's wrong?"

"Soldiers came while we were playing and took Aven. Some of us tried to stop em but they hurt us. I think Bree has a broken arm. You ave to come help," he begged.

Treena nodded. "Deek, this is Thedra, she is going to wash and dress your head while I gather some extra things for my first aid bag and then we will go with you."

Deek allowed himself to be led into the shop and sat quietly while Thedra tended his wound and Treena disappeared into the storeroom to collect extra supplies. Within a short time, he was patched up and all three were ready to go. They hurried through the streets that were busier than normal as everyone began to make their way home or to start their night shift at work. Treena constantly found her mind wondering about what had happened, and why would they take Aven? She forced herself to focus. She needed to get to the other children and find out all she could before she made decisions on what to do next.

They arrived in the darkening wide alley where the poor and street children tended to play to stay out of the way of their elders to find several children sobbing, a few more sitting on the packed earth with varying degrees of injuries, and a handful of young men blocking the entrance.

"Braith sent us," one of the older boys explained as they made room for them to pass into the alley. "He said to tell you that he has sent for a chirurgeon."

Treena clasped the speaker on the upper arm. "Thank you."

As she moved into the alley, she was quickly surrounded by the crying youngsters.

"Hush, you are safe," she attempted to reassure them. Thedra took the bag from Treena that held the first aid supplies and kept moving toward the injured children while Treena knelt on one knee and looked all of them over quickly. She hugged them all and ascertained that while they were shaken there were no obvious injuries. "Are any of you hurt?"

"Nah."

"They took Aven."

"They hurt Bree bad."

Treena spoke quietly but firmly. "I need you to calm down and help me. Can you help me?" She knew that refocusing these frightened children was the quickest way to help them. "Who knows where Bree lives?"

One of the girls, Hailey, nodded. "Me."

"Do you think you could take one of the older boys and fetch her Ma?"

Hailey squared her shoulders, sniffed, and nodded agreement.

"Thank you, Hailey. I do need you to come back too so you can tell me what happened to Aven." Treena turned to the young man she had spoken to earlier. "Can one of you please go with Hailey to fetch the injured child's Ma?"

"Ya, we can do that for ye."

Turning back to the remaining children, she said, "The rest of you need to help your friends by keeping out of the way and doing what I ask."

They all nodded in agreement. Treena moved to where Thedra was treating the obviously broken lower arm of Bree. The bone had not broken through but there was a large suspicious lump.

"How is it?"

Thedra didn't look up as she cradled Bree's arm. "I'll keep her stabilised until the chirurgeon arrives. Can you take care of the others?"

Treena looked around. There were only two children left that looked to have minor injuries.

"No problem." Treena quickly patched up the bleeding elbow of a little boy, Timmy, who was no more than six years old and what looked to be a sprained ankle of an older teen who Treena had not met before. "What's your name?"

"I'm Freya. Ma had sent me to get Deek when the soldiers came. One of em pushed Deek into the wall so I jumped on his back, and he threw me off. When I fell, I landed badly and hurt me ankle," she explained.

Treena sat back from wrapping Freya's ankle. "A couple of days on light duties and you'll be fine." The children figured out that Treena had no more people to fix so gathered around her as they usually did. "Freya, were you here when the soldiers arrived?"

"No, I only came when they were already holding Aven and the kids were yelling at them to leave her alone." Freya smiled fondly at Deek. "They were all very brave trying to help their friend."

"Deek, can you tell me what happened?" asked Treena.

"We were jus playing and Aven had come to tell us about her day wif ya. She told us she helped ya wif the flowers at the market and had lots of fun. We were jus playing and talkin," he repeated.

"Did the soldiers say anything when they came?" Treena tried to help him remember.

"I didn't hear nofing. They just came in and grabbed her."

"No, that's wrong," Timmy chimed in. "I heard the churchman say, 'that's the one,' and he pointed at her."

"A churchman was with them?"

All the children nodded.

Freya confirmed it. "By the look of his church clothes he was a Deacon."

Treena frowned. *What was a Deacon doing in the wharf sector? And why was he looking for Aven. I don't like where this appears to be going.*

"Can anyone tell me how many soldiers there were with the Deacon?"

Freya replied, "I would guess the typical squad of ten."

The children all began to agree at once. Holding up her hand, Treena tried to quiet them. "Is there anything else that happened?"

"No. It was all over fairly quickly"

The young man who seemed to be in charge of the guards sent by Braith interrupted.

"Excuse me, Treena, but the chirurgeon is ere."

Treena emptied her lap of children and stood.

"Unless anyone can think of anything else, I think it's all time you went home. Thank you for trying to help Aven." She quickly went to the doctor and introduced herself. "Please know that any costs are to be sent to the Heavenly Scents Florist Shop in the Shopping district of the Merchant Sector. The girl's name is Bree, and her mother will be here shortly."

The chirurgeon nodded and moved quickly to his patient, conferring with Thedra for several minutes. In that time, Hailey returned with Bree's Ma, who took one look at her daughter and burst into tears. Bree bravely reassured her mother that it wasn't too painful. The chirurgeon informed them that she would need to have her arm set, but that she would need to go to his offices to do it and that it would be better for Bree if she simply walked there as sitting in a cart would bump and jar the arm too much. Without being asked, the young man that had been sent with Hailey to get Bree's mother went with them when they all left for the office.

Treena helped Thedra clean up the mess that had been created, and under that guise, searched the area for any clues that might figure out what had happened.

"Do you feel anything?" Treena asked Thedra softly.

"No, just what the children reported. Many people, confusion and fear. Can you get anything?"

Treena shook her head. "There's no water here—only what we brought with us in the skins."

"Very well. There is nothing keeping us here. Thank the boy guards and let's get back to the shop."

Chapter 7
Treena

"The Lord of Thieves will see you now."

"It's about time." Treena was annoyed. They had been waiting in the foul smelling, dank sewer system for half a strike. She followed the henchman through the door and into a moderate sized room that was dominated by a large desk with several chairs placed in front. A man in his early thirties with a high forehead, square jaw, and thin lips sat behind the desk with a frown on his strong face.

As Treena and Thedra settled into the chairs, he nodded and everyone else left the room, leaving the three of them alone.

"Oh, stop looking so grumpy," Treena admonished.

Instead of responding, he stood and came around the desk and gave Thedra a warm hug. "It's been years. How have you been?"

"Why would you get a desk so large? If soldiers come snooping, how will you ever hide that?"

Braith laughed. "Ah, same old Thedra. Forever bringing me down to earth." He perched on the edge of his too large desk. "Never fear. Unless you know what to look for, the door is virtually impossible to find and can only be opened from the inside." He moved to stand in front of Treena. "Do I not get a hello from my oldest friend?"

Treena grunted but stood and quickly hugged Braith. "I'm sorry, I'm worried about Aven, and I need your help. I just got word where she is being held, and we don't have a lot of time."

"Ah, yes, your newest recruit. How big has your flock become?" He smiled warmly before changing topics. "Do you know what the church wants with her?"

"I have a question for you," interrupted Thedra. "Why did you send those young men to guard the children when Aven was taken? How did you know she was taken so quickly?"

Braith coughed uncomfortably. "Deek had been in the alley playing look-out for me for something else. When Aven was taken, he reported to his assigned contact and explained that he had to leave to get Treena as she needed to know. News gets to me quickly when necessary, and I like to be helpful to my friends so sent the guards to protect the children until you arrived."

"What was Deek doing for you, Braith?" Treena asked quietly.

"He was just keeping an eye out for someone for me." Braith tried to change subjects. "Can I offer you a refreshment? Perhaps a bite to eat?"

"You know how I feel about you using the children for your business," she warned, ignoring his offers.

Braith sighed and headed back around to his side of the desk and sat down. "Yes, Treena, I'm very aware of your attitude, we have been over this. You must realize that I'm not asking them to steal anything. Their families need money, and I need children on occasion to be places others can't. We have been over this. They could be being asked to do things far worse than reporting to me about certain people," he said defensively.

"This is not the time to argue, children," Thedra reminded them.

"Sorry, Thedra, we do like to bicker. Why does the church want Aven?" Braith didn't sound sorry at all.

Treena answered, "We don't know, but that changes nothing. We still need to get her back."

Braith frowned. "Now, don't get upset, but why? I know you like to rescue everyone, but the church obviously wants her, so is it wise to bring the church down on you? They could make you disappear too. You know every year they get more ruthless and less subtle about forcing the populace to do whatever they command."

Treena reigned in the retort she had for Braith as it wouldn't be helpful to start bickering again. He only knew half the story and she wasn't about to tell him about Aven seeing floating ghosts and that there was a connection between the two of them that Treena couldn't explain yet. From his viewpoint, avoiding the church was always a good decision and you didn't become Lord of the Thieves without making difficult choices.

"My contact in the monastery says she is in a dungeon, where they keep the 'special criminals,' and that they will be transporting her to Cynsellam before dawn tomorrow. That gives us less than a day to come up with a rescue plan." Treena glared at Braith. "And we will be rescuing her."

He held up his hands in surrender. "I didn't know you had friends in the monastery."

Treena shrugged. "He is the head chef for the Arch Deacon. I met him when I had to co-ordinate flowers for a special event a few cycles ago. He is very talented and risen through the kitchen quickly for his age."

"Do you know how she is being transported?"

"In the typical transport cart, they transfer all their 'special cargo' in. It is just a box on wheels with a single door, with a barred window, that is drawn by two horses. It would fit no more than two people," explained Treena.

"What do you mean by 'special cargo'?" asked Thedra.

Treena shook her head. "No one really knows. Rumors have been circulating for as long as I can remember, and it ranges from criminals to anything of value that has to be sent to The First Elder. But the good news is that the cart has never been attacked, so the thing is never heavily guarded. It is simply driven out of the gates of the monastery to the Wharf area with a driver and four guards and loaded onto one of the Church barges that travel to Namurrn. It is always done in the predawn before the city wakes and sailors and fisherman set sail on the morning tide out of the harbor."

"How clever of them," remarked Braith. "All this time and I, the master thief, have not heard a whisper of goods being moved. I just assumed it was people they wanted removed."

Braith whistled softly between his teeth as he sat behind his desk staring into air.

Thedra shifted in her seat but remained silent. Treena smiled to herself as she listened to Braith whistle. It drove some people crazy, but she knew it was his way of thinking over an idea, and it had never bothered her.

Eventually he stopped and nodded at them both. "It shouldn't be too difficult to ambush the cart before it is loaded onto the barge. Six men and myself should be sufficient and not draw too much attention if we move in two groups."

Thedra lent forward in her seat and shook her head. "Treena and I will be joining you."

"Out of the question. I won't put Treena in harm's way," Braith replied vehemently. "Or you, for the matter," he hastily added.

Thedra pushed on. "Aven does not need to be upset further. She will need a familiar face when you open that cart."

Braith raised his voice. "That is a stupid idea. You have no training and will only be in the way, which could jeopardize the whole operation and Aven's life. All I need to do is tell her Treena sent me, and I'm sure Aven will come."

"Thedra, maybe we shouldn't go?" interjected Treena.

"Pfft! We will be going or we will tag along behind and I'm sure that will be more of a problem. Treena knows her way around the wharf area, we won't be in the way." Thedra arched an eyebrow at Braith. "And we might surprise you with how helpful we can be."

Chapter 8
Sylvan

He had a wonderful afternoon planned, full of self con-gratulation and walking around the closest market letting other people admire him. He was after all the Master Shaymmi, and he should be out in the populace enjoying the accolades of his work. Even though no one actually knew of his most recent discovery, he did, and the First Elder did and he was satisfied with that...for now.

He had just finished brushing his hair when Jorge coughed politely at the bathroom door. "What is it, Jorge?" Sylvan asked impatiently.

"Trainee Mathias and Trainee Matteo are here to see you upon the request of Shaymmi Hadrian."

Sylvan sighed heavily but inwardly smiled as he congratulated himself on forcing Hadrian to turn to him for help with the twins. He knew it would cause her no end of frustration at having to admit she couldn't train them without his aid. *I wonder what they did to push her to this point?* he mused while fixing a stern expression on his face.

He walked into his office to find them both standing in front of his desk. One looked uncomfortable, and the other slightly defiant.

"What now?" asked Sylvan.

The defiant one promptly handed him a sealed scroll. "Sit," ordered Sylvan as he went around to sit in his hand-crafted chair behind his large desk. Quickly Sylvan scanned the content of the letter and groaned inwardly. *Why were these two so much more challenging than any other trainee they had had?* He found it difficult enough dealing with teenagers and their flippant attitudes without adding in these two's recalcitrant and insolent behavior. "Explain yourselves."

Mr. Defiant went to open his mouth but his brother spoke over the top of him. "We meant no harm. We did not realize that Shaymmi Hadrian would become so agitated with our observations and questions."

"It says here that you were rude and dismissive when she attempted to teach you the basics of entering a trance to begin Elemental Planing." Sylvan waved the parchment at them. "Do you not understand what a privileged existence you have and the ability you have been gifted with?"

"Of course, Master Shaymmi. We just wish to know why you must drink the potion and lose your eyesight to enter the trance? It seems counterproductive to have your eyesight hindered when you return. We were simply inquiring if anyone had ever tried to do it without drinking the tonic?" The boy spoke with calm authority.

Little upstarts, Sylvan thought to himself. *Why do teenagers think they know everything?*

"That is not the way it is done. The First Elder has made it abundantly clear how he expects us to use the Elemental Planes, and I am certainly not in the habit of questioning the man closest to the One God." Sylvan deliberately raised his bushy eyebrows to further his point. "Perhaps, I was mistaken. It has never happened before but I am mortal, so I am not completely infallible."

Before his brother could stop him Mr Defiant had narrowed his eyes and asked, "What exactly would you, the most celebrated Shaymmi, be wrong about?"

His words were so close to sarcastic that it took Sylvan a few moments to compose himself before he responded. Quite deliberately, he stood and straightened his impressive girth and height. "Speak to me in that tone again, young man, and right or wrong, I will have you and your brother tossed into the street with the clothes on your back and nothing more." Sylvan didn't bellow. He spoke quietly and confidently as only a man who knew exactly where his place was in the world could do. He moved around to the front of the desk and sat on the front edge facing the disobedient twins. "What I was about to say until I was rudely interrupted was that perhaps you don't have the abilities I had first sensed in you. It is quite feasible that you may only have a minor connection to the Elemental Plane and are destined to serve the Shaymmi, such as my Manservant Jorge, rather than become one, as I find it difficult to comprehend why you must question everything rather than follow the rules and learn your role."

Mr. Defiant remained seated, but his brother stood quickly and bowed deeply, his brown hair flopping over his face as he straightened. "Matteo and I meant no offense. We are deeply sorry for any angst we have caused both your esteemed self and Shaymmi Hadrian. We shall certainly strive to work harder at our studies."

Matteo took his time standing but bowed just as deeply as his brother. "It is Mathias' want to study and ask questions before we do something. He was concerned once he learned of the loss of sight. I was only attempting to help him better understand when I asked Shaymmi Hadrian what I did not, but now do, perceive as impertinent questions. It will not happen again. We are both honored to have been given these talents by the One God and do not wish to bring his ire or yours upon us."

Sylvan inclined his head at the twins. "The First Elder appreciates a sharp, analytical mind but it is never acceptable to question his teachings or decree regarding how we enter and traverse the Elemental Plane. As Mathias enjoys studying so much and you, Matteo, are content to follow his questions I want you both to spend some time in the Stronghold library learning all the rulings the First Elder has made regarding the use of the Elemental Plane and how we are to teach you to use it. I want a complete summary written and approved by me before you return to your studies with Shaymmi Hadrian."

They both bowed again, their hair landing in identical fashion across their eyes as they lifted their heads.

"You may go."

He watched as they walked out in a much more subdued state than what they had arrived in. Sylvan didn't know which one was his more overriding emotion. Was he thrilled that they had managed to irritate Hadrian so quickly that she had had to resort to having him deal with it or was he annoyed and slightly aghast at their lack of respect for the office of Shaymmi and all the glory it came with? If he was honest with himself, he was more than a little shocked at their questioning and their need for answers he had never thought to ask.

"Jorge?" he called out.

"Yes?" Jorge entered the room, and he folded his hands within the voluminous sleeves of his Shaymmi servant livery as he always did when waiting for instructions.

"What is in that vile potion I drink before I enter my trance?"

Jorge's large forehead, made larger by his receding hairline, wrinkled as he thought. "I do not know. It is brewed in the kitchen and kept in a locked cupboard in the cellar that only the Head Cook has a key to."

"Could you enquire as to what is in it...discretely?"

"I can try."

Chapter 9

Treena

Treena wrinkled her nose in distaste as the wind brought a waft of rotting fish past the alcove she stood in with Thedra, near the church docks in the Wharf Sector. *You would think I would be used to it,* she mused. *Being a fisherman's brat and all.* Treena had grown up not far from the docks with her fisherman father, mother, and two brothers. The monastery bells tolled five strikes. Predawn would arrive soon, which meant they needed to expect the cart carrying Aven to come down the road they waited near at any moment. She strained to hear any rumbling of cart wheels on rough cobblestones but could only hear the gulls that roosted in the sail masts of the boats and barges that sat gently rocking in the harbor.

Treena bent down and grabbed the hem of the left-hand side of her faded unwashed skirt and lifted it and tucked it into a garter belt at the top of her thigh, exposing a shapely long leg. She then proceeded to tug down her most revealing but slightly worn bodice to expose an unseemly amount of bust.

"You and your brilliant ideas," she muttered at Thedra, who was making several adjustments to her own shabby clothing.

Thedra laughed quietly as she quickly re-braided her hair into a much messier form. "I'm tired of being just a seamstress. I've been playing this charade for seventeen years longer than you, and just for once, I'd like to put the training we have into practice." She looked earnestly at Treena. "Katatreena, don't you yearn to be more?"

"Honestly, I don't know. I like my life, and I love helping the children."

"I understand that, but you can't tell me you don't feel something is missing?" urged Thedra.

Treena noted the glint of light from Thedra's heavy gold bracelet. "Was it a good idea to wear that? It really doesn't go with the tavern wench persona."

"It was a gift from a wealthy patron who was going to take me away from all of this. The bracelet was his promise, but the stupid bugger went and got himself killed in a river accident."

Before Treena had a chance to respond, the sound of horse hooves and the cart filled the still night air. Treena and Thedra stepped out of the alcove onto the sidewalk just as a group of four men came around a bend further up the road and staggered towards the cart, singing loudly and teasing each other raucously. Three men from across the road approached Treena and Thedra. They were sailors who had obviously been enjoying shore leave a little too much. Their clothes were rumpled and stained from too much carousing, and they were also a little unsteady on their feet. Treena noted the cart was moving slowly towards them with several swinging lanterns lighting the way.

Thedra called out loudly to the sailors crossing the road, "My fine lookin sailors, do ye care for some fun before headin out?"

One of the sailors leered at Thedra and grinned as he got closer. "What sorta fun did ye have in mind?"

Treena giggled girlishly. "That, Sir, would depend on how much ye had in ye purse."

"Hey," yelled out one of the two sailors who were still in the center of the road. "Wait for me."

"Shit!" The third sailor tripped and landed face down in front of the oncoming cart.

Treena ran out to help the fallen sailor. "Sir, are ye all right?"

There was a great deal of confusion as the horses and cart with their church soldier began to slow down to avoid the injured sailor sprawled in the center of the road. The group of drunken men that had been singing and staggering caught up to the back of the cart.

"Move," grunted one of the church soldiers moving forward.

"Oh, please, if ye could just help him to stand, we will be out ye way," asked Treena sweetly as she looked up from the fallen sailor and pushed her chest out, hoping that she didn't fall out of her too-low bodice.

The soldier's gaze was drawn to where she wanted it, and she watched as one of the other sailors came up behind him and knocked him on the side of the head with the end of his dagger. The soldier tumbled forward smacking his face on the cobblestones with a sickening sound. Before the remaining soldiers could react the drunken men at the back of the cart had silenced the two rear guards and the tripped sailor had miraculously recovered and tackled the other front guard to the ground.

Thedra, covered by the confusion, had managed to climb up next to the driver but was now struggling to get him out of his seat as they wrestled for the reins. "A little help here," she said through clenched teeth.

The driver managed to land a powerful punch to her side, and she fell forward but refused to give up the reins. Thedra responded with an elbow to his face as she straightened back up. This made the reins jerk and the horses lurch forward in response. The horses and cart ran over the prone guard and went careening down the road while Thedra and the driver exchanged blows.

Treena ran after the cart. "Aven, hang on," she yelled.

"Treena?" a voice called from inside the cart.

"Aven, can you open the door?" yelled Braith who was now running with Treena.

"I'll try."

The barge loomed before them with more church soldiers waiting on board. *This is not good,* thought Treena. As the cart moved quickly toward the end of the road and onto the docks, Treena heard someone call, "Whoa." Thankfully one of Braith's men was a fast runner and had managed to get in front of the horses. The horses instantly slowed, giving Treena, Braith, and the the other men time to catch up. As Treena reached the side of the cart with the door, she climbed up and peered through the barred opening.

"Aven, are you okay?"

A small hand reached up through the bars. "I can't get tha door open," Aven explained quickly.

Treena swore and squeezed the hand before letting go. "Hang on." She jumped back down and began to examine the door to discover a bolt and padlock firmly barring her way into Aven.

Unexpectedly the cart lurched forward, and Aven gave a little yelp.

"Treena, we have to be quick or those church soldiers on the barge are going to come investigate why their cargo has stopped moving. Get out of the way, one of my men has the tools to get that open," Braith explained.

She obligingly moved out of the way but hovered nearby.

One of the men who had been playing the role of a drunk merry maker stepped forward and opened his overcoat to reveal an assortment of tools.

Thedra moved around the other side of the cart. Treena embraced her with a great sense of relief and noticed a trickle of blood on her friend's face from a cut lip.

"Hurry it up. A few of the church soldiers from the barge are heading this way to find out what the hold up is, and it's starting to get a bit light to hide as well," a look-out called from the other side of the cart.

"Lord, we have a bit of a situation here," muttered the one trying to pick the lock.

Braith answered quietly, "What's the issue?"

"It won't budge, and I don't have a strong enough set of cutters to cut through it."

"You what?" Braith hissed.

"I can't get her out."

"Treena?" whimpered Aven, who could hear every word just as Treena had.

The look-out on the other side of the cart whispered loudly, "Whatever you have to do, do it now. Our time is about to run out."

"Everyone get out of here. We will have to find another way to get to her," ordered Braith.

The men didn't have to be told twice, they simply walked away from the cart, fading into the alleys and side streets that would take them back into the sewers and safety.

"Treena, we must go," urged Braith. "I promise we will find another way."

"No, I won't leave her."

Without warning, Braith moved to pick up Treena, but she was quicker and skipped out of the way. "What are you doing?"

"Making you leave. Thedra, tell her we have to go."

Thedra looked torn.

"What's going on here?" asked one of the two church soldiers that walked around the cart.

Braith bowed deeply and looked at his feet as he answered in a sniveling tone. "We have just come from that direction," he waved his hand to the left, "and we saw this cart just sittin here so came to find out if we could offer assistance, sir."

"And you are?" enquired the soldier.

"I am…" Braith never finished his sentence. Instead he reached up and grabbed the church soldier around the neck and pulled him into a head lock as he plunged a knife into his chest.

The other church soldier reacted by yelling before a kick to the groin and then a sharp punch to the throat by Thedra silenced him.

"Impressive," murmured Braith.

"Thank you," grinned Thedra.

"Aven, I don't want to leave you, but I can't unlock the wretched bolt." Treena couldn't keep the worry from her voice.

"There are more guards coming," warned Braith. "We must go now."

Without warning, the wooden door of the cart exploded into tiny splinters, exposing Aven standing in the doorway with her eyes screwed shut.

The guards began to run toward the cart. Braith swept Aven up and began to run. Treena turned to follow when she saw Thedra fall. Bending down to help Thedra up, she noticed a quickly spreading pool of blood. She did a quick search and found a small knife protruding from the base of her skull. Treena hesitantly reached out to find her pulse. Treena tried to hold back her tears as she stood and tried to pick up her dead friend, but she was too heavy to carry.

"I'm sorry," she whispered to Thedra before letting her fall back to the ground just as a knife whistled above her head. Without looking back, Treena ran.

Chapter 10

Treena

Aven sat curled on a pile of old blankets in the corner of the storeroom blankly staring into space. Treena was worried, as she had been that way all day. Treena refused to let her emotions get the better of her as she went about her everyday tasks of closing the florist shop for the evening. It had been a difficult day, and she had done everything possible to stop herself from thinking about Thedra and having to leave her body at the docks that morning. It had taken all her inner strength and training to follow her normal daily schedule so as to not alert the church that there was a need to come down and investigate why they didn't get their flowers for their daily services.

Elldean Stiann, the local Lore Keeper, had arrived in the morning after Treena had sent him a coded message. They had had a quick quiet conversation about what had happened, what she thought Aven was, and that while Reza had been sent for there was now a sense of urgency to it. Braith had also sent a note asking that they meet and had strongly implied that he had questions. Treena didn't want to deal with any questions as she simply couldn't explain the door exploding. Braith had also apologized for the loss of Thedra and had implied that the man who had failed to let Aven out had been dealt with. Treena was hoping it didn't mean what she thought it did. Sometimes she struggled to reconcile her childhood friend to the man and the self-made title he now carried.

Finally, all the jobs were done and she sat down heavily in the padded chair and allowed herself to cry. She hadn't meant to disturb Aven but was obviously louder than what she had intended.

"Treena, I'm sorry. It's all me fault." Aven came to stand before her.

"Oh no, Aven, none of this was your fault." Treena opened her arms and Aven climbed onto her lap. "You didn't make any of this happen."

They both cried, each holding the other, trying to give and receive comfort. The dusk sky darkened and eventually the tears ran out. Treena stood and lit a few candles against the oncoming night and offered to make Aven something to eat, but Aven, like Treena, was feeling sick and the thought of food made it worse. Bringing a blanket off her bed, Treena sat back down in the chair and Aven climbed back into her lap.

"Why me?" asked Aven. "Why take me?"

Treena shook her head. "I don't know. Did you overhear anything? What happened?"

"They put me in a tiny room with an old bed and nofing else," Aven swallowed hard but went on. "By the look of his clothes, the Arch Deacon came in."

"A short man with a large bald head and thick neck?" Treena clarified.

Aven nodded. "Ya, that's right."

"So, he came into the room they were holding you in..." Treena prompted.

"He just stared at me. It was weird."

"He didn't say anything?"

"No, nofing. But then he came back two more times. The next time he didn't say nofing again. The last time he came in he had one of his monks grab me and put me hands behind me back real tight. He came up real close to me face and asked me who I was."

"What did you answer?"

"I told him the truth. That I was a nobody from the poor quarter who just lived with me Da."

Treena gently held Aven's face and turned her to face her own. Looking into Aven's eyes, Treena noticed beautiful gold flecks that had not been there two days ago when Aven was taken. She smiled despite the situation. Treena had been right, and it explained the connection she felt for the child, if only she could have shared this moment with Thedra. "Aven, you're not a nobody. You are a very important person to me, and I'm sure your family feels the same."

Aven shrugged. "The Arch Deacon asked me questions about where I lived and with who. I tried not to tell him much." Aven rubbed her left shoulder. "Me shoulders hurt so much when he finished. He got angry and slapped me because I kept sayin the same fing.”

A large gust of wind whipped through the street causing the closed shutters to rattle unexpectedly. Treena and Aven both froze for several seconds before moving.

“It’s okay,” Treena reassured Aven. “They have no idea where you are, and they probably think you are trying to get out of the city.”

Aven continued, “It was the last time I saw him. Not long after some soldiers came in and carried me to that cart.” She sat quietly for a moment before asking in a whisper, “Do you think it has somfing to do with that ghost I seen?”

Treena was honest and said, “I don’t know. I wish I had a reason for them to take you but I don’t. The only thing I can think of is that they were mistaken and took the wrong person.” She gave her a hug. “I want to ask you something, but I don’t want you to get upset. It’s okay if you don’t have an answer.”

“Okay.”

“Do you know how the door exploded?”

Aven looked alarmed and shook her head.

“Can you explain how you were feeling when it happened?” urged Treena.

Aven kept her head down and spoke softly. “I was scared,” she faltered. “He said ye had to leave me. Somefing built up in me tummy and I closed me eyes and the door was gone.” She raised her head, and if anything, her eyes had become more golden. “Did I make it disappear?”

There is no point in lying to her, Treena thought to herself. *She is going to have to be told what she is sooner rather than later.*

"I think so, but it is nothing to be frightened of. It is a part of who you are. I will explain it all very soon, I promise." Treena paused and brushed Aven's hair away from her face. "I do think it's time we got you home. Your family must be very worried about you." Though secretly Treena wasn't sure that Aven should return home just yet. How much did she actually tell them? Was it enough information for them to track her down?

Shaking her head she said, "Can I just stay ere tonight? I will go home tomorrow. They won't be worried about me," she assured Treena.

Treena woke up tired. The morning dawned and the empty feeling in Treena's stomach had not abated. Thedra was still dead, and the world seemed wrong. She had spent several strikes last night trying to think of ways she could have changed the outcome of Aven's rescue intermingled with bouts of quiet crying. Treena just wanted to roll over and go to sleep but she needed to start her day and get everything completed quickly so she could escort Aven home.

The morning was uneventful as Treena and Aven busied themselves in what was usually the enjoyable daily tasks of being a florist, but today, they felt mundane and tiresome. Finally, all the bouquets were done for the churches, and they closed the shop for a lunch break, which was unusual but not unheard of.

"You really don't need to take me home," stated Aven as she watched Treena close the shutters. "I can walk there on me own."

"No, the church may still be looking for you, and I'm not taking any chances."

As they left the florist and walked to the end of the street, they were promptly joined by two men. "We are here to escort ye anywhere ye need to go," the younger of the two explained. Treena recognized him from when Aven had been taken. He was one of the young men Braith had sent to protect the children until she arrived.

Treena knew there was no point in arguing and they were safer in a group. "Very well." She nodded. "I am taking Aven home."

The younger man's brows shot up but he said nothing. *I wonder what brought on that reaction,* mused Treena.

It didn't take too long to walk to the shoddier part of the city and arrive at what was surprisingly a double story, unloved house pushed up against a smaller tavern on one side and a dilapidated shack on the other in a street full of neglected single-story buildings. Treena noted that all the shutters were closed against the hot season's warm sunlight.

Aven hesitated as they reached the front door. "You really don't need to come in. Me Da wont care where I've been."

Treena answered, "No, I think it's time I met your Da."

"We will wait out here," explained their escort.

Aven said nothing further as she pushed the door open and entered. Treena followed her into a large darkened room, lit only by candles. It took a few moments for her eyes to adjust.

"Oh, thank the Elementals that ye are okay," a gush of words exploded in relief as Aven was engulfed in an embrace by a taller, slightly older and heavier version of herself.

"Shhh, Lanae, ye know not to say that. What if one of them church men came in?" admonished Aven in a surprisingly firm tone.

This was a very different side to Aven that Treena had ever witnessed. Usually the girl was so reticent, quiet and hunched over that some customers didn't notice her when they came into the florist shop.

Treena stepped forward. "Hello, I'm Treena. Aven has been with me. I'm sorry we worried you. She had a fall a week ago, and I patched her up and she has been working in my florist shop as payment. She did assure me that no one would miss her if she didn't go home. I'm here to meet your Da."

"I'm Lanae, Aven's sister." The older teen curtsied ,and Treena noted that she was only wearing a very short, thread bare shift, that was too tight for the curvy girl. "Make yeself comfortable and we will find Da for ye." She caught Aven's hand

and dragged her out through the door at the back of the large room.

Instead of sitting down, Treena took the opportunity to take note of her surroundings, as she had been taught. She noted all exits and anything that could be used as a shield or weapon. The room was large and oddly furnished for someone's lounging area. It had too many over stuffed but badly worn couches and what could only be described as a bar along one wall. There was also a platform next to the door the girls had gone through that could be used for bards. Several round tables surrounded by chairs were set up next to the bar. There were bowls of fruit and other smaller bowls of nuts scattered on the tables, side tables, and bar. The atmosphere was anything but homely. A large staircase rose up to the second floor along one side wall.

A door opened up on the second floor and a man of middle years with the telltale bloated ale belly of a drunk sauntered down the stairs. His eyes were too close together and his light brown hair was oily giving him a seedy appearance.

"Ah, I didn't know we had company. Welcome to our home," he said expansively as he reached the bottom of the stairs. He frowned as he looked around. "It seems our greeter has left her post," he spoke jovially but there was an undercurrent of something else Treena could not quite pinpoint.

"I was greeted by Lanae," she assured him. "She asked me to make myself comfortable while she went to look for you."

"Good. So, me dear, what can I interest ye in?" He looked her up and down. "Dacrow!" he called up the stairway. He looked back at her and and lent forward, almost leering at her, his rancid breath making her fight to not wrinkle her nose in disgust. "Mmm, perhaps something a little younger? Oberst!"

Treena could hear more doors being opened on the upper floor.

Treena frowned. *What in all of Duthyne was he talking about?*

"I think there has been a misunderstanding. I came today because I have been taking care of Aven and I wanted to return her to your care."

His eyes lightened. "Aven? So ye like girls. Absolutely nufing to be ashamed of. I have several ages and types for ye."

With a mingling of utter shock and an overwhelming sense of outrage, Treena finally realized what was happening just as the two teenage boys came to stand before her. The older one, Dacrow, who appeared about eighteen stood stock still and stared vacantly above her head. He had the same heart shaped face as Aven but looked more like the father. The younger teen, Oberst, looked to be about twelve but could have been older as Aven also appeared younger than what she was. His features were darker and nothing like his father's. He stared at her with a brash, challenging expression that broke her heart as she knew it must be a facade. Both were very thin which was decidedly odd standing in a room with bowls of food everywhere.

Treena felt ill. This man was running a whore house, and his children were the workers. It was beyond revolting. She could feel her elemental power stirring in response to the injustice of the situation.

The door in the back of the room opened and Lanae and Aven came through. Treena watched Aven instantly withdraw into herself as a look of terror crossed her face and she took a smaller step, letting Lanae walk in front. Lanae, for her part, looked to be deliberately trying to shield Aven from her father.

Treena swallowed hard against the bile that burned her throat. She would not be leaving Aven here when she left.

"I'm sorry, I didn't introduce myself earlier. I'm Kat." Treena smiled through gritted teeth.

Aven's father took her hand and lent over, grazing his lips against it. "Fion."

It took Treena every ounce of self control to not shudder and rip her hand away. "Master Fion, I am in need of Aven's services."

A slow, slimy smile slid across his lips. "She will be expensive," he warned. "She is unused."

Treena tried not to gag at his phrasing. "You misunderstand me. I am in need of a junior assistant in my florist shop, and I think Aven would be suitable."

Fion frowned. "And how will her working for ye make me money?"

"You can have half her wage, and she will live with me. So, you earn money while not having to take care of her," Treena responded reasonably.

He shook his head in protest. "Aven also cleans for me."

"I have a cleaner come into the shop twice a week to clean. I will send her to you instead." Treena wagged her finger at him. "The cleaner is not to be touched in any way."

"Of course," agreed Fion. "What sort of person do ye take me for?"

You're a degenerate slime bag who should be caged and left to rot and die in the middle of the market square for all to see, Treena thought to herself but refrained from doing anything other than continuing to smile through her clenched teeth while her insides burned with disgust. This man was beyond vile. "Do we have an agreement?"

He held out his dirty hand. "Yes."

Chapter 11

Hadrian

She swept into the substantial silversmith shop and paused in the doorway for dramatic effect. Several customers looked around to see the commotion before hurriedly going back to their perusing. She loved doing that to people; it made her feel empowered. The general populace made it a point to know what to do when the Shaymmi went out into the city. Each Shaymmi liked to be treated differently. Some liked to be recognized and fawned over, others liked to be ignored and left to go about their business. Fortunately, there were so few Shaymmi's at any time it was not difficult for the citizens of Cynsellam to know how to treat each individual. Hadrian smiled to herself as she knew she was the enigma of the Shaymmi and the bane of the people. One could never tell what mood Hadrian was in so you could never tell how she wished to be treated. On some days she would wish to be left alone and on others she wished to be praised and admired by all. Hadrian adored the notoriety of the situation.

"Shaymmi Hadrian." The silversmith bowed. "It is a great honor to serve one who serves The First Elder. How may I assist you today?"

"I met with The First Elder yesterday, and he had the most divine set of goblets with a matching ewer that he said were a gift from someone but made by you. They had carvings of all the elemental symbols joined and encircling the cup. Is that your work?" she inquired loudly.

"I'm flattered. Yes, it is. Please be seated while I quickly deal with my other customers." He escorted her to a plush round backed chair that sat in the corner. "May I offer you a refreshment whilst you wait?"

"Perhaps later. Garm will see to my needs while you take care of your clients," she replied graciously.

Hadrian watched with amusement as he moved to each group of customers and quietly spoke to them. One young man nervously picked out a fasting ring and put a down payment on it before hurrying out the shop with a quick backward appreciative glance at Hadrian. She smiled warmly and flicked her hair back, making him blush as he exited. Her attention was drawn to an elderly couple bickering over what their gift should be for an upcoming naming day. Expertly, the silversmith intervened and agreed with both their selections before showing them a stunning silver rattle with animals engraved on it that they both admitted would be a perfect keepsake for the baby. He offered to etch the baby's name on it too. Without further bickering, the couple paid their bill and agreed to come back tomorrow to pick up the rattle. The final gentleman explained that he would come back when he had more time as he had a project he wanted to discuss and he wouldn't want to take up any of the Shaymmi's precious time, before bowing to Hadrian and leaving.

"Alone at last," Hadrian joked as she stood to take off her sleeveless black over robe, with its patterned gold brocade along the edges, that told the citizens of Duthyne that she was a Shaymmi. The removal of the robe revealed a tight fitting, strapless, black silk floor length dress with a revealing slit up one thigh. "I'm looking for a necklace to compliment this," she purred.

Cyrus laughed as he moved toward the door and flipped the open sign to closed. "Mmmm, I'm not sure I can help you. I might have to see the dress from several different angles."

"Oh really?" She ran her hand through her hair provocatively. "What sort of angle did you have in mind?"

"Well..." He drew out the word as he stalked toward her. "I have an idea but—" He kissed her deeply. His hands moved to the back of the dress and encountered a long row of tiny buttons going down her spine. Moving his head back he looked into her eyes and grinned. "I think I'm going to need some help."

"Garm, would you be so kind?" murmured Hadrian. She gathered her hair and moved it over one shoulder to give Garm better access to the buttons.

Without comment, Garm began to unbutton the dress while Cyrus went back to his kissing. He started nibbling on her exposed shoulder and slowly made his way up to her neck and finally back to her full lips. His hands found her breasts, and he grazed his thumbs against the silk across her nipples making them harden. She groaned and tugged Cyrus' tunic above his head.

With a soft hiss, her silk dress slid down her body revealing that she wore no under garments.

Cyrus took a step back and appraised her strong, naked body then looked down to the dress pooled at her feet. "Yes, that is a much better angle." He raised his eyebrows and gave her a wicked grin before addressing Garm, who still stood behind Hadrian. "Would you mind taking over for me, Garm?"

Hadrian gasped in surprise while Garm didn't move an inch, but his unusual hazel eyes shone with agreement. *The thought had never crossed her mind, but now it was there it made her groin ache.*

"Oh, come now, Hadrian. You have allowed him to watch us on many occasions, why not let him join in?" cajoled Cyrus. Without waiting for a response he went on, "Garm, I'm sure our Lady has had a stressful morning, would you be so kind as to give her a massage?"

Without waiting for direction from Hadrian, Garm placed his hands on her naked shoulders, squeezed gently, and spoke for the first time. "Yes, Cyrus."

Hadrian lent into the relaxing caress of Garm's hands while watching Cyrus move to the other side of the shop, his back now to them as he did something in one of the display cases that held his specially crafted jewelry. *What was he doing?* she thought absently, her mind on him but her body began to respond to Garm's hands that had now found their way to her breasts while he nipped gently on the back of her neck and a very pleasing erection pressed against her bottom. Giving in to her desires, she didn't turn but instead reached behind her and quickly undid the drawstring that held her manservant's trousers up.

Cyrus spun around, carrying a large gold necklace before him. He expertly placed it around her neck. Standing back, he surveyed the tableau and winked. "Yes, that suits you perfectly."

Hadrian woke to the feel of an absence of body heat at her back and realized that Cyrus must have just slipped out of bed. The bed was empty aside from herself. Garm must have gotten up without her sensing it earlier on. Without haste, she slowly stretched her arms over her head and sat up. It never ceased to surprise her when she awoke in Cyrus' bed chamber rather than her own. It was so different from her own opulent room. It was sparse, manly, and held little in the way of personal belongings with no trinkets on display. She noted that her clothes were probably still in the shop area, so wrapped the bed blanket around her like a towel and went looking for Cyrus. She found him pottering around in his kitchenette.

"Don't you look fetching," he said as she walked in and sat on one of the two chairs available.

She looked to where his eyes had fallen to see that she still had the gold necklace on. "Yes, I think it works well with the blanket."

He laughed easily, which was one of the things she enjoyed about him. He never seemed to take life too seriously. He was easygoing and willing to please. He was brilliant at what he did and was quickly becoming the favorite silversmith of the upper classes due to her patronage and The First Elders approval and display and use of his goblets.

"Where's Garm?" she asked.

"I took the liberty of sending him back to Stronghold to organize you proper transport back as it is quite late."

"That was thoughtful, thank you."

"And to get you proper clothing." He smiled as he cracked several large eggs in a bowl. "So, did you just want me for my body, or did you come for something else?"

"Rumor has it they lost the girl Sylvan found," she announced.

He paused his whisking of the eggs for a moment. "Really?"

Hadrian nodded. "The story is that several days ago the transport cart she was in was attacked and she was taken. They didn't report her missing earlier because they hoped it would be thieves who would ask for a ransom—no such thing happened. I think they waited to see if they could find her and cover their mishap at losing her."

Cyrus laughed. "Yes, that seems likely."

"Sylvan will have to try to find her again." She screwed up her nose. "And he gets to show everyone how powerful and clever he is all over again."

Cyrus put the bowl and whisk aside and sat down in the chair opposite Hadrian. He looked at her earnestly. "Maybe he doesn't."

"What do you mean?"

"Maybe it's your turn to find this girl that The First Elder wants."

"I need time to do that. I know what area Sylvan has been searching for the past season, but it has been a well-guarded secret the exact location of the child. "

Cyrus shrugged. "Then we need to get you more time."

"How?"

"I have a way, I think, but you need to trust me."

Chapter 12
Treena

Treena waited, concealed in the small, dark alcove that stood opposite the tavern her informant had chosen as their meeting point. He had gotten word to her that he had discovered information that she needed to know urgently. But Treena, being ever vigilant, as she had been trained to be, had chosen to arrive early to reconnoiter The Naughty Goat Tavern and its patrons. She had arrived at dusk, as the end of the work-day strikes chimed. She had hustled along with the rest of the people heading home, her signature, low cut peasant blouse had been pulled up onto her shoulder, covering her bosom. Wanting to blend in further, she had walked with her shoulders slightly hunched and her knees bent, which was hidden by her skirt, to hide her height.

The tavern looked more like an aged, double-door barn than an upmarket public house. The clientele of The Naughty Goat were as varied as Treena had ever encountered. Of course the poor and lower working class weren't represented as they couldn't afford the bar prices and the affluent Grandmaster Merchants and Grand Master Craftsman always felt that any frivolity created by a tavern was beneath them. However, the

Master Merchants, Guild Masters, upper and middle working class along with merchants and prosperous business owners were keen to visit the talked about tavern.

Treena noted a small party of tavern goers walking up the dark cobbled road as well as a well-appointed carriage turn the corner and make its way to the tavern doors—this would be the perfect time to join the crowd. She waited until the carriage slowed down and the footman moved to allow his passengers out before crossing the street and seamlessly joining the end of the group alighting from the carriage. The small party that had walked up the road now joined the end of the queue, and Kat became just another patron waiting her turn at the Lucky Dip game that had made the Naughty Goat Tavern the talk in Hamlyn.

The top halves of the double barn doors were open, allowing people to be lured in by the warm light, raucous laughter, and lively music that spilled onto the street. She smiled genially and casually adjusted her bodice as the line moved forward. She confidently knew that she blended into the crowd as there was such a cross section of people that it would be hard to choose a person that didn't belong. She had to admit that it was a very well thought out meeting place by her contact. Treena was astounded by the number of patrons coming and going at this time of the night. The city bells were about to peel, telling all its citizens that they had two strikes left before everything would close at midnight and curfew would be enforced once the buffer of half a strike finished to give everyone time to return home.

As the line shuffled forward, a large burst of noisy laughter could be heard—probably another patron who had received one of the funnier lucky dip prizes. The owner of The Naughty Goat had ingeniously turned a children's game of Lucky Dip into an adult version and had captured the interest and imagination of the public.

Treena took another step forward and counted only three more patrons ahead of her. It wouldn't be long before she could find her contact and find out what information he had.

Her attention was drawn back to a skinny young woman in an overly puffy sleeved dress as she moved confidently toward the small barrel that held the slips of paper with the lucky dip prizes written on them. Quickly, she put her hand in and pulled out a slip of parchment. Without looking at it, she handed it to what Treena could only describe as the Master of Ceremonies and waited for her fate to be read aloud.

"A kiss from your favorite bartender," announced the Master of Ceremonies as the tavern erupted with catcalls and jeers.

The young lady had a predatory grin as she pointed to one of the handsome young men standing behind the long redwood bar. He gallantly leapt over the bar and headed toward the door where he swept her into his arms and planted a loud, long kiss on her lips before putting her back on her feet and swaggering back to his side of the bar amid wolf whistles and laughter. Still giggling, she moved to the side to allow her friend to take her Lucky Dip.

Her friend was a small, barrel-chested man with a slight air of disdain who stepped forward and gingerly put his hand in the barrel and pulled out his "prize." The Master of Ceremonies plucked it from his hand and cleared his throat. "A round of drinks for you and four friends, on the house." This announcement was met with cheers and applause.

The Master of Ceremonies turned his mustachioed, angular face to the next patron. "Ready to try your luck?" He beamed widely as he placed his meaty hand on the barrel beside him.

The tall, well-dressed patron nodded nervously and quickly darted his hand in and out of the barrel, withdrawing his Lucky Dip paper and hastily handing it to the Master of Ceremonies, who then made a show of reading the card and sighing heavily. Someone stepped out from the inside of the tavern and behind the patron and theatrically dumped a jug of ale over the man's head. The crowd exploded with amusement as the patron sbluttered his ale everywhere. A towel was handed to him and a quiet thank you for being such a good sport was murmured before their party was led away to their table.

Treena was having second thoughts as she moved before the Master of Ceremonies and barrel. Perhaps this wasn't the best place to meet her contact. She was now the complete center of attention, which was something she had strived all her life to avoid, and it put her and her contact in the public eye far too much for her liking. She just hoped whatever prize she pulled out was quick and not too inconvenient.

Without preamble, Treena moved forward, dipped her hand into the barrel, withdrew the first card she felt and handed it to the Master of Ceremonies with a quick smile.

He cleared his throat and theatrically perused the card, frowned and rapidly scanned the card again before he passed it onto Treena without announcing anything to the waiting patrons.

She shrugged and smiled lightly as she took the proffered card, assuming it was all part of his "act." That changed instantly when she read her Lucky Dip prize.

I know what you are hiding.

"Why give it to me?" she asked calmly, though her heart raced. She casually offered the card back to the Master of Ceremonies. *What could the card possibly mean?*

He took it and cleared his throat as now every person in the main room stared at the strange exchange—even if they couldn't hear it clearly.

"I know what you are hiding," he announced dramatically.

Treena looked down at her cleavage and shrugged her shoulders several times to make her breasts jiggle. "I'm not really hiding them, am I?" she asked loudly and innocently.

The crowd roared with laughter and an impressive snort escaped from beneath his large mustache. Treena quickly made her way into the packed tavern before anything further could be said and spotted her informant sitting only a few tables away along the closest wall to the exit. It was a wise choice as most people would be busy watching the Lucky Dip game rather than what was happening a few tables away. If you didn't want to be noticed or were doing something underhanded, most people assumed you would move to the back of the room. She smiled and dodged the outstretched arm of a much older man as he tried to grab her and ordered two drinks from the passing serving girl, placing a few coins on her tray before settling into her seat.

"What was that all about, Lady Katatreena?" her companion asked.

"Ezekiel, you know you are not supposed to call me that," she quietly admonished, avoiding the question.

He wiped his hands down the front of his tightly stretched tunic before picking up and draining the dregs of his ale from the dinted metal cup.

"It's what you are," he replied stubbornly. "And if anyone asked, you could simply be my lady."

Any further discussion was interrupted with hoots of the crowd responding to the latest participant to gain entry into the Naughty Goat. Treena gazed around the room to see if anyone was paying special attention to them and found no one showing too much interest or feigning too much disinterest.

She watched the drinks server expertly weave her way from the over-sized redwood bar, through the patrons, handing out drinks in a variety of different sized metal mugs and cups to eventually arrive at their table, plonking down two drinks before moving on with a passing nod as Treena said thank you. Treena noted a large gold disc that hung behind the bar with what looked to be a large padded head blacksmith hammer hanging beside it—what could that possibly be for?

Treena took the closest tarnished cup and clinked it against Ezekiel's before taking a long drink of the expensive wine.

"Oh, that is a mighty fine choice, My Lady." Ezekiel swirled the wine in his mug before taking another sip. He was the Head Chef to Arch Deacon Ulrick and had sampled so much of his creations that his girth was forever expanding to the point his stomach almost sat upon the low table. He was a Loyalist, as his parents had been and their parents had been and so on, stretching back to a time when his ancestors had served in the kitchens of the Elemental Sky Council and their Oredmoor. Other than his exceptional cooking abilities and an eye for detail, he was average in every way, which made him the perfect informant in the Arch Deacon's staff.

As Treena drank the wine, she was only half listening to him as her mind tried to fathom what had happened at the door. *I know what you are hiding,* was quite the dramatic statement, and the way the Master of Ceremonies had behaved showed it was obviously not a normal card to be drawn.

Had the card been put there for me to pick? she wondered.

That was a thought that made her feel very uncomfortable, but she couldn't deny his reaction. *What had they been referring to?* It felt like she had so many secrets at the moment that she wasn't sure which one they meant. *Was it who she was? Was it that she had rescued Aven from the church? Was it that she knew the true identity of Braith? And we still don't know what that thing was that had scared Aven in the first place.*

Gasps of surprise and cheering brought Treena back to the present where Ezekiel sat across the table from her cheering with the rest of the crowd. She clapped enthusiastically as it would stand out if she didn't join in.

With all the noise going on, she lent forward and asked casually, "What is it you needed to see me about?"

His large, brown eyes grew sad even though he continued to smile and look like he was joining in the frivolity. "They are sending Lady Thedra's body to Cynsellam. Arch Bishop Ulrick and one of his Captains have examined her several times and are intrigued by her bracelet for some reason. I thought you should know as I know how valuable it is to the female Dalinda line."

Ezekiel and Treena both jump slightly as an unexpected, incredibly loud sound reverberated around the room. Patrons who had been before laughed openly at all the newcomers who had jumped at the startling sound. Treena scanned the room for the source and found the culprit putting away the huge blacksmith hammer next to the metal disk.

"Last round," boomed the Master of Ceremonies. There was a cacophony of sound as people rushed to place final orders with the drinks girls or made their own way to the bar.

Treena decided that if her life was not so complicated she would quite enjoy spending an evening here with her few friends. She indicated another round of drinks to the passing serving girl and turned back to Ezekiel. "I don't think it would be wise for us to take action. We still don't know why they wanted Aven. This could be a trap to find her again."

"I hadn't thought of that," he admitted. "So, is it true? Rumors throughout the Loyalists' is we have a new member to call Lady." He was cleverly circumspect in his question.

She smiled and nodded to him as their drinks were put on the table and Treena fished out a few more coins from a concealed pocket in her skirts.

"May I pass this joyful news on, Lady Katatreena?"

"Not yet. She has not been tested, but it will be good to have happy news to help ease the sad news of Thedra's passing."

"Is there any other way I can serve you before I take my leave?"

Treena lent forward, as if to say something intimate to her companion and reached across the small table to affectionately hold his hand. She knew he wouldn't confuse her sudden attraction for anything other than an act but anyone watching would think she was making an advance on the Head Chef to the man that ran the city. "Do you know if they examined Thedra's eyes?"

Chapter 13

Hadrian

Hadrian fought down panic as her consciousness battered against an invisible barrier that held her back from entering her body.

She had felt her anxiety rapidly climb once Cyrus had removed the amulet from its pouch and a mental snap had occurred and she could no longer feel a connection to her human form. It had been such a strong disconnection and disorientation that her first instinct had been to try to get back to her body. She finally managed to get her fear under control and stopped her assault on the barrier. Shaking herself mentally, Hadrian refocused to watch Cyrus as he stood over her inert body, holding a medallion in his hand as it touched her heart. He glanced at the time piece to make sure to stick to their agreed schedule then placed the medallion on her gently rising chest and walked into another room. This was the second test. The first had been him holding the amulet while she tried to return to her body after being on the elemental plane, and now they were testing to see if they could just leave the amulet on the person and it would still stop them from returning.

She gathered up her courage and glided in to join her body only to be stopped by the same invisible barrier as before. It was frustrating, yet she also felt triumphant as the amulet did exactly what Cyrus had hoped for. Hadrian concentrated all her strength and pushed hard against the shield only to be met with complete resistance. If she had a face at the moment, it would be grinning madly. Taking her time, even though she wanted it to be over so she could celebrate with Cyrus and also return to her body, as it was unsettling to know that was not in her control at the moment, she slowly glided around her body. She randomly prodded sections with her mind to see if she could find a gap, but found nothing, even when she skimmed along the floor.

Satisfied that the medallion worked, Hadrian tried to settle her survival instincts and wait patiently for Cyrus to return and remove it. Wanting to distract herself, she took the chance to study the amulet a little closer. It wasn't the most attractive piece of jewelery she'd ever seen. It was the size of her palm, and she guessed it contained several different types of metal as there were assorted distinct colors that appeared in random blob shapes on the oval, polished surface. It had a raised symbol in thick rose gold that Hadrian had never seen before. At the top of the oval was a round link that she assumed you used to hang it on a chain or leather thong. She mused that the chain would have to be thick and strong to carry what she assumed was quite heavy as Cyrus had not allowed her to touch as he said with her special Shaymmi gifts he wasn't sure what would happen.

With a sense of relief, Hadrian saw Cyrus re-enter the room and head immediately toward her body. He took the medallion from her chest and placed it back into the protective pouch, and Hadrian instantly felt the recognizable tug of her body. She plunged back into her body with an abrupt jarring sensation that was disorientating as usually everything was fluid and slow. She lay there for a moment collecting her thoughts and waiting for everything to settle.

This was a position she was not used to. No one saw her at this most vulnerable moment when she was essentially blind and her movements hindered for up to a full strike. Usually only Garm was permitted to aid her at this time. She didn't know how she felt about being this exposed to Cyrus. Hadrian startled as she felt a gentle kiss on her forehead then relaxed.

She was being paranoid. If Cyrus had wanted to betray her or hurt her, he would have done it by now. She wasn't a young girl striving to beat her peers, with any means necessary, to remain the perfect student at the prestigious school her father owned to gain his love and approval. She felt no remorse for what she had done to many pupils to remain at the pinnacle of the student body, but it had made her very wary as a few had attempted retribution. Hadrian knew this was where her need to be better than Sylvan and become the Master Shaymmi stemmed from—it was almost a compulsion.

Hadrian was impatient to have her body and consciousness return to their normal balance but didn't rush the process.

"Garm?" was all she needed to say to tell him she was ready to sit. She felt his strong hands gently take hold of her torso and sit her up. Then he began the process of massaging her feet before slowly moving to her ankles, then calves.

"Can I help?" asked Cyrus.

Garm answered, "Start with her head, then work down her neck and shoulders."

Hadrian relaxed further into the ministrations of the two men and rejoiced. "It worked perfectly."

"Even when it was left on you?" Cyrus wondered.

"Yes." She shuddered. "I will admit it was scary to not be able to get back, but it is perfect for what we plan." Hadrian laughed and flicked her fringe from her face. "It will be quite pleasant to know the pompous Master Shaymmi will suffer while I go find the girl and return triumphant."

Within a half strike, Hadrian was feeling incredible. Her sight had returned and her body tingled from the massage and the wine she now sipped. She lay on her couch with her head resting on Cyrus' shoulder, staring at the pouch that contained the medallion that was resting on the low table in front of them.

"Where did you get it from?"

Cyrus shifted slightly. "My former master left it to me, along with the shop and several other items. He told me in a letter that I found, once he had passed, that it would protect me from the Shaymmi if I ever needed it or from anyone else who could use the Elemental Planes."

"Do you know how it works?"

"No, I have no idea. I'm just happy that it did what it was supposed to."

Hadrian sat up and stretched her arms over her head before turning to Cyrus. "Now we must plan how to gain access to Sylvan. He will be searching tomorrow morning for the girl."

Chapter 14
Treena

"She's finally asleep," Treena announced absently as she walked into the front of the shop, tugging at the arm of the heavy robe she wore over her typical attire. The shoulders of the robe were a deep blue with the color gradually changing to a bright sea green at the waist before fading to a glittering white hem. With a triumphant grunt, she untangled her arm and pushed it through the long wing-like sleeve. Quickly fastening the front, Treena then moved to help Reza with the robe that he was now pulling from the traveling pack he had dropped in the corner when he had arrived just before she closed the shop for the day. His robe was made of the same heavy cloth but was a mottled collection of browns with gold thread sewn in an intricate pattern on the voluminous sleeves.

"She truly was an incredible artist," Treena murmured as she reached up and smoothed the unique, custom-made robe across Reza's wiry shoulders. It was a novelty for her to reach up, as Treena at 5'9 was tall for a Duthyne woman—the height of the average man—which made Reza's 6'2 inches enormous. Before she could firm up her resolve, silent tears slid from her unveiled golden eyes. Without saying a word, her mentor and dear friend gathered her into his arms and held her.

Treena struggled to hold onto her resolve and without warning an uncontrollable wail tore through her. She sobbed and her shoulders heaved as she tried to gulp in air as her guilt and heartbreak warred with each other. Her emotions overwhelmed her as her thoughts became a jumble and she became lost in her misery at losing Thedra. She missed her terribly. The only things that had kept Treena moving was the urgent need to protect Aven and the need to keep the church from her florist door.

When Reza had arrived, Treena had almost lost her composure as she had experienced an acute sense of relief and want to let someone else take control. It was only Aven's terrified look at the towering, silent man that brought Treena's priorities back into focus. Now, nothing would help her keep hold of her composure as the pain had finally become too much to bear.

He said nothing as she sobbed, he just held her firmly, tucked under his chin. She swallowed hard and tried to regain her equilibrium, but more random thoughts filled her mind. She couldn't fathom the years to come without Thedra's guidance and support as it was now Treena's task to train Aven, just as Reza had trained Treena. Reza had been a blessing as her mentor, and Treena had secretly had a crush on him in her late teens as he trained her and guided her in the Elemental Ways of the Dalinda, but she had grown out of that and what had remained was admiration and deep camaraderie as she became his equal and he had eventually left to resume his role as a traveling groomsmen/farrier. He was away for seasons at a time while Thedra, having finished mentoring Treena's counterpart at about the same time, had left him to his role in the country's capital and had settled only a boat trip away in Namurrn.

Her sobbing finally subsided and her eyes dried, yet he didn't let her go. She wrapped her own arms around his strong but slight waist and gently squeezed. "Thank you." Taking a step back, but not breaking the embrace, she looked up into his glorious, unconcealed golden eyes and noted the unshed tears. "What can I do to help you?" she whispered.

He paused a moment longer than bent down and softly kissed her forehead. "Be who I trained you to be."

Before Treena could respond, the church bells rang to announce that it was almost midnight.

He let her go and took the only candle in the room.

"It's time," he spoke softly.

Treena led Reza into the storeroom of the shop and moved a couple of buckets on the bottom shelf before pushing on an unseen button at the back of the shelving. Silently, the shelving and the wall it was attached to swung inward, revealing darkness. Reza passed Treena the candle and she quickly moved down the narrow stairs and entered the hidden room and set about lighting several lanterns that hung in the corners. The brighter lighting revealed a deceptively large room with three rough stone walls with the fourth wall covered in mirrors and a smooth, dark wood floor. There was an ancient table and chairs shoved in one corner, while another corner held a large bookshelf that was crammed with books, weapons, and assorted items.

They spent the time until the midnight strike preparing for the mourning ritual. In the middle of the floor, burnt into the wood, was the shape of a pentagon. Each side was the length of the average man and at each corner was a different coloured and shaped candle. In the center of the pentagon Treena laid out Thedra's heavy robe, identical to what Treena and Reza wore but in soft grays, swirling whites, and hints of silver beads.

Without any preamble, as the eldest present, Reza began the mourning ritual of the Dalinda by lighting each candle. Treena came to stand before the blue candle while Reza took his place in front of the brown candle. They raised both arms in the air, palms up and waited.

The church bells tolled to announce the midnight hour, and they began to chant.

"We evoke the Elemental Guardians who light the fire that transforms you.

Who hold the water that shapes you.

Who drive the air that moves you.

Who turn the earth that heals you.

Who shape the metal that strengthens you.

We evoke the Elemental Guardians who provide the Dalinda to protect and guide you."

They lowered their arms to their sides with their elbows bent and their palms remained up. The next full strike was supposed to be spent in silent meditation where each mourner was expected to reflect on their loss. Treena found it near impossible to remain focused as her mind warred with the loss of Thedra, the arrival of Reza, her avoidance of Braith, keeping Aven safe and her upcoming training—if Aven passed her initiation ritual. She silently chastised herself and attempted several different mediation techniques to clear her mind of the chaotic thoughts...nothing helped.

Eventually the time passed, marked by the one strike of the church bells and they lowered their arms to their sides before Reza began the ritual to the Elemental Guardian Aria, the keeper of the element Air. He intoned Aria's virtues before asking him to welcome his faithful follower, Thedra, to his realm.

Treena just stared at the beautiful robe laid out and willed herself not to cry again.

Chapter 15
Sylvan

The preparations had finally been made to Sylvan's standards and he had slept a full night's sleep to be well rested for the search. He had warned Jorge and The First Elder that he planned to take his time and find out what he could while he searched for the girl that the inept Arch Deacon Ulrick had misplaced and then tried to cover up. He also explained that it may take longer if whoever had rescued her was now, no doubt, hiding her in a way that might make it difficult to find her. *You must be patient*, he had cautioned The First Elder. *I will have Jorge report to you as soon as I wake with good news he had promised.*

Jorge handed Sylvan the tonic and for a second, they just stared at each other before Jorge almost imperceptibly shook his head. "Damn those twins," Sylvan muttered as he wondered again what was in the concoction the First Elder insisted they drink. He knew that this was not the time to worry about such things. He had a vital task to perform and if he did it right he would be celebrated throughout history as the most accomplished Shaymmi to have ever lived. Sylvan knew that that title was worth the sacrifice of following the clear instructions of the First Elder.

Without further comment, Sylvan drank the repugnant blue liquid from his customary goblet and involuntarily grimaced as he swallowed. As per their normal routine, Jorge led him to his favored chaise and settled him in as the sun began to rise. As Sylvan's eyes lost their ability to see and became covered in a milky film, he closed them and focused on his breathing. Even though he wanted to get on with his task, he was a perfectionist and knew he couldn't rush the process. Taking his time, he slowly tensed and released each muscle beginning at his toes. He refocused his mind on building an iridescent curtain that hung before him. With a final calm thought and deep breath, he rolled his consciousness out of his body and through the flimsy curtain to enter the Elemental Plane.

As always, Sylvan savored this moment as his world became clear and sharp in a way very few had experienced. Through generations of research, it had been discovered that the Master Shaymmi was more powerful than the other Shaymmi and experienced the Elemental Plane more deeply than the normal Shaymmi's. If Sylvan could find the girl again, it would prove that it wasn't by chance and that he was the most powerful that had ever lived. He paused to savor a moment of anticipated glory before he floated out of the building and quickly glided over Cynsellam and toward Hamlyn.

This time he stopped to cherish the cacophony of different vibrations that made up the city of Hamlyn. He slowly acknowledged them before ignoring the vibrations of the element metal, then he pushed the lighter vibration of the element for air aside. They of course were still there, but he could tighten his focus to the point where he could overlook them. Moving from the outer city wall and main gate, he headed toward the last place the girl had been seen. As he moved over the city, he recognized then moved to the background of conscience the elements of fire, earth, and water. He sent out his thought a little wider and found the gentle, throbbing almost hypnotic pull of the deep slow vibration that possessed the young girl. It was simpler this time, for the sounds almost called to him and he knew what he was looking for, having refined his focus.

Sylvan paused as he realized the girl was not in the wharf area where he was headed. He smiled in his mind. *Good, a challenge. I will have to find her again.*

Without haste nor hesitation, he let the insistent tugging of the vibration turn him toward the Merchant Quarter, and he slowly moved his consciousness over the assorted buildings and streets that became wider as the area become more affluent. The pull became stronger as he moved toward the Market Sector along one of the outer walls. Sylvan came to a stop and hovered high over the expanse of a multitude of flowers in every shape and color you could imagine. The element of Earth sang to him amongst the glorious array of flowers. Acknowledging the element, he pushed it back to his subconscious and slowly narrowed his search to the tainted deep, raw throbbing that the girl carried within her.

Meticulously, Sylvan studied each person before moving onto the next one as this time he didn't want to get too close and scare her. He wanted to study her and ascertain all he could before he reported back. With a triumphant mental smirk, he found the girl perched on the edge of the central fountain, eating a breakfast pastry and watching a young woman chatting to a man who was loading buckets of flowers into the back of a cart.

As he watched, he tried to dampen the throbbing vibration as it was starting to give him a slight headache. After several false starts, he managed to compartmentalize it like the other elements so the sonorous pulse became tolerable for an extended period of time.

He noticed immediately that the girl was clean and wore much finer clothing this time. Her skirt was a soft blue and the blouse a pretty pink, but both were clean and well-fitted as opposed to the tattered mess he had discovered her in. Her cheeks had color, which could have simply been that she was not being frightened by him hovering over her or she was healthier as she was eating regularly. Her hair had been washed and was now held back with a simple white headband, but he was not close enough this time to see her eyes.

Sylvan watched patiently as the girl hopped down from the side of the fountain and began walking with the young woman she had been looking at while she ate. Sylvan switched his attention to the tall woman that walked beside her. He guessed her age to be early to mid twenties. She wore her hair under a green scarf, but from this distance, it was hard to make out any fine details of her face. What he did notice immediately was her thin waist which seemed to accentuate her ample bust. She wore a full skirt in a forest green and a low-cut white blouse, with a ruffle around the shoulders. The woman looked drawn and tired even from this distance, but she smiled and chatted as they walked.

He trailed behind them, keeping a safe distance so the child wouldn't panic. They eventually came to a white-washed brick florist shop with bright red shutters and bright blue unusually deep window boxes. A sign with yellow, blue, and red flowers hung above the door where they entered. Not long after, the cart filled with the flowers that Sylvan had watched the man load, rolled up. The door opened and the girl, the young woman, and a middle-aged man came out to help unload the cart.

Sylvan took the opportunity to study the man, who was exceptionally tall, probably as tall as Sylvan which was unusual. He wore clean, brown traveling clothes with mid-calf height black leather boots. Even from this distance his face was obviously weathered, and he had short-cropped brown hair that was graying.

While the girl was occupied with her two companions, Sylvan took the chance and moved his perception so he could fully feel the tainted throb that emanated from the child. His mental eyes narrowed slightly, and he readjusted his elemental senses—there was something about these two that felt different to Sylvan but he could not fathom what it was. *Perhaps I should have three of them captured to be studied?* he pondered. No, he wouldn't risk it. What happens if there was nothing unique about the other two and he had wasted everyone's time? He would look a fool and that is something that could never be tolerated. Perhaps he would come back and study them again once the distracting baritone vibrations from the girl were removed.

In quick time, the flowers had been unloaded and the cart moved away. The Church bells tolled the strike of eight and the red shutters of the florist were opened and the man lent out to place buckets of assorted flowers in the blue window boxes. For several strikes, Sylvan watched as people came and went from the shop. Several carts turned up at certain times to take away large bouquets of flowers that looked suspiciously like the ones he saw in church when he was expected to attend.

Without warning, panic seized Sylvan. He could no longer feel his body! There was no gentle tug from the north. There was nothing!

Fear gripped his consciousness, and he tried to fight the hysteria that clawed at his mental gut. Without a second thought of exposing himself to the girl, he opened up all his elemental senses in the hope that that would link him back to his body. He was almost overwhelmed with the onslaught of textured vibrations, but he was devastated to discover there was still no connection to his physical self. He fled back to Cynsellam and arrived two heartbeats later. He plunged back through the city and into Stronghold, the home of the First Elder. Quickly, he skimmed to his suite and through the closed door and would have fainted if it was possible in his state. His body was gone.

Chapter 16

Treena

Treena was exhausted. It was predawn and she hadn't slept as the ritual hadn't been completed until the church bells had tolled five times. Now she readied herself to go to the flower market and begin her day. Reza walked into the backroom where Treena was putting things in order and handed her a large mug of steaming herbal tea.

"Drink up, it should help revive you."

"Thank you." She took a tentative sip and was rewarded with a burnt tongue and a tangy aftertaste.

Aven entered the room with a welcoming yawn and then stopped as she looked up warily at Reza. Unconsciously she took a step back and shrunk in on herself.

"Can I come wif ya to the market, please?" she asked quietly.

Treena chose to ignore Aven's behavior as there was no point in trying to reason with her that Reza would never harm her. With what Aven had experienced, she didn't blame her for being afraid and wary of strangers and men in particular. "Of course you can join me. I welcome the company. Maybe we can get you a breakfast pastry."

As they walked to the market, Aven spoke quietly, "Thank ya for me new clothes. I've never 'ad me own clothes."

Treena smiled warmly at her. "I'm glad you like them."

They walked for a few more minutes before Treena spoke again. "Reza was my teacher, and Thedra was his very dear friend too," she explained quietly. "He won't be here long, but I need you to understand that he would never hurt you. Another man will be coming to the shop tonight and he is another who you will need to learn to trust. I am not asking you to change, I understand that that is simply too much for you at the moment." Treena caught Aven's hand and gently squeezed it with reassurance. "But I do need you to trust me."

Aven looked up at Treena with a wary look in her gold flecked brown eyes. "I trust ya. Ya came for me when the church took me." She swallowed and continued, "It's real hard to trust men."

Treena squeezed her hand again in understanding.

As expected, even with Treena's reassurance, Aven had spoken little around Reza and had instead spent the day covertly watching him and had remained on alert for the man to do something. It broke Treena's heart to see her so anxious, but she hoped that over time Aven would feel less distressed, because if she was correct, after tonight her training would begin and she would learn to defend herself.

Aven and Treena were putting away the dinner dishes when there was a knock on the florist shop door.

"That will be Stiann," Treena announced. "Wait here a moment, Aven, I have to get something." Treena could hear Reza and Stiann chatting in the front of the shop as she went into her bedroom and took the beautiful robe Thedra had made out of a chest and quickly put it on. Coming back into the kitchen, she found that Aven had put the remainder of the dishes away and was standing nervously in the center of the room waiting for her.

"Come." Treena held out her hand. Aven took it without hesitation and Treena bent down to be level with her face. "Aven, the next strike is going to be very strange for you. I need you to trust me more than you ever have. Nothing bad is going to happen, but you need to do what I ask."

Aven stared at her and said nothing.

Treena went on, "If you don't want to do this, you can leave. No one is ever forced to serve."

"I trust ya," Aven whispered. "I will serve."

Treena gave her a quick hug. "Let's go."

Treena led Aven into the secret room that they had mourned in last night for Thedra. Sitting at the ancient table was Reza and Stiann, and they both stood when Treena entered. Treena took a moment to trigger something on the inside wall and the door swung shut. She tugged on Aven's hand, and they moved toward the table. Aven was hunched over and almost trembling by the time they reached the men.

Stiann was the opposite to Reza in most ways. He was at least fifteen years older, short, rotund and chatty. "Hello, Aven. My name is Stiann, and I am very happy to meet you." He absently pushed the metal rim of his square spectacles up the ridge of his large nose. He noticed Aven's curious look. "Aren't they marvelous things? I call them spectacles. They help me see better, as I spend most of my time reading scrolls or writing them." He again pushed the frame back up as it attempted to slide down his nose. "I just haven't got the fit quite right. We are still working on it."

It appeared to Treena that Aven was too fascinated to be scared of the small, chubby man in the pure white robe.

Reza stood towering over everyone in his stunning, brown hued robe, silent as usual. He cleared his throat. "Welcome, Aven. Please, sit down."

"Hang on," Treena interrupted. She went to the long, low chest of drawers and took out a small glass bowl that looked to be filled with some form of liquid. With practiced ease she took out the brown colored contacts that covered her natural eye color. It was quite a relief to blink freely, without feeling there was always a small amount of grit in her eyes. The mastermind behind the glass in Stiann's spectacles was working to make the contacts smoother, but she had to be patient.

Stiann embraced her. "There is my darling Lady Katatreena."

As Treena sat, she noticed that Aven was openly staring at her. "Dyella used ta tell me stories about the golden eyed Sky Riders who ruled Duthyne. I fought they were jus stories to help me sleep. I used ta dream that ya would fly in and rescue us."

Treena smiled encouragingly. "They are true stories that we like to keep in circulation to help people remember a better time."

"Ye are all Sky Riders?" Aven looked sideways at Reza.

Stiann laughed cheerfully. "Goodness, no. Could you imagine me as a Sky Rider? Reza, like Katatreena, is a Dalinda, and I am an Elldean."

Aven frowned, confused. "So, you are not Sky Riders?"

"Sky Riders is the common name used amongst the population. Sky Riders were known as the Dalinda and they ruled Duthyne as the Elemental Sky Council," Treena explained. "Stiann is an Elldean, and they are also known as the Lore Keepers. He keeps records of us and who came before us. He has many ancient scrolls that describe the time before the coup by the Church of the One God."

"Then ya used to fly the Sky Hunters in the stories?"

Stiann answered sadly, "Yes, according to my scrolls they were beasts to behold with beautiful long necks and a wingspan as wide as the largest ship is long. They were wise and loyal and the only people that needed to fear them were those with bad intentions. They were known as the Oredmoor."

"Where are fey now? Where are ya Oredmoor?"

Treena shook her head and spoke softly. "Gone, they no longer exist. The Oredmoor were all slaughtered by the Church of the One God."

A silent tear rolled down Aven's cheek.

Reza spoke for the first time. "It makes me sad too."

"Why are ya tellin me this?"

Treena smiled at Stiann, who nodded back at her. "Because I believe you are a Dalinda."

"Me?" Aven squeaked. "I'm not special."

"Really? Have you noticed that your eyes are slowly changing color? What do you think happened to the door on the carriage they were taking you away in when you realized that I couldn't rescue you? You got frightened or angry enough that your power did something about it. And I'm not sure at all about the spectre that you saw but not everyone sees that, so that by itself makes you special," answered Treena.

"I did that ta the door? I fought it was one of ya." Aven swallowed. "How did I do it?"

Treena shrugged but it was Stiann who answered, "We are unsure. Each of you has an affinity to an element that you can learn to manipulate. It is said the Oredmoor you rode made you more powerful when you joined together."

Reza preempted the next question. "My element is Earth, Treena is Water, and Thedra was Air."

Aven sat there for several moments and said nothing. Treena knew from her own experience that it was wise to give her a little time to process what she was being told. There would be time to fill in any blanks they left tonight. Aven would have many years of training, and any questions would be answered when they came up. She was also younger than most when they showed the signs so that had to be taken into consideration.

"How da I know which one I am?" she finally asked.

Stiann answered, "There is a ritual that we will do tonight that will show us."

Aven went to speak and then stopped.

"Go on," urged Stiann.

"I ave lots of questions but I want ta know what element I am most. Can we da the test now? Maybe I will believe it more when I ave proof."

"That sounds fair," Stiann agreed.

Reza stood and Aven jumped in her chair. He frowned slightly but said nothing to her reaction to his sudden movement.

Treena rose too. "Stay here with Stiann, it will take us a few minutes to set everything up."

"Let me tell you a little more about the Dalinda while they prepare. Two people are born every seventeen years with the abilities of the Dalinda. This has always been kept a secret. Typically around the mid-teens their eyes turn gold and their powers start to manifest in subtle ways. Interesting little side note I have noticed is that when the change occurs, the new Dalinda always seems to be able to find someone that can help them."

Aven frowned and Stiann answered the unspoken question. "Though there are few Dalinda and Elldean Lore Keepers, there are still many supporters of the Dalinda and they hope one day to restore the Elemental Council; these devotees are known as Loyalists. They are the descendants of the servants and closest confidantes who aided the Elemental Sky Council and Oredmoor."

Treena placed the final candle on one of the corners of the pentagon that was scorched into the wooden floor and straightened. "We are ready."

Aven and Stiann looked up from their conversation. "Aven, go stand in the center of the pentagon. This ritual is for the Dalinda. I am here to observe and record only," he advised her.

Cautiously Aven moved to the center of the shape, making certain not to knock over one of the five unlit candles that stood at each point. "Sit on your knees with hands on the top of your thighs," instructed Reza.

Treena smiled inwardly as she remembered the measured, quiet tone that Reza had always taken when he instructed her. She silently wished that she would be as competent a mentor as he had been.

"Close your eyes and empty your mind of all your thoughts. Push all fear outward and focus solely on taking deep breaths—three measures in and three measures out. Keep your eyes closed until you are told otherwise," Reza continued.

The room was silent as they watched Aven follow the instructions and slow her breathing. Without talking, Treena and

Reza moved to the unlit candle that represented their element. Treena stood behind a stunning crystal cut large glass bowl which contained purified water and held a round floating blue candle that represented her element of Water. Reza stood behind a large roughly hewn red brown sphere with a flat base that was placed in a pile of dirt that sat upon a black slab of marble that symbolized his element of Earth.

With a silent nod to each other, they began to chant.

"We evoke the Elemental Guardians who light the fire that transforms you

Who hold the water that shapes you

Who drive the air that moves you

Who turn the earth that heals you

Who shapes the metal that strengthens you

We evoke the Elemental Guardians who provide the Dalinda to protect and guide you.

Bring forth the Guardian we are to serve."

Treena was surprised when before they had completed the first round of chanting one of the candles had ignited. The flame of a tall, white tapered candle, in a glazed blue plain candlestick that combined signified the element Air, was burning higher than anything she had seen before. It was simple but elegant in its power. They continued onto the second round of chanting when Treena was shocked to see two more of the candles ignite. The flames on the candles that represented Water and Metal burned brightly but smaller than the first candle. Treena looked to Reza, who raised his eyebrows at her but continued with the chant for the third and final time.

As the final words were uttered the last two candles of Earth and Fire began to smolder but didn't ignite. This was the moment when usually the supplicant was asked to open their eyes so they could see which candle had ignited to show them which Guardian they would serve—only one candle was ever lit. Confounded silence filled the room.

"Oh my," breathed Stiann into the silence, breaking the spell of the ritual and the stillness.

Reza looked puzzled but not overly concerned, so Treena took her cue from him and relaxed slightly. "Open your eyes, Aven. The truth has been revealed," he instructed.

Treena let out a little gasp of astonishment as Aven opened her eyes and showed that they now shone a bright gold as if the brown had been burnt away.

Chapter 17
Sylvan

His frustration and fear were rising to a fever pitch. The Master Shaymmi struggled to maintain his composure as feelings of hopelessness and a sense that he was going to lose himself to the Elemental Plane began to once again overwhelm him. Where could his body be and why had Jorge betrayed him?

Sylvan had spent the last day traversing the rooms and corridors of Stronghold in search of his corporeal body, as each strike rang through the extensive complex he had felt a little less sure of the situation and the tiny creep of apprehension. He now hovered above his bed in a vain attempt to resemble normalcy, as his mind continued to struggle with the reality of the situation.

When he had first returned, once he had felt the disconnection between his mind and body, he had frantically swept into his suite to discover his body missing from its usual position on the chaise. He had quickly surveyed the room to only then realize that Jorge was sprawled on the ground, his chair knocked over. For the first time since becoming a Shaymmi he didn't know what to do. As his consciousness floated about his manservant, he had a choice to make. Should he stay here and wait to see if someone came to help Jorge, or should he go to

The First Elder's rooms and wait for someone to use the Spirit Mirror and give away his secret that he had discovered how to use it. He had been keeping it secret for the time being so he could reveal the new knowledge when it was most convenient and fortuitous for him to do so.

Somewhat to his own surprise, he had chosen to wait by his servant's body to make certain that he was tended to. Waiting for Jorge to be found had also given him the opportunity to take a closer look at his room before it was disturbed once everyone knew he was missing. He had left his friend and slowly glided around the room, pausing at the chaise to consider again where his body could have gone.

No one had come to check on him by the time night fell and Sylvan had become quite miffed until he had recalled that he was the one that had made it clear to all that he was not to be disturbed.

Sylvan had then hovered uselessly for several strikes before Jorge regained consciousness. *Finally! Now something can be done*, he had triumphed to himself. He had then watched in stunned disbelief as Jorge went about straightening up the knocked over chair and placing a cold cloth on the back of his head. Sylvan was bewildered by his manservant's total lack of urgency at reporting his body missing. It had taken him quite a bit longer and only once Jorge had retired for the evening to realize that he wasn't going to report anything amiss. He had then made the decision to search Stronghold himself. He found nothing.

As he battled to keep his presence of mind he gave himself a mental shake and forced himself to pull it together. I am *the most celebrated Shaymmi to ever live. I am stronger than my predecessors and are relied upon by The First Elder*, he told himself. *I can either reveal my secret and ask for help or I can figure out a way to fix this myself and find the conspirators to this horrendous crime of body snatching.* Sylvan thought about it, analyzing all the options and finally coming to the conclusion that he didn't know who he could trust in Stronghold and that he wanted to return triumphant and with answers from his search - not defeated and in need of aid.

He was startled out of his thoughts by the entrance of Jorge as he came in and set about tidying up the bed chamber. Sylvan followed him as he moved out into the sitting area and watched as Jorge opened the door for the servant who entered carrying what should have been Sylvan's breakfast. Once the servant left Jorge quickly ate half the contents of the tray and placed it outside the door to be collected later. Sylvan fumed - another betrayal. It looked like Jorge was going to keep the charade going.

Without further thought, Sylvan flew out of Stronghold and the city of Cynsellam and back toward the child he had been studying. He had an idea forming.

Chapter 18

Treena

Treena had awoken to find Reza packed and ready to leave to pass the word to those who needed to know that Aven had been discovered and tested. The word would then be passed through the Loyalist top circle and eventually filter through to the lower levels where there would be rejoicing for the continuance of the Dalinda. Sadly, he would also carry word that Thedra had been killed by the church while rescuing the young Aven. Once Reza had left, Treena had spent the next half strike reassuring Aven that no one would blame her for the death of Thedra, and if Treena knew Reza at all, he would be turning it into another tool for them to keep the Loyalists hatred simmering for the corrupt church and all it represented.

After a busy morning, Treena decided to close the shop early so they could get Aven fitted for her first training gear. Fortunately, she went to a tailor who Braith had recommended years prior so there were no questions asked when she requested black tunic and trousers to fit Aven. In hindsight, Treena thought the shopkeeper probably thought she was being outfitted like that to be an apprentice thief as Aven kept her head down and didn't make eye contact with anyone.

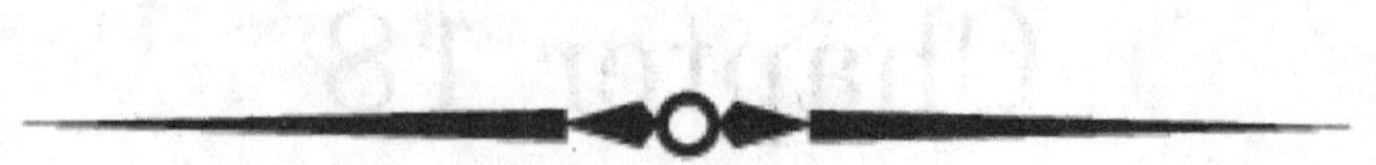

Aven adjusted her loose-fitting black trousers and tunic as she watched Treena straighten several items on the over-stuffed bookshelves. Treena wore the same style trousers and tunic but in a deep sea green with white waves cresting across the hem of the tunic and pant legs. Treena had explained that these tunic and trousers were their workout clothes and because Treena's element was Water hers were a stunning aquamarine in color. Once Aven had advanced to a certain level, she could then add her own designs and patterns onto the fabric to match her elements.

"Here, take this and put it on the table for me."

Aven moved quickly to take what Treena held out. "What is it?" Aven asked quietly as she walked to the ancient table and placed it gently in the center. Treena noted that Aven stood transfixed by the object.

"It is a bookend," Treena explained in a gentle voice. "I am told that that is what the head of an Oredmoor looks like."

Aven spun around and stared at Treena before her eyes were drawn back to the bookend. "It's beautiful, powerful...I don't ave words."

"Yes, it is those things. It was a gift from Thedra. She never told me where she got it from."

Treena finished arranging the candles and their holders along a shelf in the bookcase before handing Aven the white tapered candle in the blue candlestick that had been used in last night's ritual.

"Do you remember which point of the pentagon these sat on?"

Aven nodded and moved to put them on the correct spot.

"Good, now go kneel like you did yesterday."

Aven knelt in the center of the burnt shape while Treena knelt opposite her on the outside of the pentagon. "The elements are not always what you think they should be. Today you will hopefully learn the feel of your element that is specific to you. Air was often described by Thedra as uplifting. Reza believes the Earth feels rich and full of affirmation. I always feel an instant sense of calm when I connect with the water as if it soothes any anxiety I have," she explained.

"How can water be calm and soothin' when it rains so heavily and floods places. It can be truly terrifying?" frowned Aven.

Good, she is starting to feel comfortable enough with me to ask questions without hesitating.

"Yes, if looked at in a certain way, water is certainly all of those things, but all of the elements are terrifying and damaging when manipulated by outside forces—in their natural state they can be serene and positive to your being. Fire can destroy but it can also heat, for example. Nothing is ever as simple as it appears, particularly not an element." Treena smiled encouragingly. "Are you ready?"

"I think so."

"The first thing you need to do is light your candle. Shut out any thoughts you have, banish any doubts, acknowledge any pain then move it aside and settle your mind with the three-count breathing you did last night. Keep your focus solely on the candle in front of you." Treena settled her own breathing and gave Aven a few more moments before going on. "You need to repeat each line as I say it."

"We evoke the Elemental Guardians who light the fire that transforms you

Who hold the water that shapes you

Who drive the air that moves you

Who turn the earth that heals you

Who shapes the metal that strengthens you

We evoke the Elemental Guardians who provide the Dalinda to protect and guide you.

Bring forth the Guardian we are to serve."

Abruptly the flame on the wick of the Air candle erupted and unexpectedly again the candles for Water and Metal came to life while the two remaining candles smoked with heat. The flame from the Metal candle was too close to a pile of scrolls that were stuffed in the corner of the shelf, and they quickly caught fire. Aven jumped to her feet and began to look for something to stop the flames from spreading.

"Treena, how do ya open the door? I'll get water."

Treena laughed. "No need."

Without a second thought, Treena reached out with her mind and took control of the water that was in the crystal bowl the Water candle floated in and dumped the water onto the parchment. There was a brief sound of sizzling, and then the fire went out.

"You were so calm," exclaimed Aven in her loudest voice yet.

"It is what we are trained to do." She inclined her head to the soggy scrolls. "If truth were told, it is reassuring to know that I reacted so quickly. I think Reza would finally be happy." She stood and made her way to the bookcase, wrinkling her nose she picked up one of the limp parchment pieces. "I'm fairly confident that what we have destroyed we can get another copy from Stiann." She turned to Aven. "I think it might be safer if we put all the Elemental Candles out on the pentagon when practising for the time being." Treena smiled to take the sting from her words. "Until you have learned control."

The candles were moved to the corners of the burnt shape in the floor and the water was refilled from a flask that Treena took down from the top shelf of the bookcase. They were careful not to disturb the already lit candles as Aven resumed her place in the center.

"I am going to teach you an exercise to focus your mind and relax it from the outside world. You won't need to do this forever, but it is an excellent task to remember if you are feeling anxious and need to bring your thoughts back into line. It is called grounding, and with practice you will do it naturally.

"I want you to take a deep breath, in through your nose out through your mouth. Slowly look around you and find five things you can see. I don't need you to tell me, just say them in your mind." Treena waited a few moments before moving on. "Name four things you can touch." She paused again. Treena had always found this exercise beneficial when she wanted to quieten her mind from over thinking. "Three things you can smell."

Aven frowned before her brow cleared and she nodded.

"Two things you can hear." Treena moved to sit in front of Aven but outside the pentagon. "And finally, one emotion you feel."

A calm had appeared on Aven's face that Treena had never seen before, her shoulders were less hunched and her back and become straighter. All wonderful and encouraging signs. "Now, I want you to close your eyes and search inside for the place in your core, where you said you felt something when the door exploded. It is your center, your core. This is where your ability to manipulate your element resides." They sat quietly for several moments, and Treena watched Aven intently. "Keep your breathing calm and relaxed."

After a quarter strike of silence Treena stood. "There is no rush. Open your eyes."

Aven opened her eyes and looked at Treena with a frown. "How long did it take ya to find ya core?"

"About a week, which is fairly average. The longest it took was a season for one poor Dalinda and the shortest was two days."

Aven stood with her shoulders slumped.

"Help me blow out the candles and put them back on the shelf. Then I'm going to find out just how much work we have ahead of us with your fitness."

Aven groaned but did what she was told.

Treena smiled broadly. It was the first time that Aven had ever acted like her age and it was a joy to see.

For the next strike, Treena ran Aven through a series of tests to ascertain her strength and stamina. Her stamina ended up being average for her age while her strength was a little under and Treena surmised that it was due to a lack of food. Her lack of strength was not a serious deficit and would easily be able to be corrected and advanced with the healthy large meals Treena was feeding her and a workout plan to build muscle quickly.

"You did well. Tomorrow, after your contacts are fitted, we will start your training. Every day once the shop is closed, we will work half a strike on your elemental powers, then a full strike on getting you into shape and weapons training. Then we will stop for the evening meal before spending the night working on learning to read and write," Treena explained.

Treena didn't think it could be possible, but Aven's shoulders slumped further. "I 'ave ta learn ta read an write too?"

Giving her a quick squeeze, Treena nodded and moved the damp light brown fringe out of the girl's eyes. "And you will have to learn to speak correctly."

Aven grumbled something under her breath before smiling shyly at Treena. "If it keeps me free from Pa, I'll do anyfing ya ask."

Chapter 19

Hadrian

Slowly Hadrian allowed her body to unwind. Starting from her toes, she tensed and slackened each muscle before moving up her legs through her torso and out to her fingertips. She meticulously constructed the heavy velvet curtain in her mind's eye before slowly rolling her consciousness out of her body, feeling a distinct pop as it separated and pushing it through the curtain and entering the Elemental Plane. She exalted in the freedom she always felt when entering the Plane. Her worries fell away. Her need to prove herself to her father and her obsession with besting Sylvan became inconsequential for a few moments as the peace and harmony that she experienced when she opened up to the lower, soothing lower vibrations engulfed her. Hadrian's thoughts briefly turned to the terror she had felt when she had been cut off from returning to her body, and she paused to consider how Sylvan was faring, but it was a fleeting thought as she turned her focus toward her goal of finding the girl and returning triumphant. *Sylvan would live and hopefully be more humble when his body and mind were eventually reunited,* she justified to herself.

Hadrian refocused her thoughts and rose slowly up and out of Stronghold and hovered above the sprawling city of Cynsellam to gain her bearings before moving South East and following the road to Namurrn. She took her time, enjoying the freedom she always experienced on the Elemental Plane. Once she came upon the moderate sized town of Namurrn, she continued in a more southerly direction and followed the Hamlyn River until she reached her destination.

Jorge had confirmed that Sylvan had found the girl child in Hamlyn, but that was all the details he knew. Hadrian had never been to Hamlyn, as her assigned sectors were always to the North West, as that's where she had grown up. As she always liked to enjoy a leisurely breakfast before she entered the Elemental Plane, it was almost time for the midday strike when she arrived.

Hadrian was surprised to discover that what she had assumed to be a small harbor town was actually a large city. Hovering above the right side main gate, she took in the panorama before her and was almost overwhelmed by the cacophony of elemental tones. The city had a very different tone and texture to the capital Cynsellam, and she, like all Shaymmi, had learnt to never fully open herself to the Elemental Plane while within Cynsellam as the sheer size of the population and all that meant could overpower and confound the senses.

She faced a high curved wooden wall with two large gates allowing access into the city for the farmers who brought their goods via road rather than barge. Kets Harbour sparkled in the distance, the elemental call of the open water was far more alluring than the sluggish water to her left where the river met the bay, and the wharf area gave off the fetid vibrations of unwashed fishermans' bodies and fish. Her elemental senses were assaulted as she had not thought to dull her abilities. Hadrian could feel the tang of metal as the blacksmiths pounded it into shape, the bite of their fire as it belched heavy black smoke into the air. She could feel the vibrations of the air grow heavy with the stench it carried from the knackers and tallow makers.

Wrinkling what she considered her nose when in this state, she slowly refined her senses until she could still feel the vibrations on the Plane but they were no longer overwhelming as she would have at home in Cynsellam. She could still discern the differences in the elements but her sense of them was dimmed. *Maybe this is what not as talented Shaymmis' felt like all the time*, she mused.

Returning her focus to the view in front of her, she took in the five sturdy bell towers that truly dominated the landscape with the impressive church complex, that was run by the Arch Deacon Ulrick surrounding the center tower. She knew that each of the towers would have a church below it, as the same of every tower in Duthyne. The First Elder was fond of pointing out that if you could see the bell tower, you always knew the One God was near.

Where to begin? The sectors she had been assigned since becoming a Shaymmi had mainly consisted of farmland, small country villages, and the base of the restricted Double Ridge

Mountain Range. *How had Sylvan found the girl amongst all these others?* Maybe her recent find hadn't been as impressive as she thought compared to this.

Hadrian had exalted and gloated when she had discovered the broken shield unearthed in the newly ploughed field. The pull of the metal and something undefinable within the shield had been intoxicating as she skimmed the newly opened earth. If she was being honest with herself, she had been gliding lower than usual as she had been enjoying the sweet vibrations of the freshly turned soil when the abrupt interruption of the metal and other vibration interrupted her pleasure.

Her resolve began to waver. Hadrian began to turn her thoughts back to Cynsellam—maybe the task she had before her was too much? Softly she could hear her father's stern school master voice sigh with disappointment. "You are too quick to give up. Nothing worthwhile is easy. You must continue to push yourself. Being the best is the only acceptable outcome in this house."

Strengthening her belief in herself, she firmly turned back toward Hamlyn and chose to start to her right, as far away from the wharf and poor areas as possible.

Chapter 20

Treena

Treena sat ever so slightly slumped next to the Cartman she had hired to bring her assorted purchases of flowers back to the florist. This morning she had allowed Aven to sleep in while she visited the flower market. Aven would need all the rest she could get as her training would be extensive and intense until Treena felt that she could protect herself better. She also couldn't leave the shop or be seen as her eyes were too obvious, so she may as well rest when she could.

The cart rounded the final bend to the shop and Treena sighed inwardly; she was tired from so many things, but she couldn't rest. Her heart ached for her lost friend, and what was an acute loss was now moving into a never-ending grief and hollowness that had settled into the essence of her being. Treena had spent many strikes agonizing over what she could have done differently that night to save Thedra and rescue Aven and had come up with no answers. She had also spent many moments playing the "what if?" game—to no avail. She could not—and Thedra would never have allowed it—have left Aven in the hands of the Church, especially now her eyes had turned, confirming Treena's original suspicions.

As they approached the shop, Treena recognized Braith leaning against the red door that matched the tightly closed shutters. He wore his customary dull colored trews and collared tunic. His brown hair curled softly into the collar and his high forehead showed premature frown lines. Shaking off her fatigue, she sat a little straighter and admitted somewhere deep down that she was pleased he had come even if he was defying her wishes to be left alone until they could ascertain if the church was still looking for Aven. She had missed her friend.

He smiled warmly and helped her down from the cart by grabbing her around the waist.

"You look worn out and have lost weight," he commented.

Treena laughed. "You sound like my Ma. No hello?"

With Braith's help, they quickly had the cart unloaded and the Cartman had left with a cheerful wave. Treena had yet to open the door. "Aren't you going to let me in?"

"Why are you here?" Treena blocked the door and subconsciously rolled onto the balls of her feet and back. Her voice was soft, but he knew an answer was being demanded.

"I wanted to check on Aven." He nodded his head in the direction of the two thieves who were their acting guards across the road. "They say she hasn't been out of the shop in days. Is she sick? Have you heard that they are still looking for her?"

Treena needed to make a decision. She had often thought about revealing her identity to her friend. After all, he had earned her trust several times over their two decades of friendship. She knew his secret. He, in some way, had the right to know hers. As Aven had now been revealed, Treena was no longer the youngest Dalinda and was seen to have full voting rights and privileges, so she made her first official decision without consultation with anyone and opened the door to the shop. "Aven, Braith is here to see you."

Aven stood in the shadows of the storeroom and did not enter the shop area. "Do ya really wan me ta come out?"

"Stay there while we bring the flowers in, then you may greet Braith."

With Braith's help, the morning's purchases were brought in swiftly and the door was firmly closed and bolted to the outside world.

Aven stepped out into the room as Treena lit more candles but continued to look at her feet and keep a fair distance from the man.

Braith knelt down to Aven's level but didn't move closer. "Are you well?"

Aven lifted her heart-shaped face and looked Braith directly in the eye.

"Holy Goddess Aria!" he swore and stood quickly.

Treena moved to stand beside Aven as she knew Braith had scared her with his sudden movements.

"That's impossible...the Sky Riders don't exist anymore. The Sky Hunters died and no more came." Braith took a deep breath and looked at Treena. He narrowed his eyes and stepped forward, which in turn made Aven move behind Treena.

"You are frightening Aven," Treena spoke softly. "She is only coming into her power and her eyes have only been changed for a few days—this is as new to her as it is to you."

"You really expect me to believe this nonsense?" Braith was incredulous. "Those golden eyes are a great party trick."

"Braith, think about how she got out of the prisoner carriage." Treena remained calm but her frustration levels were rising. She had never had to convince anyone of who she was before.

Braith frowned but looked stubborn as he moved to sit on the wooden chair in the corner. Aven moved out from behind Treena just as there was a sharp tap on the door. Without being told, she scurried into the darkened storeroom and Treena went to open the door. On her way to the door, she put her pointer finger to her lips and indicated to Braith to remain quiet.

Treena unbolted the door and opened it a crack before smiling and stepping back to let the newcomer in. "Master Piress, so good of you to come so early."

A short, fine-featured middle-aged man with perfect white teeth came to stand in the center of the room. He nodded politely to Braith in the corner and peered intently at Treena.

"Master Braith, please allow me to introduce you to Master Piress."

Piress moved to Braith, who stood rapidly to receive the warm handshake Piress offered. Piress looked to Treena for confirmation, she nodded ever so slightly.

"So nice to meet a fellow Loyalist," Piress exclaimed excitedly.

"Indeed," muttered Braith as he took his seat. "Please, don't let me interrupt you. I know the shop must open soon."

"This way," Treena said brightly as she led Piress into the storeroom and lit several lanterns, giving the room much needed light and revealing Aven sitting patiently on a stool with Treena's precious hand mirror propped up on the tiny table in front of her.

"I'm going to begin on this morning's orders before it's too late and I have churchmen at the door wondering why deliveries for this morning services aren't done."

Treena left the storeroom door open and moved back into the shop where Braith waited. He remained in his chair and glared at her.

"Rather than being grumpy, you could help," she said a little too brightly. She didn't like him being angry with her and she couldn't explain any further with Piress in the adjoining room.

He grunted but stood and began to help her. They spent the next quarter strike in silence with Braith occasionally beginning to speak and then abruptly looking to the storeroom and stopping himself. He obediently trimmed the ends of the flower stems just as he had been shown years ago by Treena and then handed her the flower to put in the beautiful arrangements she created.

Piress coughed politely as he entered the room and bowed formally to Treena. "Lady Aven is ready to go back out into the world," he proudly announced. Aven trailed behind him, her head and shoulders in their usual slumped position. "The

Dalinda don't hunch, and they don't fear people. Stand up tall, Lady Aven. You can now again look people in the eye without concern of revealing yourself," he admonished in a kindly tone.

Treena was astounded to see Aven smile slightly as she lifted her head to show that her eyes were now a deep brown—very similar to Treena's. "Oh, they look lovely, Master Piress. You have done exceptional work, as usual."

"It is my pleasure, Lady Katatreena. We are here to serve." He bowed with profound respect that made Braith scowl. "Well, I shall be off to open my own store before people start wondering where I have got to."

And without further comment Piress collected his bag and exited the florist.

Braith's breath exploded from him as if he had been holding it the entire time Piress had been there. He threw down the flower he was holding and folded his arms in a very good imitation of a petulant child, or so Treena thought. She laughed lightly at her friend before instructing Aven to go fetch a bucket of water from the well at the end of the street. Once Aven was gone, Treena finally faced Braith.

"Well? Go on." Without thought, she adjusted her blouse to expose a tad more breast.

"Don't do that. You can't distract me."

Treena flushed but shrugged. "It's habit now."

"What is a Loyalist?"

"Someone who still serves the Dalinda and the Elemental Council. They are the descendants of our servants and friends who escaped when the coup occurred."

"Why did Master Piress assume that I was a Loyalist?"

Treena went back to her bouquet making. "Because you saw Aven's eyes."

"I'm not sure what I saw." Braith sounded confused. "They are brown again now." He switched topics. "Why did he call you Lady Katatreena?"

"Because that's my name."

Braith raised his voice. "Stop playing games. Aven's eyes were gold and now they are brown. We have been friends for two decades and I only now find out you have another name. I'm not finding this funny at all. Are you just having a laugh?"

"I'm not handling this very well at all, am I?" Treena was regretful. "My name is Katatreena, but my brothers couldn't say it, so it was shortened to Treena and it stuck. When I became a Dalinda, it was decided that Katatreena was too distinctive a name, so I continued to use Treena in public. All the Dalinda were known as Lords and Ladies, thus Loyalists call me Lady Katatreena. Personally, I think they get a certain satisfaction from using the secret name... as if having a secret underground society is not enough."

They both jumped as the door banged open and Aven walked in carrying her bucket of water. She placed the bucket in front of several empty buckets.

"What about Aven's eyes?" Braith persisted.

"Master Piress is a glassblower and a Loyalist. His ancestors were able to create colored glass lenses that cover our gold eyes and allow us to blend in."

Braith moved closer to Treena and leaned in to study her eyes. He was so close that their noses were almost touching. Treena found it a little unsettling for no reason she could understand.

"There is an ever so slight rim, but you would never know it if you didn't know what you were looking for." He frowned and stepped back. "I almost believe you."

Treena smirked at him. "This should help you to understand and grasp the situation.

"Aven lock the door, please." She closed her eyes for a moment and refocused her center. Calling on the cooling touch of water that was never far from her reach, she coaxed the well water from the bucket Aven had brought in and manipulated it to swirl around Braith's head before separating it into three separate waterfalls and having it gently come to settle in each empty bucket. Then with a practiced hand she removed her glass lenses to reveal her gold eyes. "Now do you believe me?"

Braith stood staring at her for several moments before he answered. "You are Dalinda."

"That's what I have been trying to tell you." Treena turned to Aven. "Can you please fetch my mirror?"

He moved to stand in front of her and again leaned in. His honey brown eyes stared hard into her gold ones. "Stunning. Your eyes are stunning."

He was so close Treena she felt his hot breath as he spoke. Aven interrupted the moment by returning with the mirror. Without preamble, Treena expertly placed the brown glass over her eyes and blinked them back into place. "Now, I know you must have a lot more questions, but they will have to wait. The bouquets for the service must be done quickly and you either need to help or leave."

Braith smiled for the first time that morning. "Fine, my questions can wait." He kissed her on the cheek, bowed to Aven, and left.

"He really likes ya." Aven giggled.

Chapter 21
Sylvan

The constant need to dim his consciousness was tiring. Sylvan had stopped on his way to Hamlyn and let down all the barriers as he gently floated over a field, next to the Hamlyn river. He found peace for a brief time. The elements on the plane aligned perfectly in such a serene surrounding, they were perfectly balanced as the Gods intended. He knew it was blasphemous to believe in the Elemental Gods as the First Elder led the Church of the One God, but his family had secretly paid homage to all the Gods when they prayed in the family chapel to the One God. The One God was supposed to represent each facet of the elements, but that had never sat well with Sylvan. He had never pondered why, as that was sacrilege, and he was grateful and didn't want to jeopardize his position as Master Shaymmi, but it didn't feel true once he had learned the secrets and experienced the wonder of the elemental plane for himself and the unique separate feel of each element. They were not facets; they were absolutes in his opinion.

He had only moved on from the blessed respite when the elemental plane was disturbed with the vibrations of a large barge packed with livestock and people could be felt making its way down the river.

Now hovering above the Florist shop, Sylvan slowly sank through the thatched roof and into what turned out to be the kitchenette. He noted that it was clean, cozy, and empty. Moving out the door, he glided into what could only be described as a storeroom. It had a large cupboard along the back wall and shelving lined with buckets, vases, colored paper, thin wire, and what he assumed were tools used to cut stems of flowers. There were two more doors leading from the storeroom.

Sylvan chose the one opposite the one he had just come from and slid through the door to discover a bedroom beyond. It was a simple room with a large bed that looked surprisingly and extraordinarily welcoming and soft. Pushed up against the far wall was another bed but this one was smaller and not so well appointed in its bedding. He assumed it was the child's bed. Like the kitchenette, this room was neat, sparse, and empty.

Moving out of the room, he made his way into the florist shop at the front of the dwelling. With his elemental senses dulled he could only just acknowledge the underlying element of earth that permeated the room. Being a florist shop, it only stood to reason that he would feel the warmth and healing strength of the earth.

He looked around the larger room and noted the wooden chair in the back corner, buckets lined up in neat rows, ready to receive the morning's delivery and a huge scarred work bench that dominated one side of the room.

Sylvan felt his frustrations flare as the girl was not in this room either. He was a little confused. He had been watching the shop for several days and had come to know their routines well. They should be home. The young men that rotated their watch had not left to follow them. It was after supper and typically they didn't leave once they closed the shutters and door to the shop for the evening.

He quickly swept through the rooms again, only to remain disappointed. How was it possible that she was not here? He knew he had not seen her leave. He felt his panic rise again. *Where was she? Maybe this was a mistake.*

Stop it! he admonished. *This is not the time for hysterics.* He could almost hear his Grantha speak those words to his eldest sister, who favored immediately over-reacting when events didn't happen the way she felt they should.

If he narrowed his focus, he could feel the deep undeniable hum that she emitted. She was near, but where? Letting down his barriers to allow him to experience all of the elemental plane, the unmistakable vibration became more pronounced and he could feel it, of all places, under him. Without further thought, he sank through the floor.

The backlash of her terror as he appeared in the room almost drove him out again. This time he was slightly more prepared and gradually dulled his senses until the waves of whatever she was emitting were dampened enough to no longer cause pain. He could concentrate on looking around the room and trying to find a way to communicate now that the heat from her fear was not as harsh.

He was shocked to find a large room, with a complete mirrored wall at one end and on the opposite wall a large bookshelf crammed with many items, some of which he could discern no use for. In the middle of the smooth floor was some form of pattern burnt into the wood, but it was difficult to see exactly what the shape was because the young girl was kneeling on it, with the woman kneeling beside her, her arms wrapped protectively around the waif's slim shoulders. The young girl stared at him, while the woman talked quietly in her ear and looked around the room occasionally but obviously couldn't see him.

He hovered there, his insubstantial hand held open, hoping that if he didn't move the young girl would eventually see he wasn't about to attack or harm her and calm down enough that he could try to communicate with her. As he waited for her to stop screaming, he noted that she was wearing clean, new clothing in a style of black tunic and loose pants that reminded him of the elite warrior monks training attire. The woman wore the same type of clothing but in a sea green with white on the hems. *How very odd,* he thought to himself. *Why would they be wearing that style of clothing and be in this strange, hidden room?*

No one can scream forever and eventually and thankfully she ran out of puff and subsided. He felt the dull throb of her terror but he could also sense it had eased slightly. He saw that the woman continued to talk to her but was now helping her to rise. He was shocked to discover that what they had been kneeling on was an Elemental Pentagon burnt into the floor. *Oh, this is even better.* He felt triumphant. His choice to not contact the First Elder about his situation and rather go and seek out the child and find out all he could was becoming quite fortuitous. Now, he had to put his next step of the plan into place. By the end of this he would be covered in glory at what he had survived and gleaned.

Slowly, as to not set off more screaming, he began to move toward the bookshelf, in the hope he could find something to help him reach the girl. His luck held as he spotted a set of learning alphabet tiles on the table situated in the corner. He floated above the table and waited.

The woman watched intently as the girl lifted a shaky hand and pointed in his direction. After another discussion, they both moved towards the table, the girl walking slightly behind the woman. He pointed to the tiles. The girl bravely nodded at him and set out the alphabet tiles in order while the woman took the parchment and quill that sat beside them. They both took a step back and waited.

Deliberately he pointed toward a single tile. As if confirming his choice, the waif slowly crept forward and touched the same tile. The woman wrote it down.

It took half a strike to signal each letter clearly. By the end of it, he was exhausted and the girl no less wary. He needed to remove himself from her presence as having to keep up so many shields was exhausting, and he felt he was losing grip on his essence. He again took great care to move slowly, but once he was through the ceiling and then the thatched roof, he let his barriers down slightly and between thoughts he was again approaching the haven of his rooms in Cynsellam.

Chapter 22

Hadrian

The vista was glorious as the last of the sun's rays fell across the gently rolling hills in the distant as it headed toward the horizon. It was still hot but thankfully a breeze had started to take the sting out of the heat of the day. Hadrian absently twirled the stunning gold bracelet between her pointer fingers as she reflected on her frustrations and triumphs of the day. It was day three in her search, and she had only just moved out of the wealthiest Guildsmen and merchant quarter and onto the area where the majority of the Guildhalls stood in a large square all facing each other with the internal section being used for markets and fairs. She did have to admit that she had spent several chimes on the second day, when the sky had been clear, absorbing the elements that flowed in from Kets Harbor, that Hamlyn looked over. The richest quarter sat on the cliffs facing out to the large harbor and beyond and Hadrian had found the elemental flow of the water mesmerizing.

The search was slow-going with her need to check every mansion from the cellars to the attic, to the work sheds and stables. She had felt no unusual pull within the elemental plane and returned each day exhausted. None of the Shaymmi did more than three days Elemental planing in a row because the concentration it took was enormous and mistakes were made when you were tired. Mistakes were to be avoided at all costs while entering and exiting the plane as your consciousness could be lost forever to wither and die, consumed by the elements if you didn't handle the separation expertly. But she had no choice; she would go out again tomorrow in search of the girl as she knew she only had limited time before Sylvan would be missed and Jorge, his manservant, would not be able to cover it up.

Her father had said he would arrive at the beginning of the next season and she wanted to impress him with being the First Elder's favored Shaymmi because she had found the latest relic and would by then have rediscovered the girl that was highly sought after. It would prove that Hadrian was keeping the citizens of Duthyne safe in a way that only a handful could and that she was the best at it at the present time.

The day had started out perfectly with the First Elder calling her to his office a full chime ago and consulting her on the bracelet she now held. If Hadrian could solve the puzzle to the bracelet riddle, then it would be a triumphant moment that she had striven for for so long. Her father would finally be proud of her without condition. It still rankled her that even when she had succeeded at school and got perfect marks, he would say that the exam was marked on a curve or her tutors were being influenced by the fact that he was the Dean and wanted to appease and impress him. Nothing was ever good enough, but this time would be different. He would finally be proud.

A gasp from behind her quickly evaporated her daydreaming and she turned in her chair to find Cyrus standing there staring at the bracelet she played with.

"Where did you get that?" he asked in a voice barely above a whisper.

Hadrian was relieved; she had made the right choice. "So, you know what this is?"

"Yes, it's a trinket bracelet and very rare." He sat down beside her without being invited and continued to stare at the jewelry.

"May I?" he held out his hand.

Hadrian shrugged and pooled it gently in his palm. "What can you tell me about it?"

Cyrus held the piece in his hand, as if weighing it for several moments before laying it flat on the table. The bracelet was yellow gold and as thick as Hadrian's little finger. It was exquisite and heavy and when the First Elder had asked her to see if she could discover anything from it, she had immediately sensed what could only be described as a warmth to it. Being tired from her daily journey to Hamlyn, she had asked him if she could perhaps take it to study and when she was rested she would then travel the plane to see if she felt anything from it that way. She had then audaciously suggested that perhaps she could take it to Cyrus to see if he could tell them anything further. The First Elder had agreed to both requests. It was a heady feeling to know he trusted her.

"It's old," he began. "Perhaps even ancient. But it's well cared for and has been added to over the centuries." He pointed to several large, circular links. "Here and here, if you have a practiced eye, you can just pick up where it has been reinforced where obviously it has worn over the years." He carefully turned it over. "And here also. The fastening loop has been repaired several times by an expert hand."

"What about the... what did you call them?"

"The trinkets?"

"Yes, the trinkets. What are they?"

Cyrus picked up the bracelet and pointed to a trinket that was attached to the bracelet. "They were typically decorative pendants that usually signified something important in the wearer's life. Take this one, for example." He pointed to what looked to be a tiny gold cup. "This is a fairly new one, only a decade or two old by my estimations. I would guess it is a thimble, like those used by seamstresses. Was the owner a seamstress?"

Hadrian shrugged but continued to look earnestly at the bracelet. "I have no idea. I got it from The First Elder. What do you think this one was?" She pointed to a worn charm with very little detail.

Cyrus held the trinket up to the fading light of the sun and turned it from side to side. "My closest guess would be an instrument of some type. Perhaps a fiddle or gittern?"

"What about that one? It looks to be so old that it is thinner than the rest."

"Maybe a type of bird? I think those are wings and the long tail bit could be trailing feathers." Cyrus looked away from the bracelet and straight at Hadrian. "Why did he give this to you?"

Hadrian met his eyes. "He wanted to know if I could sense anything from it. I guess with everyone believing that Sylvan is still unavailable, as he searches for that damn girl, I was his next choice. So if I can learn anything about the bracelet, my status will continue to rise. I asked him if I could show it to you as you may have an idea of what it is, and I was correct."

"Did you sense something from it, like he hoped?"

They both returned to looking at the bracelet. "It's odd. There is something coming from it, but I have no idea what it is and it is very faint. Tomorrow morning, before I head toward Hamlyn for the day, I will take a closer look at it while I am on the Elemental Plane."

"Would it be possible for me to take it back to my shop once you have looked at it? There should be maker marks on each trinket. I could see if I can find anything that is clear enough, and I might be able to recognize one of the marks."

Taking it from Cyrus, Hadrian laid it on her wrist. "I would be the envy of everyone if I had one of these. Imagine how famous you would be if you brought them back into fashion. How long would it take you to make me one?"

Cyrus smiled as he looked at the bracelet on her wrist. "It would depend on how many trinkets you wanted made to go on it."

Chapter 23

Treena

Treena always felt content in the Scribe shop that served Elldean Stiann, a Lore Keeper of the Dalinda. She felt content sitting at the large ink-stained table as the final rays of the sun streamed through a cleverly designed window that sat in the middle of the roof in the back area of the shop, hidden from view from the patrons that entered by floor to ceiling bookshelves that sat in rows along one wall. It was a private spot that was reserved for his most auspicious patrons and occasional students. As Aven settled into a chair with a beginner's book she had chosen, Treena sighed. "This was where I learned to read and write too."

She recalled spending late afternoons bent over the parchment, practicing her letters with Stiann sitting patiently beside her. It had been discovered after several weeks of frustration that Reza had a learning disability, and he kept teaching her to write the letters backwards, which she then compared to her letter tiles. He couldn't perceive what he was doing wrong. Stiann had fortunately visited to check on things and offer his assistance in training the newly discovered Dalinda when Treena had asked for clarification and the issue had come to light. He had taken over that part of her education, which Reza had been grateful for, and she had proved to be an excellent student.

The Scribe's shop was still calm, quiet and smelled wonderful to Treena, a vast difference to her home life as a teen where she lived in the Fishermen's part of town, as it always smelled of rotting fish; and where, when her three brothers were home, was overwhelmingly noisy. It was a corner shop with large meticulously cleaned windows along the two exposed walls to allow as much light as possible in to work by. In front of the windows were four desks—two along each window, which typically sat four young men, one per desk, with parchment and quill carefully scribing their work. What people did not know was that two of the men were doing other people's paid scribing work, while the other two were copying the latest saucy romance novels that were in great demand from the wealthy women of the city.

This, of course, was strictly forbidden by the Church so it made it even more tantalizing to own one and gossip about it with female friends and dream about a different life where love was more important than money and prestige. Though, if the wives were perfectly honest with themselves, none would be willing to give up their pampered existence now that they had grown accustomed to having the best. But it was fun to dream and sigh longingly about the perfect love of a handsome man. What the wives did not know was that the servants who could read were taking the already used copies and reading them to the other staff members of the house in hushed tones when the masters were asleep or out, returning the book each morning before anyone was up to discover their secret. Churning out the lusty page turners had become such a significant money maker for Stiann that he funneled back into the continuing works of expanding his library and learning all he could that might help the Dalinda one day to rule again.

She sat, sipping her hot lemon drink and watching Aven slowly move her fingers across the page and sounding out any unfamiliar words, correcting her when she had to. It was a perfect rest day afternoon. All the shops were closed, and she had done her morning ritual of going to the required church attendance with her family and having lunch with them in a local tavern near the market district. It was her great delight to be able to treat them once a week to a scrumptious meal and to give thanks for them being so understanding about keeping her secret and the extra hours that training and caring for Aven now took up. Her mother, in particular, had welcomed Aven to the rest day lunches, continually tutting in dismay at her under-fed frame.

Stiann came around the over-sized bookshelf with two aged and relatively small scrolls and placed them carefully on the table.

"I think I have found what you seek." It had been a few days since the spectre had interrupted their training and Treena had gone to Stiann for help in finding the words he had slowly spelt out to Aven. "I think what you want to know should be in one of these scrolls. Take one and start reading, but be careful," he warned. "These predate the coup."

Treena was extremely careful as she took the scroll closest to her and slowly untied the string that held the two rolled ends together. She took in the brittle parchment and fine, neat writing as she carefully unrolled each end over the table. Treena sat and brought the lantern closer to the scroll to see the faded writing as dusk approached overhead.

It was a letter from a trainee Dalinda to their family. He spoke of his training and growing love for his Oredmoor and profound respect for the rest of the Dalinda Council, his Shomma, and the Den Keepers assigned to his Oredmoor. He missed home and was hoping that the use of a Spirit Mirror, to contact them directly and see their faces, would be available to him once he had completed his training and proved his worth.

"It's not much, but yes, Spirit Mirror is in here," Treena announced excitedly.

"I seem to have something in this one too," Stiann added. "This is an entry made by the Elemental Sky Council Chronicler approximately 160 years before the rise of the First Elder and his corrupt cohorts. It was reported in the Council meeting that the Spirit Mirror had been successfully installed in its new location in Hamlyn and that Lord Aydan had tested it at dawn to confirm that communication had been established with the Arch Deacon of Hamlyn." He looked up from the scroll. "That's it, that's all that is written about it but they go on to talk about patrols and an upcoming Elemental Earth Festival."

"Patrols?" interrupted Aven. "What does it mean?"

There was a heavy sigh from Stiann. "It is often discussed that the Dalinda patrols were not the smartest way to help rule Duthyne. The Dalinda and their Oredmoor would go out on fortnightly patrols and visit different areas of the country to make certain that the Higher ranked priests and their monks were being trained and doing their job effectively and to punish any miscreants with major transgressions. They were also there to protect our borders, which are vast. Only half of the Elemental Council ever went out, while the remainder stayed at the Compound and saw to the daily business of running the country."

"How was goin out ta help people bad?" Aven frowned.

Treena answered, "It's never bad to help someone. The Dalinda of the time were revered but also, if we are being blunt, seen as aloof and unapproachable as they lived in the Compound so far from most cities and towns. They left it up to the priests and monks to take care of the general population and were only reported to or called upon in times of greater need. Yes, they did patrols but that never truly brought them into contact with the common folk for very long so they lost touch with what was important and also couldn't see how the First Elder and his corrupt priests were insinuating that the Elemental Scriptures were misinterpreted and that they knew the true way." She paused to sip her lemon tea. "There has been much debate over the years as to how we would run the country differently if we ever regained power."

"Do you fink that will appen?"

"Without the Oredmoor I don't see how. All we do is hope and train and continue to believe that the Elemental Sky Council can be resurrected before the First Elder and his lackeys completely deplete Duthyne's resources and do irreparable damage to the poor and under class, when their job as church members was to take care of those very same people". Treena expelled her breath in a frustrated rush. "This is a discussion for another time. I want you to keep asking questions but for now we should get back to the spectre and its request of the Spirit Mirror."

Stiann refilled her teacup before taking a seat. "It seems fairly clear now we know what a Spirit Mirror is that this visitor you have had, Aven, is wanting us to find one so it can communicate with us. What we need to think about is whether we should trust it or simply ignore it?"

Treena shrugged. "What's the harm in finding the Spirit Mirror? We can decide what to do once we get it." She turned to Aven. "What do you think? You are the one who can see the spectre."

Aven swallowed and fidgeted in her seat, though she didn't shrink away from the question or Stiann's gaze noted Treena. "I don't get a feelin that the fing wants ta hurt me. The first time I saw it, I jus got a fright."

"That settles it. Find the Spirit Mirror and then we decide what to do next," agreed Stain. "I am intrigued to see one work."

Chapter 24
Sylvan

Albin stood in front of the Spirit Mirror in his office and moved his head from side to side. Sylvan was fascinated. It was just like watching a lady of advancing years stare into a mirror and look at the toll time was taking on her features. Albin slowly drew back the skin from his thick jawline toward his ear with his thumb while pulling the skin above his manicured greying eyebrow upward with his forefinger, in the process smoothing out the lines on his, what Sylvan guessed to be his, mid-sixties face.

Abruptly, the morning sun blazed over the horizon and the Spirit Mirror's frame pulsed with what Sylvan would describe as elemental power. Without preamble, Albin lit a taper from the nearest lantern and swiftly lit the unique candle that sat on the ornate thin table that stood in front of the mirror. Sylvan could see Albin's lips move in what he assumed was prayer but without the aid of an activated Spirit Mirror could not hear the words spoken. Within heartbeats, the surface of the Spirit Mirror began to glow azure in the center before expanding its circle and changing colors several times before reaching the sides of the mirror.

A short ruddy-faced man with bright eyes in the deep yellow Alb and adornments of an Arch Deacon filled the frame. Sylvan had seen the bushy-eyebrowed man several times but could not recall his name. The Arch Deacon bowed deeply, revealing a weather worn woman in warrior monk clothing with an aggrieved expression across her face behind him.

The First Elder inclined his head to the servile bowing of the Arch Deacon. "Report, Arch Deacon Illyius."

"The next intake of recruits are ready to begin training. Arch Deacon Jocastta continues to do an exceptional job of running the monastery and training our Monk Warriors. I will be bringing back your new elite guards when I return to the capital."

Sylvan noted that Arch Deacon Illyius was concise but spoke with a zeal in his voice that you didn't often hear.

"Arch Deacon Jocastta, do you have anything to add?" asked The First Elder.

The woman stepped forward and bowed effortlessly. Her sleeveless clothing revealed well-defined sun-kissed arms with several scars on them. "I won't waste your time on the mirror. A full report on the year's training has been given to Arch Deacon Illyius for you."

"Very well, we will speak again next week."

Sylvan was astonished as Albin spoke a few words he couldn't quite hear and waved his arm across the mirror to see the faces swirl and change to another room and face.

A much younger Arch Deacon waited in the mirror. He smiled broadly and bowed sincerely to the First Elder. Sylvan was shocked at his age and casual demeanor and was further astounded when The First Elder returned the smile. "How are you settling into your newly appointed role, Arch Deacon Nels?"

"It has been a challenge to win over some of the older warrior monks who have been serving here so faithfully, but I think I have managed to convince them of my probity to our faith. My sermons are slowly growing with many younger faces, as you had hoped."

"That is excellent news. I look forward to your report next week." Albin dismissed him and before Nels could return the farewell the imposing form of Arch Deacon Ulrick appeared in the Mirror.

"Report," ordered The First Elder.

With a perfunctory nod of his large bald head, Arch Deacon Ulrick brusquely answered, "The girl and those that aided in her escape have yet to be found. Has your Master Haughty uncovered anything of use yet?"

Sylvan was stung to hear himself referred to like that.

The First Elder shook his head. "No, Master Shaymmi Sylvan will inform me immediately when he finds the girl. I have no doubt of that as one of the Shaymmi has done well for herself of late and taken the gleam off his own star. I am certain he is out there scurrying around"—Albin waved his hand in the air—"doing everything to find the girl so he can again be the most superior and celebrated."

Arch Deacon Ulrick scowled. "Why do you allow such pompous behavior?"

"He serves his purpose."

Sylvan was affronted by The First Elder's answer. The flippant words hurt in a way he didn't think they would.

He watched as the mirror went blank as the sun slipped fully over the horizon and dawn ended and Albin again took several minutes to peer into the now normal mirror and frown unhappily at what he saw. As if deciding something, he snuffed the candle in front of the Spirit Mirror and took hold of the lantern sitting at the corner of his desk and quickly exited his inner office.

Sylvan's curiosity warred with his piqued pride as he watched Albin leave the room. Quickly he made the decision to follow The First Elder...it wasn't as if he had other pressing matters. He could only hover around the girl and her mentor in Hamlyn for so long without the girl becoming uncomfortable. She had never fully relaxed in his presence, and as his plans involved her trusting him, he needed her to not be so wary of him.

He was led down several corridors where he watched everyone bow deeply or scurry out the way as Albin swept past, mostly oblivious to the fawning. Sylvan was not surprised when they arrived at the double open doors of the monastery library. What he was surprised with was when Albin stopped to converse with one of the Trainee Shaymmi twins. Sylvan couldn't decide if it was Matteo or Mathias. After a brief pause to wave away his elite guards, Albin moved through several long heavy laden bookcases of scrolls and ancient tomes to come to a secluded area that had several lushly padded chairs and low side tables. He moved to the wall behind a large chaise lounge and pushed on the center of the large bas-relief elemental symbol.

Sylvan watched in wonder as a section of the nearest book-shelf swung outward, exposing a dark opening. Holding the lantern from his office high, Albin began to descend the stairs that appeared a few steps in from the hidden doorway. Sylvan felt an instant change in elemental energy as he followed Albin. It reminded him of what he experienced when he discovered an artifact but as if it had lost its potency. It was a disconcerting feeling.

The descent didn't take long, and the stairs ended with a short corridor with two doors on each side and a large open archway at the other end. Albin made his way to the second door on the right and took the symbol of his office that he wore around his neck, and placed it in the center of the door where there seems to be a gap and slowly twisted it. The door swung inward and Albin stepped in with Sylvan gliding in behind him. The ancient pull of elemental vibrations assaulted Sylvan, and it took him several moments to adjust his conscious state to block out the more piercing reverberations. By this time, Albin had hung the lantern on a hook on the wall and had turned to the over-sized metal banded wooden chest in the corner of the small room.

Sylvan took a quick look around to find a sturdy chair with restraining straps on the armrests and front legs "*Well, that is disturbing,*" he thought to himself. The only other things in the room were a highly polished floor-length free-standing mirror and an unusually large pile of dust and dirt next to it. A small broom and shovel were tucked behind the mirror.

The First Elder struggled to lift the lid on the heavy chest but eventually got it open to expose something wrapped in soft gray cloth. As Albin lifted out the covered item, Sylvan surmised by the number of emanations coming from it, even with his senses dulled, it was the latest artifact that Shaymmi Hadrian had uncovered. It wasn't as powerful as the last two he had personally unearthed, but it was still exactly what they were charged with looking for. He had noticed that over the years the power of the relics found were weaker in general as well as much fewer in frequency than what he had studied when in training.

Albin placed the covered item on the odd chair then removed the heavy gray cloth to reveal an ornate helmet that was incredible in its craftsmanship and unlike anything that Sylvan had uncovered. He had seen photos in ancient tomes that were on his family's estates. The tomes were forbidden, but his mother loved them and she didn't care that she was flouting the law and could honestly see no harm in keeping them in the vast family library. This magnificent sky-blue helmet had once belonged to a Dalinda, the fabled leaders of Duthyne and the riders of the Oredmoor.

Without stopping to admire the elaborate details of the helmet, Albin picked it up and walked to stand in front of the mirror. Sylvan expected him to put it on but he simply stood there holding it in front of him. After several moments, Albin closed his eyes and began to hum. Sylvan was flabbergasted to hear the deep baritone, so similar to the emanations that thrummed within the helmet. He wished that he could drop his guard but knew that he would be overwhelmed by the helmet's elemental vibrations. He had not realized how much weaker he was until this moment. The Elemental plane was obviously syphoning his strength the longer he stayed here.

He would ponder that later. For now, he watched The First Elder to try to fathom what he was doing. For what Sylvan guessed to be a quarter bell chime, Albin hummed until the helmet began to darken in color. It was almost sad to see the vibrant hues fade from the scaled helm until it was all a dull gray. The humming continued and tiny fractures appeared on the surface, quickly spreading and becoming larger cracks until the helmet crumbled into dust and floated to the floor. *That explains the dust pile,* Sylvan thought absently.

Albin wiped his hands on the cloth and threw it back into the chest before closing the heavy lid with a thud. He then took the lantern from the hook on the wall and moved closer to the mirror. He slowly leaned in and examined his face like he had earlier that day.

Sylvan floated forward and hovered near the lantern to also look at Albin's face and was astonished at what he saw. It took him several moments to understand what he was seeing. It was in the tiny details that you took in when you looked at someone without even knowing it. The crows feet around his eyes weren't as deep, the same with his forehead lines. His jowls and neck weren't as loose and the white of his eyes were brighter. Albin appeared to be a decade younger than when he had entered the room!

Chapter 25

Treena

"So, that's it." Treena sat back and waited for Braith to absorb all she had told him. She had patiently answered each of his questions as honestly as she could regarding the Dalinda and Oredmoor. She had again shown him a small measure of her elemental powers by heating the water in the kettle without putting it over the stove fire and then having it flow from the kettle spout and into his teacup. And then she had told him about the spectre who had visited Aven and the Spirit Mirror they now searched for.

"Lady Aven, may I ask you what you think of all of this?" Braith inclined his head in a formal manner.

Aven giggled and shyly looked up from the empty plate she had been looking at in front of her. "Master Thief Braith, I like it. I feel safe an I sleep at night wifout worrin if me Da is gonna decide tonight is me night ta earn me keep."

He chuckled. "Master Thief, indeed." He turned serious. "You are still in danger from the church, as we still have no clue as to why they took you," he reminded her.

Aven stopped smiling and hunched in her seat but didn't lower her gaze from his face. "Treena is teachin me ta take care of meself an one day I will be able ta use me powers too."

Treena was proud of Aven. She had grown in confidence and continued to work hard to learn all that was being taught to her. "She is safe from the church here, I think. I am a simple florist, who is good at my job and trusted by the church. They have no need to suspect me of anything."

"True," acceded Braith. "And to them Aven is your newest florist apprentice."

"Yes, for now."

Aven interrupted. "For now?" Frown lines appeared on her young, heart-shaped face.

Treena stood and started clearing the kitchen table. "Yes, for now. You aren't meant to be a florist. You are not needed in that capacity. I am here and established; there is no need for another Dalinda to be established here. I have access to the monastery here, and as mentioned, am trusted by the church. Every one of us have different roles and positions across the country."

Aven, without being asked, moved to the large sink and waited for Treena to elementally heat the water before starting to wash the dinner dishes. "What will I do then?" she asked hesitantly.

Braith hurried to lend a hand. He rolled up his sleeves and took a towel from a hook near the doorway and took the wet but clean plate from Aven.

Treena answered, "The Council need someone mobile as Lady Calantha retired a little while ago. She was a Master Story Teller and Bard. It gave her freedom to travel and connect with the Loyalists and to continue to spread the word that the Dalinda continue to serve and train and find ways to help the general populace, even if the majority don't know we exist." She stared earnestly at Aven, who had stopped washing the dishes. "How do you feel about studying to become a dancer? There is a professional troupe that have an academy here. Once the church stop looking for you, I want to enroll you. You have picked up your self defense quickly and your training drills have already strengthened your body. You are strong, lean, and quite graceful."

Aven just stared at Treena. "I dunno."

"If you don't like it you can try something else. It's important for you to enjoy what you do."

Braith interrupted. "Who will help you run the shop?"

"I have someone else in mind," Treena answered cryptically before changing the subject. "Now, onto other important things. Where do we find a Spirit Mirror?"

They finished the dishes and tidied the kitchen in silence as they separately pondered Treena's question. Once they were all seated back at the small table, Braith broke the silence by whistling through his teeth, which Treena knew he did when he was concentrating. It drove some people crazy but never seemed to bother her.

He stopped whistling mid trill and frowned. "There is no other place. It has to be in Arch Deacon Ulrick's office in the monastery."

Treena grimaced but nodded her head. "I have looked at it from every angle and I have to agree. The scrolls we found both indicated that it was used to communicate and the monastery is where the Dalinda and Oredmoor would stay when they came to Hamlyn. The Arch Deacon is an arrogant man, and his office would be in what he would perceive to be the most important room in the monastery, where the vanquished heathens once ruled from."

Braith snickered. "Vanquished heathens."

Chapter 26

Hadrian

Hadrian carefully twirled the delicate stemmed goblet in her hand. "You are a genius!"

Cyrus shrugged in a nonchalant fashion, but Hadrian guessed by the slight self-satisfied smirk that he was thrilled with the results.

"I was having drinks with Artious, the glass blower, and as the night went on, we were throwing around some rather ridiculous ideas when we stumbled upon this one." He waved his hand toward the goblet.

The drinking vessel was beautiful. Hadrian held it toward the bright summer sunlight that poured through the window of the closed shop and watched the glass sparkle. The receptacle was far more bulbous than normal and was incredibly made from flawless clear glass. The entwined stem was created from white, yellow, and rose gold. Each vein of gold twisted around the other to create a beautiful cradle for the glass receptacle to fit snugly in. It was half the weight of a typical goblet and impressive in its simple but drastic design changes.

Cyrus poured a large amount of the light rose wine Hadrian had brought with her into the goblet.

"What do you think about drinking from it?"

She took a deep drink and was pleased to discover the bridge of her overly broad nose didn't hit the rim as she drained the goblet.

Cyrus raised his eyebrows. "Thirsty?"

She grimaced. "No. Annoyed. Exasperated. Frustrated. Pick one."

"The search not going well?" he asked as he refilled her glass before filling his own plain silver goblet.

This time Hadrian took a large gulp but didn't drain it. "I'm exhausted. I have never worked so hard to find anything on the Elemental Plane. I thought it would be easy," she admitted grudgingly. "The girl is only in Hamlyn, but now, if I'm honest, maybe we didn't think this through? What happens if they have moved her out of the city?"

Cyrus grunted. "I hadn't thought of that."

Hadrian didn't want to admit that she may not be powerful enough to find the girl. It irked her that she may have to concede that Sylvan does have the superior power and deserve his title of Master.

"How is your guest?" Cyrus inquired.

She snorted in a very unladylike manner that her father would have been mortified to witness. "My guest? His body seems to be perfectly fine. I do occasionally feel a twinge of regret for the distress he must be feeling at being separated from his body for so long. But it can't be helped." She drained her glass. "Besides, it should bring his ego down a peg or two—he certainly

to the Arch Deacon's outer office? I know you have done it
fore. Just pop them onto the Pastor's desk. She will deal with
m when they have completed the service."

"How could I say no as it's completely my fault they are late?"
e agreed to his request.

Treena placed the fresh flowers on the messy desk belonging
Pastor Parisa in the outer office. The outer office was sparsely
nished with plain, hard surfaced furniture, that made it very
r that if you intended to intrude upon the Arch Deacons'
e you would be in for an uncomfortable wait. There was a
e chunky desk with papers strewn all over it. Two sturdy
k wood chairs sat before the desk on one side of the office
along the opposite wall stood a long, heavy church pew.
placed her ear against the cool, smooth wood of the inter-
door to make certain that no one was in the office. Treena
iently unlocked the door with the key Ezekiel had surrep-
usly given her and slowly opened it, closing and locking
ftly behind her. She paused to make certain there was no
e other than the wind, which had surprisingly picked up as
art had made its way into the monastery grounds, and the
murs of the congregation attending morning service. Her
nd ability to block out the sound of the wind told her that
one was still in the chapel on the lower floor listening to
Deacon Ulrick lecture about sin.

owly she turned her head without moving her slender,
d body as she had been trained to do and allowed her eyes
am the room for some form of trap. The Archbishop was

could use it." Hadrian tossed her beautiful auburn hair over her
shoulder and stood. "I need to find that girl!" Her voice rose
several decibels, showing her frustration.

"How long do you think he can survive on the plane before
he starts to lose himself?" Cyrus asked.

"To be honest, I am unsure. His body seems to be holding up
as if it is in some sort of stasis, but his consciousness won't be."

Cyrus said nothing as he refilled her glass. He leaned forward
and gently kissed her forehead.

She moved restlessly around the room. "Father has delayed
his visit. Something more important has come up." She tried
to say it lightly, but the slight still stung. Absently, Hadrian
began to take jewelery off a display shelf and try it on. She would
then discard it back to Cyrus who would place it carefully in its
display position.

"It seems we are both frustrated," Cyrus said, interrupting
her browsing. He left the room and went into what Hadrian
knew as his workroom for a moment before returning with the
bracelet he was charged with discovering its secrets. He placed
the unique bracelet on her wrist and clipped it into place. Deftly
he spun the bracelet until he stopped at the intricately created
tree. "This is made by Master Silversmith Thoreau. He died two
years ago in a workshop accident." He then touched the bell two
places from the tree. The bell tinkled prettily when it moved.
"This superb piece is done by the famous Master Goldsmith
Kassian. He lived a hundred years ago." His hand then moved
the bracelet around to a heavy anchor. "This was certainly made

by Master Silversmith Mignus. He is rumored to have retired in Ostville with one of his children once his wife had died. He is too far away to make easy contact with." Cyrus held Hadrian's wrist with one hand and traced her vein into the palm of her hand before leaning in and kissing it. He then gently removed the bracelet.

"Lots of information but it answers nothing," Hadrian summed up.

"Exactly my dilemma and source of frustration."

Hadrian touched the bracelet and gently held a charm. "This looks to be the newest. Should it not be the easiest to track down its creator?"

Cyrus sighed. "I think that one is the most frustrating of all. Yes, that thimble appears the newest by several decades but irritatingly it is the only one without a creator's mark."

Hadrian emptied the remaining wine into their glasses and held Cyrus' out to him. "Here is to being able to achieve nothing more today." She raised her glass in a toast, the unique goblet catching the sun's final rays. She stopped to admire it again. "I think this might just get you the Master title you have been so eagerly working towards."

"Mmm, fingers crossed." He took the goblet from her fingers and placed it next to his on a shelf. "I can think of several ways we can relieve frustrations as well as celebrate my new creation," admitted Cyrus as he gave her hand a tug and pulled her towards his bedroom.

Hadrian put up no resistance.

Chapter 27

Treena

The bells tolled to announce the time a
services were about to commence throu
Treena took the last bouquet of flowers from
hired cart, thanked the driver and sent him on
gizing profusely that she had been running la
miss this morning's service.

Treena stopped outside the kitchen door ar
low-cut green blouse, so her shoulders were re
had chosen to wear no layers of petticoats
brown skirt—they were too cumbersome.
back with a simple green ribbon. She walked b
kitchen to Chef Ezekiel, who was quietly but
ing the under cooks and kitchen hands throu
tasks. "This is for the Arch Deacon's office, a
find Pastor Parisa," Treena explained clearly
He turned from the bread kneading he had
wiping his hands down the front of his apro
Treena. "I have no one to spare to take them
hands over hers, that still held the stems of th
them a pleading squeeze. "Would you be so

could use it." Hadrian tossed her beautiful auburn hair over her shoulder and stood. "I need to find that girl!" Her voice rose several decibels, showing her frustration.

"How long do you think he can survive on the plane before he starts to lose himself?" Cyrus asked.

"To be honest, I am unsure. His body seems to be holding up as if it is in some sort of stasis, but his consciousness won't be."

Cyrus said nothing as he refilled her glass. He leaned forward and gently kissed her forehead.

She moved restlessly around the room. "Father has delayed his visit. Something more important has come up." She tried to say it lightly, but the slight still stung. Absently, Hadrian began to take jewelery off a display shelf and try it on. She would then discard it back to Cyrus who would place it carefully in its display position.

"It seems we are both frustrated," Cyrus said, interrupting her browsing. He left the room and went into what Hadrian knew as his workroom for a moment before returning with the bracelet he was charged with discovering its secrets. He placed the unique bracelet on her wrist and clipped it into place. Deftly he spun the bracelet until he stopped at the intricately created tree. "This is made by Master Silversmith Thoreau. He died two years ago in a workshop accident." He then touched the bell two places from the tree. The bell tinkled prettily when it moved. "This superb piece is done by the famous Master Goldsmith Kassian. He lived a hundred years ago." His hand then moved the bracelet around to a heavy anchor. "This was certainly made by Master Silversmith Mignus. He is rumored to have retired in Ostville with one of his children once his wife had died. He is too far away to make easy contact with." Cyrus held Hadrian's wrist with one hand and traced her vein into the palm of her hand before leaning in and kissing it. He then gently removed the bracelet.

"Lots of information but it answers nothing," Hadrian summed up.

"Exactly my dilemma and source of frustration."

Hadrian touched the bracelet and gently held a charm. "This looks to be the newest. Should it not be the easiest to track down its creator?"

Cyrus sighed. "I think that one is the most frustrating of all. Yes, that thimble appears the newest by several decades but irritatingly it is the only one without a creator's mark."

Hadrian emptied the remaining wine into their glasses and held Cyrus' out to him. "Here is to being able to achieve nothing more today." She raised her glass in a toast, the unique goblet catching the sun's final rays. She stopped to admire it again. "I think this might just get you the Master title you have been so eagerly working towards."

"Mmm, fingers crossed." He took the goblet from her fingers and placed it next to his on a shelf. "I can think of several ways we can relieve frustrations as well as celebrate my new creation," admitted Cyrus as he gave her hand a tug and pulled her towards his bedroom.

Hadrian put up no resistance.

Chapter 27

Treena

The bells tolled to announce the time and that church services were about to commence throughout Hamlyn. Treena took the last bouquet of flowers from the back of the hired cart, thanked the driver and sent him on his way, apologizing profusely that she had been running late and he would miss this morning's service.

Treena stopped outside the kitchen door and readjusted her low-cut green blouse, so her shoulders were revealed. Today she had chosen to wear no layers of petticoats under her simple brown skirt—they were too cumbersome. Her hair was tied back with a simple green ribbon. She walked boldly through the kitchen to Chef Ezekiel, who was quietly but confidently guiding the under cooks and kitchen hands through their assigned tasks. "This is for the Arch Deacon's office, and I can't seem to find Pastor Parisa," Treena explained clearly to Ezekiel.

He turned from the bread kneading he had been supervising, wiping his hands down the front of his apron before answering Treena. "I have no one to spare to take them." He put his larger hands over hers, that still held the stems of the bouquet and gave them a pleading squeeze. "Would you be so kind as to take them up to the Arch Deacon's outer office? I know you have done it before. Just pop them onto the Pastor's desk. She will deal with them when they have completed the service."

"How could I say no as it's completely my fault they are late?" She agreed to his request.

Treena placed the fresh flowers on the messy desk belonging to Pastor Parisa in the outer office. The outer office was sparsely furnished with plain, hard surfaced furniture, that made it very clear that if you intended to intrude upon the Arch Deacons' time you would be in for an uncomfortable wait. There was a large chunky desk with papers strewn all over it. Two sturdy dark wood chairs sat before the desk on one side of the office and along the opposite wall stood a long, heavy church pew. She placed her ear against the cool, smooth wood of the internal door to make certain that no one was in the office. Treena efficiently unlocked the door with the key Ezekiel had surreptitiously given her and slowly opened it, closing and locking it softly behind her. She paused to make certain there was no noise other than the wind, which had surprisingly picked up as the cart had made its way into the monastery grounds, and the murmurs of the congregation attending morning service. Her ears and ability to block out the sound of the wind told her that everyone was still in the chapel on the lower floor listening to Arch Deacon Ulrick lecture about sin.

Slowly she turned her head without moving her slender, toned body as she had been trained to do and allowed her eyes to roam the room for some form of trap. The Archbishop was a powerful man and very cautious and Treena was not about to risk all she had achieved by getting caught. Her large dark brown eyes swept over a massive teak desk that dominated the middle of the room, making the plush dark velvet lounge off to the left side appear undersized. A rectangular teakwood low table, with a fine porcelain tea set, sat in front of the lounge and a slender, tall, ornate oil lamp stood to one side. Above the couch was a large oil painting in muted colors. The right wall of the office was covered in bookshelves with leather bound books filling every shelf. After seeing the severity of the outer office, Treena was mildly surprised at the opulence but knew she shouldn't be. The church had become greedy, and the amount of money spent in the office could have fed all her street children for a year.

Feeling confident that there were no traps, Treena moved away from the door and towards the over-sized desk. The smell of incense, parchment, and leather filled her nostrils, all adding to the sense of wealth. She contemplated drawing the heavy cream brocade curtains across the four narrow windows that allowed the mid-morning sun in but thought better of it as she didn't want to attract attention from any passersby. The windows rattled as she assumed the wind continued to pick up. *Perhaps there was a storm coming.* They were known to sweep across Kets Harbor with little warning.

Where could it be? Who knew how big a Spirit Mirror was? Her eyes swept over the room again, hoping an idea would formulate...nothing happened. Treena noted that for all its richness and beauty, the room felt cold and barren with no hint of welcoming or warmth. She crept to the desk. There were several fountain pens and two inkwells as well as piles of neatly stacked papers, which held no secrets, just sermon ideas, budgets for spending in areas of the city, menu lists for upcoming meals with visiting ranking clergymen and so forth—nothing caught her attention. She turned her focus to the beautiful desk, noticing the smell of varnish and the sheen it created. After several minutes of further searching, Treena ascertained that there was no hidden compartment. She checked under the couch and low table, behind the painting, even going so far as to lift the tall brass lamp. Nothing.

This is taking too long, Treena thought to herself as there was a slight lull in the whistling wind and she heard the congregation downstairs begin their final hymn. The sermon would soon be complete, and she needed to be out of here well before the Arch Deacon returned and found her where she wasn't meant to be. Moving quickly to the bookshelves she began to scan the stamped spines in the hope that a title might trigger something.

Unexpectedly, she heard footsteps on the floorboards in the corridor coming towards the office. Moving quickly, Treena made her way to the heavy floor length curtains and pulled one aside only to smile triumphantly. She had found the Spirit Mirror! Her joy turned to worry as she heard the key turn in the lock of the office door.

Chapter 28

Hadrian

"Do you have them?" Shaymmi Hadrian asked quietly as she was shown into the antechamber of The First Elder's office. Her elaborate robe of office open at the front to reveal a stunning, form-fitting gown in rich green to compliment her glorious deep auburn hair, piled in curls on the top of her head. She insisted on always wearing obviously feminine clothing under her robe of office as she was proud to be one of the few women who were Shaymmi's.

"Right here." Cyrus patted the bundle of velvet material that sat on one side of him.

"And the bracelet?" She settled into the seat on the other side of him, her leg brushing against his and just a fraction too close for any semblance of being only acquaintances.

He fished around in his very best tunic pocket before holding up the trinket bracelet. "I think I have identified another adornment." He smiled coyly at her, choosing to ignore the monks stationed at the inner doors just as she had done. "I have started your first trinket."

Hadrian beamed as she took the bracelet from him. "Thank you."

"Ah, wonderful, you have the bracelet. I hope you bring tidings," commented The First Elder as he strode into the room unannounced. He wore his typical robes of office. A deep yellow Alb with a white tippet that had olive green and gold embroidery which ended at the hem of the Alb. A tasseled cincture and white chasuble with a large gold and green symbol of the church on the back finished the ensemble. His soft, supple leather slippers made no sound on the hard white marble floor.

Cyrus quickly rose to his feet and bowed deeply. Hadrian secretly smirked at the depth of his bow as she too rose and bowed to The First Elder. As she straightened, she was startled to discover the changes in Albin's face. He had somehow managed to reduce a decade of lines and aging from his face overnight—how was this possible? There were potions and salves always peddled by questionable characters in the markets that claimed to be able to rejuvenate you, but even they couldn't claim this.

"You are looking remarkably well." She spoke slowly. Unsure of the etiquette at this time.

"I communed with my Master overnight and have been blessed that The One True God has chosen to again sanctify my leadership by bestowing me this fine gift of regressing my age so I may continue to serve in His name. If you had been at Service this morning you would have known this, Shaymmi Hadrian," he explained and admonished in a way that reminded her of her father.

"A most joyous occasion that I have missed." She curtsied deeply and attempted to lighten the mood. "Perhaps, I will try to commune with The One True God a little more frequently if that can be the result."

It worked. Albin's features softened slightly. He turned to Cyrus. "And did you manage to get to a Service this morning, young man?"

"Yes, I try to attend a Service at least twice a week."

Hadrian was shocked. She had no idea that Cyrus was so pious regarding The One True God. She tended to be more of the opinion that if he left her alone, she would leave him alone and secretly she had always liked the appeal of the Elemental Gods, but it was death to talk of them other than to hear the Priests in Services denounce them. She knew people did or there would be no need for the continued denouncing, but she had never had a friend close enough to trust to share her thoughts on why she felt drawn to them.

"Maybe you could take Shaymmi Hadrian with you soon," suggested The First Elder.

Hadrian thought it best to change the subject. "How remiss of me. I haven't formally introduced you. First Elder Albin, please may I introduce the gifted Master Silversmith Cyrus."

Albin frowned. "I thought you were a Goldsmith?"

"I am. I am still a Journeyman Goldsmith, but I have already attained the title of Master Silversmith. With my latest creation I hope to attain my Master Goldsmith title," explained Cyrus.

Hadrian noticed his nervousness had disappeared as he spoke about his craft. He waved his hands with enthusiasm to punctuate his words and spoke rapidly.

"You hope to become a Grandmaster Craftsman?" inquired Albin.

Cyrus nodded vigorously. "Very much so. It would be an honor to run a Guild in this beautiful city."

"I have commissioned a gift for you, First Elder," Hadrian interrupted while indicating to Cyrus to get the velvet wrapped bundle. "I am aware that you have received a few items created by Cyrus before but nothing like this. I do hope you like them." She was genuine in her want for him to like them. It still took her by surprise occasionally that she wanted good things for another person.

Cyrus placed the gift on a nearby table and they booth stood patiently by as The First Elder carefully unfolded the fabric. The material held a set of four matching gold and glass goblets. It was the same stunning three types of gold entwined stem that ended cradling a clear glass receptacle that had enchanted Hadrian. All goblets to now had been made of metal, no one had ever thought to use glass.

"I think the title of Master Goldsmith will not be far off and you are about to become a very rich man." Albin picked a glass and held it up. "It is quite beautiful. Bring the bracelet and a goblet and we shall enjoy some wine out on my personal balcony."

They quickly followed The First Elder through his spacious office and into the afternoon's waning sunlight that lingered on the simple balcony. Hadrian took in the plain white wooden chairs and low small tables that were scattered around the open space. A few green leafy plants in low pots stood in the corners and lanterns ready to be lit were lined up against a side wall. A serving monk followed them out with a wine skin and very carefully filled their unique glasses while they settled into their chairs.

"Shaymmi Hadrian has told me what you have discovered so far regarding the bracelet. Do you have any further news?" asked Albin.

Cyrus went through the trinkets until he came to a certain one before handing it to The First Elder by that ornament. "I originally thought it was a flute or other instrument. I now think it is a scroll. The details are worn but still there under the right light. The mark was also very faint but was oddly familiar yet different and it took me a while to figure out why. The scroll was created by the same person that made the bell— Master Goldsmith Kassian. But the scroll was created when he was an apprentice, so his mark is slightly different than the one on the bell. A hundred years ago that was common practice. Now we tend to have the same mark throughout our career to avoid just this confusion." He gestured enthusiastically.

"So, you have now identified four of the eight trinkets and who crafted them?" confirmed Albin.

"Yes, but I will need time and perhaps access to your more extensive library if I am to find the others," suggested Cyrus.

"What about sending someone to find Master Silversmith Mignus in..." Hadrian turned to Cyrus. "Where did you say he was?"

"Ostville."

Their conversation was interrupted by a voice that was becoming louder and more insistent as it echoed through The First Elder's office.

"I must see him now!" someone was yelling. "It is urgent."

Hadrian's stomach roiled in terror. Had they been caught? Had someone found Silvan's body? She looked quickly at Cyrus and noted his anxious expression before trying to school her face into something resembling curiosity.

"Please excuse the interruption." Albin stood and moved into the office, closing the door behind him. But to Hadrian's relief, it didn't latch properly, and she made a show of standing and moving to pour some wine when she really moved closer to the door and ever so gently pushed it further ajar. She gestured to Cyrus to come closer.

"Let him through." The First Elder's voice had changed from his typical convivial tone to a demanding hiss. Hadrian blinked with surprise. "This had better be as important as you claim."

"Forgive me, First Elder, but this couldn't wait," the man spoke excitedly. "Someone in confessional today directed a Priest to check the eyes of the body you have in the catacombs. It was a curious enough statement that the Priest chose to send someone to follow it through, but neglected to remember to try to find out who would know you had a body down there in the first place." The man spoke so quickly that his words tumbled onto each other and Hadrian had trouble deciphering all he said through the door.

"I take it you found something worthy of you shrieking your way in here?" Albin had modulated his tone slightly.

"They are back!" he blurted loudly.

"Who?"

"The Dalinda. The Elemental Council."

Albin's voice was a furious shout. "What are you blithering about? To utter those words means death."

"Her eyes were gold. They were covered by some form of brown glass, but once we removed them, we found gold eyes."

Chapter 29

Treena

Treena held her breath as the key rattled in the keyhole. She was elated to have found the Spirit Mirror and was calculating how she was going to remain hidden until she had the opportunity to leave. Abruptly the air was filled with the sound of the church bells—they were different to the normal peeling to tell the time. She concentrated on the pitch and frequency of the tolling. It was a warning, but she was having trouble remembering for what.

As the church bells settled into silence, she knew she didn't have much time as they would start again, as a warning sequence was always repeated five times so the populace at least knew that there was a problem. She breathed deeply and closed her eyes, focusing her attention on her hearing, hoping to ascertain if whoever had put the key in the lock had entered the room while the bells tolled.

She could hear several lots of running footsteps further away, which indicated that the office door and the outer door were open. This was good if she needed to make a run for it, though she preferred to remain unseen. There was no excuse for being in here and hiding where the spirit mirror was—she would be taken and tortured if discovered and captured, but if she was seen yet escaped, she would have to leave the city forever. In this area her face was too familiar, unlike Aven she was recognizable. Both of those options were unacceptable. Her only choice was getting out of this office unseen.

"Your Grace, I am sorry to interrupt you, but there are several Guildmasters requesting to remain until the hurricane has passed. I am uncertain on the protocol of who is most important in these situations..." The servant's voice trailed off.

"How many are there?"

"There were five plus wives and children when I left."

"When you left? Speak plainly."

"As I was leaving to find you, I overheard several lower ranking Guildmasters making comments that perhaps they too should stay."

Arch Deacon Ulrick swore softly. Treena could just make out the words, which meant he was further into the office than what she had hoped. Now that everything was quiet, and she knew the bells were warning of a hurricane, she could clearly hear the wind outside and she realized that's why her body was experiencing the pins and needles sensation. Her element was Water, and the air was filled with it. She had made several errors tonight that she would have to assess, but now was not the time for self-reprimand.

The bells began their tolling again.

Treena strained to hear anything over the clamor.

"—open—hall. I'll meet—monks securing—city. Find Chef—prepare—guests."

No further voices were heard as the bells continued their ominous message. The wind was slowly picking up in strength and rain pelted the rare clear glass windows of the building's turret office. Treena waited until the bells ceased and silently counted to thirty before cautiously moving the heavy curtain aside. The room was empty, and the door was closed. She quickly moved to the door and pressed her ear to it. She heard footsteps and voices. One she knew. It was Pastor Parisa brusquely issuing orders as people arrived with requests or questions.

"Ah, Holy Torrent, think," muttered Treena. How was she going to get out of here?

She looked around the room, already knowing the answer, but not liking it. She had known coming into the room that if she got locked in with no means of escape through the door that she would have to climb out through the window. Though she didn't think she would have to do it in the middle of a hurricane. With little difficulty, as Thedra had expertly made the skirt and had Treena practice several times, she lifted the skirt hem on her right side to find a small piece of cloth with a hole near its end, Treena brought the little tag up and attached it to the button that was at the base of the side pocket. The button looked like a decoration, but in reality, it was there for this purpose. Treena quickly found the tag on the left and repeated the action. Now both her legs were exposed to mid-thigh, and without all the petticoats, her legs were free for climbing. Thinking about

Thedra made her heart constrict for a moment, but she pushed it aside. Escaping was paramount, and Thedra's spirit would be furious if Treena got caught.

The bells resumed their clanging as Treena headed to the window. She noted that the tolling was no longer a warning sound but just a clanging lacking any syncopation as the wind was now strong enough to move it. She was grateful to find that the window had a view of the harbor in the distance and immediately below and to the left the barracks and stables and not of the immense sprawling gardens. Most people would be huddled in the center of buildings, not near windows, and the few that would be about would have their heads lowered against the stinging rain so would not be looking up as they ran in between buildings. The stables would be crowded with monks there to calm and take care of the horses while the barracks were probably full of the lazy warrior monks who remained safe in the barracks, rather than out helping the citizens of Hamlyn. At least today their apathetic behavior would aid her escape.

Bracing for the onslaught and hoping the bells continued for a few more counts to cover the sounds, Treena braced against the jerk she knew would come when she unlatched the window. Something went right as she unlatched the glass pane and pushed it open. She was expecting it to jerk out of her hands and smash against the wall, sending shards of glass everywhere and creating a distinct noise. Instead, the wind took hold of the frame, ripped it out of her hands and off its hinges and out into the howling winds without a sound. Wind and rain filled the room, quickly scattering papers, but the tolling bells covered the noise for now. She needed to be out of the window and out of sight before anyone came to inspect the sounds coming from the office.

The rain stung as it hit her face and Treena pulled back in and made a quick decision as she moved the heavy desk chair to the narrow window. She gathered her thoughts and called on the water that stung her face and body to instead create a soft bubble that she could put her hands and feet through and that would protect her from the winds. Instantly there was relief as she climbed out the window and clung to the windowsill as she strove to find footing in the huge blue-stone blocks of the monastery. Without the wind and rain punishing her, she found the climb difficult as the stones were slippery, and she had no time to waste but no longer impossible. Below Treena and to the left was a small copse of shrubs that she slowly angled towards. Almost immediately her fingers began to ache as they fought to hold onto the slippery bluestone wall. For one heart-stopping moment, her feet and one hand all slipped at once and she dangled precariously by one hand before her toes found purchase in a crevice. Thankfully, only being on the second story and without too much further interference from the buffeting winds, she made her way to the bottom and jumped the final few feet into the bushes dispelling the protective bubble as she did.

Immediately her hair was whipped into her face and the wind tore at her clothes. The bushes gave her no protection from the raging wind. She felt exhilarated. It was the first time she had used her powers outside of the confines of her training areas and in an emergency. It was satisfying to know that she hadn't panicked and that they had worked the way she intended. But this was not the time for self-congratulations or reflection. She had to return the key to Chef Ezekiel and get back to Aven.

Treena attempted to pull away the wet hair that clung to her face but to little avail as the wind tore it from her hand. She didn't bother to undo her skirt as it would only be in the way. Not willing to risk using the water to protect her again while so close to the enemy, she stood and braced her legs against the wind and slowly followed the wall to the right, away from the barracks, figuring at some point she would encounter a door. As she fought to move along the wall, bent double against the wind and trying to find bricks to pull herself forward with, it registered that she had not heard the church bells for longer than usual. The shrieking wind was so powerful that it drowned out all other sound.

With great determination, Treena gritted her teeth and kept her head low to give the rain a smaller target as the rain stung against her cheeks and ran into her eyes. Several times as she fought to stay on her feet, she considered using her ability to create her rain bubble but her training and years hiding her powers stopped her. Thankfully, the strength and weapons training did come into play, and she was able to keep her feet until her hands moved forward and she no longer had a blue-stone wall to help steady her. Treena squinted through the rain and found she had come upon a tiny alcove. She slipped in to find a terrified child of about eight huddled in the far corner.

Treena moved to the other corner and grimaced at him as she pulled her hair from her face. He stared at her in terror as the rain continued to pound the world outside their little space. Treena wanted to assure him that he was safe, but the noise was too loud to bother attempting to shout. Instead, she did what she would do for any of her street kids. She opened her arms and gestured with her hands for him to come closer. She smiled kindly and kept eye contact with him. After hesitating for only a few moments, he took three steps toward her and allowed himself to be wrapped up in her arms. He quivered against her as she stroked his head. Just as he was settling down, there was a large crash as an uprooted tree flew into the side of the wall and landed across the opening. He yelled in fright and buried his head into her rib cage as the alcove was plunged into darkness.

Chapter 30

Sylvan

Sylvan spent the day in what turned out to be a futile search for his body. He had concentrated on the servant monk area of the compound but had discovered nothing suspicious. Though, if he was honest with himself, he really didn't know what he was looking for. He had never taken much notice of the comings and goings of the servant monks, so didn't know if any were acting strangely or not. Floating around the servants' area had given him the chance to consider what he had witnessed in the secluded chamber yesterday. It had been an astonishing occurrence; one he was still having trouble digesting. In some inexplicable manner, The First Elder had grown younger, and the beautiful helm of the Dalinda had disintegrated. It was an interesting development and one that Sylvan hoped to use to his advantage once he was back in his body, though he would have to be exceedingly clever about it as even though he was favored for his power, he now knew that Albin put up with his behavior for his own means. It was just another piece of information he could put away for use at a different time if needed. Much like his ability to use the Spirit Mirror at dawn and dusk without the candle and spells the First Elder had required, and that it gave him the ability to hear in the room it was placed in.

He moved slowly back through the compound, heading toward Albin's office. It was close to sunset, and he wanted to be there if he used the Spirit Mirror. For some reason, it was comforting to hear a voice. The Elemental Plane's usual vibrations that had once calmed and soothed Sylvan, he now saw them as leaching his strength. He worried he would one day soon stop being able to control them and instead be unraveled by them, even though in some small part they were what sustained him also. He fought the urge to panic, as he did at least once every strike. After checking on The First Elder, Sylvan intended to head back to Hamlyn and see if the girl and her mentor had had any success with their current search for the Spirit Mirror.

Skimming lazily through the air, Sylvan came to an abrupt halt as he entered the private office of The First Elder. Unexpectedly, it was full of people. Albin's more youthful appearance was contorted with rage. Sylvan had never seen him this way. The man was typically in control of everything and everyone. What could possibly have happened to make him so angry? A Deacon, who Sylvan had never seen before, stood with his shoulders hunched as if the First Elder's ire was making him wilt. Several of Albin's personal guards stood at attention, blocking the door. Hadrian and a man he didn't know stood at the door to the balcony. He noted that both their faces showed shock. What was happening? He was bewildered and he tightened his shields against the seeping of elements as he thought he felt a stronger pull of metal in the room. Sylvan longed for rest; everything was becoming distorted, and he no longer trusted his instincts. He was constantly feeling stronger elemental vibrations when he shouldn't be. Maybe he had been exposed to something when he had witnessed Albin's transformation?

Sylvan floated high along the ceiling, coming to rest near the spirit mirror. He had an idea. He was tired of not being able to hear people. Slowly, he extended his consciousness out to the mirror and felt it pulse under his touch. He looked out the window and realized the sun was close enough to the horizon that he should be able to activate it like he had when he had been experimenting once while waiting for the First Elder. He waited until everyone's attention was focused on the priest as he spread his hands wide as if to say he did not know more and gently touched the mirror with his thoughts. There was a slight ripple along its surface.

The room was filled with a cacophony of loud voices. Albin was furious, the Deacon wary, and Hadrian asked him to repeat what he had just said. The Deacon looked to the First Elder for guidance. Sylvan watched as Albin scrutinized Hadrian and her companion for several moments before nodding his head to the priest.

"At confessions this morning, someone gave a tip off about checking the eyes of the body that was being kept here in the compound." He eyed the First Elder nervously but went on. "There was much discussion about whether there was a body here, but I decided to come see rather than continue an endless discussion. I have a cousin in the warrior monk ranks who let me in and introduced me to the captain. I explained the situation and told him that if there happened to be a body being kept here that it was suggested that they check the eyes. I thought that would be dismissed but he insisted that I accompany him into the bowels of the compound to where indeed there is a dead lady. He then made me wait several strikes before a doctor arrived and pried her eyes open and then he got tweezers out..." He trailed off and Sylvan noted he looked a little pale. "Anyway, it turns out she had some brown glass covering her eye and that underneath, her eye was gold."

"Impossible," Albin muttered. "They are gone. The Ored-moor died because the One God willed it. There are no more, so there is no need for their riders. They died once their Ordemoor died and never returned. It is told in the scriptures."

"There must be great need if they have returned now," the Deacon reasoned, his voice almost reverential. "The One God must believe it is time for their reappearance."

"Nonsense," dismissed Albin as he looked to the captain. "Take the good Deacon and reward his excellent service by find-ing him a comfortable resting place."

"Oh, thank you, Your Excellency. I have always wanted to spend some time in your compound." He bowed and followed the captain from the study.

Everyone remained standing as the First Elder stalked around the room. To Sylvan, he seemed overly agitated. He was unsure why the news would bother Albin so greatly. The probability that the Dalinda had really returned was infinitesimal. No Oredmoor roamed the skies, so why were their riders being born?

Finally, Albin went to the office door and ordered another warrior monk into the room. "Go retrieve Master Shaymmi Sylvan. Tell him I need him immediately."

If Sylvan had a voice, he would have yelled for joy. Finally something would be done about his missing body. As he silently celebrated the order, he noticed both Hadrian and her companion look uncomfortably at each other before they hid their concern. *What did they know?* Sylvan wondered.

"Excuse me, Your Excellency, but I am certain I can help you if you just tell me what you need Sylvan to do." Hadrian bowed obsequiously.

"Shaymmi Hadrian, I want you and Master Cyrus to continue to keep your focus on the bracelet as it comes from the same person with the purported gold eyes. You stated that you couldn't feel a great deal from the bracelet while on the elemental plane, so I would like Master Shaymmi Sylvan to try. After I speak to Sylvan, I will visit the body myself. I highly doubt the eyes were gold. Probably just a trick of the light. I have a feeling if we figure out the bracelet, we might learn that it once belonged to the forbidden and its residual power may have rubbed off on the wearer. The One God spoke almost two centuries ago and destroyed the forbidden, I doubt he has changed his mind on their existence."

There was the sound of whispered voices in the outer chamber and Sylvan assumed the captain or the warrior monk who had been sent to get him had returned. He watched with growing interest as Hadrian became more agitated and continued to shoot Cyrus worrying glances.

Just as the warrior monk stepped through the door, Hadrian cleared her throat. "Please, forgive me but there is something you need to be aware of. I have avoided interrupting you as I know how hectic your schedule is..." Her voice petered out.

"Go on."

She looked toward the warrior monk then back to the First Elder. "Sylvan is missing."

Sylvan was ecstatic. Finally, something would be done.

Chapter 31

Treena

The city of Hamlyn was silent. At least where Treena stood it was, but she knew that in the poorer sectors there would be screaming with loved ones trapped or dead. The shrieking of the ferocious winds had given way to peaceful humid stillness and fading blue skies as the sun began to set that belied the damage done to the coastal city. The harbor no longer wildly churned, having already thrown ships and pleasure crafts without care into each other and the warehouses lining the wharfs. The storm water surge that accompanied the hurricane had broken the sturdy sea walls and now continued to slowly creep closer to the abandoned and ruined market square in the center of Hamlyn. The smell of sewerage that floated in the storm surge was nauseating, having come up from the tunnels and through the grates as they had been the first to fill when the ocean began its unrelenting march into the city.

It was as if Hamlyn and all its terrified inhabitants held its breath as the eye of the storm advanced over it. Most of the church bells, that told the city the time every strike, had fallen and smashed during the mighty onslaught. The few that re-mained were now eerily silent, when only a short time before they had been pealing frantically in warning before the hurricane hit and then had rapidly changed to a haphazard clangor as the violent winds had begun.

In the poorer and working-class sections, few buildings remained intact. Many had had window shutters ripped off. Countless walls and roofs had collapsed, and with the buildings being so tightly packed, once one building had fallen, it had taken its neighboring houses with it and devastatingly crushed all those sheltering within. Debris floated in the ever-rising water surge along with the revolting sewerage, and sadly on occasion a lifeless, swollen body.

The monastery on top of the hill that overlooked the city was high enough to escape the water surge, yet the smell of rotten sewerage and death still lingered in the air. The once glorious stained-glass windows of the main cathedral were shattered and the magnificent ancient bell tower in the middle of the decimated gardens was now in ruins as the golden bell of Hamlyn lay embedded halfway down in the pockmarked tower wall.

Nobles' houses fared no better. The perfectly manicured gardens and mazes were in disarray. Tree branches had snapped off, fragrant flowers denuded of their colorful petals and many smaller trees in private fruit orchards had been uprooted. Several grand houses were now missing large parts of their roofs.

Carriages and carts lay on their sides or smashed into piles of wood throughout the city, having come to land randomly after being caught in the powerful hurricane and thrown aside as if discarded like a child's toy.

Without warning, a fierce, hot wind whipped across the harbor and down the empty streets. It howled past the ruined town center and whistled loudly as it swept through the broken wrought iron gates and abandoned guard house before it entered the nearby woods, making the trees bend to almost breaking point.

Treena knew she didn't have much time before the eye of the storm passed and they were once again plunged into the nightmare of a hurricane. She needed to get back to Aven. She made the decision that the return of the key could wait, as Ezekiel could no doubt explain it away with so much panic and extra people in the kitchen to serve the added Guildmasters and their families in the monastery. Once the winds had settled and the sun returned, it was easy to see through the tree and realize they could quickly climb through its branches.

"It's fine for the moment. The eye of the storm is overhead. We need to hurry, and we can get inside and you back to your family," she assured the small boy as she attempted to gently unlock the hands around her waist. "Come on, you can hold my hand instead," Treena offered.

Instantly he unlocked his arms and grasped her proffered hand. "You look strong enough that you will have no problem climbing through that tree," she encouraged. His eyes showed a little pride, and he stood a little straighter.

In quick order, they negotiated the fallen tree and Treena was grateful that its trunk was thin and not heavily populated with branches. "Can you run?" she asked the boy as they emerged from the final branches.

He nodded but remained silent. He held out his hand.

She smiled kindly at him but just like the street kids, he still needed reassurance and comfort. His rich fabric clothes told her that this boy came from a wealthy family but that didn't mean he was any more loved. Early on, Treena had learned that money didn't buy you love. Rich or poor, parents, for many reasons, took their frustrations of their situation out on their children in varying ways. *This was not the place for reflection,* she reminded herself as she stood, considering her options, before deciding to keep moving along the wall away from the stables and barracks, the boy in tow.

They jogged along the wall, occasionally having to move around fallen debris. At one point she noted the boy look up at the sky fearfully. "Nothing to be frightened of at the moment. We will get you to safety before it hits," she assured him over her shoulder.

It didn't take long for them to reach a door which was hanging half off its hinges. Treena carefully opened the door enough to look inside and discover it was a side door into one of the corridors the servant monks used. The hallway was full of people scurrying around, some calm, some alarmed but all were moving swiftly, except one poor young girl who looked to be close to tears and terrified—everyone avoided her. Treena walked up to her and placed a gentle hand on her shoulder. The girl yelped with fright but remained still. "Are you hurt?"

She shook her head no.

"Do you know how to get to the kitchens from here?"

This time she nodded.

"You need to go to the kitchens and see Chef Ezekiel. He will need help with all the extra people stuck here. I want you to take this boy with you as he has lost his parents. If you run into anyone who can help him find his parents, he may leave your side. Otherwise, he can go to the kitchens and wait until someone has time to figure out where his parents are." Treena took his hand and gave it a squeeze before putting it into the young girl's hand. "Do you both understand?"

They looked at each and were both scared enough that any protests remained silent. "Don't let go of each other and stay to the side of the walls, then you won't be in the way. Now off you go," she urged. Treena didn't have time, but she stood there and watched them scurry off. They each looked back and she shooed them with her hand and an encouraging smile. They disappeared around a corner.

Moving quickly, Treena returned to the broken door and fled into the still air. Taking a second to gain her bearings and thanking the Goddess Torrent for Elldean Stiann making her study the complete layout of the monastery that overlooked the city, she decided on the quickest way back to the shop and set out at a run to the closest gate.

As she ran, she took note of the debris that scattered the grounds. Now she understood how the stunning golden bell became embedded in the wall when it had withstood all prior hurricanes. Treena knew this one was not as severe as the last two that they had had within the last five years. The base section of the bell tower stood straight and proud as if completely unaware that the top section was gone and in its place was a large carriage skewered by a single strong post. That was going to be a story to entertain when this was all over. If the tail end of the storm didn't budge it, it would be interesting to see how they would get it down.

Treena encountered no one as she left through a side gate, noting the guardhouse was still intact aside from a lone shutter. She considered readjusting her skirts to what a lady should be wearing but decided against it. If she encountered anyone, they would not be looking that closely at her as they would have their own concerns. She ran down the hill, taking no notice of the stunning properties that she passed, only vaguely noting the destruction that littered their streets and a few sections where their high walls had tumbled into the paved roads. As she passed through the walls that separated the elite from the merchant housing section, the wind picked up. By this time, Treena was puffing hard and was grateful that this section of the city had leveled out. The destruction here was the same as the elite guilds section. It would appear that money could buy you safety from almost anything. In this area, she did see a few guards and servants out in the streets. They were inspecting the perimeters of the properties to report back to the owners, she assumed. No one took a second glance at her.

The wind was steadily growing stronger as the sky darkened. Treena felt the first few drops of rain as the eye of the storm moved further away. The trailing storm would hopefully not last as long and blow itself out. Treena's side hurt and she had started to slow down as she began to find more debris strewn across the cobblestone roads and on occasion had to climb over broken detritus. Sadly, she came around a corner to discover a carriage with its horses still attached in a twisted pile. Both horses were dead with limbs broken and one's neck contorted to a sickening degree. There was nothing she could do but keep jogging and offer a silent prayer to the God Loam. Lightning cracked overhead and she heard a young child begin to cry as Treena fought to keep her dress from flying up as the wind blew harder. If she was out here for much longer, she was going to have to start looking out for debris. There was not enough time to reach her shop. She would have to trust that Braith would keep Aven safe.

Treena looked around. She needed to get under cover; she was dead if she stayed outside much longer. She calculated how far she was from Elldean Stiann's shop—she was only a block over. It was a risk but one she felt she could take. Doing her best to ignore the thunder overhead and lightning that illuminated the dark sky, she made her way, occasionally avoiding the assorted debris that scooted along the street. Treena tried not to consider the damaged buildings and shop fronts she jogged past. It was going to take weeks, months even, to clean up and get back to normal and the church was taking more taxes all the time. The citizens of Hamlyn were going to be even worse off than they had been as all the money the Church of the One God collected went to their own luxuries. The payment of the warrior monks and then the rest went to the First Elder in Cynsellam. There would be no help, just pointless prayers to a god that didn't exist.

She wasn't paying attention as she rounded her final corner and came to the front door of the scribe's shop and didn't duck in time to have a chunk of something hit her in the shoulder. She cried out in pain, but no one heard as it was carried away on the howling wind. Holding her bleeding shoulder, Treena banged on the front door, noting that all the wooden shutters were down over the clear glass windows that typically gave the shop front a unique view of the passersby. No one was going to hear her pounding on the door. She huddled in the thin alcove and tried to think while attempting to not think about her throbbing shoulder. How was she going to get Stiann to hear her?

Another huge chunk of debris came hurtling toward her and she used her power to push it away through instinct. The water simply did what it was told and formed a shield that she pushed against. It was in that moment that she recalled the feeling of peace and quiet when she had created the water bubble to aid her in climbing down the wall before. It gave her an idea.

Slowly Treena gathered the heavy rain above the shop, creating a shield with it over the roof before picturing it draped over the building like a large canvas. It was taking a lot of effort, and she had never tried anything so large before, especially while other elements were in the mix. As the water created a wavering shield in front of her, the sounds of the hurricane decreased. She hoped that this was the same inside the shop. Taking the opportunity, Treena pounded on the door and yelled for Stiann to open it.

She was growing weak, her shoulder ached, and she couldn't guess how much blood she had lost as the water made it run everywhere. Treena lifted her hand to pound again, knowing that she only had this chance before her power would give out and the storm would again be in control. As she went to slam her fist onto the wooden door, it was wrenched open and she stumbled forward into one of the apprentice scribes before blacking out.

Chapter 32

Hadrian

"**S**ylvan is missing," she repeated. "His Servant, Jorge, came to me a few days ago to report that while he had been out getting a meal Sylvan had vanished. We have been making discreet inquiries as I believed you would not want the capital to know that the Master Shaymmi had disappeared."

"It is true," confirmed the warrior monk.

"Get me his Servant," ordered Albin. He glowered at everyone in the room before moving to his impressive pale oak desk and taking a seat in the hard matching chair. He told no one to sit so they all stood awkwardly, waiting for the warrior monk to return with Jorge. The First Elder steepled his fingertips, resting them on his lips, just below his large, hooked nose and said nothing.

Hadrian silently sent a prayer to her favorite Elemental Goddess, Pyre. *Please help me get out of this one and I promise to go to church.* She didn't know what to think of the whole Dalinda returning and didn't much care now if it was true. She was thinking fast on how she was going to save herself from keeping her involvement regarding Sylvan from the First Elder. She surreptitiously looked at Cyrus, who appeared to be more interested in his fingernails than the happenings in the room. She was amazed at his calm exterior. Somewhere in the compound, the bell tower began to ring, joining the other towers in Cynsellam reminding the citizens that they were expected to say their prayers to the One God before beginning their supper.

It felt like an eternity with the four of them locked in a tableau, the First Elder sitting behind his desk, Hadrian and Cyrus standing near the balcony door they had come through when they had first heard the words "gold eyes," and Albin's loyal serving monk standing at the double doors that led back out into the other rooms of the suite. Hadrian longed to settle into one of the plush olive-green lounges that stood so welcoming. She was not used to standing in one place for so long on such hard marble floors. Her rooms were filled with thick carpets, and she spent the majority of her day lying down as she searched the elemental planes.

Eventually Jorge was escorted into the room. Hadrian noticed that his typically rosy cheeks are flushed even further than normal. He was ushered to stand before the desk of the First Elder and bowed formally before folding his hands into the voluminous sleeves of his servant robe. Hadrian decided to take this moment to move to a serving table close to the desk to place her now empty wine goblet on it. This gave her a better view of the proceedings and allowed her to take the advantage of holding Jorge's eyes for a moment before he looked back at Albin.

The First Elder finally removed his steepled fingers from his lips and cleared his throat. "I want to know exactly what happened and when. I am the leader of the Church of the One God, and I will know when you are lying. Be very clear on the truth. I want my Master Shaymmi back, do you understand me?"

Hadrian suppressed a shudder. She was fairly certain that everyone in the room understood him. Jorge nodded solemnly and Hadrian fought the urge to flee from the room. *What was he going to say? Whose threat would hold more sway with him?* Everything she had worked towards could come crashing down in the next few strikes.

Jorge began. "Master Shaymmi Sylvan had entered his trance, just like normal. I tidied his suite then went to give some directions to the kitchen staff regarding his requested meal for the evening. I did take my time and have some lunch with the twins who were working off some latest misdemeanor in the kitchens. When I returned, I discovered the body was missing and I immediately went to Shaymmi Hadrian to report it as she is next in line of the Shaymmi. I was then going to come to you, but Shaymmi Hadrian convinced me that we could take care of it without you because you were too busy and we didn't want it leaked that the Master Shaymmi of the Church of the One God was missing. She felt it would look bad for everyone." Jorge finished his speech in a rush.

Hadrian was pleased none of that appeared to be too damning toward her. She looked to be caring about the Church and not her own self-interest.

Albin turned to face Hadrian. She noticed his strong nose appeared sharper in the fading daylight. "Why did you not come to me? This is important. Sylvan is too valuable to lose. There is no one as strong as him to serve."

The last stung her ego but she just nodded assent. "I know how important he is to you—to us." It hit a nerve to say it but Hadrian had a role to play just like Jorge. "I am sorry if I overstepped. I just felt it vital to try to find him without drawing too much attention to the situation. I have been out on the plane looking for the girl as well as directing the search with Jorge's aid. I was only going to give it a few more days before I accepted that we may need to bring it to you to get help." She took a deep breath and tried to look innocent and concerned. "I have also considered that he may not want to be found and that he is hiding something, that this is not a kidnapping but an unstable man who has chosen to leave."

Jorge snorted, drawing everyone's attention. "Begging your pardon, Shaymmi Hadrian, but that is ludicrous. Have you ever met a vainer man? This is where his power is, this his home. He is worshiped in the streets and the First Elder gives him everything he desires. He is the strongest Shaymmi and there is no reason for him to leave. Something has happened to him; I can feel it."

The trap shut and Hadrian hid her smile. "You know it? How are you so sure of this?" She turned and raised an eyebrow at the First Elder. He didn't disappoint.

"I think you might know more than you are saying, Jorge."

The Monk Captain strode back into the room and surveyed the situation before choosing to return to his post by the double doors of the inner office to mirror the guard on the other side.

"As always, perfect timing," Albin acknowledged the captain before turning to the other guard. "Please take Jorge to a quiet room and question him in more detail regarding what happened on the day. I want a full report and a plan on what you will do to find my Master Shaymmi."

Hadrian held back her smirk but didn't hide her threatening glare at Jorge as he was escorted from the room. He glared back with equal ferocity but said nothing as he walked, head held high, from the room.

Albin laughed. "It seems you have a way with people, Hadrian."

She shrugged. "He is not the first male to underestimate me. I did my best to find Master Shaymmi Sylvan, but I believe if I had my time again, I would have brought this to you immediately." She bowed. "Forgive my hubris in thinking I could handle the situation alone."

"You will continue your normal duties while Sylvan is missing. The girl can wait while I deal with this and the alleged gold-eyed monster." He turned to Cyrus, who had managed to remain removed from all the revelations thus far. "Keep searching for the makers of that bracelet; it is important. You have my permission to send someone to inquire after that Silversmith you spoke of."

Neither Hadrian nor Cyrus needed to be told it was time to leave.

Chapter 33

Treena

"The shoulder seems to be healing well. The stitches can come out in a few days." Elldean Stiann wrapped Treena's shoulder up. "You might have to think about changing your everyday outfits for a while as that scar is going to be distinctive and draw attention and make you memorable for the wrong reasons."

"I'll think about it."

It had been five days since the hurricane had swept through Hamlyn, and the people and city were slowly recovering. The areas around the wharf and poor quarters were the worst hit as they had to deal with the storm surge as well as the killing winds. The church was carrying out mass funerals in the center of the large market square so people could carry their loved ones there to feed the pyres. There was no waiting as a body left to mourn over could rot and spread disease in these conditions. The citizens of Hamlyn knew the consequences of not disposing of bodies quickly. One could mourn their loved ones later, when houses and livelihoods were rebuilt. It was a bitter truth.

Both Treena's and Stiann's shops had survived mostly unscathed. Stiann was missing only his sign, and Treena had lost her flower boxes and signs. All their strong wooden shutters showed signs of damage, but they had held. Nothing a few slats and a coat of paint wouldn't fix. They had paid for a Master Builder to build those shutters, and it showed. Not that it mattered since her shop was closed for the week on orders from the Church. If it wasn't essential items you were selling, you were to remain closed and take the time to clean up and help those around you. Because of her shoulder, she hadn't been able to help but she had spent several days checking in with her horde of street children to make sure their families were okay, and she took the time to travel to the edges of the wharf area to check in on her family. The family home was a large warehouse with the ground floor separated into two sections where her father sold his fish that he caught on his boat and where her mother sold her simple handmade undergarments for the women of the area. The upstairs section was converted into the family home and due to Treena's status, they had many little luxuries that the neighbors didn't possess. Due to the same Master Builder, their home had fared well from the hurricane though the storm surge had reached them enough to fill the ground floor with several inches of water that both her older brothers grumbled about as they had to sweep out the water as their precious fishing boat had sustained major damage on the wharf and would take months to repair. They would also have to wait until the wharf was opened and deemed safe before they could start their repairs.

Treena was still waiting to discover if the flower suppliers in the region had been badly hit by the storm. Hopefully word would reach her tomorrow, or she would have to go down to the first reopened market the day after and hope flowers were there for sale. Thankfully her major client, the church, didn't care what they paid as long as pretty flowers turned up daily in certain places and bi-weekly in the churches for services. She was loath to charge them more because she knew the money came from taxes, which the people already struggled to pay, but in another way, she was regaining some of those taxes and putting them back in the economy by giving to her parents and the street children she cared for.

Aven sat quietly as she practiced her letters, while Stiann and Treena chatted of inconsequential matters as she made them both lemon tea. Treena cupped the steaming mug in her hands and let the heat soothe her, watching the steam lazily swirl up and away. Once her mind was calm, she began to talk to the Elldean.

"There are a few things I need to discuss, and I think you might be my best option." She paused thinking everything through. "And it probably needs to be recorded somewhere."

Elldean Stiann nodded but didn't say anything.

Treena had always liked that about him. He was willing to wait rather than push you to say something when you weren't ready.

"I used my powers while I was in public. I got trapped in the office of the Arch Deacon and had to climb out the window, by then the storm had begun and the stone wall was too slippery to navigate while the wind was that strong."

"How did you use them?"

"I drew the water around me to form a protective bubble."

"And did it work the way you planned? Did you struggle to create it amongst the panic of being trapped and in the middle of a devastating storm?"

Treena was relieved he hadn't scolded her. "It worked perfectly. There was plenty of water in the air, so it was simple to manipulate." She took a hesitant breath and kept going. "There is more. I found a child and stayed to protect him rather than make my way to Aven as quickly as possible."

Stiann shook his head and smiled kindly at her. "You chose to protect a child rather than rush back to a child that has powers and was already protected?"

Treena hung her head. "Yes."

"That is what you are supposed to do." His tone had turned into his patient lecture tone she had become so familiar with when he taught her to read. "Aven has Braith and her powers. What did this child have?"

"Nothing. He was stuck in a tiny alcove."

"Oh, my darling Katatreena, that is what you were born to do. You are a Dalinda. Your whole existence is to protect. Though, you do appear to have an affinity with children. Aven is important but was in no immediate danger and had someone very competent looking out for her." He looked into her uncovered gold eyes. "You made almost every decision correctly. That doesn't mean that you will next time as we all make mistakes, but you must trust in your training and yourself. There may come a time when you can't afford to second guess yourself as it will cost you or someone else dearly."

"Almost every decision? What did I mess up?"

A thump on the door made them all jump.

"I'll get it," said Stiann as Treena reached for her contacts and Aven handed her a mirror.

As Treena swiftly put in her second contact with a practiced hand, Stiann called, "It's just Braith."

The two entered the kitchen and Treena noted that Aven smiled openly at them. It made her heart sing to know that the young girl now felt comfortable with two men in her life. After her harrowing up-bringing by her revolting father, men were only there to use you in any way they saw fit, was her opinion. It was taking time, but Treena was slowly seeing the changes in the girl as she became less wary. She still didn't speak a great deal and only when addressed, but she didn't hunch and cower when they entered the room anymore. The time that Aven and Braith had spent together while the storm raged must have broken through another barrier and the smile was the proof.

"Aven, how are the letters coming along?" Braith inquired as he accepted a hot lemon tea from Treena before seating himself at the small kitchen table.

She shrugged. "Fine. Borin, but I learn cause I ave to."

"Maybe we should put the words on a deck of cards? I am certain you will pick it up extraordinarily quickly then." He looked amused but didn't elaborate.

Aven giggled just like any other eleven-year-old with a cheeky secret, and all three adults smiled at her indulgently, though only one knew what she was giggling about.

"Do either of you care to explain?" asked Stiann.

"Oh no. I wouldn't want to ruin the fun." Braith winked. "How is the shoulder?"

"Healing well." Treena resisted the urge to reach up and touch it.

"Sorry I haven't been here. I have had some trouble with a few enterprising individuals who thought this would be the best time to rob our citizens. I knew you were healing and Stiann was to keep the boys across the way informed if you needed anything."

"You are upset that a few of your men are doing their job at this time?" Treena was confused. Had he finally grown a conscience?

"No, no. It is the perfect time to be out helping ourselves to the things we lackor other people lack. It is the absolute wrong time to steal from our poorest because they are weak and exposed." Braith looked indignant. "My street urchins are out pickpocketing the rich who are charging a fortune to rebuild the homes of the poor. The older ones are taking the opportunity to visit the richer guildsmens' homes as part of clean-up crews to either case the place or pilfer what they can, especially food.

They drop half to the makeshift kitchens that have been set up in the poor and dock areas and the rest comes to me."

Stiann looked impressed. "A thief with ethics? How unusual."

Treena coughed into her tea mug. "Hardly."

Braith smiled blandly but refused to be baited.

Stiann missed the sarcasm in her voice. "Oh, I think it is rare for a thief to consider where he steals from."

"She was implying that it isn't ethics that makes me pick targets, it's the payload. Most of the time that is true, and over the years we have had some huge disagreements about my trade, but not today. I am here about the Spirit Mirror." He took out a small hip flask and poured a nip of clear liquid into his lemon tea, took a sip, and leaned back into his chair.

Treena chose to not dwell on what he had said. They had rehashed this discussion so many times. She loved to irritate him, so asked innocently, "What about the Spirit Mirror?"

Braith expelled his breath loudly, as if losing patience. "Did you find it?"

"Oh that. Yes, of course I did," she replied nonchalantly. "It is behind a curtain in Arch Deacon Ulrick's office. It hangs on a wall but I didn't have the chance to find out how it is hung and if I can remove it."

"Why?"

"I was interrupted by Ulrick, then the hurricane, then I was locked in and had to get out before someone got back—that sort of became my top priority." She kept up the charade of nonchalance, ignoring the memory of her heart pounding as she learned she was trapped.

"How did you get out?"

She shrugged. "I climbed out the window and down a wall."

He stared at her as if deciding whether she was telling him the truth. "You climbed down the monastery wall in the middle of the hurricane?"

"How else was I going to get out and back to you?" she asked. "And Aven."

"Impressive."

"Thank you."

Stiann interrupted their exchange. "What do you think we should do now? Sneak in and take it or sneak in and use it to communicate with whoever this thing is that visits Aven?"

"I don't know if I can take it. I'm not sure how it is attached to the wall, or it might be too heavy to carry."

Braith leaned forward, putting his elbows on the table and looking directly at Treena. "Then we will have to go take a look and decide while we are in there."

"I'm not taking Aven in there."

Stiann said, "I don't think you will have to. You are Dalinda, so the mirror should work for you. It was built for you to communicate with others over long distances."

"I guess that is our best option. Aven can go with you to the shop and practice her letters there."

Aven's face brightened at the thought of being in the scholar's workshop. Treena knew how she felt; she had loved being surrounded by books too.

"All we have to do is figure out how to get back in there again."

Braith nodded. "I have a few ideas."

Chapter 34
Sylvan

Sylvan floated down the hidden corridor in the library as he couldn't find the First Elder in his usual places, and he had now started to keep tabs on him. His days had become quite routine, though he now fought against the feeling that he should just lay down and rest. Sylvan didn't know if he was becoming despondent to not being able to do anything or if the pull of the elemental plane to join it completely was becoming more dominant as he grew weaker. He had never noticed it before.

His morning started with him checking on the girl and her mentor in Hamlyn before heading back to Cynsellam to be in Albin's office, at sunrise, to hear the reports from the ruling clergy across the country. He was learning a lot about how strict Albin's rule truly was. He had always thought the First Elder was an old man who ruled in Cynsellam, but the outlying cities and towns ruled themselves, this was not the case. Albin knew everything and was consulted on most decisions before they were made. He was also far more ruthless than what Sylvan had understood, even though Albin was calm in appearance, everything had to be done to his exacting ways.

After listening to the morning reports, Sylvan had taken to finding Hadrian. He had uncovered her affair with the silversmith and on occasion her servant joined them in bed. Sylvan had never understood the need for a carnal relationship and after watching a few moments of all three in bed he had fled her suite. He now checked in a little later in the day and always found her reclined on her chaise, performing her Shaymmi duties diligently.

To fill his time, Sylvan had taken to checking in on the twins, Matteo and Matthias, who he usually found either sparring in the yard with the warrior monks or in the library. He was furious that they were missing out on vital training but there was little he could do to rectify the situation while he was stuck on the elemental plane. After that, he would move around the monastery to see if anything was out of place, then he would check on Albin one more time before heading back to Hamlyn in the hope they had found the Spirit Mirror.

Today on his second check of the First Elder, he had found him missing. He had checked all the places he typically visited but could find no hint of him. His only thought was that perhaps he had gone back to the hidden corridor and Sylvan had always meant to go back and search it more thoroughly—he may as well do it now.

Sylvan now found himself floating outside the door of the room Albin had used to channel the power of the uncovered helmet, having just stuck his head through the door to find the room the same as the last time they had been there. Sylvan moved further down the corridor, checking behind any door he came across. He found empty rooms and rooms filled with crates and a room full of skeletons and piles of clothes. *What the hell was going on in here?* he thought as he slowly pulled out of the bone-filled room.

He moved deeper down the corridor, which opened into a large room that looked to be full of junk. Sylvan moved into the dark room, using the elemental vibrations to feel that there were life forms to his right. He slowly floated over to the area, to discover Jorge, his servant, hanging from a heavy, upright wooden pole, with his arms drawn up and chained to a metal loop at the top. His usually round face was bloody and swollen, his left eye was completely closed, and he had several open wounds on his chest that slowly wept blood. Two warrior monks flanked him, their faces stoic, giving away no emotion. Albin stood to the side, smiling in a calm, friendly fashion, as if he was having a chat with friends. Another warrior monk stood in front of Jorge, a whip in his hand. Sylvan noticed that his knuckles were bloody. Sylvan felt sick, though he had no stomach, his brain still thought he did, and it roiled in disgust at what had been done to his personal servant. No matter how he had betrayed him, Sylvan couldn't help but feel alarmed and worried for Jorge.

Sylvan watched, frustrated, as Albin spoke, but he was unable to understand what was being said. He had tried to learn to lip read, but it was more difficult than what he had thought it would be. Jorge shook his head, and he received another lashing for the effort. It was obvious that he was being questioned and punished for not revealing his secrets. Sylvan longed to know who Jorge was protecting. That might lead him to who had taken his body and blocked him from returning to it.

Another question was asked and was refused to be answered, resulting in another lash with the whip, making Sylvan squint at the resulting pain that he knew Jorge must have felt. Sylvan hovered there for several chimings of the bells, watching in horror as the wounds accumulated on his servant's body. Eventually Jorge lost consciousness and slumped down, limply dangling from the chain that held him to the pole. One of the warrior monks grabbed a bucket of water and threw it over him. Nothing happened. They had pushed him too far and his body didn't respond to the shock of icy water.

The First Elder stood with his odd, calm smile still on his face. He spoke and raised his hand in a wave. All three warrior monks bowed formally and began to move away. Sylvan assumed he had dismissed them. Sylvan waited to see what would happen next. He was upset with Jorge's betrayal but felt the need to witness what would come of his manservant.

Albin walked around the servant, his lips moving. He then checked to make sure that the warrior monks had left the cavernous hidden room before coming to stand in front of Jorge. The First Elder moved forward and took Jorge's mangled face in between his hands. He closed his eyes and the smiled finally disappeared from his lips.

Sylvan felt the stirring of the elements on the plane. What was happening? It was vague, just a hint. It reminded him of the child and the helmet when Albin had drained it to dust, but weaker. Both had odd vibrations that he hadn't felt at any other time, even when he found an ancient artifact that he now knew belonged to the Dalinda. Jorge's face began to distort, his mouth opened wide like a silent scream, his eyelids flew open, but Sylvan knew he couldn't see anything as the pupils had become milky.

Sylvan tried to understand what he was seeing. Could Albin possibly be trying to drain Jorge in some way, just like he had the helmet? It seemed completely implausible, but what else could it be? He studied the First Elder's face to see if there was any change occurring. There was no difference to his already altered face.

Albin opened his eyes and threw Jorge's head back with enough force that it hit the pole that held him. He glared at the servant before spinning on his heels and stalking away. Sylvan didn't follow him, his attention focused on Jorge. He watched with dawning horror that his servant, and if he was honest with himself, the only person who he thought cared about him at the monastery, was dead. His chest no longer rose and fell with his breathing. He was still and Sylvan wished him to be at peace. It was an odd moment. He knew he should be glad, Jorge had betrayed him, but at this time all he felt was sadness. He knew the anger and frustration at one more person who could now not help uncover his body would come, but all there was was an empty feeling he couldn't explain.

Chapter 35

Treena

The pile of leaves stirred. Treena held her breath and remained as still as possible. This was wonderful progress, and she didn't want to disturb Aven as she continued to move the air enough to gently lift the leaves from their pile. The leaves rose higher and began to spin in a slow circle. Aven's golden eyes blazed as she fought to keep her power controlled. It was a battle to not allow the element to take over. You had to bring it under your control and slowly bend its natural want to your desire. It was like coaxing an animal to trust you. This got easier till you eventually manipulated the element without thought until it was tremendous amounts, then it took all your energy and internal will. You also had to be aware of the interconnecting elements around you. If you moved the earth in the wrong place, you could change the course of a river or create a whirlwind near a fire and you could inadvertently start a forest fire. At the moment, Aven controlled the air without disturbing the water in the pail next to the swirling leaves or the small amount of dirt that lay on a tray to the other side. What she was trying to achieve was to get the leaves near enough to the tiny fire that was burning brightly in a brazier in the corner, so they could float into the fire without disturbing it with the air that carried the leaves. It took a gentle touch to do this.

Leaves began to spin a little too quickly and careen around the training room, the water in the pail rippled and the dirt on the tray scattered as Aven lost control of the air element. All the candles in the room were snuffed out, but the fire in the brazier was bigger, so withstood the gust before it settled by Aven letting go of the element.

The frustration on Aven's face was clear, even in the soft light the fire threw off. "You did well," Treena tried to soothe her.

"I ain't learnin quick enuf." Aven's speech went back to its worst when she was upset.

"Quick enough for who? You have only been in training such a short time. What we are doing is difficult." Treena was calm, but worried as to why Aven couldn't see how well she was doing.

Aven took a deep, settling breath and closed her eyes. All the candles reignited at once.

"I cannot explain enough how extraordinary it is for you to be able to do that. The only candle you should be able to light is the one that represents your element, yet you can light any candle, which means you have some control over fire."

Aven had herself under control a little more. "I am not strong enough in anyfing."

Treena scoffed. "You blew the door off the prison wagon. That was impressive and took huge amounts of power and focus."

"But I don't know how I did it. I need to learn that."

Treena came to sit next to Aven in the middle of the training room floor and slowly took her hand, reminding herself to go gently. Aven became more trusting every day and Treena didn't want her to backslide by pushing too hard. "I understand you want to learn it, but why are you pushing yourself so hard? You will get there. You have shown great ability already, but you are young; one of the youngest ever to gain your powers, and we don't want to burn you out. We have years to do this."

"They don't ave years." Aven sat staring at the fire in the corner. She didn't resist Treena's handholding.

"Who?" Treena spoke barely above a whisper.

"Me family."

Understanding finally came to Treena. "You want to rescue your brothers and sisters?"

"I will rescue them." Aven spoke in the strongest voice she had ever used. "They will not die like Dyella or Aleeya or be broken like Dacrow." She swiped the tears that began to fall.

Treena sat and waited. She wanted Aven to know that whatever she said or didn't say was going to be on her terms. She was in control of this situation, and she would not be forced to do or share anything she didn't want to.

Slowly Aven stood and untied the string that held her training pants in place. She allowed the pants to drop to the floor and with her shoulders and head bent in shame or sorrow, Treena couldn't pick which one, Aven turned to expose the back of her skinny thighs. They were covered in horrifying healed welts.

"Oh, Aven." Treena expelled her breath slowly, as she fought her natural instinct to hold the child and soothe her.

Aven pulled her trousers back up and tied the waist before she turned to face Treena. She lifted her face, and her Dalinda eyes shone with more tears. Without being invited, she took the few short steps that closed the gap and collapsed into Treena's lap. The force of her misery finally overflowed, and she sobbed. Heartwrenching, heaving grief poured forth and Treena held her tight, willing her to understand that she had found a safe place that would never change.

Eventually the sobs turned to quiet tears and finally subsided into soft hiccups, causing them both to laugh softly. Aven spoke in an even quieter voice than normal. "Ma died when I was four. I don't remember her, only what I been told. Dyella was me eldest sister and when the customer came for Ma, Da just gave thirteen-year-old Dyella to him instead. Over the last seven years all but me has been given to customers." Aven shuddered.

Treena couldn't hide her revulsion. She waited to see if Aven would go on.

With a deep breath, Aven slid off Treena's lap and knelt in front of her, she grasped both of Treena's hands and continued to look in her eyes. "Dyella died trying to save me and me youngest sister, Jeska. Bout two years ago a customer fell in love with her and told her he would take her away, she said she would only go if he took us too. Da catched us sneakin out. He killed both Dyella and her lover and whipped both me and Jeska. Jeska was me age now and the next night was given to her first customer. She cries herself to sleep every night." Aven's voice had become flat, monotonous as she recounted her father's degradation of his children. "Another sister died about half a year ago at the hands of a client who liked to play games. My oldest brother is not right in the head because he refused to be used when he was twelve. Da beat him until he was just lying on the floor, then left him to the customer."

"How many are still being used by your father?"

"Dacrow, Lanae—she is allowed to eat as much as she wants but was beaten when she tried to share her food with us, some men want round girls. Oberst and Jeska."

"So, two boys and two girls and two sisters dead?"

Aven nodded. "I can't let him hurt em anymore. I have to save em."

"Yes, we do. But we need to plan this and figure out the best way. I don't want you losing anyone else you love." Treena squeezed Aven's hands. "You have to trust me. I want to help. We are family now. But you need to train, the spirit that visits tells us that they still search for you. I know this is hard for you to hear, but you cannot be lost. You are Dalinda and one day we will be restored as rightful rulers, it may not be in our lifetime, but we need to be ready."

"Why does it matter so much if it ain't gonna be us?"

Treena smiled. She remembered asking the same question. Being older now and taking care of young ones, she had come to understand that at some point every Dalinda-in-training prob-ably asked that question. It was a huge, daunting commitment that appeared to be for nothing sometimes. Every decision you made was for a greater good, that probably wouldn't happen in your lifetime. At any age it was hard to see the point at times.

"If I don't train you properly and then you don't train the next Dalinda properly, what happens when we are needed? We will not be ready to rule in good faith and take back the tyranny of the One Church. The people of Duthyne need us to be strong and hold true to the Elemental Gods and their teachings. We are still being born, so there is hope."

"How can we take back Duthyne without the Oredmoor?"

Treena sighed and stood up, groaning as her knees protested from sitting on the hard wooden training floor for so long.

"That, Aven, is the question no one can answer. Every year the First Elder creates more warrior monks and makes the populace pay dearly for the privilege. They are cruel and greedy, and everyone grows more fearful. The Loyalists grow also, but we must be careful who we let into our ranks as we cannot be discovered. We will be hunted to death like we were when the original First Elder had us all slaughtered. The only advantage we have this time is that we are hidden well and spread throughout the country."

Aven bowed in a very formal manner to Treena. "I promise I will keep the secret and train hard as I can, so I can help more than jus me family."

"You are so brave and smart. Yes, everyone needs protecting, not just the people we know."

Aven bent down to pick up the few books that she had been learning to read from before the elemental training had begun for the day. "Where do you want these?"

"Over on the shelf, next to the Oredmoor head bookend on the left."

Aven's heart-shaped face filled with wonder. "I love that bookend."

Treena laughed. "I have two and, well, obviously they are not really the heads of Oredmoor."

"Can I touch it?"

They moved to the large set of shelves that spanned one wall of the underground training room. Treena took down one of the bookends, replacing it with a heavy unused candle. She then moved to another section of books and replaced that book-end with a large, uncut, clear crystal. She gave one to Aven and held one herself. She had forgotten how heavy they were. They had been given to her by Stiann, but he couldn't tell her anything about them. They looked like white marble, but they were tougher. Treena was embarrassed to admit it, but she had dropped one while she was tidying the shelves at one point. It had not been chipped or scratched much to her relief and thankfully had not shattered.

Aven held hers up to the nearest candle to examine it. Her face was in awe. "Is this what they really look like?"

"I'm not sure. If you look at this one, it is different from the one you hold." She held it up to the candlelight next to Aven's. "See, the horns on this one are much smoother than the horns on yours and yours has a single eyebrow ridge whereas mine is double."

"They even have slightly different scales." Aven stroked the side of its neck. "This one has more rounded scales while yours have a pointier end. They are both beautiful." Aven continued to hold hers with reverence. "Could I hold yours too please?"

"Sure, give me yours." Aven handed the bookend over and then carefully took the new one in both her small hands.

"Um, Treena, was this really cold to touch?" Aven asked.

"No, it felt the same as this one. Why?"

Aven's eyes were wide, but she didn't look scared. "This one feels strange. It feels cold and almost wet." She moved it closer to her face for a look, expelling her breath as she did. Instantly the eyes began to glow a dull gold, slowly building to the same bright gold as the Dalinda.

Treena slowly put down the bookend she was holding. "Aven, can you please slowly pass it to me?"

Aven nodded and gently placed it back into Treena's waiting hands. As soon as Aven's hands no longer had contact, the eyes faded and it returned to its normal temperature. Treena held it up and looked at it intently. "Are you comfortable holding it again?"

"Yeah." Her little hands didn't show any hesitation when they took the Oredmoor head. "It feels cold and almost wet again, but the eyes ain't changin." Aven spoke softly.

Treena frowned as she thought about it. An idea dawned on her. "You have equal ability in water and air. It feels cold and wet, like water, I think it needs air too."

"I didn't move the air last time." Aven didn't understand.

"No, but you breathed on it."

Aven drew in a breath and slowly expelled it onto the book-end. Immediately the eyes returned to a glowing gold. "What does it mean?"

"It means I think we need to talk to Elldean Stiann."

Chapter 36
Sylvan

Hadrian walked into her suite. She looked annoyed. Her lips were pursed and high forehead furrowed. The warrior monk, who guarded her, closed the door quickly behind her, as if he did not want to be caught up in her mood. Sylvan floated along beside her, his thoughts split between curiosity of her movements and profound sadness for what had happened to Jorge yesterday at the hands of the First Elder.

Sylvan noted that while her suite and his were the same in size, they were decorated differently. She pushed open the double bedroom doors to reveal the silversmith, who had been with her in The First Elder's office, and her manservant asleep in the tangled sheets of her overly large bed. Sex was something Sylvan rarely thought about and having it so blatantly displayed in front of him was making him feel incredibly uncomfortable. He had been far too busy to engage in things of that matter and didn't trust anyone that had shown interest because he never knew why they would be interested in him. He knew he was nothing to look at. So it must be his wealth and title that made the pursuer want him and he didn't want to share his position with anyone.

Sylvan turned his back to the scene on the bed and watched Hadrian instead. She gestured to the two sleeping men and spoke at some length. Sylvan wished he had a spirit mirror with him, and it was dawn or dusk instead of mid-morning, so he could hear her words. He assumed she was waking them up.

He looked around the room, noting that there were clothes strewn everywhere, with several empty wine skins and three glasses with the dregs of red wine in the bottom. The clothes were quickly being snatched up by the men and Sylvan turned once he had counted to one hundred, assuming by then that they had enough time to at least get their breeches on.

Hadrian spoke directly to her manservant. Sylvan wished he could remember his name, but it had always been something he just didn't need to know but now he thought perhaps he should be more aware of things going on around him. He might need to rethink his idea of what he needed to know. The servant bowed formally and hurried from the room.

The Silversmith—Sylvan did remember that his name was Cyrus—was finished dressing and now helped himself to the fruit that had been left on the serving board in the bedroom, before taking a long draught of wine. Hadrian looked to be worried and trying to convince Cyrus of something. She moved to her large dressing robe and yanked open the doors to expose Sylvan's body unceremoniously tangled up in her discarded clothing.

Sylvan rejoiced and immediately swooped down to enter his body. He stopped abruptly as he slammed into an invisible wall. It was like the air had hardened and created a barrier. He battered against it, his frustration growing while his energy weakened further. He moved back and took a huge sweeping motion, attempting to reconnect with his body and recoiled instantly as he rebounded heavily off the barricade. He noticed at the same moment that he was flung backward that Cyrus flinched.

He collected his thoughts and calmed his emotions. He positioned himself so that he could watch Cyrus and floated above his body. Slowly he lowered himself until he came up against the hard surface. He pushed against it, watching Cyrus the whole time. The harder he pushed, the more Cyrus looked alarmed, before his eyes narrowed and looked toward Sylvan's supine body.

Hadrian spoke to Cyrus, who shook his head and turned from the inert body. He moved to Hadrian and kissed her softly on the cheek before he spoke. It wouldn't be the last time that Sylvan wished he could hear on the Elemental Plane. Sylvan slowly exerted his consciousness against the invisible barrier and Cyrus frowned. *What does this mean?* Sylvan wondered. Does this Cyrus Silversmith have something to do with how he is being kept from returning to his body?

Sylvan floated away from his body and higher up to the ceiling as he followed them both from the bedroom and out into Hadrian's study, where she had her chaise to lie on to enter the Elemental Plane. He was torn. Sylvan wanted to know what these two were doing but hesitated to leave his newly discovered body. He watched in fascination as Hadrian and Cyrus began to move the furniture to the outer corners of the room. Side tables, couches, and low tables were all shunted aside. A barely stocked small bookshelf was moved into the bedroom and several large plants were taken out to the private balcony area.

What are they doing? pondered Sylvan. It was all so strange. Why would Hadrian take his body? Could it be as simple as her wanting to be the best? Did she not understand that just because he wasn't able to get back to his body, he was still stronger and more capable than she was?

Cyrus went back into the bedroom and Sylvan followed. He was disappointed to discover that Cyrus was getting himself another glass of red wine. How could they drink so early in the morning? Cyrus carried the glass out to Hadrian, and they spoke for a few more minutes before without warning Hadrian dumped the full content of wine onto the now exposed beautifully crafted rug. Sylvan was completely confused by this.

Chapter 37

Hadrian

Hadrian watched the red wine spread through the expensive rug. *Maybe I should have used white wine, it looks like blood,* she thought absently. The wine continued to inch its way outward. She looked around the room, taking note that there was nothing else to do but wait for Garm to return. She was becoming anxious. Keeping the body in her wardrobe had been a good idea at first, but now it was a liability. There was too much at stake for her to be caught. Hadrian needed to keep searching for the girl. She still hadn't proved herself, and if anything, she had dinted her reputation with the First Elder. She would rectify that by any means necessary. She needed to concentrate on finding somewhere else to store Sylvan's body. Shaymmi Hadrian knew there was an ancient cellar in the stronghold. She had visited there several times with Garm to choose a wine. Perhaps there might be somewhere down there she could hide Sylvan? Perhaps Garm might know of somewhere. She would ask when he returned with the new rug.

She turned to Cyrus to find him looking back at her bedroom with a strange look on his face.

"What's wrong?" she asked. It was the third she had voiced her concern. "And don't tell me nothing."

"I'm not sure." He spoke slowly. "There is something not right. I think the Master Shaymmi is trying to return to his body."

Hadrian tried to calm her sudden influx of nerves. "How do you know?"

"I feel pressure around the body. Like when we practiced, and you were trying to return."

She pushed past him and rushed back into the bedroom and came to stand in front of Sylvan's body. It looked the same. It was tangled in her clothes, with the ugly amulet resting on his chest. The body still breathed and didn't look anything other than being asleep. She closed her eyes and attempted to calm her racing thoughts and breathing. She didn't know what she hoped to sense by doing this, but she strained to find some trace of disturbance even though she wasn't on the elemental plane. Hadrian pushed her breath out in a big rush, frustration making her swear. "For the love of Pyre."

Cyrus raised his eyebrows at her, but did not chastise her for breaking one of the Founding Rules.

"Don't panic." He moved closer to her and took her hand. "It's just a pressure I am feeling. I don't feel anything weakening." He looked at the body. "I do wish Garm would hurry back with that rug. The sooner we get that out of here the more comfortable I will feel." He squeezed her hand. "I don't mind admitting that the First Elder's cold ire was unnerving to witness. I wouldn't like to be Jorge at the moment."

Hadrian felt uneasy as she thought of Sylvan's manservant. He had better hold up his end of the deal.

There was a sound from the outer rooms and both Hadrian and Cyrus rushed to see who it was. Fortunately, it was Garm returning with a new rug, carried in a large wheelbarrow.

"I thought we could use the wheelbarrow rather than carry the old rug."

"That is a wonderful idea." Hadrian was relieved that they didn't have to lug the heavy body of Sylvan anywhere. She moved to lock the doors to the suite. "Grab his body and bring it out. Let's get this over and done with."

Cyrus and Garm half carried, half dragged the inert body of the Master Shaymmi out of the bedroom and into the main room. Garm had his feet, while Cyrus carefully held Sylvan's shoulders, dragging him slowly on his bottom so as not to dislodge the amulet that stopped Sylvan from entering his body.

The men gently lowered the heavy body to the center of the ornate now-stained rug.

Hadrian frowned. "How are we going to keep the amulet from slipping once he is rolled up in that rug?"

They all stood there and stared at each other. Hadrian looked around the room, as if searching for inspiration.

"Could we glue it?" she suggested.

"What about tying it onto him?" Garm queried.

"Mmmm... I'm not sure either of those will work." Cyrus bent down to look at the amulet. "Gluing it may affect how it works, and we will have to lift it to get the glue on it."

"We can't lift it even for a second. Sylvan is good enough that he could re-enter his body in that short amount of time. It would be disorientating, but not impossible," Hadrian warned them.

"I don't think tying it on is feasible either for the same reason," remarked Cyrus. He continued to study the amulet, hovering closer to the chest of Sylvan.

"Well?" Hadrian asked impatiently.

"Give me a minute. I'm thinking as fast as I can," muttered Cyrus. "Do you have a pin? Maybe a hair pin? I think we might be able to fasten it to his clothing. It does have those two rings for, what I assume, is a chain to go through."

By the time Cyrus had straightened, he discovered that Garm had disappeared. He assumed either to the bathroom or the bedroom to see what he could find in Hadrian's belongings.

In a very short time, he entered the room holding out his open palm with several things on it. "Will any of these do?"

Cyrus took the two fastening pins and knelt by the body. "This should do it." He looked up at Hadrian and said in the most serious voice she had ever heard, "Perhaps you and Garm should grab something, just in case this doesn't work, and he somehow re-enters his body and is able to wake up. He will need to be silenced quickly." His face was solemn. "This should work, but we need to be prepared. We have come so far to be caught now."

Garm didn't need to be asked. He moved swiftly to the antique hutch that had been pushed into the corner and grabbed a hefty wooden carving of the One God. Hadrian looked around the room before settling on a stunning marble bowl that typically held fruit. She dumped its contents on the floor.

"Ready?" asked Cyrus.

They both moved closer to Cyrus and Sylvan's still body. "Ready," answered Hadrian.

Garm just nodded.

Hadrian held her breath as she watched Cyrus carefully thread the pin through one of the eyelets of the amulet. She kept watch over Sylvan's pale face, noting that his once clean-shaven square jaw now sprouted a brown beard, with a scattering of gray through it. His usually perfectly braided, chestnut hair was unkempt from being tangled in the clothes and dragged around the suite. She would have snickered if the situation wasn't so serious. *How low had she brought her enemy?* She wondered how his pride was holding up under all the strain of not being able to do anything about the current circumstances. It reminded her of her final year at school, before her abilities as a Shaymmi had manifested, when she had finally discovered her rival's secret and had managed to find a way for them to be late to their final exam and have points deducted, thus giving her the opportunity to get the highest results. She couldn't recall another time when her father had been prouder of her as when he read out her name as the highest achieving student that year.

Cyrus expertly threaded through the second fastening pin and very softly gave the hideous amulet a tug to make sure it was secure.

"It appears to have worked," he announced. "Let's get him out of here."

Hadrian stood in one corner of the room and hovered, unable to help as Garm and Cyrus delicately tucked the edges of the rug around the heavy, barrel-chested, six-foot frame of the Master Shaymmi. They had effectively rolled him up without moving his body to either side. Cautiously they then lifted him and placed him in the wheelbarrow, arranging it to look like just a rolled-up rug with an evident wine stain.

"Garm, we will follow you. Let us find a place for him in one of the storage rooms. If you are challenged, let me handle it."

Hadrian and Cyrus followed the manservant through the lavishly decorated corridors of the Shaymmi and into the sparse corridors of the servants that ran Stronghold. They were about to be stopped, when one of the warrior monks recognized Shaymmi Hadrian and quickly bowed and moved him and his companion out of the way. She flicked her auburn, glossy hair over her shoulder as they moved by them, hopefully distracting the monks further and having them focus on her rather than what they carried.

In Hadrian's opinion, it took far too long to reach the storage rooms they were after. Garm cleared his throat and spoke softly.

"My Lady, here are stored all the furnishings not in use at the moment. They are yours to be used at your whim, I am told by the Housekeeper. Each storage room contains different items."

"Excellent. I wonder why I wasn't informed about this earlier?"

"My Lady, it has always been assumed that with your exquisite taste and sound bargaining skills that you were happy to take care of your own purchases to furnish your suite and always just been reimbursed," explained Garm.

"Can we discuss this later, maybe?" Cyrus interrupted. He kept looking around to check if anyone was coming.

"Of course, gentlemen, let's find me a new rug," she announced expansively.

The first door they opened revealed a large room that contained open shelves, much like those found in the Stronghold library, but these contained plates, bowls, cups, mugs, ewers, and an assortment of huge serving platters and such. Closing this door, they moved onto the next room, which contained nothing but dining room chairs, row upon row of them in different fabrics and styles. The following room held stacked tables of varying sizes, and then the next room held side boards and desks.

"When all this is over, I am coming down here to have a good look around. Some of these things are beautiful." Hadrian spoke quietly as they closed the door of a room that contained nothing but sculptures and paintings.

The next door was exactly what they were looking for—rugs and other floor furnishings. Garm pushed the wheelbarrow into the room, and they firmly closed the door behind them. Spreading out quickly, Cyrus and Garm searched for a place to hide Sylvan's body.

"I've found something that might work," announced Garm from the far-right corner of the over-sized storage room. Cyrus came back and got the wheelbarrow before joining Garm and Hadrian. "What do you think, Cyrus?" Garm asked.

Hadrian went to admonish Garm asking for Cyrus' opinion rather than hers, when she realized it had to do with his knowledge with metals.

They stood before a large, deep, metal chest. She watched as Cyrus gingerly opened the lid to expose a pile of ash in the bottom of it. "Well, that is odd," Hadrian remarked.

"Very," agreed Cyrus. He was running his hands over the chest as if trying to feel something. "This should be fine. It is solid enough and doesn't look to have been used in a long time. We could also prop a few rolled up rugs in front of it to obscure it from view," he suggested.

"You two be as quick as possible. I am going to stand by the door to make sure we are not interrupted."

Hadrian watched from the door as the two men slowly unwrapped the Master Shaymmi's body and carefully placed him in the chest. They had to rearrange his limbs several times for his body to fit, but they eventually managed it, all the while being careful not to dislodge the amulet. With a quiet thud, they closed the chest and began to move a few rolled-up lengths of carpet in front of it. Hadrian let out the breath she was holding, then looked around the room for something suitable to replace the rug she had spilled the wine on. She finally settled on two smaller rugs. One for under the dining table and one for the seating area. They were then piled onto the wheelbarrow, and they dumped the soiled rug at the door.

"These two will have to do," she announced loudly as she opened the door and allowed her servant to wheel the barrow out first. "Garm, let whoever needs to know where the ruined rug is so they can deal with it."

Chapter 38
Sylvan

Panic rose to terror as Sylvan watched Cyrus and the servant shove his body into the metal chest and close the lid. As the lid sealed, Sylvan's mind spiraled out of control. His body felt weaker, as if the chest was leaching his senses. He watched with growing horror as the men piled large rolls of carpet around the chest to conceal it. Maybe it was time to reveal his secret and contact the First Elder? He fled the room and floated through the sparse corridors of the servant's area.

As he made his way back to the offices of the First Elder, it occurred to him that there was nothing he could do until sunset. The midday chimes had only rung a short time ago. Sylvan slowed his gliding down to hover in the middle of a hallway that was decorated with carved alabaster marble busts of The First Elder. He had never considered that they were all of the same man before. *And everyone thinks I have a huge ego,* he mused as he tried to make up his mind what he should do next.

He began to move again with no real end destination in mind. He just felt that he should continue moving. It made him feel like he had slightly more control over the situation when in reality he had none. Sylvan hoped that the young girl and the instructor in Hamlyn would be able to access the Spirit Mirror soon, so he could communicate more freely with them, and they would then trust him a little more. Sylvan had still not even managed to earn their trust enough for them to spell out their names on the alphabet blocks they used to communicate.

Sylvan found himself at a crossroads. He was going to have to make a decision soon, but he had calmed down a fraction and realized he could afford to put it off a little longer for now. His body was getting a trickle of air through a tiny gap in the lid so he wouldn't suffocate. *I think I need to know a bit more about what Albin is doing. I also want to see these golden eyes for myself.* This made up Sylvan's mind and he glided toward the library.

Within a few heartbeats, Sylvan was in the library and heading toward the concealed door at the back. He was almost there when he noticed movement in the shadows of an overstuffed bookcase to find the twins, Matteo and Matthias, looking over an old, brittle scroll. *What are those two up to?* He glided lower to see if he could read what they were looking at. The light was dim in the recess of the shelves, and he couldn't make out many words. Book ends, access, time, and elements were the only words that stood out. He couldn't even fathom what all that was about.

When everything returned to normal, and Hadrian had been revealed and removed from the Stronghold, he would have to take on the training of the twins himself. He was curious about a few things, and once they were able to enter the elemental plane, he wanted to know if they could sense each other. And he wanted to know why they thought they didn't need to drink the elixir. Sylvan's opinions of The First Elder had been compromised and he no longer trusted the supreme leader of the church. Now that he thought about it, did he really want to hand over the little girl and her teacher now he had seen what happened to Jorge? It was all very unsettling.

One minute he had been the most powerful Shaymmi and unconcerned with affairs that didn't matter to him, and now he was putting his own comfort aside for others. Though, if he was honest with himself, and he usually was, he still could end this at any time, so the stakes weren't that high. He could expose Hadrian, Cyrus, and the servant as well as lead The First Elder to the girl and her friends in a matter of moments if it suited him. It just didn't suit him right now.

Moving on from the twins, he found the door and floated down the corridor, passing quickly into the large room that held Jorge. He deliberately didn't go near Jorge. Even though he felt deeply betrayed by his servant he was conflicted and was struggling to come to terms with his death and the way he died. The body of the woman that had caused so much trouble was further back in the room, behind a curtain and guarded by two powerfully built warrior monks. He floated closer until he hovered inches above her. She had slender brows and high cheekbones, and her chin was tilted in a way that she looked like she had a slightly superior attitude, even in death. Her eyes were wide and unseeing, but they were breathtaking in their brilliance. There was no denying what lay before him.

These were the eyes of a Dalinda, a fabled Sky Rider, who could control an element with no more than a thought. He wondered what element she had been able to manipulate and didn't feel guilty for doing it. This woman was a legend, a myth, a hero that the Church of the One God had spent several hundred years attempting to erase the existence of.

Albin's response now made sense. This could not get out. The First Elder's job was clear: he would stop at nothing to have this remain a secret. Sylvan did precisely what he presumed Albin would have wanted him to do and why he was sent for. He opened his senses on the Elemental Plane. It was there and slight. It had probably been stronger when she was alive, but he felt the smallest trace of varying vibration than what he felt when he was close to and examining any particular human. He was now certain that her element had been water. It also explained why her body was decomposing at a much slower rate than a normal human.

Several ideas were starting to form in his head, and he wasn't happy with any of them. He put a few things together such as the twins thought they were being given the elixir for a different reason other than it was required to enter the Elemental Plane. Sylvan had always been guided by the First Elder and now things were becoming unclear. He also could not help but consider what Albin had achieved with the helmet that had been discovered and how it had been reduced to ash. Had more than one First Elder known this secret? Is that what the Shaymmi were really doing for the church? Sustaining First Elders? *Was there something wrong with that?* Sylvan would have to take a lot more time to answer that one. He wanted nothing more than to return to his rightful place as Master Shaymmi and have Hadrian removed for her vile betrayal, but another part of him now argued that if this was only what he had found out in a few weeks, what else was Albin hiding?

Sylvan heard a voice whispering on the elemental plane.

"Hello?" it called.

Rapidly he rose through the building and recognized that with all his musings and meanderings, sunset had arrived.

"Hello?" the voice called again.

How could there be someone on the elemental plane? It is impossible. He opened his senses and found the pull coming from the direction of Hamlyn. Another thought dawned on him. *Could they have activated the Spirit Mirror and that's what I am hearing?*

Sylvan was surprised to discover that while he had been sorting through his thoughts, his subconscious mind had taken him out of Stronghold and he was now facing the direction of Hamlyn. *I need to check the Spirit Mirror.*

Chapter 39

Treena

Treena stood in front of the Spirit Mirror, grateful that they had finally thought of a plan to get everyone away from the Arch Deacon's office area for at least two chimes around sunset.

It had been Chef Ezekiel who had come up with the brilliant idea to poison everyone with bad meat. He could blame someone else and even feign illness himself. Braith had accompanied Treena that morning to deliver flowers rather than the usual delivery service, and they had stayed by taking their time in the set up of the church and then had sat through the boring service conducted by the Arch Deacon himself. They then had gone to the kitchen on the pretence that they needed a bucket for the water, as the flowers were drooping. This got them out of the kitchen as the noon meal was served, which gave them the excuse not to eat it. Instead, they took their time drawing water from the well in the kitchen and walked around the beautiful garden, with Treena pointing out different plants to Braith. To anyone that came by, they looked as if they belonged there and were perhaps a courting couple, stealing a few minutes from their usual chores.

Braith carried the bucket as they made their way back to the chapel and took an extraordinarily long time to refill the vases that contained the floral arrangements. They had then returned to the kitchen to find the place in the chaos.

"Could I possibly impose on both of you to bring a fresh bucket of water in each? There seems to be an outbreak of illness and most of my staff have come down with it," Chef Ezekiel asked as soon as they entered. This, of course, gave them further chance to waste time until sunset and to make certain that the staff and Arch Deacon Ulrick were truly too ill to move from their chambers.

Within a chime, it was confirmed that most of the senior members of the monastery had taken ill, and a doctor had been sent for. Sunset was not far away. Chef Ezekiel openly handed the key to Treena and had said loudly, "I know you re-watered all the bouquets in the chapel, but did you remember the one that was sent up to the office of the Arch Deacon?"

"I did not. It completely slipped my mind. Would you like us to attend to that so he will have bright flowers ready to greet him tomorrow when he hopefully feels better?" Treena had volunteered.

"That would be much appreciated. I am beginning to feel unwell myself. If you return, and I am not here, please put the keys on the desk in my office, just through that door." He had indicated a door off to the right of them.

The sun hit the horizon and Braith turned the key in the lock, leaving it there, so no one could use it from the other side.

Treena pulled back the curtain that hid the Spirit Mirror and watched as a ripple moved over its surface. She pulled at her water element and reached out to the mirror—it vibrated under her touch. Something was happening, but what?

"Hello?" She spoke softly to the mirror's surface. She paused for a few heartbeats before she tried again. "Hello?"

Treena turned to look at Braith, who shrugged at her and hovered in the middle of the room, in case something happened in the outer office. She turned back and gasped. There was a man in the mirror. He had a large barrel chest, pale skin, and a short brown beard that matched his chestnut hair, which hung in a messy braid. His clothing was rumpled and the whole image was blurry, and she felt slightly queasy as she could almost see through him.

"You're the one who has been talking to the girl?" blurted Treena. "You are fuzzy and almost transparent."

"I would imagine I am. I am only a consciousness on the elemental plane. My body, as you know, has been stolen."

"Who or what are you?" asked Treena.

"I am Master Shaymmi Sylvan." His round, deep brown eyes took on a haughty appearance as he spoke.

Treena was astonished. Anyone who lived in Duthyne had heard of the man in the mirror. Though no one really knew what he did for The First Elder.

"What do you want with the girl?"

"I am required by the First Elder to search for artifacts from the time of Dalinda and Oredmoor. I was searching the area when I felt an unusual pull on the elemental plane that had never been there before. That is when I found the girl the first time. I quickly reported my find, as is required." He answered without inflection.

Treena did her best to not react to the name Dalinda and Oredmoor. They were forbidden words and she was surprised to hear them used so casually. He was part of the Church of the One God's inner circle, and the punishment, she was sure, would be swift and severe if he was heard speaking of them.

Was this him showing her that she could trust him? Did he know who she was? These thoughts frightened Treena and she lost track of the questions she wanted to ask. Stalling while she attempted to understand what was happening she asked, "How is your body surviving all this time without food or water?"

"My body is being fed by the energy I draw from the Elemental Plane. It is not a lot as I cannot truly manipulate the elements, but I can draw a small amount of each of the five elements to sustain me for a short amount of time. I don't know of anyone else who has been out here as long as I have—it is not something I would ever have thought I needed. I can only tell you that everyday I grow weaker as if it is leaching my very essence, even though it sustains me at the same time. I think the chest they have stuck my body in is making it worse. I truly don't know how much longer I can survive."

Treena considered his words, but said nothing.

"Will you help me?"

"I'm not sure I should. What would stop you from exposing the girl again as soon as you get your body back?"

"I won't do that." Sylvan's eyes widened with what Treena could only describe as horror for a moment. "I have seen what he does to those he thinks have any power he can use."

"I have responsibilities here. How am I supposed to leave everything and come to Cynsellam to find a body that you don't even know is the location of?"

"But I do know now." He became more animated which made his appearance blur further. "I know who has done it and why. I just have no way to get help aside from you to come and find it."

Treena frowned. She felt like he wasn't telling her everything. He was hiding something.

"Aren't the Dalinda supposed to help everyone?" he asked her pointedly.

She held her ground and attempted to look cool. "The name is forbidden. Why do you use it so casually?"

"Because that is what you are. You are a Water Elemental Dalinda. Under those brown glass discs, your eyes would be the same stunning gold as that of the dead Air Elemental Dalinda, whose body is currently lying in the secret chambers of Stronghold."

"You can tell that about me from this mirror?" she whispered.

"Yes. It makes sense now. I thought you were vibrating a little differently because you were near the girl. But once I saw the eyes of your friend, I opened my senses and could immediately tell what she was. The mirror makes everything clearer. There is something else you should know. They are very interested in her bracelet. Does that have any significance?"

Treena fought to breathe normally—this was moving too fast. She had expected a very different conversation when this began. Now she didn't know what to think about this spectre who needed her help. Treea felt trapped. She needed to think this through but knew that she would find it difficult to come up with another plan to get into the room to use the Spirit Mirror.

"If I agree, where is your body?" She stalled for thinking time. She hoped Braith was able to hear everything in case she missed something.

"In Stronghold, in the rug storage room. They have put it in a chest and piled rolls of carpets and rugs around it. It is along the far right wall when you are standing in and looking from the door." He continued to lose his shape.

Treena looked out the window to realize the sun was setting. The Master Shaymmi could disappear at any moment.

"I need to discuss this with people. I will send you my answer soon, through the tiles you have been using to communicate with the girl."

"Very well, but if you can find a way to communicate better, as the tiles are rudimentary. There are things about the First Elder you need to know..." As he spoke his body and voice faded, and the sun finally dipped over the horizon.

Chapter 40
Treena

The following morning, Treena decided to make a side trip while coming back from the flower markets and stopped at Aven's favorite pastry vendor. The young girl was working hard and learning as fast as she could. Aven never complained and was progressing better than what she thought, and Treena hoped a treat might bring a smile to her pretty face. The girl constantly fretted about her siblings' predicament. And that might not change. Treena had a feeling that after she discussed the Spirit Mirror conversation with Stiann, she would be traveling to the capital. Treena was feeling trapped about the situation, as if she was being forced on a course she didn't want. *Maybe that is what being a Dalinda truly was.*

As Treena rounded the corner to her shop, she found her delivery cart driver bloody and angry. Her flowers from the market were all over the road. One of Braith's bodyguards was helping to pick up the flowers and put them in piles at the front of her shop.

"What happened?"

The young thief answered first. "I was takin' a leak around the corner, so didn't see nuffin'. But Russ got clobbered and then came runnin', sayin' that Aven been took and he was gonna tell the boss." He was careful not to mention names with the cart driver in hearing distance.

Treena barely stopped herself from accosting the cart driver.

"What happened?" she demanded.

"I arrived to find the young lass being dragged out of the shop by a filthy, scrawny man, with loads of missing teeth, and who appeared to have already started drinking." He wrinkled his nose to show what he thought of such a creature. "When I tried to stop him, he punched me and pushed me to the ground, yelling at me that he was her Da and that he owned her."

"Anything else you remember?" She was desperate for any clue to help her track Aven quickly.

"Sorry, Miss Treena." He looked around at the mess of flowers. "This is going to take you some time to clean up, do you want any help?"

"Thank you for the offer, but once we get your cart righted with the buckets unloaded, you can be on your way."

The thief continued to pick up flowers as Treena stood there trying to figure out the next step. "What's your name?"

The young man, barely seventeen she guessed, straightened and bowed his head. "Eddie, Ma'am."

"Eddie, do you know the area near the poor quarter where the little ones play out of the way?"

"Yes, it's where you helped Freya's brother when he got hurt lookin' out for Aven."

Treena was relieved. "Yes! That's exactly where I want you to go now. I want you to bring back all the children that can keep up with you when you run. Send the little ones home. Tell them I need help cleaning up the flowers and that Aven has been taken by her Da. Can you do that for me?"

He was off and running without bothering to answer. Treena looked at the flowers and went to help the cart driver with unloading the flowers that hadn't been disturbed in the ruckus. As she moved into the shop, she noticed with dawning terror that a mirror was propped up on the pruning bench and an open box lay next to it. Quickly, she put the bucket down and moved to the box. Aven's brown eye discs were inside. Treena groaned and tried to keep a tight reign on her growing fear. She closed the box and put it in her pocket.

Treena finished helping the cart driver unload the cart and made sure that no flowers would be crushed when he drove away. Slowly, she continued to sort through the flowers. She opened the front window shutters and put out the buckets that usually held bouquets into their window boxes and began to collect flowers and sort them into lots.

Within a short time, a gaggle of children arrived at her shop, huffing and puffing and talking over each other. Eddie stood in the middle of them.

"Well, that was quick," said Treena. "Shh." She held up her hands for them to be quiet. They instantly did what they were told. "Does anyone here know where Aven's Da lives?" Freya and Zad put their hands in the air.

Treena assessed the situation and quickly came to some decisions. She didn't know what was happening to Aven or what her father had in mind to punish her for running away. She didn't have time to wait for Braith. Freya was the oldest here, and the children would follow her instructions.

"Freya, I need you to stay here and get the children to clear up all these flowers and put them into the buckets. If someone comes to buy flowers, just tell them there has been an emergency with my apprentice and you are not sure when I will be back." She turned to Eddie. "I know you are supposed to protect me, but I need you to stay here and tell Braith everything when he arrives, because we both know he will be here soon. Freya can give him directions on where I am going."

"What you all you gawkin' at? You 'eard Treena. Get them flowers off the dirty ground and make sure to be gentle and don't break any." Freya spoke firmly to the worried children. "Treena has never let us down. She will get Aven, but we gotta do our bit."

Eddie stood beside the buckets, instructing anyone who couldn't decide which flower should go where.

"Zad." Treena looked at the skinny, unkempt street kid, who she had been keeping an eye on since his family had perished in a fire that engulfed a row of houses several years prior. He was about eleven, but like most street kids, he was undersized due to lack of food. "Can you show me where Aven used to live, please? You won't need to come in with me. I just need to know where her Da has taken her." This of course, wasn't true, she had been there before when she had taken Aven home for the first time only to discover that her Aven's father was using his children in the most degrading vile way to make his living. What she needed was an unassuming lookout for when Braith arrived.

"Yes, um. We used to play nearby when we were little and not allowed to go far." He squared his shoulders bravely.

"Would it be okay if I took your hand? I don't want to lose you." Treena felt his anxiety and hoped to spare him as much as she could. She asked to take his hand because she knew boys of that age were sensitive to appearances of being carefree and strong.

His small hand snuck into her proffered one, and they were off at a jog.

Chapter 41

Hadrian

"Do you really go to church service several times a week?" Hadrian asked Cyrus as she snuggled further under the blanket. The days were still hot, but the nights were growing cooler as the season slowly changed.

"Of course. I can't believe you don't." He caressed her naked shoulder, slowly moving up to her neck and gently massaging it.

"Mmm, that feels good," she said while her thoughts raced with complications, knowing that this man was far more devout than she had thought. It could be a problem. Hadrian was grateful that she had not confided her attraction to the forbidden Elemental Gods. "So, what do you confess?" she half joked.

"Oh, you know. That a celebrated Shaymmi, her servant, and I do some kinky things in our spare time." His voice was serious.

Hadrian sat up and glared at him. "You do not!?"

"You are right. I do not." He looked amused and pulled her back down to lie next to him. It was just the two of them. Hadrian had sent Garm off to fetch wine and clothing from her suite. "Could you imagine the monk if I told him that? No, what is in my heart is between the One God and myself. It is not the church's or the confessional monk's business to judge my choices."

Hadrian relaxed a little after that statement. Perhaps he isn't as pious as she thought. He just did what was right for him. *Don't we all, really?* she admitted to herself. She decided to go ahead with the plan she had made when she had sent Garm off for the afternoon.

"My turn," she announced as she rolled Cyrus onto his stomach and straddled his bare bottom. Slowly and sensuously, she began to massage his neck and shoulders, giving him time to relax before she brought up the delicate subject.

"Cyrus, I've been thinking."

"Mmm, that is always dangerous." He sounded bemused.

Normally that would have brought a laugh from her, but not today.

"I think we have a problem."

"Just one?"

This time she did laugh. "Stop that, I'm serious."

"Okay. What's the problem?" came the muffled reply from the depth of the pillow.

"It's all unraveling, and I think it is dangerous for Garm to know our secrets. There is a rumor circulating that Jorge was tortured and killed." She paused, fighting her instinct to demand and order him to do what she wanted. Hadrian knew that she would have to do this delicately. "I can only assume that as there has been no one knocking our doors down that he stuck to his part of the bargain and kept his mouth shut."

"Bargain sounds so much better than blackmail," observed Cyrus. "That feels amazing."

Hadrian ran her hands slowly down the entirety of his back and rested them on the top of his bottom.

"With Jorge gone, that leaves the three of us who know what we have done to Sylvan."

"Get to the point, Hadrian, or at least keep moving those hands." He wiggled his torso impatiently.

She started to slowly press in a circular motion up his spine.

"Does there really need to be three of us who know what is happening?"

"What are you suggesting? That we get rid of Garm?" joked Cyrus.

"Yes."

"Yes?"

"Yes." Hadrian emphasised the word.

"Don't you think another person missing might bring more attention to you?"

"Don't you mean to *us*?" she corrected.

He pushed himself up onto his elbows. "No, I mean *you*. I have nothing to gain by Sylvan going missing. You do. And then if your manservant goes missing, that will look like you have got rid of him because you have something to hide."

"They will think you helped me for your own advancement," she countered.

"That is true. But he does things you don't," he said wickedly.

Hadrian moved one of her knees to pry open Cyrus's thighs. Then she moved the other leg so she was now kneeling in between his legs, her hands slowly snaking down his back again. She reached his beautifully shaped bottom and began to knead it. She sucked on one of her thumbs and then trailed it down the crevice of the perfect cheeks and swirled it around his anus. Cyrus moaned softly and lowered his chest back to the bed. As she played with his anus and slowly slid her thumb in, she began to take small nips with her front teeth up his lower back.

"Well?" she breathed against his back. "Should I stop?"

"If Garm went missing, it might also indicate that he is guilty of Sylvan's disappearance. If we made it look like he left in a hurry and maybe put out a few 'clues'..." Cyrus let the thought hang there.

"So, you will do this for me?"

"Only if you let me turn over so I can have you."

Hadrian laughed. "Done." Hadrian moved to allow Cyrus to turn over, before she slowly lowered herself onto him.

Cyrus groaned with pleasure. "Done," he agreed.

Chapter 42

Treena

She clenched her fists and not for the first time wished for Thedra to be there with her. *I don't know if I am ready for this.*

"Do you want me to go in with you?" asked Zad.

"It is kind of you to ask, but no. I want you to stand just to the side of the door, and when Braith arrives, tell him I have already gone in." Treena took a deep breath, squeezed Zad on the shoulder, positioned him to the side of the dilapidated door, and whispered, "Stay here."

Treena pushed the open door, not knowing what to expect, but it certainly wasn't the vile stench that assaulted her senses. She almost gagged as the smell of human degradation filled her nostrils.

"Can I help ya?" a bored female voice asked.

Treena scanned the downstairs area. It was dirty and almost empty. It was filled with a few grotty lounges that had lost their padding years prior, a bar that took up the left hand wall, and several small round tables with rickety chairs. A set of stairs ran up the right-hand wall and two doors were on the opposite wall to where Treena stood. There was a manky looking barman with stringy brown hair, and a single obese man in his middle years that she assumed was a patron. Quickly ascertaining that Aven wasn't there, Treena turned to the owner of the voice. She was a larger shaped girl in her later teens, but with the same heart shaped face as Aven.

"Lanae, where's Aven?" she spoke quietly.

"Who wants ta know?"

"It's me, Kat. I have been taking care of Aven, remember?"

One of the doors opened and a boy in his early-teens came out carrying a plate that held a bread trencher filled with some form of stew. Treena guessed that the door led to the kitchen—she doubted that Aven was in there. He slid the plate in front of the obese man and moved toward them. He was underfed, like Aven was, but carried himself with a bravado that Aven hadn't learned.

"Oberst?" Treena asked.

"You lookin for some fun?" he leered at her.

Ignoring the comment, Treena spoke softly. "I'm looking for Aven. Your Da broke into my shop and took her. Is she here?"

They stared at her, frightened, and her heart hurt at their despair. To do this to your kin was beyond depraved. Her resolve hardened, and she knew that when she left here today she would take all of Aven's siblings with her.

"Boy, come here. Sit with me while I eat," ordered the repugnant obese man.

Oberst's eyes filled with contempt for a moment before it was replaced with false bravado.

"Sure, Chunky, but will cost ya more."

"I'm lonely. Come sit nice and close." Chunky took another bite of his trencher and stew dribbled down his many chins.

Treena tried not to gag as she watched Oberst pull a chair opposite the man and sit with one leg on either side of his. Chunky continued to shovel food into his mouth with one hand while the other slowly made its way down to Oberst's crotch.

She couldn't watch anymore and turned her attention back to Lanae. "Did he bring Aven here?"

Lanae looked at her then back at Oberst, as if deciding something. "Ya must save her. Take her somewhere he can never find her. She is the only one that can be saved. The rest of us are ruined now."

Treena gently took Lanae's hand. "I don't believe that. You are all worth saving."

"No touchin' until ya pay," announced an arrogant voice from the staircase.

Lanae's hand trembled in Treena's. She quickly let go as she didn't want to get the girl in trouble.

"Da, I was just explainin' that as ya came down." Lanae's brown eyes were filled with fear.

Something welled in Treena, and she felt her power stir in a way that had never happened before. This man was a monster; he made his own children feel worthless. They were terrified of him and with good reason. He rented them out like animals and had killed his eldest when she had tried to escape. Treena looked at the pale-skinned man—his hair was greasy and his round brown eyes were bloodshot. Rage boiled up in Treena as he sneered at Lanae as he reached the bottom of the stairs. He turned his full attention to Treena. "Thought you might turn up."

A short, sharp scream of a scared little girl filled the air and something snapped in Treena. She moved swiftly to the stairs, but was blocked by Fion.

"Oh, I don't think so."

She tried to shove past him. Treena was taller and no doubt stronger, but he had the advantage of just having to brace his feet. Quicker than she had expected Fion lashed out and punched her in the face. He connected with her cheekbone and she stepped back at the force of it. Treena reached up to touch her cheek and her fingers came away covered with blood.

"I did warn ya to stay away." Fion glowered.

"What are you talking about?"

"The note at the Naughty Goat. I paid a lot of money to scare ya off and ya stupid bitch jus ignored me." Spittle formed in the sides of his mouth.

"Move," warned Treena. She didn't have time for this.

"Make me." Spit flew as he taunted her.

There was another loud, terrified scream, followed by a thud from the upper floor. Fury engulfed Treena and instinct took over. It was time to end this once and for all. Aven needed to be safe. The Dalinda stepped forward. This time she was ready for the swing and ducked easily under the arm of Fion. Her arm shot out and she connected upwards with the disgusting man's throat and he crumpled to the ground, his brown eyes bulging as he grabbed at his neck. She didn't wait to see if he would die. The gurgling sound as blood trickled from his mouth told her that he would probably die before she got back to him.

"Aven?" Treena called as she reached the top of the stairs and took in a hallway that had several doors on each side. "Aven?"

A door opened at the far end on the right, and a young man with a beautiful smile that matched Aven's in her rare moments of unguardedness, stepped out. It was Dacrow, the brother beaten so badly that his mind no longer worked the way it should. Treena didn't know if he would understand her, but she had to try.

"I'm looking for Aven."

She could hear feet running up the stairs. She didn't know who it was. She needed to find Aven before whoever it was could interfere. Dacrow raised his fingers to his lips, and then pointed to the middle door on the right. Treena hoped he knew what she had asked as she studied the old door. Slowly, she grasped the knob and turned it to find it locked. The feet had reached the top of the staircase and the corridor became crowded as both Lanae and Oberst came to a stop a little away from Treena.

"Da is dead," announced Oberst. "You better hurry. Barman Derkop has run off. We don't know if he left to get the warrior monks or just hide."

Treena nodded her thanks and turned again to the door. She took a step back and gathered her full skirts and hitched them up a little higher before taking aim and gave the door a powerful kick near the handle. The door burst inward, remaining intact but the frame had buckled considerably.

Aven huddled in a corner, her golden eyes blazed with power, yet her young face remained frozen in fear, her mouth open in a silent scream. The content of the room was being hurtled around in a minor whirlwind. Lying at the base of the whirlwind was a churchman, his face was covered in blood and his eyes vacant. Death had taken him.

"Aven? You need to stop now. You are safe," Treena called softly. She warily watched the items flying around. She inched into the room, hugging the wall. Treena had to duck as a plate sailed past her head and crashed near her, shattering into razor sharp shards that now joined the rest of the swirling mass. She continued to reassure Aven as she moved into the room. "Aven, you need to listen. I need you to focus on my voice and find your center."

Treena noted that Aven blinked and her mouth closed. The whirlwind lost some of its intensity. "Good girl. Can you look at me?"

Aven slowly moved her eyes to look at Treena, who remained against the wall.

"You are safe. Your Da can never hurt you again. You are safe," Treena repeated. "You need to bring your power within you, or you will burn out. You must be tired."

The whirlwind slowed even further and some of the heavier pieces fell to the floor. An unusually large, metal paperweight landed on the churchman's chest. Treena guessed by the large open wound on his head that that is what had killed him. She finally reached Aven, and without further thought to her safety, engulfed her into a firm hug.

"You are safe. I am here," she murmured repeatedly into the young girl's hair.

The remaining items fell as Aven surrendered to Treena's voice. The wind stopped and everything went quiet. Treena took the moment to look above Aven's head to discover that they were in a small room that had been Fion's. A dirty bed sat in one corner and a desk in another, with a chair lying on its side. Papers, filthy clothes, broken crockery, and shattered glass covered the floor. Blood pooled around the churchman's head, slowly creeping outward. Aven's siblings crowded the doorway—all eyes were wide with shock, though Treena wasn't certain what Dacrow was understanding. She picked up Aven and turned her face away—the already traumatised girl didn't need to see what she had done to the churchman's head as she was carried out of the room.

"Is there another way downstairs?" Treena asked them. She didn't need Aven seeing her dead father. Treena didn't know what her reaction would be.

"Yes, there are stairs behind that door. They lead down to the kitchen," answered Oberst. All bravado had disappeared.

"Is there anyone else up here?"

"No, things are always slow in the mornin'. Jeska is in the kitchen. She cooks til the cook for the dinner crowd turns up around the mid afternoon chime."

"What happened to Chunky?" Treena asked.

"He waddled off as soon as Da started chokin'. He don't want no trouble."

Treena handed Aven over to Lanae, who took her and held her close.

"I will be down soon. Stay in the kitchen. I will come and get you."

There was a heavy bang and many footsteps downstairs that made several of Aven's siblings cry out in fear.

"Treena?" a male voice yelled.

"It's okay. He's my friend. He will have brought people to protect you. Go now to the kitchen. I will be down shortly." She urged them toward the door. "Oberst, wait."

The boy hesitated, but did what he was asked.

Treena put her hand in her skirt pocket and took out the case she had brought with her. "Give this to Aven when you get down there. She will know what to do, but you must not let anyone into the kitchen until she tells you too. Friend or foe," she warned. He took the case without comment and headed for the door.

Braith yelled, "Treena?" His voice held an edge she had never heard before.

"I'm up here," she called as she moved back into Fion's bedroom and studied the dead churchman.

Heavy footsteps thudded up the stairs and down the hallway until they came to an abrupt halt in the doorway. She looked up from her inspection to find Braith staring at her.

"You're hurt." He hurried to her side and looked like he was ready to hug her.

"I'm fine."

"You're bleeding." He reached up and gently touched her face.

"Aven's Da hit me."

Braith's eyes were angry. "Is that the dead body downstairs?"

"Yes, he wouldn't let me by." She pulled her eyes away from his. "Do you know who this is?" She indicated the dead body.

Braith studied the large, bald-headed man with his huge bull neck for a few moments.

"Holy Pyre, that is Arch Deacon Ulrick. You killed the Arch Deacon of Hamlyn?"

"No," Treena whispered. "Aven did."

Chapter 43
Treena

Exhaustion warred with uncertainty. Treena sat at her mother's kitchen table. Aven and her siblings sat around the family table. Some ate the cheese, fruit, and fresh bread that had been laid out for them while others sat in stunned silence, but all the siblings continued to stare at Treena and Aven as if not knowing what to say. Treena understood exactly how they felt as she felt the same way. She had no idea where to start with the tangle of emotions that churned within her. She had killed their father and she didn't know how they felt about that. He was a monster, but he was still their father.

It had been a long day filled with dread and hasty decisions. Once Braith had arrived and confirmed what Treena knew, that Aven had inadvertently killed the Arch Deacon of Hamlyn, they decided to get the children out of there as quickly as possible. No one knew if anyone knew where Arch Deacon Ulrick was, or if they would be searching for him if he didn't turn up at a certain time. He might have had a troop of warriors monks coming back for him at any moment. Braith had put men at the front door to give warning while the children gathered anything they wanted to take with them before Treena had ushered them all out the back door and into the garbage-filled back alley. Zad had met them out the back, as asked by Braith. The stench had been revolting and they had covered their mouths as they set out looking like any other day when Treena came to check on the poor children. Sometimes she was known to also make sure the older children were fine, so being with Lanae and Oberst was not unusual.

Treena had led them on a circuitous route and gathered a few smaller children along the way for appearances sake. For several blocks, they had all acted like everything was as it should be before she had sent them back to their parents or guardians. Finally, they arrived at her parents' house and were greeted by her mother, who had been notified by one of Braith's thieves that Treena was on her way with five children ranging in age from eleven to eighteen.

She sat there and pondered how to start the conversation she knew they had to have.

"Thank ya." Aven looked at her, her golden eyes once again covered by brown glass. "That is the second time ya 'ave risked your life to save me." The small girl stood and came to Treena's side. Without a word, Treena opened her arms and Aven climbed up onto her lap, like she was a child of five. There would be a discussion at some point about what exactly had happened with Ulrick, but not in front of her siblings.

Treena kissed the top of Aven's head. "I told you I would always protect you." She looked to the siblings at the table. "I'm just sorry I couldn't help you all earlier."

"You killed our Da." It was Jeska who spoke. She was only a few years older than Aven and looked to be as badly underfed as Aven had been those few months prior. One side of her small face was covered in a smudge of dirt and she wore clothes that were loose and threadbare, just like the others. Her hair was matted and cropped short, like her two brothers'. For some reason, Lanae's hair was longer and her clothes appeared to be in a slightly better condition.

"Yes, I killed him. He took Aven, and I had made a promise to protect her. She is very important to me," explained Treena.

"You are a Sky Hunter." It was a statement from Oberst as he looked at his youngest sister.

Aven got off Treena's lap and went to Oberst. "No, no, you are wrong. Sky Hunters don't exist—they are folk tales."

Oberst's lips set into a stubborn line. "I know what I saw. Ya eyes were glowin' gold and ya were makin' things fly round the room. We all saw you put those things in ya eyes that she made me give ya."

Jeska interrupted. "Ya made things fly? Could ya do it again? I always miss stuff," she pouted.

"It's okay, we won't tell anyone," Lanae reassured them. "Who would believe us?"

Rather than confirm or deny who Aven was, Treena changed the subject. "I am sorry for having to kill your Da."

Oberst snorted and Lanae frowned at her. "Don't be," they both said at once.

Lanae added, "Do ya know what the monster used ta do? He would put out a bowl of fruit on the table for the customers. I was welcome ta eat my fill, and when it got too old for the customers, he would leave it on the kitchen table in front of the rest of em and just let it rot. He would rather waste food than feed his family. We were nothing but bodies to sell, and I will not shed a tear for the man." She almost spat the final words out.

Treena looked at the faces of Aven's siblings. Dacrow, the eldest, sat there smiling at her while continuing to pick at the food laid out for them. She wondered if he truly understood any of what had happened. Lanae glared at nothing while she sat, almost absently stroking Jeska's hand. Oberst continued his glances at Aven—he knew what he had seen and was obviously the most curious about it. They may have to tell him the truth, but not tonight.

"What 'appens now?" Jeska asked. "And what do we call you?"

"You call me Treena, I only used Kat to keep your father from tracking Aven." She smiled gently at her. "And now you tell me what you would like to do." Treena sat back in her chair and looked at them. "Do any of you dream about doing something?"

"Nah, we just always talked about escapin'. We never thought it would happen so didn't think further ahead than that," Lanae explained.

Treena noted that her speech was slightly better than her siblings too. She had obviously been trained for a different clientele.

"If you are willing to trust me, and are happy for me to make arrangements, I think I can help you."

"We stay together," warned Oberst.

"Yes, except for Aven. She remains with me."

Oberst looked ready to protest, but Aven stared him down. "I want to stay with Treena."

Treena stared into space, attempting to find her center and control her emotions. There was too much to do to let her remorse decide the next course of action. Her thoughts moved between needing to figure out what to do with Aven's four siblings, the need to protect Aven herself, and the need to decide what to do with Master Shaymmi Sylvan and his missing body. There was a soft tap on the door and Treena went to open it just a hint to check who it was before opening it wider to let Braith slip in. He followed her back to the kitchen.

"Would you like a drink?" she offered.

"Whatever you're having is fine."

Grinning wickedly, she handed him her dinted, metal mug.

"Be careful, it is a little warm." She turned her back and began to prepare herself another drink, while she waited for him to take a sip.

"Dear Guardian Torrent," he swore. "You didn't tell me that it had whiskey in it."

"Coffee and whiskey make a perfect match on a night like this. I think sometimes you forget I am all grown up."

"No." His voice was serious. "I am in awe of what you can do." He took another sip. "The bodies have been dealt with." He spoke in a whisper not wanting anyone to hear him. "Fion is in the harbor, in someone's fishing nets, and will be taken out to sea and used as bait without their knowledge. Ulrick has been left in a compromising state in a back alley near the central markets."

Treena smiled tremulously at him; she barely controlled the overwhelming want to fall into his arms and hide from everything that had happened today.

"I never knew that having a best friend as a criminal could be so useful," she whispered. "Thank you for being there for us all today. I don't think I can ever repay you for risking exposure to help us."

"You." He drew her into his arms, and for once she didn't hesitate. She needed comfort and love and he had always given her both. "Help you," he repeated. "I would do anything for you. You are my best friend." They stood still for several more moments until Treena finally felt better and pulled away. He let her go. "What are you going to do with this lot?" Braith nodded to the huddle of children asleep in front of the low burning fire. The night was cool, so the fire had been allowed to burn out rather than be put out to keep the house from being a furnace.

"I've got some ideas, but I need to speak with Stiann and my parents first." She blew out a big breath and looked at his concerned face.

"You don't need to make all these decisions on your own."

Treena straightened and stood eye to eye with the man who would always be so precious to her. "Actually, I do. I am Dalinda, it is my duty to make these decisions. And I have to live with the consequences of my choices."

They both knew she spoke of killing Fion. He was a man that deserved to die. His offspring had, in every way possible, told her that it wasn't her fault, and they were able to forgive her, for in their eyes she had saved them all. But to Treena, it was more complicated. She had taken a life, while her role, her instinct, was to protect, and she didn't know if she could ever forgive herself.

Chapter 44

Treena

Ezekiel was late, and Treena was worried. He had requested the meeting through the normal channels and had suggested the fruit and veg morning market as he was always there. Treena wandered around the stalls, pretending to browse by picking up the fruit to test it and smell it like Ezekiel had shown her, and chatting with the sellers. Food was still in short supply and what was on offer was not the usual standard, much the same as the flowers she sold. The recovery from the hurricane would take many more months.

It had been two days since Aven had been kidnapped and Arch Deacon Ulrick killed. His body had been discovered by a passerby late in the afternoon on the same day it had been dumped by Braith's men, and the city of Hamlyn held its breath for the ramifications they knew would come. The make-shift monastery bell, the only one able to be used since the hurricane, chimed the early morning alert. Treena decided to give Ezekiel to the quarter chime and then she would need to leave or risk looking suspicious. As she meandered, she found fresh apples and decided to buy them for her family as a treat—her mother always loved to have them with hard cheese.

Treena found it unsettling that she didn't need to be any-where for a while. She had planned to meet Stiann at his shop after the meeting, and Braith would bring Aven there. Aven had been kept out of sight since the incident and had either been guarded by Braith and his thieves, or Treena at her parents place, or in the sewers. The florist shop was being attended by a Loyalist, Emilia, the original owner who had taught Treena everything about the business, before handing it over as Treena's cover. Jeska, Aven's youngest sister, was now the apprentice. She looked enough like Aven and was only a year older, so most people wouldn't notice the difference if she dressed in the same clothes. As long as the flower arrangements kept turning up for services, it was hoped that no one would notice the change.

Braith had offered to find the rest of Aven's siblings roles within his gang, but Treena had been aghast at the idea. Lanae had told him loudly and vehemently that she would never be owned nor answer to a man again. Treena's mother ran a laun-dry business and offered Lanae the chance to work with her while she decided what she would like to do. Surprisingly, it had been discovered that Dacrow, who was no longer right in the head, thanks to his father's beatings, was extraordinarily gifted at fine needle point. Treena's mother had been thrilled to find someone to take over that work, as she had been complaining about her fading eyesight making it more difficult each year, and Oberst had appeared to be happy to do it. Oberst had been offered work with Treena's father and brothers and was trying his hand repairing the family's fishing boat that had been damaged in the hurricane. After it was repaired, he would join them and learn about being a fisherman to see if he liked it.

The quarter bell chimed and Treena swore under breath. She didn't know where Ezekiel was, but she couldn't afford to loiter any longer. Taking her cloth bag full of apples, Treena began to make her way out of the market and back towards Stiann's shop. Passing by a dark alley, Treena heard her name softly whispered. She assumed it was one of Braith's bodyguards, who had been set to watch her, and didn't hesitate to step in the alley. What she found made her cry out.

"Ezekiel. Guardian Torrent," Treena swore and rushed to the chef's aid as he lay covered in blood, holding the side of his neck with one hand and his rotund gut with the other. The alley was dark, but not dark enough to hide the fact her friend would soon be dead. "Who did this?" She knelt beside him, not knowing what to hold first.

"Closer," he breathed shallowly.

Treena bent closer. "Tell me."

"Locking city down," he struggled to say. "To find killer." He made a gurgling sound as blood trickled from the corner of his mouth. "Get out today," he rasped before his eyes rolled into his head and his body went limp.

Shadows fell across Ezekiel, and Treena tensed. She had been so intent on her friend that she had not considered that the culprits who had done this could still be hidden in the depths of the alley. Treena ran through her options, She knew this was no training drill and that her choices could cause her death and or further exposure regarding the Dalinda. She looked up to find two short-cropped hair warrior monks looking over her. All she could think was that she was grateful that neither had the flowing scalp lock, indicating that they were of the elite warrior monks.

"Oh, thank goodness. You must get help. This man has been attacked," she said with feigned relief.

"Do you know him?" one of the monks asked.

"No, I just heard a noise as I walked by. Why aren't you helping him?" Treena demanded.

Both of them looked at her, but no one moved.

"Fine, I'll go and get someone myself," she went to stand.

"Stay where you are," commanded the same monk. "How do we know you didn't attack him?"

Treena noted the blade he held, its tip pointed toward the ground, coated in blood. She looked to the other monk to discover his weapon was still sheathed. "If that is the case then one of you stay here with me and the other go get help."

"By the look of it, he doesn't need help, just a priest to bury him."

Treena looked at her friend and realized that he no longer breathed. He had died in her arms while she was talking. Softly lowering him to the ground, her anger rose. She grabbed the bag of apples beside her and twisted it around her hand. Treena swept around in a low crouch and the bag thudded into the knees of the monk standing closest to her. He toppled over, howling in pain. Treena completed the turn and came up standing in front of the monk with his blood covered sword. He blocked the alley exit.

The monk responded quickly and lunged at her with his sword. She held out the bag of apples like a shield and the sword plunged into it, coming out the other side and narrowly missing Treena's torso. She jumped back, letting the bag go. Apples fell everywhere as the monk shook his sword to dislodge the bag—this gave Treena the chance to pull her knife from beneath her skirts. Her knife was shorter than his sword, but she was taller, evening up any advantage he had. He also probably didn't expect her to know what she was doing, so if she fumbled a little to begin with, he might give her an opening because he wasn't as alert as he should be. *Just keep an eye on those apples,* she reminded herself as she stood there, trying to look like she didn't know how to hold the knife properly. *And the other guard,* she warned. Thankfully he was behind the monk she faced, and was only now starting to rise. Treena noted he was favoring one leg as he leaned against the stone wall with his outstretched hand.

The monk got tired of waiting for Treena to do something and attacked. She jumped and squealed in pretend fear and allowed him to push her deeper into the alley. Treena swung at him several times and he responded. She gave ground each time. The monk with the injured knee now stood with his sword out, but didn't engage as there wasn't enough room in the alley for both of them to fight side by side. Treena felt for the blood that pooled on the ground under the feet of the monk that had killed her friend, while she parried another strike. She had never manipulated anything other than water and was hoping that liquid was liquid. *Please, Torrent, help a girl out,* she prayed.

As Treena continued to avoid the thrusts and parries of the monk, she reached out her mind and felt the heavy fluid that had spread out from Ezekiel's wounds. In the same way she manipulated water, she manipulated the blood, finding it easier than she thought it would be—perhaps there is more water in blood than she thought. She shaped the liquid to feel like ice, hoping that it would harden to the same degree. Treena counted on it being enough.

With practiced timing, she dropped any pretense of inability and harried the monk with her knife, stepping in closer, so he couldn't swing his sword. He was taken by surprise and took a quick step back, slipping on the now icy blood, giving her enough of an opening to plunge her knife into his side, perfectly placed to puncture a lung and kill him. Treena grabbed his sword as he fell backward over Ezekiel and advanced on the monk with the injured knee.

She was careful to avoid the apples still strewn on the hard packed dirt of the alley. The monk moved to meet her. He attempted to look like he wasn't favoring one leg. Treena smiled coyly at him, and he blinked in confusion, before she threw the knife and it embedded itself in his stomach. It wasn't a killing blow, but it would be enough to slow him down further and be more wary of her. He lifted his sword and beckoned her to him. Treena nodded her head and moved toward him, as she did she realized that she would have to kill this man. She had been thinking that if she could simply get around him she would be able to run, as he was in no condition to keep up with her, but now she understood that he couldn't leave the alley alive or he would have them looking for her immediately.

"You know we only wanted to see who he was meeting. We just followed him out of curiosity," the monk tried to reason with her. "You don't have to die for your friend. Just put down the sword, and we can figure something out."

Treena gave a forced laugh. "You want me to put down my weapon? I think I have the upperhand." She was impressed with his hubris. "Why did you kill him if you were just curious?" She stalled, putting off the inevitable. Treena felt ill. It was one thing to kill Aven's dad in self-defense or the other monk, as he had obviously killed her friend and would have killed her. The man standing in front of her was already sufficiently injured to allow her to escape, but that wouldn't be enough now. *Just do it quickly*, she told herself. *You are Dalinda, your job is to protect and you must survive to get Aven out of the city.*

He didn't have an answer for her, and she couldn't wait any longer. Ignoring the guilt that was rising within her, she did what she was trained to do: assess the situation and what was at hand to help her. The apples still lay on the ground and he was already unsteady on his feet. Thinking rapidly, she spun, raising the sword in an overhead arc. While he focused on that, she kicked an apple in his direction. He stepped toward her to block the sword descending toward his head, and when he stood on the apple with his injured leg his knee buckled. The monk went down in a heap, grunting as he hit the ground. He parried one last time as Treena stepped closer and plunged the sword into his chest. Blood spurted everywhere, and she was sprayed with it. Barely holding down her breakfast, she grabbed her knife out of his stomach and wiped it on his top before sheathing it back into her leg holder. She tore her blouse and rubbed blood on her face as she ran out of the alley, being careful not to trip on the helpful apples.

Treena huddled over, looking like she was scurrying away from someone. "Miss? Are you aright?" a kind voice interrupted her hurried steps.

An elderly man and his wife stood in her path, both with concerned looks on their weathered faces.

"Someone attacked me," she whispered, and held a trembling hand to her mouth. It helped keep the bile from rising with what she had done, but they just saw the distress and reacted to it.

"Can we help you?" he offered.

"Nah, just wanna get home." Treena went to move past them and stopped. "Thank ya." As she moved by them, someone caught her elbow and she spun with her fist raised.

"Woah." Braith let go and danced back. "What the Pyre happened? Are you okay?" His face instantly changed to concern. He took her elbow again.

"It's not my blood," she whispered. "I made it look worse, so people would think I was assaulted." Treena frowned at him. "Why are you here?" She finally registered that it wasn't one of his thieves. They continued to move through the streets. Treena hunched over and Braith looking like he was supporting her.

"There was an incident with the boy watching you. He decided to pickpocket while you wandered the market and chose the wrong mark. I was on my way to try and smooth over the mess when we realized no one knew where you were."

"We have to get to Aven. I have to get her out of here now. She's with Stiann."

"Why? No, don't answer that. Fill me in when we get there. No point in repeating it." Braith gripped her elbow a little tighter in support and they hurried through the street.

Chapter 45
Treena

"There are still so many things that we don't know about him," Treena voiced her concern, again, as she continued to throw a few things into her travel pack.

Elldean Stiann nodded his agreement as he sat at the old table in the training room. "I know, but there are too many reasons for us to find him. We need to know what he knows about The First Elder. I also want to know what he meant when he said he had seen what Albin does to people when they have power he can use."

"Aren't we putting Aven in unnecessary danger? Should we not be hiding her and seeing to her training?"

"Aven's safety and continued training is a priority," conceded Stiann. "But I think the rescuing of the Master Shaymmi is just as important."

"Really? Why?" Treena was astounded that Stiann felt this way. She had completed her packing and joined him at the table. Aven was upstairs, spending the last few chimes with her sister before they left. They were now only waiting for Braith, who had gone to pack and see to turning his business over to his second. Treena was impatient to leave and terrified to leave at the same time.

Stiann leaned forward and looked earnestly at Treena. "Now that we have discovered the Shaymmi's are employed by The First Elder to find the ancient treasures of the Dalinda and Oredmoor, and they do it via elemental vibrations, it leads me to believe that the Shaymmi aren't what they think they are."

"You are talking in riddles. Who are the Shaymmi then?"

"Think about it." Stiann's voice had risen an octave with excitement. "He could use the Spirit Mirror, he could see your elemental power, and was able to see Thedra's too." He ticked off each point with a finger. "He has an affinity for finding Oredmoor and Dalinda tainted items." Stiann sat back in his chair, as if waiting for her to figure it out.

Treena tried to understand what he was saying, but the last few days had been exhausting and her heart ached for the loss of Ezekiel this morning and their need to leave the city now. It didn't have room to fathom what Stiann was leading her towards. "I'm too tired, Stiann. Perhaps another day I could figure it out," she apologized.

He patted her hand and plunged on. "I think the renowned Shaymmi are actually the missing Shomma. And the power that Sylvan has displayed to discover Aven and use the mirror, while his peers are able to enter the elemental plane but not sense you, shows him to be the Master Shomma. The most powerful and the one able to find and understand all Oredmoor on the elemental plane."

"That is a lot to get my head around," admitted Treena. "If what you say is true, then we most definitely need to rescue him and tell him who he really is. I don't know if it helps the Loyalist cause, but it won't hurt it to know the fabled Shomma still exist."

Stiann stood and Treena stood with him. She was several inches taller than him. He grasped her shoulders and his excited expression changed to severe.

"You must understand something. If he refuses to go with you, or it appears his loyalties are suspect, he must be silenced. This news is too precious to have known. I don't know if The First Elder is aware of who he really employs, but from now on, we must begin to keep our sources looking for the traits of a Shomma a few years before a Dalinda pair are due to have their powers manifest."

Treena closed her eyes against the harsh reality of what Stiann was asking her to do. She knew it to be the correct course of action, but the thought of killing again made her somber. She had killed three men in less than a week—that was enough for a lifetime for her.

"Treena?"

"Yes, I know, and will do it, but I must admit I don't understand the people who can take a life without thought." She knew her eyes glistened with unshed tears.

Stiann reached up and cupped her cheek. "You are so strong and brave. Your compassion and warmth are the things that matter. They are things that keep your little gaggle of children secure. But you are more than that. You were born to protect more than a small group of children, and even though you hate every moment of the violence, you will always do what is right, because there is always more children needing your help."

"Will you look after the children while I am gone?" Treena asked. She felt guilty that only now she was remembering that they needed to be cared for.

"I am leaving too, but it will take me several weeks to pack up the shop. It is too dangerous to stay here. Hamlyn has become the focus because of the search for Aven and now the death of Ulrick. I will make arrangements for the children to be cared for," he assured her.

"Thank you." Treena was grateful. She picked up her now heavy pack and made a promise to herself that she would one day return and retrieve all of the precious items. Including the stunning robes Thedra had made.

As they moved out of the training room, Treena asked, "How will I contact you?"

"Through the usual channels. You know what to look for as you go through towns. And you know how to contact any of your fellow Dalinda. I'll send word through the network once I meet with my fellow Elldean and tell them about my suspicions of the Shaymmi."

Braith walked into the storeroom and smiled charmingly as he spun in a circle for Treena, who raised an eyebrow but didn't mention his change in appearance. His usual clothing of soft, dull tones, but of the highest quality, designed to not attract attention from the authorities had been replaced by a cloak of the darkest green, which covered a black leather vest and coarse dark grey trousers. The only thing that remained the same were his clean leather boots.

"You ready?" he asked.

"Almost." Treena grabbed her boots and cloak, took one final look around her bedroom, and closed the door. "You sure you want to come? Can you trust your thieves to run everything while you're gone?"

Braith laughed as they settled around the kitchen table. Aven and her sister hovered around the kitchen door.

"They're thieves, so there is a certain amount of skimming off the top. As long as my profits don't fall and no one does anything stupid to attract attention to us, all will be well." He changed the subject. "I've made arrangements for us to leave via the river rather than the city gates."

"Excellent," Stiann announced from his seat at the table. "Looks like you're ready to leave."

"Do you have everything you want to take, Aven?" Treena asked as they gathered in the kitchen. Time was getting away from them. It was mid-afternoon and Treena was concerned that the person in charge of the monastery at any moment would change their mind and close the gates early. Even though she now knew they would be leaving by the river, they could still search the river crafts for anyone trying to hide or escape. Treena was trying not to let her worrying thoughts overwhelm her.

"I 'ave left somefin in the trainin' room. Would it be okay if I went and got it?" Aven asked timidly.

Treena smiled kindly, hoping to make the girl feel less scared. She had noticed that Aven's speech had backslid since she had been kidnapped by her father. Hopefully, once they were on the road and away from the overbearing fear of being discovered, she might be able to enjoy being a child for a while. They of course, would continue her education and weapons training, but there would be time for stories and seeing new things.

"Yes, get what you need, but be quick. We have lingered long enough."

Aven moved quickly out of the kitchen, taking her travel pack with her. "Thank ya."

Chapter 46

Hadrian

Hadrian sat on her balcony and admired the view of the city. She lifted her heavy auburn hair up and twisted it around until it sat on top of her head and held it there, allowing the late evening breeze to cool her long neck. The city bustled away and twinkled prettily as the street lamps flickered, beyond the low walls of Stronghold. Hadrian looked outward past the outer walls of Cynsellam to the sparsely forested, gently rolling hills that reached the horizon.

She rolled her head around to ease the tension in her neck. It had been another long day of searching for the girl, and Hadrian was becoming desperate. She needed to find the child and prove she was as strong as Sylvan to appease The First Elder as his demands to find the missing Master Shaymmi grew more forceful and widespread. She knew word had been sent to his family to ask if they had been in contact with him and that his usual places to visit within the city had all been searched and people questioned. Hadrian wished that Cyrus was here to enjoy the view and reassure her that she was up to the task, and maybe help alleviate some of her tension with the distraction of the bedroom, but he had been keeping his distance.

They had discussed it and had decided that he should keep his visits to her only when he was bringing something to Stronghold that had been ordered and she would stop going to his shop until things settled down. They didn't need any extra attention now that people were discovering that her servant had disappeared, just like Sylvan. Hadrian had been assigned a new personal servant and she had let it be overheard that perhaps Garm had run away because he had had something to do with Master Shaymmi's Sylvan disappearing. She knew that the servants would soon spread that gossip and hoped that it would divert attention from her.

Hadrian briefly considered the possibility that perhaps Cyrus had not wanted to see her because he was now feeling guilty about Garm. Hadrian felt torn with what to do about it. She wanted to see him to explain how grateful she was that he cared enough about her to have taken a life for her, but she also didn't want him to dwell on it and make himself feel worse. This was all new territory for her—considering other people's feelings did not come naturally.

As she heard her new servant, Castriel, enter the sitting room, with what she assumed would be her evening meal, Hadrian stood, letting her hair unwind and stretched her arms over her head. Her shoulders protested and she slowly swung her arms in wide circles. Her body needed to rest and recover. Her eyes felt gritty and ached constantly as the elixir they drank to enter the elemental realm took her sight every morning.

"I need to find that girl now," she muttered to herself. *You also need to consider what to do regarding Sylvan's body,* she thought to herself, as those thoughts could never be uttered aloud, except to Cyrus. Hadrian had almost conceded that she would need to choose between some fairly abhorrent choices in the very near future regarding Sylvan. The situation had almost got to the point that leaving his body in the trunk for eternity might be the best course of action. She had first thought that she would swoop in, find the girl, prove she was as gifted as Sylvan, and then allow his essence to return to his body, but they would now be on level footing. None of that had happened and weeks had passed. *I wonder how long you can stay on the elemental plane without it adversely affecting you forever?*

"Excuse me, Shaymmi Hadrian, there are people here to see you." Castriel interrupted her.

Hadrian frowned as she lowered her arms and adjusted her loose fitting, lounging robe. She wasn't expecting anyone. "Very well, have them wait in the sitting room."

Castriel nodded and left to carry out her instructions. Hadrian took a few moments longer to admire the view as more stars appeared in the night sky, before she figured she had made the visitors wait long enough for one of the esteemed Shaymmi of Duthyne. Carefully running her fingers through her hair, she walked into her suite to discover the twins, Matteo and Matthias, Shyammi's-in-training, waiting for her. They both stood and bowed as she entered the room. Matteo's usual arrogance showed as he bowed less deeply than his brother. That was how she told them apart.

"Sit," she told them as she moved to the side board and poured herself another glass of red. Hadrian offered neither a drink. "What can I do for you both?" She settled herself across from the young men.

Matthias answered, "We were hoping you could let us know when we will start studying with you properly. We understand there is much to learn, and we are keen to begin."

"I understand that you have not had the opportunity, but you have to acknowledge that you brought much of that on yourself." Hadrian paused and took a sip of the strong wine.

"But..." Matteo began.

Hadrian spoke over the top of him. "You are too quick to temper and you—" She nodded to Matthias. "—have too many questions. You were both told to understand your place. Have you?"

Matteo's chin jutted out and he spoke between clenched teeth. "We have done all we have been asked."

"We simply wish to further our education and were hoping that, as you appear to be in charge, would take on the responsibility." Matthias impatiently pushed the dark brown hair that hung in his eyes away from his face.

Hadrian considered the young men for a few moments. She didn't want to have the responsibility of training them. Perhaps she could palm it off to another—maybe the Shaymmi who had trained her? At the moment, there were too many other things that were taking her time and she needed to focus on that.

"The last time I tried to teach you, you were rude and aggressive and kept asking irrelevant questions. I do not have time for that."

Matteo's eyes locked with hers before he acceded to her dominance and looked away. Matthias leaned forward on the couch and cleared his throat. "I will try to curb my curiosity until I am fully trained and can discover the answers for myself."

"Very well, I will speak to Tiago, the Shaymmi who trained me, and have them begin your training as soon as they are able." Hadrian knew that could be a few weeks away as Tiago was notoriously lazy, and Hadrian didn't want the twins coming back to bother her for a while. "It may take a little while for Tiago to be ready for you. In the meantime, I want you both to study the logs of where all the artifacts we search for have been discovered and cross reference it with a map of Duthyne and our search areas to make certain that we are not missing anywhere vital. You will also clarify with each Shaymmi their current search location. Is that clear?"

"Yes." Matteo scowled.

"Thank you, it is much appreciated." Matthias was more polite.

"Wonderful," she said with grace and rose from her seat. Hadrian noted that the young men had grown over the summer and were now almost as tall as her. The Shaymmi, for some reason, were always taller than the average citizen of Duthyne.

"See yourselves out. I am going to eat the supper that you interrupted."

As they both bowed, she noted with satisfaction that Matteo's bow was a fraction deeper than it had been earlier. They would all grovel to her eventually, when she became the Master Shaymmi.

Chapter 47

Treena

As the heavy barge slid along the slow moving river, aided by the poling of six bulky men, the small town of River's Edge appeared. It was the halfway mark between Hamlyn and Namurrn and many stopped there to spend the night as it was illegal to move upon the river between sunrise and sunset. There were crafts on both sides of the river of varying sizes docked to several rickety looking piers or tied to poles that stuck up out of the water with a metal ring at the top of it.

Aven and Treena sat in the cabin that had been assigned to them and looked out the open slated shutters. As they floated by, they were able to see more of the town, and Treena could feel the overwhelming helplessness that pervaded the place. No one smiled. There were no jovial greetings of neighbors, nor children laughing as they ignored their parents' instructions and ran down the roads. The churches greed was palpable as well as visible here.

"What's wrong with em?" asked Aven.

"They have almost lost hope. Their lives no longer have meaning, as everything is taken from them. This is happening in the bigger cities too, and we will see more crime and desperate people. People in the cities pay taxes usually—when you sell goods you can also pay a tithe. This was common with farmers. Rather than pay a fee they would pay in whatever they farmed—grain, meat, leather. My father would pay his expected tithe with fish he had caught once a season, and my mother would mend clothes of the clergy for free on one day per season. The church got skills to use or foods to feed themselves and the poor. The poor were expected to do their part by cleaning, aiding with harvests, keeping the street swept or helping to repair church run buildings. This was how everything was run when the Dalinda ruled, and it was fair and just. People were cared for and everyone could play their part and felt they had a purpose. It also made towns and villages fairly self-sufficient. Now, everything is hoarded by the church and only the monasteries are maintained. People are expected to still give their day of work plus pay taxes and those that paid in farmed product were now being expected to provide those products and the tithe too."

"What happens if you can't pay?" Aven whispered.

Treena drew in a breath between her teeth and settled her mind. She could feel the barge rocking a little more than normal under them and knew that she was probably the cause.

"There is no such thing as can't. They expect you to sell anything to pay your taxes or you can become a servant until you work off your debt." She looked down at Aven and tucked a few stray hairs behind the girl's ear. "Or they take one of their children as payment and that child has to pay off the debt."

As Treena watched, a young woman, probably in her late teens, was accosted by two monks who were bullying anyone and everyone as they moved around the piers. The woman looked terrified as they were backing her up against a shed wall. No one stepped in to help, instead they scurried away in the hope they didn't attract their vile attention. Treena felt bile rise as one of the monks grabbed the girl around the throat, while the other roughly grabbed at her breast.

Braith moved in front of the shuttered window and blocked their view. "Don't even think about it. They will not do too much more than what they are doing. If it was night, it would be a different scenario." He spoke rapidly. "You can not put yourself in danger to save her."

He moved out of the way, and Treena found that the young woman still stood against the wall, as if paralyzed, while the monks had moved off to accost the next person. She was relieved when River's Edge finally slid out of view and they found an empty pole to moor to for the night as the sun was dimming.

"Treena, why do we not do more to stop it?"

"I don't think any of us knows how bad it is. Only a few of us travel and we never all get together. Perhaps if we did, we would compare notes to find that it is not just happening in our area, it is like a disease spreading across Duthyne." She looked at the innocent face of the youngest Dalinda, and grimaced. "I think we are also scared that we won't be strong enough to take back what is ours because our Oredmoor are dead and people won't follow us."

Treena felt a small hand slide into hers and looked down at Aven's hand grasping hers. "I will help you, if you want to try."

"First we rescue Sylvan, then we get you to safety and finish your training and hope your counterpart comes to his powers sooner rather than later, and then we take on the church, okay?"

They both stared out the window, but Treena didn't take in the dry, dull brown grassed hills or the farmstead or two she could see in the far distance. She knew that both of them were thinking how much the populace were still going to have to endure before Aven would be in a position to aid Treena and whichever of the Dalinda had had enough of waiting and were prepared to do what they were born to do. Not hide, but rule and protect and take care of the citizens of Duthyne. Treena knew that the Loyalists were still waiting for the day to come. Perhaps it was closer than anyone knew?

Aven hung on tightly to Treena's hand as they made their way through the streets of Namurrn. It had been a few years since Treena's last visit, when she had come to surprise Thedra and she was trying to remember how to get to the shop that Thedra had owned. It was late morning, and after spending almost three days on the barge, hidden in the barge captain's cramped quarters, Treena was grateful to be off the rocking craft and walking freely through the city.

Namurrn had a different feel to it than Hamlyn. It had a smaller population, and was spaced out because it wasn't set against a sharp rock face and river. This allowed for wider streets which resulted in less congested thoroughfares. Everything around the port area was dull and dirty. Typically as they moved out of the poorer areas the markets, shops and housing became cleaner and brighter.

After several false turns, Treena finally came to the street she was searching for. People strolled down the cobbled road, stopping to browse in the warped windows and occasionally entering a shop. Treena lifted her head and stood tall, her usual stoop to avoid attention would not work here. It was warmer in the center of the city and no breeze from the river or the wide open hills could penetrate to cool anyone. She pushed her travelling cloak back over her shoulders and pulled down her blouse to expose her shoulders and more of her bosom.

Treena squeezed Aven's hand to get her attention. The small girl looked up. "Stand tall, look like you belong here. When you look timid, rich people think you have something to hide," she instructed.

Aven nodded and squared her shoulders.

"We need to find the perfect dress for your party next week." Treena pursed her lips and looked at Aven's sweet face, ignoring the surprised look. "I think a lovely periwinkle blue will look very becoming on you," she announced loudly.

While Treena had flung her cloak over her shoulders to show her clothing, Braith had drawn his dark green cloak across his chest to hide his. He plastered the universal resigned look of a man who was forced to shop with his family on his handsome features and walked dutifully next to Aven. Treena winked at him, before turning to a display full of brightly colored ribbons. Aven oohed and aahed with Treena before they moved on to another shop a few stores down that had a wonderful scent wafting through the open shutters.

"We must come back if we have time. I am indeed in need of several more bars of scented soap."

They strolled by more shops and stopped to admire ladies slippers, fine leather bound books, and stunning tapestries of flying lizards, that looked suspiciously like Oredmoor. Eventually they came to stand in front of a store with a clearer glass window than anyone else in the row and a swinging sign that said 'Thedra's' and had a picture of a thimble on it. On display was a dress that no one would ever have the courage to wear. It was a dress that defied current fashion, and Treena knew instantly it had been created for her. The material was silky and the color of the sun-kissed dark sea of Kets Harbour. It had a halter neck that joined the tight bodice to a thick collar, that Thedra had hung sparkling clear crystals from and the edging of the top had matching intricately detailed silver embroidery. The over-sized bell sleeves, that were carefully attached at the sides of the dress, began just above the elbow and gathered tightly at the wrist. The floor-sweeping gown was cinched at the waist with a silver embroidered sash that showed the design of a perfect drop of water at its center.

"Thedra did this?" asked Braith. "I just assumed she was a seamstress on much the same level as your mother," he told Treena.

Treena continued to look at the beautiful creation. "When we get back to Hamlyn, remind me to show you my ceremonial robe."

"I wonder who it was designed for?" Braith seemed as enchanted by the gown as she was.

"The Lady Katatreena," Aven spoke softly.

"Yes," agreed Treena.

"You?" Braith frowned and looked from Treena to the gown and back.

Treena laughed, wondering if she should be insulted. "Not this me." She swept her hands downward. "The one that could have been."

A sign in the window said 'available' which Treena was relieved to learn. This shop was by appointment only, catering to the most exclusive of clients, which were usually the ones who knew the most about what was going on in the upper echelons of the church hierarchy. If the sign said 'available', it meant that no one was in there and you were free to enter to make your own appointment. With a heavy sigh, Treena turned from the dress and opened the solid timber door. A bell tinkled, announcing their arrival.

"Make yourselves comfortable, I'll be there in a moment," a female voice called.

Treena looked around the store to find little had changed. Perfectly crafted dresses hung on racks along the back wall, all sorted into shades. Along the left-hand wall were several luxurious velvet couches and a low table. In the center of the room was a raised circular dais. The right wall contained a highly polished mirror, a small stand for cloaks and hats, and a doorway. Treena knew that beyond that doorway was a small kitchenette, similar to her own, and a large workroom that contained all the fabrics in all the colors you could wish for. Thedra's secret training room was hidden behind the bolts of fabric on a shelf much the same as Treena's. As Reza had built both, it stood to reason they would be different versions of the same thing.

They all stood near the dais, well aware that they would dirty anything they touched in this perfect room. A woman of advancing years waddled in. She had steel gray hair that curled around her deeply wrinkled face. Her clothing was impeccable, but simple compared to what was on offer in the shop. Her aged hand flew to her mouth as she recognized Treena.

"Lady Katatreena." Nikolina curtsied gracefully. The matronly woman turned to Aven, who was still holding Treena's hand. "And this must be Lady Aven." She curtsied again. "It is an honor to meet you."

"Nikolina, this is Braith."

Braith nodded his head in greeting. "This is a fine establishment."

"This was all Thedra's work. I now run it for the Loyalists, but she was the creative force of the place. Thankfully, she crafted so many gowns that I can simply copy them and make little changes in material texture and embroidery that the women here think they are getting the latest fashion." Nikolina turned back to Treena. "What brings you to Namurrn?"

"I hope it was fine to come here unannounced. There were some complications in Hamlyn that we needed to avoid, so we left in a hurry. We need to be on the road to Cynsellam by tomorrow morning and we have to resupply our food and look for a safe place to stay. Can you help us?"

"I will see to the supplies. I live with my family so Thedra's bed and everything is free to be used. When she became popular she moved it out of the storeroom and into the training room, to create more space and give the appearance that she didn't sleep in her shop. There is a bathing tub in there too. She used it both for bathing and dyeing the fabrics."

"Sounds perfect."

"Wonderful. And I insist you come to dinner tonight," Nikolina said brightly.

Treena knew from experience that sometimes Loyalists became a little too enthusiastic when a Dalinda visited their city, town, or village and too many people were invited to attend a 'dinner.' This could draw unwanted attention, and at the moment, the last thing they needed were the authorities noticing anything. Treena also wasn't sure if Aven was ready for the adoration some Loyalists displayed when being close to a Dalinda. It was flattering, but unnerving the first few times it happened.

"I am not sure if that is a good idea." Treena looked down at Aven, hoping that the matronly woman understood the hint.

Nikolina smiled kindly. "It will just be my husband and myself. Our children are all grown and left, and no one needs to know you passed through if you don't want them too."

"A home-cooked meal would be greatly appreciated. If you could write down clear instructions, we would all love to visit your home."

Nikolina beamed, adding more crinkles to her already heavily lined face. "Splendid. Now, let us get the bath full so the Lady Aven can clean herself, and you two can give me a list of what you require. My new assistant will be back soon, and I can send her off to get a few things. Then I think I will close the shop early today and finish getting your supplies and leave you to rest."

The training room was certainly more cramped than Treena's. Though the room was larger, it held an over-sized wooden tub, that had been coated in resin to make it water tight, and a comfortable looking bed along one wall. A huge pile of cushions in varied colors and fabrics filled a corner. Treena studied several of the cushions and realized that by the look of the embroidery on the tops and edges this was where Thedra had practiced her designs. The usual bookcase full of oddities, candles and weapons took up another wall and the large symbol of the Elemental Gods was burnt into the well worn wooden floor. At some point, Thedra had strung up a rope with a sheet, like a curtain attached to it, so it could be pulled across to hide the tub and bed.

It hadn't taken long to fill the tub as Aven didn't need as much water and they would add a little more once she was done. Braith had excused himself while Aven bathed and Treena took a few moments to go through Thedra's things and make certain they were all in order. She knew they would need to be packed up and many of them would be passed to Aven and the male Dalinda once he was discovered and trained, but that was not necessary yet.

Treena smiled as she listened to Aven hum softly as she climbed out of the tub and dried herself. In no time, the girl was dressed and standing in the middle of the room holding a book.

"Would it be all right if I sat on those cushions and practiced my reading?"

"That is a great idea." Treena went out to the kitchen and took the big kettle off the fire, lugging it to the tub and adding it in, before refilling it from a bucket in the kitchen and putting it back on the fire to heat for Braith. Returning to the training room, Treena pulled the sheet across and peeled off the rank clothing she had been wearing on the barge for several days.

Aside from the cloak, she tossed the clothes onto the pile with Aven's dirty clothes. Once Braith's were added, she would wash them and hang them out to dry. The cloaks would take too long to dry, so they could only take the time to air them.

Braith cleared his throat from behind the makeshift hanging sheet. "I have something for you," he spoke quietly.

She hadn't heard him come in and gave a little start when he had coughed. "Hang on." Treena grabbed the towel that had been left hanging on a wall peg and quickly wrapped it around herself. She pulled the sheet aside and noted Aven already napping on a pile of cushions. Braith's cloak covered her.

It was moments like these when Treena stood in a towel and Braith stood so close to her, his muscular arms and chest hair exposed by the leather vest, that she realized how grown up they were. Most of the time Braith was just Braith, her childhood friend. The one who had protected her before she knew what she was. She didn't typically see him as the man who stood in front of her now, but being this close and with just a towel between them it was in the forefront of her mind.

"Here." He held out his hand, a bar of lavender soap in his palm. "I thought you might like this."

Treena took the bar and held it to her nose. The smell was enchanting. She leant forward and kissed his cheek, noting the roughness from his three-day growth.

"Thank you," she whispered, not wanting to wake Aven. "That was most thoughtful."

"Take your time bathing. Nikolina has left with her apprentice so the shop is locked up. I will be outside, guarding the door." Braith kissed her cheek and stepped back, moving the sheet back into position.

Treena refrained from pointing out that she didn't need guarding. She was quite capable of taking care of herself. But what would be the point? He would sit out the front of the door regardless of what she said. If she was honest with herself, when it came his turn to bathe, she would choose to sit and guard the door for him too. That's what friends did.

The door clicked closed, and Treena hung the towel back up on the hook. As she settled into the delicious warm water, a little voice piped up. "He really does like you."

"Go to sleep, Aven."

Treena liked to think that the heat from the warm water was making her face flush.

Chapter 48
Sylvan

The languid feeling of floating over the open fields and low lying hills near Namurrn had lost all of its appeal to Sylvan. He was tired. If he had a body, he would have said he was bone weary. He would do almost anything to feel the comfort of a bed under him and to taste food again. His thoughts were growing darker as time dragged on. He tried to summon some enthusiasm since it looked like the Dalinda and her young charge were on their way to Cynsellam to help him, but he didn't want to have false hope.

Sylvan had gone to check on the pair when he had felt a tug near Namurrn. He was struggling to keep all of the elemental vibrations under control, and it was the only reason he had felt the girl's unmistakable call. He had followed the elemental power, until the softer and more subtle power of the older Dalinda appeared and he knew that the pair were in Namurrn.

He had found himself in an awkward situation when he had swooped into the dress shop's hidden room to discover the beautiful woman in the bath. Thankfully, the girl has been curled up asleep and hadn't witnessed him arrive and warn her to cover up. He had not stayed in the room. Sylvan had rapidly exited and hovered near the door, taking note that the man, who had no elemental power but that was often with them, was waiting at the front of the room.

It was a full chime before the man rose and went into the hidden room. Sylvan surmised it would be safe for him to enter too. He was correct. The woman was now clothed and the girl awake. Immediately the young girl pointed at him and spoke words he could not hear. She delved into her backpack and came out with the alphabet tiles that they had been using to communicate. She deftly lay them out on the floor and the woman found parchment and quill to mark down what was spelled out.

Sylvan slowly pointed at three tiles. W...H...Y

He waited while they spoke before the woman scrawled, *had to run,* across the page in neat script.

He again pointed at the same three letters. He got another short response. *Doesn't matter. On our way to find you.*

If he could have smiled he would have. He felt relieved. He knew that they still had insurmountable odds to overcome, but at least they were planning on trying. He pointed out more letters.

H...O...W L...O...N...G

Two/three days, was the answer.

T...H...A...N...K...Y...O...U T...I...R...E...D

He finished spelling his message and formally bowed to the girl and the Dalinda and slowly moved up through the ceiling and back toward Cynsellam.

Sylvan wondered why he still kept himself from going to the First Elder and revealing all. It would be over. His body would be found and Hadrian punished, but something held him back. The sight of Jorge's body floated to the front of his thoughts. He was still conflicted about his feelings for his servant. Jorge had betrayed him, but had he truly deserved to die being tortured and having Albin attempt to suck his energy from him? Somewhere along the way, it had occurred to Sylvan that if the First Elder had tried it with Jorge, when would he try it with one of the Shaymmi?

Feeling no need to exert himself more than he had to, he eventually glided into the monastery and through the corridors. He checked on the First Elder who was eating a meal at his desk while reading over a scroll. Sylvan then moved on to Shaymmi Hadrian and was surprised to find her alone. The silversmith who had helped her move his body had not visited for a while. He also noted that she had a new servant. Where had the other one got to? Now, that was intriguing. Should he try to find the servant or the silversmith just in case he needed them to corroborate his story when he was eventually free?

It was probably easier to find the silversmith than the servant, as the monastery was a warren of tunnels and narrow passage ways that the servants used to stay out of sight. He could roam around forever and not find the right servant. He recalled that the silversmith was named Cyrus, and he was gaining quite a reputation for crafting beautiful items. Sylvan decided that he would check out the Guildsmen areas near the craft markets and investigate anyone who had stunning glass goblets on display. As Cyrus had caught Albin's attention with one, he would definitely be using that to his advantage.

It was nearing the end of the day, but as Sylvan had nowhere to be, what did it matter if he started his search now? Slowly he floated out across the city, taking note of the packed residences and clean streets. He made his way to the vast market square, which at this time was full of people buying food stuffs for dinner, or little trinkets to take home to apologize to their partners for some misconstrued drama. The glass fronted shops that ran along the outer rim of the market all had lights shining brightly inside, inviting customers to drop by on their way past. Sylvan missed spending time here. Being worshipped and renowned for working with the First Elder was auspicious—he missed the accolades. But now that he knew his work was only to keep Albin looking young he felt cheated.

He admired the many different baubles and clothing items that were displayed and wished he could smell the food that was being brought to tavern tables. He found a silversmith's shop with stunningly crafted pewter goblets but not the blown glass and entwined metal stems that had caused so much fuss. Sylvan moved on. He went by two more silversmith's shops before coming to the right shop. A small anvil with a flame sitting atop it was the sign—a creative sign for a silversmith, he thought.

Sylvan noted that while a lantern sat in the window, allowing all to admire the goblets, curtains were pulled to hide the interior of the shop and it looked to be closed. He moved through the door and into the shop and took a moment to adjust to the darkness. Sylvan floated slowly through the room and into another that turned out to be an empty kitchenette. There were two more doors. Sylvan assumed one to be Cyrus's bed chamber and the other to be his workshop. A hint of light flickered from under one of the doors.

Without any further thought, Sylvan moved to the light and glided effortlessly through the door. *Well, that is unexpected,* he thought as he took everything in.

Chapter 49

Treena

"I think this is it." Treena looked up and down the tightly packed street and up at the obviously well-loved house. They had followed Nikolina's instruction to her house to discover she lived in a middle-class section of the city with other lower ranked guildsmen families. Treena wondered which Nikolina's husband belonged to.

Before they had begun to move up the well-tended path, Nikolina opened the door and beckoned them in. She smiled a big welcome as they walked through the door and into the overstuffed house. Treena was a tiny bit overwhelmed with the amount of ornaments there were crowded on the hutch and didn't want to think about the rest of the house surfaces.

"Come and meet my husband, Jodan. He had an accident a few years back and doesn't walk well."

They followed the heavy, older woman through the sitting room and into a kitchen that held an eight seater square table and smelled of roasted pig. Treena noted there were six places set at the table. Nikolina showed them where to sit as she made introductions, apologizing when Jodan didn't stand to greet them.

"Are we expecting someone?" Treena nodded toward the sixth setting.

"I thought you might like to meet Thedra's friend," Nikolina answered evasively.

Treena stared at her for a minute before she comprehended what was being implied.

"The one she wanted to get back to see that she didn't want to stay as long as she normally did?"

Treena wasn't sure why they were speaking so cryptically, but assumed it may be that Nikolina thought Aven innocent of the happenings of men and women. Sadly Treena thought Aven's views on coupling were tainted and would remain so for a very long time.

There was a polite knock on the door, and Nikolina went to answer it while they stayed in the kitchen and made small talk with Jodan. Within a few moments, the seamstress returned with the mystery guest and chaos broke out.

A man of middle years with a balding head and rounded shoulders strode into the kitchen. He wore the deep yellow Alb and olive green cord cinture that girdled his ample waist of the Church of the One. Aven squealed with fright and hid behind Braith, who she had been seated next to. Braith rose slowly, a knife instantly appearing in his hand. Treena stood abruptly, causing her seat to tumble onto the stone floor and add to the noise. She stood ready to attack, taking note of all the things in the room she could use as a weapon.

The churchman held his hands up, revealing he held no weapon.

"Nikolina, you didn't tell them who was coming, I assume?" He spoke quietly.

The older woman had paled considerably and grasped her husband's shoulders.

"I...I...ummm—" She tried several times to speak. "Thedra didn't react this way when you met her."

"I am certain there is a reason for the behavior," the churchman assured his host as he took the seat closest to the standing Treena. "Please, be calm and understand I am an ally."

Treena ignored the man and looked at Braith, Aven cowering behind him.

"I'll check the front." Walking out of the room, Treena moved to the front window and carefully pulled aside the curtain a fraction. Two warrior monks stood at the end of the path, but there were no patrols and the street looked clear of all other people. Treena frowned and went back to the kitchen. "There are only two guards out there."

"Yes," the churchman explained. "They are my bodyguards. I can usually convince them that I don't need them and am able to travel freely around the city, but with the trouble in Hamlyn and the death of Arch Deacon Ulrick, I can't go anywhere unattended at the moment."

Braith held his free hand out behind him and Aven took it.

"We will check the back." The tension in the kitchen mounted as Treena waited for Braith to return or call for her assistance.

Nikolina stood with her husband, still pale and nervous. The churchman appeared calm and sat relaxed in his seat. Treena watched his leg shake slightly under the table—he wasn't as calm as he wanted them to believe. Braith returned with Aven in tow. "Nothing out back."

Treena stood over the unwanted guest and spoke in a deadly tone, "Who are you and what do you want with us?"

"I am Deacon Titus. I was Thedra's partner, companion, lover...whatever you wish to use as a label. It will never be enough for what she meant to me."

No one moved. Thoughts raced in Treena's mind. Was this a trap or the truth? How was she to know?

"Nikolina? Is this true?"

"Yes. For the past year I know that they have been more than friends."

"How did they meet?" Treena asked.

Deacon Titus interrupted. "Why don't you ask me those questions?"

"I have other questions for you. Now, be quiet." Treena was abrupt in her delivery, causing Braith to hide a smirk and Titus to look uncomfortable.

"You can't talk to Deacon Titus like that, Treena. Thedra would be appalled." Nikolina looked shocked.

"Thedra is dead and monks killed her. I'm not concerned with being polite to someone I have no reason to trust and every reason to be suspicious of."

"Jodan worked as the monastery groundskeeper and had a fall from his ladder and has never been able to walk properly since. Thedra was over to check in and offer her help when Deacon Titus stopped by with a meal for us and to reassure us that we would be taken care of." Nikolina looked nervously at Treena while Jodan reached up and patted his wife's hand, that still gripped his shoulder.

"And how long ago did you say your accident was?" Treena looked to Jodan.

"About three years."

Treena turned to the seated Deacon, towering over him, her face commanding. "Now, you may tell me about your relationship with Thedra."

If the Deacon was put out with her surly demands, he didn't display it. His broad face was solemn but sad as he spoke. His voice gentle. "At first she was polite, but avoided me. I was instantly fascinated with her, but it was not reciprocated. I understand now why that was, but at the time, I don't mind admitting I was a little put out." He smiled fondly at Nikolina. "These two friends were hesitant to help me find common ground with Thedra. They told me that perhaps she wasn't the one for me. They were wrong. She was vibrant and clever and kind, and I just wanted to get to know her."

"How did you win her over?"

"She found me serving food one night to the street kids and told me that I reminded her of a dear friend." He looked at

Treena shrewdly. "That was you, Treena. She spoke of you often."

"And since when does a Deacon get his hands dirty and serve food to the poor?" Treena asked, sarcasm obvious in her voice.

Titus threw his head back and laughed. "That's almost word for word what Thedra said." He grew solemn as pain crossed his face. "If you all sit and promise to listen without prejudice, I will tell you what I told her."

Treena looked to Braith, who gave the slightest shrug of his shoulders. It looked like the decision would be hers. She looked to Aven, still standing behind Braith, but no longer cowering. Treena raised an eyebrow at her. Aven gave the briefest of nods. Treena was relieved to know that the girl would not be adverse to continuing to be in the presence of the Deacon. He had piqued Treena's curiosity enough to hear what he had to say.

"Very well."

Slowly she sat next to Titus, turning her chair so she could see his whole face as he spoke. Braith and Aven returned to their seats on the opposite side of the table, and Nikolina left her husband's side and began to finish serving the evening meal.

Deacon Titus wasted no time with preamble. "I joined the church in my youth with grand ideas to help those less fortunate and to create change in this town." He paused and frowned at the table. "But I have managed to do very little. Things gradually grow worse, year by year. The taxes and tithes the monks demand on behalf of The First Elder, plus their own extortion money is sending our town broke, and from what I can gather, the rest of the country with it." Titus spoke softly and melancholy filled his voice. "The church was not created to drain the citizens of Duthyne for its own benefit. Whether it is the Church of the Elemental Gods or the One God, it is there to serve those less fortunate, to guide those in need of understanding and to teach others that we should be inclusive."

His speech moved Treena in ways that she never thought a churchman could. Not even the mention of Elemental Gods made her panic. She sat astounded that this man understood that the church was created to serve, not to demand and take. Even before she had learned her true identity she had served. Taking care of others made her happy and fulfilled.

Nikolina began to place bowls of thick, rich stew, full of root vegetables and meat in front of them. She put a plate filled with warmed rolls in the center of the table and everyone murmured their thanks. Deacon Titus didn't offer to say a prayer of gratitude—Treena thought it odd but didn't comment. Once their immediate hunger was satiated, Titus continued his speech.

"I do what I can to lessen the demands of the church on the Namurrn people, but the warrior monks grow more violent. Not only do they collect the tithes and taxes for the church, they demand their own collection fee, and if you don't pay something bad happens to a loved one or your business. Even though I am the head of the church in Namurrn, in reality, I am just the figurehead. The one that gets to lecture the upper classes about charity beginning at home and such. Now they aren't even exempt from the extortions of the warrior monks, and I have very little power to do anything about it all as I don't control those monks—they come under another's jurisdiction."

"And Thedra comes into this, how?"

"After six months of superficial talking, she began to tell me ways in which I could help that wouldn't be noticed by the monks. Over those first two years, we developed a deep friendship and great trust. I finally admitted that I was in love with her and we embarked on a beautiful affair that only Nikolina and Jodan knew about." He sighed and clasped his hands together. "I miss her."

"We all do," Treena said.

"I wanted to come meet you and tell you our story, and let you know that you have the support of one churchman. I don't have a lot of power, but my office still carries weight." Titus looked at Treena. "I just wish I had had the courage to tell her that I knew her secret and that I didn't care—if anything, I tend to agree with her."

Treena tried not to look startled. "Her secret?" She wondered if the Deacon had noticed how everyone held their breath.

"That she worshiped the Elemental Gods. I saw the candles and the forbidden sign burnt into the floor of her bedroom. I tripped on the rug that covered it. She never knew. I wish I had spoken to her about it. She could have perhaps told me about the old ways and how the Dalinda and the Oredmoor led with better qualities than what I see in our current situation."

Her hand had covered his before she realized what she was doing. "I think Thedra was ready to confide in you. One of the last conversations I had with her was about her wanting to get back here as quickly as possible. I teased her about having a secret lover."

"Is that really wise?" asked Braith.

Treena withdrew her hand. "If he didn't betray her after three years, I don't believe he will betray us."

"You know more about it than I do," admitted Braith.

Deacon Titus looked at Braith in surprise.

"I am only here to help Treena. She calls the shots—since we were kids, really."

Titus looked at Treena. "You seem to inspire faithful friendships, much the same as Thedra did."

They sat in silence, finishing the last of the stew. Aven stood to help Nikolina remove the plates. Treena watched Titus watch Aven.

"Does the child have the same quality?" he asked.

"I am not sure," Treena lied. She changed the subject. "Why didn't you denounce Thedra when you found the symbol on her floor?"

"The Church of the One God has failed its congregation in every way. The more I was around Thedra, the more I realized that she lived with values that I considered noble and just, which I believed stemmed from her religious choices." It was his turn to grasp the hand Treena had laid on the table. "Will you tell me the truth about my beloved? Did she worship the Elemental Gods?"

Treena closed her eyes. Should she tell him the truth? Could he possibly be an ally in all of this? There was no point in looking at anyone else in the room for their opinion. This choice was entirely hers to make.

"Yes," Treena whispered. She silently prayed to Torrent that she had made the correct choice.

"And you?" he pressed.

This time, she did open her eyes and look around the room, seeking consent from each person before she spoke. All four nodded.

"We all do."

Titus sat still for a moment, his face gave away nothing. "Thank you for trusting me. I hope to repay that trust one day."

The rest of the evening was filled with stories of Thedra and eating the apple pie Nikolina had made. They parted company, with Deacon Titus leaving first, and taking his escort with him. No one the wiser that he had visited with anyone but the oc-cupants of the house, and he had been there regularly enough over the years that none in the street took any notice. The other three left a chime later.

Chapter 50

Treena

The sun was setting as Treena unpacked her bedroll and laid it out under a canopy of tall trees that were set far enough back from the main road to Duthyne that no one would see their campfire. She settled her back against a tree and watched the small fire throw shadows, making Aven's training routine appear like a ritualistic ancient dance.

"As you move through the second thrust, make sure to raise your other forearm high enough to cover yourself. It is dangling a little too low," Treena corrected.

Braith laid out his bedroll next to Aven's as they had taken to having Aven sleep between them on the barge. The young girl was jittery being out in the open, after only being in small confined rooms all her life. This would be their only night in the open as they would reach Cynsellam by tomorrow night, if everything went according to plan. Having two horses pull the cart they had acquired in Namurrn was far more efficient than one and they had made good time.

Instead of joining Treena at the campfire, Braith moved to Aven. "May I show you a few things?"

Aven nodded and stopped her movements.

"Treena has so far done a great job at showing you the basics, but I think her morals will not allow for her to teach you some of the street fighting and dirty tactics that will get you out of trouble quicker," he explained.

Treena raised an eyebrow, but refrained from commenting. If he could help Aven gain a little more confidence and a single new move that aided her in protecting herself, Treena would not quibble over what Braith thought he knew about her and her training. She tended the fire and continued to keep an eye on the bubbling stew pot as Braith showed Aven a few of his 'street' tricks. It was all things that Aven would have eventually been taught, once she understood the basics, but Treena kept her silence.

Aven quietly thanked Braith and moved to get a water skin from the cart.

"Supper shall be soon, rest a little," Treena told her. "You push yourself too hard."

"Would you care to spar a little, Treena?" asked Braith. He brandished his weapon in a flourish.

"Careful you don't hurt yourself with that," she warned.

Aven giggled. It was a lovely sound to Treena's ears. She wished the girl could laugh more, but her life had been so traumatic it was hard to find silly humor in things.

Treena stood slowly and stretched her arms over her head, releasing the tension in her shoulders.

"As long as you promise to be gentle with me," Treena mocked Braith.

Braith snorted. He backed up to allow more space for the two of them. He had only been instructing Aven, but now they would need room.

"Ready?"

"Do you always talk so much before accosting someone?"

Braith grinned at Treena. She felt herself relax. It had been a while since they had talked and teased with such ease. Everything had become far more complicated since the arrival of Aven. Braith launched a series of parries at her.

"It distracts your opponent."

"Only if your opponent is stupid." Treena evaded the attack with confidence, finishing with a roll that almost took Braith's feet out from under him.

He leapt over her and she came to her feet.

"Bravo." He bowed slightly, never taking his eyes off her.

Again he moved forward, pressing his attack. Their knives glinted in the firelight as they thrust and parried and grappled for supremacy. Treena felt good. It was exhilarating to spar again. She knew she was more adept and trained than Braith, but he was stronger than her, which helped put the fight on equal footing, if she didn't use her elemental abilities. There was also no desperation to win, so there was that to consider, though she knew his ego would take a bruising if she came out the victor. He still didn't quite understand what type of training she had. To him she would always be Treena, the girl he had rescued years ago, and she had allowed it to stay that way to protect her true identity.

Quickly he stepped in close behind her and wrapped an arm around her shoulders, while bringing his other arm, holding the knife toward her throat. She brought up her empty hand to stop the knife coming at her.

"Yield?" he breathed in her ear.

She laughed and moved the knife to her other hand, pressing it gently against his groin.

"I could ask you the same thing."

Aven laughed loud enough to distract Braith, and Treena took full advantage of it. She took a step back, planting her foot in between his and thrust her hips backward, while turning the hand that held his knife arm at bay and grasping his forearm instead. With all of her strength, she bent forward in one fluid motion pulling his knife arm with her. Before he could respond, he was flying over her head and landing with a heavy thump on the ground.

Treena stood up and winked at Aven.

"Action will always beat reaction when one underestimates his opponent." She held out her hand to Braith to help him off the ground.

As Braith stood, dusting himself off, he looked shrewdly at Treena. "You play dirty. A knife to the groin I would never had anticipated."

"I am full of surprises," she said airily as she returned to the campfire. Treena stirred the stew one last time and placed a loaf of bread by the fire as Aven helped get the plates out.

As they sat and ate their meal, Treena enjoyed the sounds of the night. The leaves rustled softly in the light breeze, while several nocturnal birds spread their wings and called to their fellow night friends. The horses snickered and the fire crackled and any sounds from the road were lost in the shadows.

"You have come a long way very quickly, Aven. You must train very hard," Braith noted as they finished their meal.

Aven shrugged in her typical hunched manner. "I don't wanna be useless. I don't wanna 'ave ta be rescued for a third time."

"From what I saw, you did a fairly good job of rescuing yourself against Arch Deacon Ulrick," said Braith.

"I panicked and lost control of meself. Not really the same fing." She stared blankly at the fire. "Treena still rescued me. I jus' stood there."

"Aven, take the compliment that Braith gave you." Treena reached over and took the fine hand of the young Dalinda. "You are remarkable and have learned so much in a brief time."

Aven blushed. "Thank ya." She looked at Braith. "Can I ask ya a question?"

"Sure."

"What 'appened to the man who couldn't unlock the cart?"

"He was punished. I can't have incompetence in my line of business. If you hadn't of did what you did, Treena would probably have died trying to get to you, and you would most likely be in the hands of the church."

Treena had an uncomfortable feeling in the pit of her stomach at Braith's words. She prayed to all five Gods that Aven didn't ask another question.

"How was he punished?"

Braith coughed and looked over Aven's head to Treena. She pleaded in her head that he didn't do what she thought he did.

"He was killed, as a lesson to everyone."

Treena closed her eyes against the words.

Aven gasped, "Why?"

"The assignment and stakes were clear, and he brought the wrong tools to the job. Shoddy work is not tolerated, and an example had to be set."

"You are cruel." Treena spoke quietly. "Could you not have disciplined him in another way? Thrown him out of your crew?"

"No. He knew too much. Once you begin to rise through the ranks, the more you know, the more you are valued, but the more you also become a liability." Braith was cool as he stood and took the plates from the ladies. "Are we that different, Treena?"

"What makes you say that?" she asked.

"If the situation had gone differently in Namurrn, would you have hesitated in permanently silencing Nikolina and Jodan to protect your cause?"

An uncomfortable silence filled the air. Treena considered his words. Would she have killed the two Loyalists if it was necessary to keep the secret? It was a daunting question she had no easy answer to.

"I don't know," she said it softly.

He returned to the fire and settled on his bedroll. Aven snuggled into hers as Treena lay down and rested her head on her backpack so she could watch the glowing embers.

"Braith?" Aven spoke.

"Mmm?"

"Would you please tell me how you met Treena?"

"Do you want the version she would tell you or the truth?"

Treena laughed. "Be nice," she warned. "I was just a little older than you, but had been sheltered and had no real experience with the truth of the streets at night," Treena explained to Aven. "This should be interesting to hear your version of events."

Braith put the final small log they had on the fire and took a swig of the water skin. "If I remember, the weather was miserable that night, which made it the perfect time for pickpockets. It was drizzling and heavy clouds skidded across the night sky, so the moon cast little shadow and people hurried with their heads down, trying to stay dry. I was around fifteen and very sure of my abilities to pick any pocket presented to me. I was working on my breaking and entering skillset at a warehouse on the docks. I had heard that a large shipment of illegal spices had just arrived, and I wanted to show my prowess by breaking in and stealing a variety for the boss of the thieves at the time. I waited patiently in the rain when I noticed someone skulking down the side of the wharf. My curiosity got the better of me, because they were just so bad at hiding and I wondered what they were up to. I abandoned my break and enter plan to follow the fellow with the suspicious behavior to discover if they had a secret worth stealing.

"It didn't take me long to catch up with the skulker, as they never thought to look behind them and they were moving very quickly. We came to a fisherman's boat that was tied up to the wharf, and the person just stopped and stared at it. The clouds cleared at that moment, and for the first time, I saw the beautiful face of the Lady Katatreena. I thought she was my age or older as she was as tall as me, but it turns out she was several years younger. Her clothing was well-tended and she didn't look underfed, so I quickly figured that she wasn't a street kid and she certainly didn't have the look of a whore. She looked upset and confused and I just couldn't help it. I stepped out of the darkness so she could see me. That didn't go quite so well." Braith chuckled.

"Why?"

"I screamed. I was terrified. I had been so focused on getting to my father's boat, and was dismayed to find there was no way to get on board, that when he rose from the shadows I just screamed."

Braith took another swig of water before passing it to the ladies. "The scream caught the attention of the spice smugglers, and I could just make out two of them start to walk down towards us. I don't even want to think what would have happened if we had been caught. I told her that I wouldn't hurt her but that she had to be quiet. She looked so scared. I tried to explain that she needed to hide, either with me or by herself, but she needed to hide now." Braith sat up on one elbow and looked over at Treena. "Why did you choose to follow me rather than hide by yourself?"

"I figured that if you really wanted to hurt me, you wouldn't have offered for me to hide alone. You would have done everything to persuade me to go with you."

Braith continued his story. "Along the wharf are ladders over the side, so the sailors and fisherman can fix their hulls and clean them. That is where I took her to hide. We huddled under the wharf, both hanging tightly to the slippery ladder, no longer get rained on but drenched by the sea water that sprayed around us. The footsteps of the two searchers came and retreated, and eventually I deemed it safe for us to come out of hiding. As I escorted the sodden girl back down the wharf, keeping us to the shadows, I asked her a few questions and was shocked to find out how young she was. I insisted on walking her all the way home and made her promise not to go out at night by herself again. After that, I would go to her place every few days to check that she was keeping her promise and we became friends."

"Why did you want to get on your father's boat?"

"I wanted to be a fisherman, but because I was a girl, I wasn't allowed to go to sea with my brothers. Staying at home, helping my mother, sounded dreadfully dull."

"That was a wonderful story. Thank you for telling it to me." Aven's voice was sleepy and she yawned. "When do you think we will be in Cynsellam by tomorrow?"

"I am guessing a few chimes after the midday meal." Treena looked across to find Aven already asleep.

"I'll take first watch." Braith smiled at her. "You look like you are fighting sleep."

"Thank you, but make sure you wake me when it is my turn. I am no little girl in need of coddling any more."

"Have no fear, I am well aware of that."

"Night, Braith."

"Pleasant dreams, my friend."

Chapter 51
Sylvan

Sylvan attempted to rest, even though it was a futile exercise. The constant battle to block the strong pull of the elemental vibrations was becoming unbearable and overwhelming. He had almost lost his ability to manipulate his consciousness to keep it all down to a dull intrusion. He was weak and could feel his essence slowly being leached away. Each day he battled to not give in to his desire to be done with this situation and get his body back. Something was holding him back. With a mental shrug of his non-existent shoulders, he gave up the pretense of resting and moved away from his bed and again noticed how his suite felt different without Jorge pottering around in it.

For reasons unknown, he made the quick decision to make sure his once-friend had been taken care of in death. After all, these were church men—they should have prayed over his body and respected his body by burning it or returning it to the earth. With his strength diminished, he could no longer move upon the elemental plane as instantly as he was accustomed, and he felt that sting his pride. Eventually, and presumably still more than likely quicker than his cohorts, the Master Shaymmi arrived at the hideous room that The First Elder used to torture Jorge.

The room was lifeless. Filled with items that had lost or had their basic elemental patterns removed or disfigured. What had Albin done? Sylvan carefully dropped his elemental shields to a fraction of their usual strength and was astounded at the muted tone that greeted him. He stopped at a table and poured his full focus onto an ornate sword that lay upon it. Typically a sword of this beauty, crafted in fire and with obvious skill, would have greeted him with the strong vibrations of metal and an undertone of fire. Now Sylvan was filled with a flat monotone that made his heart ache.

The sudden realization that the First Elder was clearly trying to experiment at draining other items was shocking. The man had obviously become desperate in his search as Sylvan knew that the Shaymmi were not discovering Oredmoor tainted items as frequently as they used to. Albin's experiment on Jorge had not worked...Sylvan had a sickening thought. He stopped studying the sword and scanned the room for the Dalinda's body.

Swiftly, he glided to the table he had last viewed the body of the Air Dalinda to find, to his horror, her clothes in a rumpled pile and scattered with blackened ash. His mind froze and wouldn't fathom what he had found. *Is it even possible?* he thought to himself. *Has the First Elder reduced a Dalinda to ash to drain them of their elemental force?* His mind recoiled from the abhorrent concept and knew it to be true, no matter how much he wished for it not to be. *This is why he is desperate to get the girl. He probably knows now that she is a Dalinda, because of the discovery of the golden eyes and obvious draining of the body.*

Through the sickened feeling that Sylvan was experiencing, a familiar vibration entered his subconscious. She had arrived in Cynsellam. They were here. Her power had grown, and she was like a beacon to him. It was four chimes past noon day and he hoped that all the Shaymmi had finished their searching task for the day and were returned to their body and off the elemental plane. Most were lazy and only ever did a half day's work, usually in the morning. He wished for today to be no different. Sylvan realized that the only true threat would be Hadrian—she was pushing herself hard to find the girl and could possibly still be out on the plane.

With a fleeting prayer to the Air Elemental Goddess, Aria, for the heap of ashes on the table, Sylvan shored up his shields and moved with as much speed as possible to Hadrian's suite. He was relieved to discover that she was there and awake. Her face looked drawn and resentful as she stared at the two young men who stood in front of her. Her new servant was holding a goblet out to one of the twins and he stood there with his arms crossed, lips in a thin line. Obviously they were still refusing to drink the elixir that was part of the preparation to enter the Elemental Plane. This was not his problem today.

Sylvan decided to check in on the other Shaymmi to make certain that none lingered on the Elemental Plane. What he found made him feel guilty and ashamed of the group he led.

Not one of the five Shaymmi he checked on were doing anything other than self-indulgent past times. Having spent so much time watching the Water Dalinda and her charge, he had come to understand that aiding others could be satisfying and fulfilling in a way that adoration by many for superficial reasons was no longer desirable. He was slowly coming to terms with the knowledge that the time he had spent on the Elemental Plane had changed him in more than one way. He had come to consider others and their needs above his own. He now knew that his ego had been stopping him from first going to Albin and revealing his secret ability to use the Spirit Mirror, but now changed into not telling because it was not his desire to hunt down the girl for The First Elder's macabre needs.

It was only once he had returned to his suite that he belatedly realized he had not uncovered if Jorge was still down in the room, still tied to the pole. It would have to wait. Jorge was gone, he couldn't save him and didn't know if he would have if given the chance to, after being betrayed. But Aven did deserve his aid. He would save her, if it was in his power. Sylvan had finally chosen his side.

Chapter 52
Treena

The noise and chaos of the animal yards that stood outside the heavy walls of Cynsellam were staggering. Treena felt overwhelmed at the sheer size of the pens and again felt a little self-doubt creep in before banishing it. They had been waiting in the sluggishly moving line for over a chime and Treena was grateful that they could all rest in the cart, rather than stand to wait for further instructions. Eventually their turn came and a man with a bored voice and scrawny body told them to take their cart over to the indicated area on his left, where they then needed to unhitch their horses and join the line to the large open stables at the other end of the yards.

Treena took full advantage of the wait and examined the area that opened in front of her as they passed into what was once a large arena where the Oredmoor and their Dalinda lived and ruled when they stayed in Cynsellam, away from the Compound, the main Dalinda base in the foothills of a massive mountain range, north west of Hurlirenn. The original First Elder had allegedly wanted to destroy the structure, but that had proven too difficult, so instead he had turned it into animal yards. Nothing of the standing walls indicated that the once mighty Oredmoor had been housed there. No elemental symbols to represent the five Gods or their chosen Dalinda. The walls were still sturdy, but anything that may have been of interest had been removed or destroyed. It was an unsettling feeling to be here—a place where her kind ruled but had no true value to her in this current time.

Another full chime came and went before they joined the line that allowed them entrance to the city. Treena now held two painted wooden chits that showed the aisle and number of their cart and horses. It didn't take them long to enter the city proper, passing under the portcullis that would cut a man in half if it was dropped at the wrong time. The walls were ten feet high and painted white. Several bored looking monks nodded and took the bribe that was placed in their hand, as every group bent to acknowledge their presence and take their hand in homage. Treena felt revolted by it, but held her tongue, doing her best to simply to get Aven through the gate and into the city without incident.

"It smells different." Aven frowned, trying to figure out what it was.

Braith answered, "Yes, there are no animals allowed in the city. No animals, means no droppings. You can smell the unwashed and the layer of smoke that covers everything. You will notice everything is cleaner because there are no animals."

"Really? No animals at all?" Aven was doubtful.

"Well, yes, there are animals. People can have cats," amended Treena.

"Cats? I didn't know that. Why just cats?"

"To kill the vermin. With all those animals there is a lot of feed out there, and of course, all the waste that comes with a city. Vermin is always a problem. I think it was the second First Elder that changed the law that outlawed all animals in Cynsellam that the original First Elder had created when everyone in the city was getting sick because of the rats and the diseases they carry. Cats were then allowed."

"You know so much," Braith snorted.

Treena shrugged. "I guess, but it's not very useful stuff."

"I disagree. It's things that will allow you to not stand out when you are in a different place. Simple things that people who live in a certain area would know, that would surprise others. It's actually very clever."

"Here is another interesting tidbit for you then...have you noticed there are no beggars?"

"I think I feel ill," Braith joked.

Treena laughed lightly while Aven frowned at both of them, not understanding the levity.

"Isn't that a good fing?" she asked.

"You might think so. Everyone has a job here; no one is to loiter. The beggars get to sleep in shelters, out of sight of the sensitive people who might be offended by their presence. For the rough blanket they receive, plus watered stew and a roof over their head, they are tasked with cleaning the streets and doing anything where there is no skill involved."

"But isn't that good?" Aven insisted.

"Yes, on the surface. What it really does is keep the beggar a beggar. He never has the opportunity to better himself." Treena looked slyly at Braith. "Though, I think Braith doesn't like it for another reason—which is what we were laughing at."

"Half the beggars in Hamlyn aren't actually beggars," explained Braith. "They are pickpockets, lookouts and such. Beggars can loiter and no one notices them on purpose, especially the wealthy. It makes them feel uncomfortable." He looked around curiously. "The thieves here must have to get truly creative."

Treena led them through the city. She was attempting to reconcile the directions she had received from Elldean Stiann regarding the abode of her counterpart to what lay before her. It took them another chime to wind their way through the busy city streets until she brought them out into the vast, bustling market square. Treena took Aven's hand and gave it a squeeze.

"You hungry?"

The young girl nodded vigorously.

"I think we should eat at one of those taverns with the wide windows that look out on the goings on and watch the world go by for a little while."

"I think that is a marvellous idea. How about over there?" He pointed to a brightly colored tavern that had a large woman standing out the front, chatting to passersby. Music poured out of the open windows and there were enough people around that they could get lost in the crowd if necessary.

"Great. Let's go," said Treena.

"What a beautiful little girl you have," the large woman complimented them as they approached.

"Thank you," both Treena and Braith answered in unison.

"Would you like a table out in the front or inside?"

"Inside but near the window, please," Braith responded.

A child not much older than Aven scurried up to the rotund woman and bobbed his head at the group.

"Table ten," she instructed the boy. "Try the steak and kidney pie, it is the chef special. Enjoy your meal," she told them cheerfully as they were led inside.

They chose the recommended pie and a pint of cider for the adults, while Aven was given goat's milk. Treena took the chance to take a deep breath and let the noise and everyday life of the capital city wash over her. She let her mind rest and tried not to think about the next situation. She still had no idea how they were going to enter the monastery and find Sylvan's body. *You are safe and Aven is safe, take a moment to just be,* she reminded herself. It wasn't long before the gold crusted pies were placed in front of them, and Braith entertained them by pointing out a petty thief who was trying to look like he wasn't trailing a target. It was enlightening to watch the thief pause and inspect things, or bend down to adjust a shoe while he stalked his prey. A large man, with a bull neck and broad shoulders, who wore a rich brocaded robe, that was far too heavy to be worn in this weather, but he obviously wanted people to know his wealth status, was the target. He had a servant that followed him and carried the parcels he purchased. Before they could see the end result, they had passed out of sight. Treena had to admit she was a little disappointed.

The pies were as delicious as the woman had claimed, and they finished them quickly. Treena knew that they didn't have time to linger over another drink, as the day was wearing on, so with great reluctance they stood, while Braith paid and they left the tavern. With the directions firmly in mind, she led them over to the far right of the market to a row of glass fronted shops that held wonders not seen in Hamlyn. Stunningly carved alabaster statues stood next to a rug bizarre with eye dazzling illusions within the rugs. Pewter goblets that were so delicate that they begged to be drunk from sat beside leather saddles with intricate tooling. Treena continued to look up at signs above the shops, looking to see the symbol that had been on Thedra's sign too.

"This is it," she announced as she peered into the shop to see if there were any customers. It appeared to be empty.

Treena pushed the door open and a bell rang within the shop.

"Make yourselves comfortable. I will be out in a moment," a male voice called from one of the backrooms.

The shop was filled with beautifully crafted items all set out in pigeonhole style shelves, allowing each piece to be displayed without detracting from another.

"Wow." Braith grinned at Treena. "My fingers itch just being in here."

Before she could answer with more than a laugh, a man entered the room. He was shorter than Treena and had the beginnings of a receding hairline, but it wouldn't stop women from admiring his handsome features, chocolate brown eyes, and well-defined build.

"Katatreena!" She was engulfed in a strong hug. "It is so wonderful to see you."

She returned the hug with feeling. He could be difficult and stubborn, just like his element, metal. But, he was her other half, her male Dalinda. Once she finished the hug, she stood back to introduce him.

"This is Cyrus."

"It is so wonderful to see you, but you could not have come at a more difficult time," said Cyrus.

"This is Aven," Treena announced.

Cyrus moved to Aven, who looked to be trying very hard not to hide behind Braith. Her shoulders were hunched but her eyes were not downcast and she smiled tremulously.

"You must be the one that is causing so much trouble." He knelt in front of her and took her hand, holding it gently in his for a few moments. He cocked his head at Treena. "Now, that is interesting." He spoke cryptically as he looked at Braith.

"And this is Braith. He is aware of everything." Treena was just as cryptic, not knowing if they were truly alone in the shop.

"Your childhood friend, who you used to gush about?" Cyrus stood and took Braith's offered hand.

Braith grinned at Treena. "You gushed about me?"

Cyrus answered, "Constantly."

Treena felt herself flush. "He is my best friend." She defended herself. Treena changed the subject. "Why have we picked a bad time to come, and why would you think Aven is causing issues?"

"I was just about to lock up the shop and head out." He began to move around the shop, closing blinds and lighting lanterns now the shop was darker. "I have been summonsed to an audience with the First Elder."

Aven gasped and then tried to cover it by covering her mouth. She ducked behind Treena. Cyrus frowned at the reaction.

"Is there something I am not aware of?"

Treena ignored his query. "Why would you be summonsed?"

"I may have meddled a little too much in the affairs of the Shaymmi," he admitted.

"Oh, Cyrus, what have you done? We are not supposed to draw attention to ourselves."

"It was all going wonderfully well until the Master Shaymmi found a girl with power in Hamlyn. She was found and picked up, but later escaped. Is that girl Aven?"

"Yes. Thedra died in the rescue of her."

Real pain crossed Cyrus' face. She was his mentor, much as Reza was Treena's.

"I tried to stop the Master Shaymmi finding her again, by helping a power-hungry Shaymmi, Hadrian. That plan was working perfectly, but things are starting to unravel and the First Elder wants to know where his favored Shaymmi is." He studied Treena. "You look different."

"I've been traveling. I'm covered in dirt and haven't bathed in a few days."

"No, that is not it. You appear more collected. It's hard to pinpoint."

"I've had to do some things I wish I hadn't." She grimaced. "I am learning to make decisions, but they don't always sit well with me."

"I have been laying low but have heard rumors that Arch Deacon Ulrick is no longer with us. Would that be what you speak of?"

Aven peered out from behind Treena's body and spoke slowly, taking the time to pronounce her words.

"That was me. I got scared."

Treena explained, "She is powerful when she is cornered, but has no control."

Braith chimed in with a lighter tone. "I've seen it once; it was quite spectacular."

"I don't have long, but I am intrigued." Cyrus knelt again. "Lady Aven, would you be so kind as to give me your hand again?"

Aven held out her small hand, he took it in his calloused but surprisingly delicate hand. He closed his eyes and everyone in the room fell silent. Treena knew he was trying to guess the child's elemental power—it was a game they played amongst themselves. It was something they had not been able to master, only the candles and the revealing ceremony were capable of it, even though she had now learned that Master Shaymmi Sylvan could ascertain their element. Perhaps he really was the missing Shomma.

Cyrus sighed and let go of her hand. "Thank you for trusting me." He looked to Treena. "She feels different to everyone else. Do you know why?"

"Are we alone?" Treena looked to the closed doors.

She thought she noted a moment of hesitation, but he said, "Yes."

"Aven is gifted with more than one element. She has the ability to manipulate both air and water, plus has a little control over the other three."

"How is that possible?"

"That, we don't know. Elldean Stiann was researching it, but is now having to pack up and move because of what happened in Hamlyn. He is contacting other Elldean to see what they know."

"I really do need to get going, but why are you here? Why bring Aven closer to the people who want her?" Cyrus grabbed a cloak and started toward the door.

"We are here to free Master Shaymmi Sylvan."

"In the name of Chalyx, why?" he exclaimed.

"It is complicated, but he has information regarding the First Elder and we think he is not what he seems. It can wait until you get back." Treena pushed him toward the door. "While you are there, try to figure out a way to get us into the monastery. We know where his body is being kept, but need to get in."

Cyrus looked flummoxed. "You know where his body is?"

"We have had minor contact with him. There is much to tell, but it can wait."

"Fine. Hopefully this won't take too long, and Shaymmi Hadrian sticks to the plan or you could be rescuing me too." Cyrus gave Treena another hug and told them where the kitchen was before he left.

Chapter 53
Hadrian

It was dark by the time Hadrian was escorted into the First Elder's inner office. She was shown a seat and offered refreshments, but refused as her stomach was queasy. Hadrian settled the hand-crafted cape around her, fidgeting with the clasp that held it together at her throat. She looked around the empty room—there was a personal guard stationed on the other side of the doorway, but she noted that there was still enough respect for her that none were in the room with her. This gave Hadrian hope that the situation just might be salvageable if Cyrus sticks to the plan.

Footsteps disturbed her thoughts as someone approached. She stood and turned in case it was Albin. Cyrus was escorted in and told to wait. Interestingly he was not offered refreshments. Hadrian settled back into her chair opposite the large desk, and Cyrus took the one next to her. They didn't speak. She wanted to warn him to keep his mouth shut but remained silent.

Hadrian looked at the man she had come to care for—not enough to jeopardize her status, but there was an undeniable connection there. From the moment she had stepped into his shop, drawn in by the swirling patterns he had created in the beaten flat collar necklace that stood on display in his window, she had felt a bond with him. It was something she didn't understand and had never spoken of with him, frightened that it was one-sided. She didn't want to appear vulnerable or weak. The recognition had been almost instantaneous. Hadrian refused to think about it further and looked away, instead focusing on the view from the open doors onto the balcony and beyond, noting that more stars were appearing as the night deepened.

Several pairs of boots could be heard entering the outer room, and both Hadrian and Cyrus rose quickly, turning to see the First Elder enter. They bowed deeply and stayed standing until he divested himself of his ceremonial trimmings and indicated they could sit. As he sorted through a few parchments and scrolls on his desk, Hadrian studied him. Was he younger again or was her mind just playing tricks? This time it was not as discernible, but being a woman of a certain age, one took notice of things others didn't. She found it unsettling, but didn't question it. Hadrian decided that she would try to find out his secret to reversing the aging process when this saga was over.

The First Elder cleared his throat and looked up at the two of them. He steepled his pointer fingers and held them to his mouth for several moments before speaking. "There appears to be another missing person around the two of you," he began, raising his brows. "Hadrian, where is your servant?"

Hadrian refused to look down, it might make him believe she was guilty of something. "I wasn't aware that you were so acquainted with the comings and going of our servants." She attempted to deflect his statement.

"Did you not think with all the mystery surrounding the disappearance of the Master Shaymmi that another missing person would most certainly be reported? Everyone is covering themselves, and there are people every where willing to tell what they know to avoid being cast out of the monastery in disgrace."

The undertone of a threat was obvious to Hadrian. *Was he implying that someone had told him something that incriminated them?* She chose to say nothing until he asked her a direct question—he would get no information he didn't specifically request.

An uncomfortable silence began to build. The First Elder finally broke it. "Hadrian, I will ask you one more time. Where is your servant?"

"He mentioned something about visiting his mother." She waved her hand dismissively. "He is a servant, I barely take notice of him."

"That is not quite the story I was told." For the first time since entering, he addressed Cyrus. "Do you know where Hadrian's servant is?"

Hadrian watched Cyrus from the corner of her eye. He had more to lose than Hadrian in many ways, as he was the one to have actually killed Garm. Though she had been the mastermind, he was the one to have done the deed, and of course, she was far more valuable to the First Elder. As long as he didn't find out her part in the disappearance of Sylvan.

"I am sorry, Your Holiness. I only know what Hadrian told me—that he had gone to visit family."

Albin sat back in his chair, again raising his steepled fingers to his mouth as he waited for someone to add something. The office filled with the noises of outside as no one in the room moved.

"It has been rumored that the three of you were carrying on an illicit affair."

Neither spoke and Hadrian found herself holding her breath, waiting for the First Elder to ask his question. "Were you?"

Hadrian took the opportunity to move in her chair, uncrossing and recrossing her legs.

"I was sleeping with both men, if that is what you want to know. Hardly an illicit affair," she scoffed. "I didn't realize my sex life was that interesting to everyone."

"Normally, with whom you spend your time and share your favors is not my concern and certainly not something I care to know about, but Master Shaymmi Sylvan is still missing and I find it odd that now your servant is also missing."

"I told you that he went to visit his mother," she reiterated, breaking her own rule of speaking without being asked a question.

"Would it interest you to know that Garm is an orphan? His mother died many years ago and he was raised here."

Hadrian tried not to show her mounting panic. Everything was beginning to unravel. Cyrus was so still, he could have been mistaken for a stone statue.

Albin turned to look at Cyrus. "Did you have anything to add, Master Silversmith?"

"No, Your Holiness. Hadrian advised me that Garm had left to visit family. I can only tell you what she told me."

Hadrian strained to keep herself in check. *What was he doing? Was he implying that she was keeping things from him and he was innocent?* She had the distinct feeling that she was being set up to take the fall. *This can't happen,* she told herself. Thinking quickly, Hadrian made a decision to protect herself before things became more complicated. She uncrossed her legs and sat forward on the chair.

"Your Holiness, please forgive me for I have lied." She heard Cyrus draw in a breath, but plunged on. "We have been lying to you. I fell in love with Garm and in a jealous rage Cyrus killed him. I have been too scared to come forward as I didn't feel safe."

"You bitch," Cyrus muttered.

"Do you deny the claim?" Albin asked.

"I deny that I killed Garm in a fit of jealousy. Could I possibly speak with you without Hadrian present, Your Holiness?"

Hadrian gave him a sharp look, but Cyrus ignored her and kept focused on Albin. "As I would like to get to the bottom of this, I think that is fair." He turned to his personal guard. "Escort Shaymmi Hadrian out to the sitting room and make certain she doesn't leave. Have someone come in here and stand guard while I have a chat with the silversmith."

I think I am now in trouble, she admitted to herself as she was taken from the room. *Maybe it wasn't the wisest decision to blame Cyrus.*

Chapter 54
Treena

Night had completely fallen. The market sounds outside of the curtained window had taken on a different feel. Now they could hear raucous voices filled with song and the laughter of people passing by. Treena longed for that carefree life for a moment, but knowing that underneath it was a facade that many lived with to escape the ever encroaching demands of the church. They had settled around the small kitchen table, and Treena had made them lemon tea while they discussed what Cyrus had revealed. It had been startling to hear that Cyrus had helped in the kidnapping of Sylvan's body. They would have to wait until he returned so they could fully understand how he had been involved, and how much trouble he was in. With the unearthing of Thedra's eyes, the need for cautious behavior had never been greater, and he was at this moment sitting in the office of the First Elder. Treena felt a little queasy at the thought. She needed something to occupy her mind.

"Grab your packs, I want to check what we need from the market tomorrow."

Aven went to move but Braith had already stood up. "Stay there I will grab everyone's."

"Ta," said Aven. "I mean, thank you," she amended.

It took Braith only a few minutes to return with the packs.

"What in the name of all five elements do you have in your pack, Aven?" he asked as he plonked them on the floor in the kitchen. He selected Aven's and put it on the table in front of her.

"How heavy is it?" Treena asked. She picked it up out of curiosity. "I wasn't expecting it to be that heavy. How have you managed it all this time?"

"You can open it. They are really yours." Aven answered cryptically.

Carefully, Treena opened the backpack and discovered the matching Oredmoor bookends from her training room nestled in amongst the clothes. She pulled them out and placed them on the table.

"Why?" she asked.

"I'm not sure. They react to me, so I figure they must be important."

"They are Oredmoor head bookends," Braith exclaimed like both of the girls wouldn't know. He bent down to examine them and whistled in appreciation of their beauty. "Do you have any concept of how much these would be worth on the black market?" He looked at both of them and then looked sheepish as he probably recalled who he spoke to. "Hang on, you said it reacts to you, Aven. How?"

Aven looked to Treena, who gave the smallest nod of permission and moved them so both bookends were facing Aven.

"Stand behind her," Treena told him. "Whenever you are ready, Aven."

Aven put out her two hands and touched the bookends. "Lean over and feel them now," Treena told Braith.

Braith stepped to the side of Aven and put his hands on the side of each book end. "This one feels cold and wet."

"It does to me too," agreed Aven. "Take your hands off now." He watched closely as Aven leaned forward and blew her breath out slowly. The bookend that had felt wet appeared to be changing. Its eyes began to glow the same golden hue that Dalinda eyes had.

A thumping on the front door made them all jump and Aven squealed. Quickly they stuffed the Oredmoor heads in the pack and shoved it under the table, piling the other packs on top. They all moved out of the kitchen and into the main area of the shop. The thumping continued. Braith opened the door and stood back.

"May I help you?"

"Where is he?" a monk marched into the room, followed by three more.

Aven shrank behind Treena, who attempted to look angry at the interruption. "Who are you looking for? Cyrus has gone to the monastery. I demand to know the meaning of this?" She used a shrill voice.

Three of the monks took no notice of her and began opening and closing doors. The fourth monk, the one who had original-ly spoken, stood watching Treena, Braith, and Aven.

"Who are you?"

"I am Cyrus' sister, and this is my husband and daughter."

"You are taller than your brother," the monk observed.

"Yes, we had different mothers." She sniffed with disdain. "Our father liked the challenge of bedding women, not so much the keeping of them."

There was a commotion from one of the rooms Treena had not been in before, and the three monks escorted out a servant in the livery of the church. He had long dark brown hair that hung in a single braid down his back and terrified look on his plain features.

"Do you know this man?" demanded the monk.

"Should I?" countered Treena. She found it best to answer a question with a question when dealing with authority. She raised her head in a haughty manner as if she were the one in control.

The monk stared at her for a few seconds. "I think you will all come with me to the monastery for the moment."

"Very well," Treena agreed readily. "But I insist on getting our packs. My daughter is quite sickly and her medicines are in them."

Treena guessed that the monk was so relieved that she hadn't put up any resistance to being taken to the monastery that he was quick to agree with the taking of the packs.

"You," he pointed to Braith, "grab your packs."

He lied, Treena fumed in her head. *He told us no one was here. We spoke about Aven's abilities and that we were here to rescue*

Sylvan. She had no idea who this man was and how he fit in with the game Cyrus had been playing. *What is Cyrus up to?*

Treena gathered her cloak and Aven's from the rack near the door and put hers on before bending down to help Aven.

"Stay close and look weak," she murmured to the girl.

"Shall we," Treena stood and held out her arm for Braith. "Come along, dear." With as much primness as she could manage Treena swept out of the door and allowed the monks to follow in her wake with the man who had been hiding.

Her last thought as she entered the cool night air was, *let me have made the right choice by not arguing.*

Chapter 55

Hadrian

Hadrian did everything she could to not fidget. *What was happening? Why was it taking so long?* She had watched guards come and go since she had been escorted out into the sitting room of the First Elder. She tried not to worry about Cyrus giving away their secrets. What had she been thinking telling the First Elder that Cyrus had killed Garm in a jealous rage? Now, she had exposed herself to Cyrus's retaliation. She had miscalculated on many different levels and now it was time to pay up. Hadrian only hoped that she was up to the challenge.

Another monk hurried through the room and into the office of Albin. He stepped out of the office and looked to her guards.

"Bring her back in."

Hadrian stood—she would not be 'escorted' anywhere.

Settling back into her seat, she took the chance to look at Cyrus. He returned her look and slowly shook his head. *Is he trying to give me a signal that he has said nothing or is he telling me that he is ashamed at how I betrayed him to save myself?* She was about to find out.

Time moved slowly and she heard the dinner bell in the monastery courtyard begin its tolling. Her stomach grumbled in response and she placed her hands over it to hide the sound. Moments dragged on and Hadrian repeatedly told herself to remain calm, that she was still in control. Many loud footsteps were heard outside the room before a group of people were escorted in. A man and woman in their mid-to-late twenties and a young girl around eight were escorted into the room. She wondered who they were. They were ushered to one side to reveal Garm, and Hadrian gasped in response. She quickly swung her head to Cyrus, who deliberately ignored her.

"Well, it would seem that Cyrus didn't trust you as much as you thought he did, Shaymmi Hadrian," The First Elder spoke. He stared at her, waiting for a response.

Her mind tried to work. How was she going to get out of this? Why hadn't Cyrus followed through with her request? She remained silent as she attempted to sort through what she thought she knew.

The First Elder chose not to wait any longer, instead turning to the other people who had been brought in with Garm.

"And who are these people?" he asked the monk who had brought them in.

"They claim to be the silversmith's sister, her husband, and their daughter."

Cyrus spoke before being asked anything. "They had only just arrived when I was requested to attend you," he explained. "They had no idea about Garm, or what has been happening."

"They did seem quite surprised when we found Garm hiding in Cyrus's wardrobe," added the monk.

The First Elder appraised each of Cyrus's family members.

"Very well. You three will sit over there and remain silent until I ascertain the whole truth." He pointed to a sumptuous couch in the corner of the room. "Keep the child quiet," he warned.

Obediently, all three hurried to the couch and sat. Hadrian turned back to the First Elder, her mind already forgetting Cyrus's kin as she focused on saving her own skin.

"Now, where were we?" Albin asked no one in particular. "Cyrus, why did Hadrian think you had killed Garm?"

Cyrus sat forward. "I told her I had because I promised her I would, but when it came time to do it, I couldn't go through with it. I am not a killer. I did fall in love with her, and I wanted to please her so have done things I am ashamed of, but in the end I couldn't kill for him."

"Why did she want Garm killed?"

Cyrus remained silent and Hadrian held her breath. Whatever he said would incriminate him too. How much truth was he prepared to share?

"I can only tell you what she told me, but that may not be the truth." Cyrus spread his hands wide. "I think it best if she told you why."

The First Elder looked to Cyrus and nodded before turning to Hadrian. "I think Cyrus is being most gracious in allowing you to answer for yourself. What do you say?"

"I was trying to help Cyrus. He had brought in an artifact that still radiated elemental power and Garm knew about it. I have fallen in love with Cyrus and wanted to protect him, so thought it best to get rid of the only person who would betray us," she explained.

"Why did you not come to me with the artifact?" Albin's voice had become harsher.

"It was the same time as Master Shaymmi went missing and you charged me with finding the missing child. I felt it was the wrong time to tell you about the artifact until after the child was recovered."

Albin arched an eyebrow at her. "So, it was for my benefit?"

"No, it was wholly for mine and Cyrus's benefit," she admitted. Hadrian was wise enough to not try to place any blame on the First Elder.

"And yet, you betrayed Cyrus at the first sign of trouble, by informing me that he had killed Garm."

Hadrian lowered her head in the hope it looked like she was ashamed, when in reality she was trying to figure out a way to not hand over the artifact. Maybe she could find another similar pendant and then be embarrassed when she realizes she is mistaken and the pendant has no power?

"Garm, what do you have to say? Is Hadrian telling the truth?"

"Yes and no," the servant answered. Ignoring the glare Hadrian shot him.

"Go on," urged Albin.

"Cyrus did bring in some kind of pendant that Hadrian got all excited about."

The First Elder sat back in his chair again steepling his pointer fingers and holding them against his lips. He looked at Hadrian then Cyrus and finally returned his threatening gaze to Garm.

"Let me ask it this way...and let me be clear that I will not tolerate any more lies or dissembling. I want the truth."

Garm bowed deeply.

"Do you know something that would make Hadrian want you dead?"

"Yes."

Chapter 56
Hadrian

There was a collective gasp at Garm's answer.

"He's a liar and a servant. Why would you believe anything he tells you?" scoffed Hadrian, thinking quickly. She knew where this was heading, and she didn't know if she could extricate herself from all the deceit, but she needed to try.

"You attempted to have him silenced. That alone shows there is something to hide," countered Albin.

"I told you that I thought Cyrus had killed him out of jealousy. You just heard him admit that he loves me."

"And I heard you admit that you loved him. I think you are both manipulating the truth to serve your purpose." The First Elder returned his focus to Garm. "What is Hadrian hiding that would make her want you gone?"

"Sylvan is trapped on the Elemental Plane, and it is her doing."

This time the gasp from everyone in the room was followed by several people talking at once.

Hadrian spoke loudly, "You liar."

Cyrus muttered quietly, "Here we go."

Hadrian heard someone say, "Finally," but couldn't place the voice.

"Silence!" roared a monk.

"Thank you." Albin nodded his head to his bodyguard. "Garm, please explain that statement."

"I am not sure of all the details, but I was there when Cyrus brought in the pendant they spoke of and tested it on Hadrian. The amulet thing seems to stop them from re-entering their body once out on the plane." He stopped talking and looked at Hadrian before turning back to Albin. "I also helped them steal Sylvan's body and was there when she blackmailed Jorge into not reporting it."

"Jorge had nothing to do with it?"

"No. Hadrian told him that as long as he remained quiet and kept pretending everything was fine that she would guarantee that Sylvan would be safe. If he told, she would destroy Sylvan's body and he would never be able to return."

"Is there anything else?"

"Once Sylvan was found to be missing, we moved his body from Hadrian's room to a storage room, where as far as I know he still lies."

"It's all lies. Why are you lying?" She stood up and was instantly surrounded by warrior monks. "Why would I do such a thing?"

"Sit down, Shaymmi Hadrian," commanded the First Elder. "I intend to find out why you would do such things."

The warrior monks took a step forward and she raised her hands in supplication, retaking her seat but staring at everyone with a defiant glare. *Think of something,* she pleaded with her subconscious.

"Cyrus, you have just been implicated in some very serious accusations. What do you have to say?"

Cyrus looked calm as he inclined his head in acceptance of the statement. "I gave Shaymmi Hadrian the pendant. I had inherited it from the silversmith that was my master. I do not understand about the elemental power you are all referring to, but was told that it could be used against someone on the elemental plane if needed. It had no import to me, so I just left it in a drawer for many years." He paused as if gathering his thoughts.

Hadrian felt the tension build and prayed for a miracle to save her from the next words he would utter.

"Hadrian was complaining one night about the Master Shaymmi and the accolades he receives and that it wasn't fair, as she is just as capable. She confessed that he had found a girl with unique elemental vibrations, but somehow she had escaped and was now on the hunt for her again. Hadrian was convinced that if she had the chance, she would be able to find the girl and be your favorite." He shrugged and readjusted his shirt cuffs. "I remembered the amulet I had been given and offered her the use of it. We tested it, as Garm has already stated, and it worked. The rest is fairly close to what Garm has said, but as the search for Sylvan intensified, Hadrian began to worry and thought it best that I kill Garm so it was only the two of us who carried the secret. I love Hadrian, but I don't trust her, and I have grown fond of Garm, so I chose to spare his life and help him hide."

"Why? Why lie? Maybe it is you and Garm who are trying to get rid of me?" she accused.

"I will admit that I used you." Cyrus looked sorry.

Hadrian frowned. Where was he going with this? She felt trapped.

"I wanted the fame and fortune as much as you did. You were a means to get the attention of the First Elder and it worked. I wanted to be rich and renowned. I crave comfort and recognition." He looked guiltily at Albin. "Not charming qualities to admit to, but it is the truth. We both wanted the same thing. It turns out that the Shaymmi is far more ruthless than I am."

Albin inclined his head in acknowledgment but didn't absolve him. "Oh, I am not sure, but I think there is more to you than you want to admit."

Hadrian didn't know what he was hinting at, but she felt a glimmer of hope that it might help her cause. She would wait and see if it could be used to her advantage.

"Your Holiness, I am not sure what you are alluding to?" Cyrus said.

"If you wanted to curry my favor and make a good impression, why not come to me with your knowledge, rather than use the anonymity of the confessional?"

The room fell silent. No one moved. It was as if each person held their breath, waiting to discover what the First Elder implied. Until this moment, Hadrian had forgotten about Cyrus's family that sat huddled in the corner, witnessing the revelations. She wondered how much they understood and why Albin was allowing them to witness it.

Cyrus cleared his throat. "I am not sure what you are implying. I go to church and confessional bi-weekly, as all the faithful should."

"Ah, yes, and I applaud the effort. What I want to know is how you knew and why did you tell us to check the traitor's eyes?"

Everyone began to talk at once, but Hadrian was more interested in the loud, shocked gasp that came from the back corner. How would they know what that last sentence meant?

Chapter 57
Sylvan

Sylvan had been astonished as he witnessed the young girl and her Dalinda trainer and the man that accompanied them be escorted into the First Elder's office. What had been even more startling was that the moment the child entered the room, the Spirit Mirror activated. He didn't know if it was the accumulation of three Dalinda in one room or just the child, but incredibly, he could now hear the conversation. The child acknowledged that she could see him with a quick nod of her head.

He observed with growing wonder the complete machinations of Shaymmi Hadrian and the lengths she would go to have his role. He mourned for his friend all over again when he finally learned the truth that Jorge had not betrayed him but had protected him and had given up his life to save Sylvan's. He watched the web of lies unravel as first her servant then her lover chose to tell the truth as she had shown her willingness to come out on top at all costs. It was satisfying to see Hadrian look humbled, but that had swiftly changed with the last words of the First Elder. Had the First Elder just implied that he knew

Cyrus had been the one to inform the church to check the eyes of the dead Dalinda who had rescued the young girl?

For his own selfish reasons, he wanted the conversation to return to finding his body and punishing Hadrian, but he also wanted to deflect from what had just been revealed. He couldn't bare to see the young girl or the female be drained and turned to dust for the vanity of the First Elder. It was time to step in.

He cleared his non-existent throat and floated into the area of the Spirit Mirror.

"I think it's about time we all stopped talking and went to find my body. I am bored being out on this plane, and I would like the opportunity to express my side of the story."

Chaos ensued, which Sylvan felt was completely satisfying. He had made a fine entrance and by the look on Hadrian's face, had ended any ideas of her redeeming herself.

Albin cleared his throat and nodded his head to a monk. The monk again used his booming voice to tell everyone to be silent.

"Master Shaymmi, it is good to finally have contact with you. We have been most concerned." The First Elder looked intently in the Spirit Mirror. "Why have you not contacted me sooner through the mirror?"

"It has taken me this long to learn what I required to use it while out here on the Elemental Plane, and I think this will be my only time as it is too difficult," he lied. "I have been watching, but not able to hear or contact you until now. I will admit I grow weaker daily, and I urge you to find my body now."

"Yes, but I have one question," Albin spoke. "From what you know, who tells the truth? Is Hadrian behind the scheme?"

Sylvan decided to throw a little confusion into the mix. "My understanding is that Hadrian is behind all of it." He emphasized the 'all.'

Predictably she stood and yelled, "He lies!"

"I think it is time to return Sylvan to his body."

"It would be appreciated," admitted Sylvan.

"May I offer to show you where the body is stored, Your Holiness?" offered Cyrus.

The First Elder stood and took in the room with a sweeping gaze. "The three culprits will all escort us to the Master Shaymmi's body. Leave a few monks here with Cyrus's family."

Sylvan noted that they were doing an excellent job of looking scared and non-threatening.

"Master Shaymmi, you will meet us at your body." Albin asked as the monks took hold of each accused and marched them toward the hallway.

"Yes, I will meet you there. Thank you, Your Holiness." Sylvan allowed himself to move away from the mirror and fade from view. He did not leave the room. He waited and watched as the room emptied, leaving two warrior monks to guard the three. He moved to the outer rooms and found the usual two monks at the entrance to his suite and that was it. Sylvan quickly returned to the inner office and swiftly reappeared in the mirror. The child saw him re-enter the room and nudged her companion when he appeared in the mirror.

"Excuse me?" he said politely, which was totally out of character for him, but the effect he wanted. The two monks turned to face the mirror.

The Dalinda and the man didn't need anything more than that distraction. Both pounced. The man snapped the neck of his guard and caught him before he made any noise falling to the ground and knocking anything over. The woman had knocked out the other guard with the hilt of her knife and had caught him before he hit the ground. Sylvan watched with growing admiration as they swiftly worked together to move both monks out onto the balcony and closed and locked the door.

Once they were back in the room he whispered, "Two at the outer door."

"Thank you," the woman responded.

"You need to get out of here. Once the Shaymmi enter the Elemental Plane tomorrow morning, they will know the girl is here. She has grown more powerful and this close she will be obvious." The girl paled and it hurt to see her scared. He was surprised at how much he cared for her now.

"My name is Aven," she said in a tiny voice. "Can we help you first?"

"It is nice to meet you properly, Aven. I will go now and reunite with my body." He looked to the woman. "Head toward Haslet, my family has land there where they raise goats. I will say that I am going home to rest. I will be in touch with Aven if anything changes."

"I am Treena, we will need to go to East Monns first. I will need to check in and meet with a few people."

"Very well. I must go. They should be at my body by now. Thank you for saving me Treena, Aven and..."

"Braith." The head of thieves reluctantly gave up his name.

"Heed my warning, leave the city now." He quickly gave them directions to get out of the monastery and didn't linger to see what they did. He had to get to his body before they removed the blocking pendant.

He ignored all the feelings of fatigue and the almost overwhelming vibrations of the elements around him as his mental shields continued to hold by the most tenuous of threads. He glided as quickly as he could to where his body was hidden. Sylvan arrived in time to see Garm and Cyrus remove the rolled rugs and carpets they had piled up to hide the large metal chest. Hadrian stood to one side scowling. He took a moment to savor the witnessing of her plans being completely unraveled. Why couldn't she have just known her place and none of this would have happened? A voice within his inner most thoughts whispered back at him, *if she didn't do what she had, Aven would either be dead, drained of her powers, or been held and tortured by*

the First Elder, for I would have found her again and not thought twice regarding the consequences.

Sylvan watched with growing excitement as the chest was opened and his body exposed. Albin casually moved to inspect the body, while Sylvan's mind shrieked for him to just get on with it. The First Elder stood up and looked at Shaymmi Hadrian and asked her a question.

Hadrian looked like she would refuse to answer for a moment before replying.

Albin looked dissatisfied with the answer, but Cyrus spoke quickly.

As always, Sylvan was frustrated with not being able to hear what was happening, and really, at the moment, he didn't care. He just wanted to know why they were taking so long to remove the pendant. He hovered close to the chest and watched with growing anticipation as the Master Silversmith lifted the hideous amulet from Sylvan's chest. Instantly he felt the connection that tethered his body and consciousness meld as one, and with practiced ease, he rolled through the veil that separated the Elemental Plane to his corporal body. He sighed both physically and mentally as the joining was completed and slowly opened his eyes. Relief at the situation quickly turned to pain as his mind registered the damage his body had endured. His muscles cramped and his stomach felt like it had wrapped itself around his spine, his head throbbed, probably from a combination of dehydration and backlash from the reconnect. Sylvan absently noted that his eyes weren't filmed over, as the elixir they usually drank would have long left his system, and there seemed to be no ill affect from that. Though it pained him to show his vulnerability, he didn't have a choice.

"I can't move. Someone will need to help me get out," he announced in his most imperious voice.

The First Elder quickly assigned several warrior monks to aid Sylvan. While he was being carefully lifted out, Albin ordered the removal of Hadrian, Cyrus, and Garm from the room. As Sylvan stood on his wobbly legs, being held up by two shorter, but far more powerful men than he, he watched with barely concealed contempt as all three were marched out, with their arms held tightly behind their backs. He moved to walk but his muscles cramped. Thankfully the monks who supported him felt his legs give way and caught him before he fell.

"Take him back to his room and see to his needs," ordered Albin.

Sylvan's mind raced. He needed to plan ahead. "I think it best, as I have no manservant, that the twins are sent to me. Having both of them should suffice until my body is working properly."

"Very wise," agreed the First Elder. He turned to the monk closest to the door. "Find the twins and send them to Master Shaymmi Sylvan's suites."

"And get me some food. I am famished," Sylvan added.

In a brief amount of time, Sylvan was carried to his suites and laid on his finely upholstered work chaise. The twins arrived, with surly but curious looks on their matching faces, and a plethora of trays filled with a variety of food were placed on a sideboard. Sylvan ordered one of the young men to start filling the bath for him, while the other was sent into his sitting room to find Sylvan's favorite red wine. The First Elder and Sylvan were finally alone. As Sylvan attempted to find a more comfortable position on the chaise, his mind raced with all the things he needed to accomplish to aid the only people who had risked everything aid him.

"I have news of the girl, if you are interested?"

"Very much so."

"I continued to monitor her movements while on the Plane as I worked on a way to communicate with you. This morning she was in the forests to the east of Namurrn. She has been there for several days, with a group of four men. I'm not sure if she is hiding or heading for Croile."

Albin frowned and lines appeared on his typically smooth forehead, thanks to the draining of the artefacts. Sylvan tried not to stare. "Do you know how she escaped through the lock down of Hamlyn?"

Sylvan feigned surprise and hoped his acting abilities were up for the challenge. "I had no idea that Hamlyn is in lock down. She must have left before that occured." He hoped that with that misdirection, Albin might assume she had nothing to do with the demise of Arch Deacon Ulrick.

"Is this it?" One of the twins walked back into the room, not caring if he interrupted a conversation. He held up a wineskin.

"Yes. Would you care for a glass, Your Holiness?"

"Thank you, but no. There is much to be done, and I still have those three miscreants to deal with. Perhaps in a few days when you are feeling more like your usual self and are ready to return to the Elemental Plane." He left without any further comment.

As soon as the First Elder left the suite, Sylvan struggled to pull himself up into a sitting position.

"Pour me a glass then go make sure the door is locked," he told the young man.

Without a word, his orders were carried out.

"Go fetch your brother, tell him to stop running the water. I will do that later."

Sylvan sipped on the wine and savored the spiced liquid as it heated the back of his throat. He slowly placed his feet on the ground and holding onto the back of the lounge for support stood up. His legs shook, but didn't collapse. Experimentally, he bent his knees slightly. They protested, but the cramping had finally eased. He carefully let go of the lounge and took the few steps to the sideboard where the food platters sat. Though he wanted to gorge on the rich meats and gravies, he knew it wise to start off with something plain. He took the flat bread and dipped it into a mild paste before beginning to nibble on it.

He turned back to walk to his chaise when the twins came out of the bathroom. One moved quickly to help him but Sylvan shooed him away.

"I am better than what I appear." He looked at both of them and felt mildly ashamed that he still couldn't tell them apart.

He sat down slowly and chewed thoughtfully on his flat bread. "I am going to ask you a favor, but it will put you in a compromising position if you are caught. I will not force you to do anything, and I am putting great trust in you just by speaking of it."

The twins looked at each before turning back to him. "We will hear the request."

"Let me start by apologizing. The First Elder is not to be trusted. You were right about the elixir, after having survived on the Elemental Plane and returning to my body without it in my system, I can honestly say that I think there is another reason he wants us to take it. I don't know what that is, but hope now to help you find out." Sylvan took another sip of the wine, as his throat was dry from not being used. "There is a woman, man, and child trying to get out of the city. They must be helped at all costs. The First Elder has horrifying plans for the young girl, and I won't let that happen if I can help it. They will be at the docks, looking for passage to East Monns. I need you to aid them in securing safe passage and be out of the city by dawn." The Master Shaymmi, who was renowned for expecting his whims to be indulged and his orders to be followed, looked earnestly at the two young men before him and uttered the word no one would ever foresee him using. "Please."

Chapter 58

Treena

The chimes rang through Cynsellam, announcing to everyone that curfew had begun until the fifth chime rang in the morning. The only people allowed out carried special chits or were patrolling warrior monks. Anyone discovered out without valid cause would be locked up and made to pay a fine the following day. If you were caught more than once, you would then be expected to pay your dues in other ways. Treena tried not to dwell on any of that as she huddled under the awning of a dockside warehouse waiting for her contact to arrive. As she had been trained to do by Reza, on the way through the city earlier that day, she had taken note of two shop fronts that had the Loyalist emblem painted on their sign. The one closest to the docks was a tavern, and they had arrived just on closing. Although the owner had not known Treena and she had not told him who she was, she did reveal to him the correct password and the name of Lord Cyrus. She then explained that they needed a boat or raft to get to East Monns immediately. The tavern owner left his wife to close up and led them down to the dock area himself, telling them to wait while he organized a few things.

Two male figures loomed out of the darkness and Treena instinctively crouched into a fighting stance.

"Don't come any closer," warned Braith.

"It's okay. They are not here to harm us," Aven announced.

Treena was dumbfounded. Aven was typically the one cowering behind them, but instead she stood and walked out of the shadow.

"Are you Treena?" one of them asked.

"Yes, and you are?"

"We were sent by Master Shaymmi Sylvan," the young man announced.

"Keep your voice down," whispered Braith. "Night air carries sound."

The other young man stepped forward and knelt before Aven. "I am Matthias. How may we aid you in escaping?"

"Hi Matthias, I am Aven." She curtsied.

Treena watched with growing understanding the interesting turn of events. The gruffer young man didn't appear happy with what was obviously his identical twin brother, and how he was behaving regarding Aven.

"Did you have any plans on how you were going to aid us?" she asked the frowning one.

"I am Matteo. We thought we could commandeer a craft for you through using Master Shaymmi's name and the proof of our clothing." He raised his hand to the neckline of his dark tunic, indicating the silver threaded embroidery of the Shaymmi of the Church of the One God.

"A grand idea, but one small drawback. We don't want any-one to remember us or where we went. Everyone remembers the goings on of the Shaymmi as it is an honor to serve them," Treena explained. "I would suggest you turn your cloaks inside out and fasten them so no-one sees your tunic."

"But" Matteo began to protest.

Treena spoke over him in a firm but low voice, "Or you can go back to Sylvan, tell him that you offered us aid as asked, but that you weren't willing to follow instructions. I can't have anyone come with us who can't follow orders."

Matthias had stood and moved under the awning to stand next to Aven while his brother was complaining. Treena watched as he quickly complied with her request.

"You are going with them?" Matteo asked his twin.

"I think he wanted us to. He was very clear that he doesn't trust the First Elder and we were to help these people. I feel drawn to her, them...don't you?"

Mathias scowled. "And since when do you make decisions without discussing them with me first?"

"Aren't we discussing it now?" Matteo kept his voice down. "What are your objections to going? You were miserable. The Master who is to train us is telling us that he no longer trusts the man we are to work for. We know that he has been lying to the Shaymmi about the elixir. If we don't like where we end up, we go back or move on."

Braith stepped in. "If Sylvan sent you to help then do as asked or leave."

"Fine, I'll help. For now." Matteo reversed his cloak and moved into the shadow of the awning beside his brother.

They stood quietly for a moment. Treena listened for the sound of footsteps. While they waited, she realized that the sound of the river docks were vastly different to the docks she had grown up with in Hamlyn. In Hamlyn there were always the sounds of the powerful waves in the bay echoing in from the cliff side to the right of the port city. Here in the capital the river found its end. It was gentle, and waves lapped quietly against the huge stone blocks that created the wharf area. The noises from the animals, kept in the old Oredmoor Arena, that stood next to the river, drifted through the still air. Treena fretted that they would have to leave the horses and cart behind, but she would take heed of Sylvan's warning that Aven was in danger if they didn't get out now. He had no reason to lie. He could have simply told the First Elder who they were as soon as he appeared in the Spirit Mirror; instead, he had deflected and given them instructions on the best way to leave the monastery without incident. Treena thought they would still be meandering around all those marble corridors without that knowledge.

As they waited, she considered the two young men who had apparently joined them on their escape. By the way Aven and Matthias were behaving, the twins would be joining them permanently. Treena needed to get to the Elldean of East Monns to confirm her hunches. But now she had a decision to make. How much should be revealed to them? Usually the vetting of Loyalists was long and protracted, and most came down through lineage of those who served the Dalinda and Oredmoor before the Subversion. Treena felt uncomfortable as Braith's words from their conversation on the road resurfaced—wouldn't she kill to protect their secrets?.

No solid decisions were made as her thoughts were interrupted by the sound of footsteps. She ignored the sudden rapid beating of her heart as she tried to fathom how many sets of feet walked toward them. Was it the Inn owner with the owner of the vessel they would use, or was it a small patrol of warrior monks?

"If it comes to it, I hope you two are prepared to fight," she whispered.

No one answered as the footsteps came closer. Treena could now make out that there were three people approaching. If the twins didn't help, she felt confident that they would be able to take care of it.

"Hello? I have brought a fellow such as myself—a boat owner that is willing to risk leaving now and running at night with no lights. The price will be high though, as he risks much, though we both understand that it is an honor to serve."

Treena spoke softly, but did not emerge from the shadows of the awning.

"You both will be well compensated once I have reached East Monns and alerted them to who has aided me. How quickly can we get to this craft? And who is the other person with you."

A new voice spoke up. "He is my son and old enough to understand and serve. His oaths have been sworn."

"Very well. We need to leave immediately." As if to make the point, the monastery bells rang out across the night air, announcing that it was one chime after midnight. The chimes disturbed the birds as they roosted in their nests and startled the animals in the pens near by. Creating a great deal of sound to cover their movements.

"I keep the boat tethered at the end of the dock to make it easier to slip away. Our tavern owner friend will distract the monk at the end of the pier while we get going. Stay in the shadows as much as you can. We have chits to be out here, you do not. If a patrol comes, keep moving while we stop to talk to them."

Before they began to move, Treena spoke. "There has been a change in passengers and there will now be five traveling. Is this an issue?"

"No, that is fine. Move along while there is still noise; the animals will settle quickly."

Treena felt like it was taking forever as they slowly made their way down the large expanse of dock, leapfrogging from build-ing to building, remaining in the shadows. They encountered two patrols of six men and both times the hidden group moved ahead while the boat owner kept the patrols busy. A small bribe for each patrol and they were moving again. Eventually the warehouses gave way to a wide pier that held ships, boats, and rafts of all sizes tied to the both sides. She indicated for Braith to take up the rear, while she took point. The sulky twin, Matteo, moved lithely on his feet—he had obviously had some training in fighting. Unfortunately his brother, Matthias, was heavy footed and had to be rescued by Aven as his foot got tangled in the mooring ropes of one of the ships. It would have been amusing if the stakes were not so high.

Without further incident, they reached the end of the pier and the tavern keeper came to her. He held up a bottle and smiled. "I am off to entertain the monk on duty. Have a safe trip and remember me to Lord Cyrus when you next see him."

Treena took the man a few steps away from the twins and leaned in to speak to him. "Thank you for your service. Do not tally here overly long. I have a feeling that you will be needed again to give aid. Lord Cyrus will need to leave as quickly as we do, maybe more so. He will too be traveling to East Monns." She placed her hand the man's cheek. "Please, let him know that the Lady Katatreena and the Lady Aven are safely away."

He went to kneel and Treena caught him. "No, no, not here."

"Yes, my Lady. Have a safe journey. I will see to your wishes as soon as you are safely away. I will spill the bottle and have to go back for more." He turned and left, calling out to the monk in the small box at the end of the pier. As he disappeared into the guard house, the boat owner's son led them to the craft that would hopefully see them to safety.

It didn't take them long to board and settle into the captain's cabin. It was a tight fit, but no one complained, and Treena was grateful that she didn't have to witness what she knew would be a scowl on Matteo's face. She had no patience for sulky teens at the moment. The boat rocked as the son poled away from the dock. It would be slow going, so no noise would be made until they were free of the area.

The second chimes of the day were faintly heard from the city as they slid past the now awakened animals in the ancient Oredmoor Arena. Treena peeked out the window to see less boats were anchored to the sides of the river and guessed it would only be another league or so before they were free from Cynsellam enough for her to use her elemental powers to control the currents and make their journey swifter.

Chapter 59
Sylvan

The fives chimes announced to the citizens of Cynsellam that they could once again move freely about the city. What it announced to Sylvan was that the twins had either chosen to leave with the others or had been caught. He hoped they had been wise enough to understand his warning and had decided to go. The feeling of his body joined with his mind and lying in his bed was sheer bliss, but the few hours he had slept had been filled with dreams of being trapped and slowly suffocating. Sylvan stretched and found that even though his body ached for not being moved for such a length of time it had stopped cramping. He slowly got out of bed and stood still as a feeling of light headedness swept over him. He closed his eyes and took a few deep breaths and allowed his equilibrium to return. He made his way to the bathroom where he threw cold water on his face and again marveled at the changes that had happened while he was trapped on the elemental plane. His once barrel chest and slightly paunched stomach had diminished, and he noted the slight sag of his gut with a frown. He now had a brown beard and his hair had grown long enough that it was easy for him to tie it back. In the right clothes, he would be unrecognizable from who he was and that suited his next move perfectly.

There was still a large amount of food under cloches on the side board, and Sylvan grazed from them as he reflected. His first thought was that he should check to see how far away Aven was, but just couldn't bring himself to enter the Elemental Plane so soon. To accomplish it without the elixir and no one to watch over him that he trusted was a combination he wasn't willing to try. His stomach from not eating for so long had shrunk and he was quickly satiated by the small amount of food he ate.

He went back to his closet and chose the plainest outfit he owned and quickly put it on. Pulling boots onto his feet and doing everything manually was odd, and he again thought of his manservant and friend Jorge. A deep twinge of regret and pain filled his heart, but now was not the time to mourn. Grabbing his luxurious and highly visible cloak that clearly announced his status, he laid it on the lounge in the sitting room and then stuck his head out of his suite door.

"You, get me another bottle of wine, but leave it in the sitting room. I do not wish to be disturbed today. I am tired and will be seeking my bed again soon." Sylvan used his most demanding voice and the guard quickly moved. He turned to the other guard. "I need you to inform the First Elder that I wish to have dinner with him tonight. I have much to tell him about what I discovered. I will need to rest till then."

The guard looked at him and hesitated. Sylvan knew he was not supposed to leave the door unguarded and would prefer his fellow officer to get back before he left his post.

"I think I am perfectly safe now the perpetrators have been caught. We both know how the First Elder will feel if I told him you made me wait for instructions to be followed." Sylvan raised his heavy brows and gave him a penetrating look. He was amazed that he now had to think about how to behave when just a short time ago this would have been his natural behavior. He had to actually fight the urge to say please. Having to rely on Aven to communicate for so long, and to discover what Albin really thought of him, had made him reassess his behavior towards people. If only he had had the chance to show his new side to Jorge.

He waited and continued to stare at the guard, who began to fidget.

"I will carry your message, Master Shyammi."

Sylvan nodded and closed the door. He grabbed the cloak and put it on and counted to twenty before slowly opening the door again. The corridor was now empty and he slowly crept out and made his way as swiftly as possible in his weakened state to the monastery library. He encountered upon a few servants and they all scurried out of his way, keeping their head down as soon as they recognized who he was. Being so early in the morning, no one was in the library and he moved to the very back of the expansive room. He wasn't interrupted as he found the large chaise lounge and moved to the wall behind it where he gingerly pushed on the center of the large bas-relief elemental symbol that would allow the closest bookshelf to swing open and expose the entrance to the underground dungeons.

He wasn't expecting the rank air that greeted him at the top of the steps to the passage below. Wrinkling his nose and wishing he had a way to conjure light, he held his hand against the wall as he slowly took his first step into the darkness. Sylvan had traveled this corridor several times on the Elemental Plane and was grateful for it as it gave him some what of an idea as to what to expect. A dull light at the end of the corridor didn't grow much brighter as he entered the huge room. He was relieved to find what he thought he would.

Shaymmi Hadrian, Dalinda Cyrus, and the servant, Garm, were all with their hands stretched over their heads and tied to a metal ring at the top of poles. Their feet barely grazed the ground and all three had wads of material shoved in their mouth. They were alert and watching him with wild eyes as he moved closer. Sylvan couldn't help it, a satisfied smirk crossed his face as he looked at Hadrian.

He moved to stand directly before Hadrian and noted her torn and unkempt appearance.

"You couldn't just be the second best? You let your greed and want for recognition bring you so low. Look what you have become." He moved his arm expansively to take in the room. "You have changed things that can never be unchanged and put in motion a new era, all with complete ignorance."

Sylvan moved to Cyrus and stood there feeling the vibrations that came from him. Like Treena, his vibrations were subtle, and if you didn't know what to look for they would be easily overlooked, which is probably why the Dalinda had managed to survive for so long without discovery.

"I am surprised at you, Master Silversmith. Why would you betray your own kind?"

The disguised brown eyes of Cyrus grew wide as he warily watched Sylvan draw nearer. Sylvan reached into his fancy cloak and withdrew the ornamental dagger he had concealed. Cyrus strained against his restraints, his feet trying to find purchase on the floor so he could scuttle back, it didn't work.

"Stop moving. I don't want to hurt you."

Cyrus stopped struggling and held still, he looked at Sylvan suspiciously.

"Much better," commented Sylvan as he raised the knife and cut through the rope that bound the silversmith to the pole. The dagger was remarkably sharp, and Sylvan sent a silent thanks to Jorge's spirit that he had maintained the sharp edge even though it was never used.

The rope gave way and Cyrus rocked as he settled on his feet. Bringing his still-bound hands down to pull the material out of his mouth.

"Why?" was the first word he spoke once he was free.

Sylvan didn't answer it. Instead, he moved to Garm and cut him down too.

"Hold out your hands," he ordered. They both held out their hands, and Sylvan quickly cut the rope that bound their wrists. They were both completely free. "Wait over there." Surprisingly, neither argued and moved to the indicated spot. Sylvan came to stand before Hadrian again. "I have to go now, but I need you to remember something." He leaned in closer and lowered his voice. "You will pay for what you did, but not in the way you think. You will always be second best, even if I no longer serve the First Elder, and I will always be able to find the girl and you won't."

Hadrian growled through the cloth and Sylvan chuckled. He turned on his heels and moved to the two waiting men. He had many misgivings about aiding them after what they had done to him, but both were not to blame— that was on Hadrian. He lowered his voice, so as the Shaymmi could not hear him.

"Do you know where the pendant is that you used?"

"Over there," Cyrus spoke quietly. He nodded his head to a table.

Sylvan moved to the table and quickly picked up the unattractive amulet and pocketed it. He had an idea that he wanted to try once they were safely away. He walked by both the men and said, "Let's go."

As they moved down the dark corridor with Sylvan in the lead, he told them what was happening. "Cyrus, I saved you because of Aven and Treena. Do not think it for any other reason. I plan on joining them and know where they are heading."

"You know my family?" Cyrus sounded suspicious.

Sylvan stopped and turned. "I know Aven is the girl I searched for. I know she will grow in power once she learns to harness it, and I know it won't be long until the other Shyammi will find her, because she will be like a beacon. I know her trainer is Treena." Sylvan was still careful with his word choice as Garm stood with them. "I can reveal your secret and betrayal if you are happy for Garm to know who you are?"

"No, I believe you." Cyrus gestured forward. "Lead the way. We need to stop at my shop before we head out of Cynsellam."

Sylvan looked over to Garm. "Can you get us out of the monastery quickly and as unseen as possible?"

"Yes," Garm spoke. "Thank you for rescuing me," he added.

"You are a servant and have no say over how you are used. I should have treated mine better," was all Sylvan said in way of explanation as to why he had rescued Garm. "I will lead us out into the library, as I am allowed there. Once out of the library, Garm, you take the lead. By my estimations, the half sixth chime is about to peel and we need to be away before the place starts to have monks moving around everywhere."

With Garm in the lead, it had not taken them long to exit the monastery via the servant entrance and reach Cyrus's shop. Garm and Cyrus waited outside, pretending to peruse the window while they waited for the Silversmith to grab whatever he needed. While they waited, a patrol of monks walked by. Thankfully the market square had begun to fill with the stall holders and workers and they took little notice of the two looking into the window of the silversmith shop. Finally Cyrus emerged, a heavy cloak now around his shoulders, even though the morning was turning warm, and handed Sylvan and Garm cloaks.

"Did my family head toward the docks?" Cyrus asked Sylvan.

"That was where they were planning on going." Sylvan reluctantly took off his fine cloak and looked around. A street cleaner nearby looked to be finishing up his shift and heading home. Sylvan handed him the cloak.

The man bobbed his head and scuttled away.

Cyrus watched the exchange and then went to the subject of Treena. "I have a good idea where they would have gone to get help." Cyrus then took the lead and they made their way to the wharf side of Cynsellam. As they passed a double storied tavern, an Inn keeper with a green apron and round face called to them from the open window. "Master Silversmith, my wife has baked your favourite. Come and try a morning pie before you start your day," he beckoned.

"Very well." Cyrus changed direction and walked into the tavern, Sylvan and Garm followed. There were two other patrons in the tavern and Sylvan guessed that they were regulars as they were tucked into a corner, eating their morning pie and taking no heed of what was occurring.

They were shown to a table in the front corner. As they settled into their seats, the green-aproned man lowered his voice as he swiped the water marked table with a cloth. "I got your friends away and was warned to have a craft ready for you. I will escort you to the boat as it should be prepared by the time you have finished the breakfast pie."

"Thank you. You have done exceptionally well on such short notice."

Sylvan spoke quietly. "Can I enquire as to how many of his friends left together?"

"Five." The round-faced man stood and asked loudly, "Ale, cider, tea, goat's milk?"

Sylvan ordered tea, while the other two ordered cider. They sat, tensely waiting for something to happen. No one spoke.

Thankfully, a thin, friendly looking woman emerged from the kitchen expertly carrying three metal plates.

"Here ye go." She plonked the pies down and walked away to retrieve the jugs of cider from the bar. "The tea 'll take a moment longer," she announced and left again.

They quickly ate the pies and Sylvan marveled at the flaky pastry and egg and pork filling. It was light, yet hearty and quickly filled his stomach. His tea arrived and he was happy to find it strong and sweet, just the way he liked it. Within a quarter chime, their meal was done and they were ready to leave when a patrol of monks stood out the front of the tavern. The men waited for them to leave, but they didn't budge. They attempted to look nonchalant as they took it in turns to look out the window, but in reality, they were getting desperate. Sylvan had made arrangements to not be disturbed for the majority of the day so he would not be missed, but he had no idea how long it would be until Cyrus and Garm's disappearance would be discovered.

Garm stood up and looked at the two men. He turned to Sylvan. "Thank you, for rescuing me, I will forever be grateful." He turned to Cyrus, "Thank you for being my friend and disobeying Hadrian. I too will always owe you a debt."

Cyrus's eyes narrowed. "What are you planning on doing?"

"I'm going to cause a distraction."

"You'll get yourself killed. I can't have that."

Sylvan noted the real concern in the Master Silversmith's voice.

"Just be ready to leave. I have places I can hide."

Before more could be said, Garm moved to the tavern keeper and spoke to him quietly. The round-faced man frowned but nodded his head. They both moved toward the door. The inn keeper handed Garm a bottle and shook his hand. Sylvan watched with growing understanding. Garm walked out the door and moved past the patrol of monks. Once he was clear of them and several yards away, the inn keeper stepped out the door and yelled, "Thief! Stop him!"

The monks reacted instantly, and with Garm taking off at a sprint and the inn keeper bellowing and pointing in his direction, there could be no confusion with who he was accusing. Sylvan quickly gathered his cloak around him and followed Cyrus to the door. They waited until the people who had stopped to gawk went back to their business and then left the tavern. Around the corner they waited for the tavern keeper to join them and lead them down to the docks.

Without preamble or further issues, they boarded a small boat and were ushered below deck where they stayed until they reached East Monns. Sylvan spent a great deal of that journey sleeping or reflecting on his choice to throw everything away for an unknown future. It still baffled him as to why he had done it.

Chapter 60
Hadrian

Shaymmi Hadrian was terrified. She couldn't recall a time where fear gripped her so tightly. The dawning of what could happen to her was making it hard for her to breathe. She swayed from ever increasing dread of her current situation to loathing the man who could have freed her and chose not to. Sylvan had swept in, released the two men who had betrayed her and then left. While Hadrian hung there, she tried to think through why he had done it. They had all been complicit in their actions against him. And he freed them of his own accord, simply to punish her, or had he done it on orders of the First Elder, so she could fully understand her predicament? She moved slightly and whimpered through the material stuffed into her mouth as her shoulders blazed with sharp pain. Hadrian didn't know what time it was, how long she had been there or how much more she could endure. She would cry if she could, but terror had robbed her of that reaction.

Hadrian slowly lifted her head, as to attempt to not cause further pain, for she thought she heard footsteps coming toward her. A flaming torch flickered its telling light down the corridor and soon the glow of it filled her space of the dungeon. There were exclamations and accusations as it became apparent that the First Elder had not ordered the release of Cyrus and Garm.

"What happened?" Albin demanded

The wad of material was taken from her mouth by one of the monks. Hadrian's mouth was so dry that she could do no more than cough and wheeze out a few syllables. A flask of water was brought to her and poured into her mouth—they didn't care how much they spilled on her in the process. After a few gulps they stopped and she tried again. "It was Sylvan." She took great delight in speaking those words.

"I beg your pardon." Albin stepped threateningly closer.

Hadrian laughed—she no longer had anything to lose. If she played this right, she might still get out of this with more than just her life.

"It was your precious Master Shaymmi. I told you that they were lying, and that I was telling the truth. They were all in it together, and I was set up."

The First Elder looked at her and they both knew she was lying, but what he did about it was what mattered. Would he take the opportunity to save face?

"It would seem that you have revealed a great travesty, a plan to discredit you," he finally spoke. "Get her off that thing."

Once Hadrian had been cut off the pole and her limbs had stopped trembling, she spoke. "He came in very early and let them go and took something off that table—I am assuming the amulet—and left again. He didn't linger and said very little, but he did take a few moments to gloat." Hadrian seethed with the thought of Sylvan standing before her, his words playing through her thoughts.

Quickly, Albin moved to the table and swore loudly. No one but Hadrian was shocked with his language. He obviously used it more frequently when he was alone and his guards witnessed it regularly. "He did take the amulet. I wonder what he could want with it?"

Hadrian remained silent, choosing not to risk saying anything wrong at this time.

Albin moved closer to her and studied her for several moments. "You will be taken to your suite. You will stay there and do my bidding and work to find the girl. Sylvan gave me directions on where to find her when he woke up, and I have been directing the search in that area. It has not yielded anything as of yet."

"He could have given you misleading information on purpose," she said cautiously. "The girl could still be in Hamlyn or somewhere completely different." Another thought occurred to her and she tossed up whether to say anything.

"Go on, you look like you want to add something."

"What happens if there is no girl and it was all a hoax?"

"To what end?"

Hadrian lowered her eyes and studied the floor. She didn't like what she was about to say. "To draw me out, to make me jealous enough to push me to play the game." She didn't know whether it was true or not, but she wanted the First Elder to believe it as she was worn out trying to find the girl and had bitterly come to terms while hanging on the pole that she would never be capable of finding her.

"That is appearing more probable."

"While we all now look for the girl, we are not doing our primary task for you." She continued to look at the ground. "Maybe that is part of Sylvan's plan?"

"Look up, Master Shaymmi Hadrian, and listen to me carefully."

Master Shaymmi Hadrian hid her satisfied smile with the elevation of her status as she raised her head. "Yes, Your Holiness. I live to serve."

"See that you do. I will not tolerate any more of this behavior. I want the twins trained. There is to be no more delaying of that because you feel it an inconvenience. Is that clear?"

"Yes, Your Holiness." Hadrian curtsied deeply. "I am grateful that you have chosen forgiveness for faults." As she stood straight, she considered her options and the best way to ingratiate her way back into his good graces.

"The church forgives, Master Shaymmi, and I must lead by example," he said with a complete lack of real compassion in his tone.

"While Sylvan let the others go, he said something to me which I don't understand, and I thought perhaps you might want to hear it to make your own judgment on?"

"Go on."

"He looked at me and said, 'You have changed things that can never be unchanged and put in motion a new era.'" She omitted the part regarding her complete lack of ignorance. "What do you think he meant?" She shivered as the combination of the cold of the underground room and the wet top section of her dress from the careless monk with his water flask began to chill her skin.

"Are you cold, my Master Shaymmi?" He completely ignored what she had just said. *Did he already know what Sylvan had alluded to?* She wandered.

"Yes," she spoke quietly, not certain of the tone of his voice and the implications.

"Good, remember that. Remember the ache of your arms and shoulders and the dryness of your mouth and standing there in your own filth, because if you defy me in any way, I shall drag you down here, strip you naked, and leave you tied to that pole to rot forever."

Hadrian closed her eyes against the humiliation she felt at knowing that everyone in the room could probably smell her soiled body. Tears threatened as they hadn't before, but she swallowed them down, her father's face floating before her. *Never let them see your fears or tears, be stronger, be better.* He would bark those words at her if she got upset growing up. Straightening her shoulders and opening her eyes, she reminded herself that she was now the Master Shaymmi and all of Duthyne would soon know that, including the disgraced Sylvan. No one need know the price she would pay for the title and that it had cost her a man she had come to care for greatly.

Chapter 61

Treena

The morning light shone through the slightly ajar window on the second floor of the farmhouse. It warmed Treena's face and pushed her into wakefulness. The owners of the farmhouse were Elldean Stignasfon and Elldean Ferron, a middle-aged married couple who ran a peach tree plantation on the outskirts of East Monns. It was a delight to be able to stretch and roll over to allow the sun to fully cross her face, but to not have to get up and be anywhere.

Treena lay in the bed thinking. She considered all the information she had and what she had risked and accomplished since Aven had entered her life. Decisions needed to be made and the quiet, unassuming florist was not capable of making the difficult ones. However, the trained Dalinda with the ability to manipulate water was more than capable of taking on the wrath that the Church of the One True God was about to hurl at them. It was a daunting idea, but after seeing the way in which Aven's father had treated his children and the way the Deacon of Namurrn had wanted to protect his people, it was time to stop doubting herself and her choices, and just get on with it.

It was the fourth morning since their escape from Cynsellam and Treena finally felt that she may have a better understanding of what had transpired and who had betrayed whom. Sylvan and Cyrus had arrived two days prior. The first thing Sylvan had done was get a ribbon from Treena and tie the ugly pendant around Aven's wrist. He had explained that he didn't have the strength to enter the Elemental Plane at the moment but believed that she would be safe from the searching Shaymmi while she wore it. He would make certain of this when he felt better. After that, Sylvan had undertaken the task of explaining what had happened to him, from the first time he had encountered Aven till now. He had then taken to his bed, and other than eating he had slept. The toll his body and spirit had taken being separated for so long was obviously harder on him than first thought.

There was a polite tap on the door and Braith's voice called softly, "Are you awake?"

"Yes, you can open the door."

The door creaked open and Braith stuck his head in and smiled at her. "I thought you might like to know that Elldean Stiann arrived about a chime ago. They are waiting for you, but didn't want to disturb you."

"Thanks, I'll be there shortly. Do you think you can grab me something to eat, please?"

"I am forever doing favors for you." Braith pretended to be aggrieved. "Yes, I suppose I could find you some food." He closed the door before she could come back with a witty response.

Treena pulled the covers back and quickly washed herself and got dressed. She was hoping to speak to Stiann to confirm her suspicions regarding Aven and Matthias. She had waited until now to broach it but she wanted to know why the First Elder had been sure that Cyrus was the one to blame for revealing that Thedra was a Dalinda. That thought made her nauseous so she had put it off. Now, she could no longer do that. Decisions needed to be made.

She made her way down the stairs and into the large area where they had been taking their meetings. Braith handed her a plate with bread, cheese, and peach slices on it as she came to the last step.

He bowed mockingly and muttered, "My Lady."

"Thank you, kind sir." She pretended he was being genuine and inclined her head in thanks.

Treena sat at the large table and took a slice of peach. Aven came to join her, she carried a book.

"I see you are continuing your reading practice."

The others that had been standing around the room, talking in groups, came to sit around the table. Cyrus and the twins joined them as well as their hosts Elldean Stignafson and his wife Elldean Ferron. A few moments later, Stiann came down the stairs and was followed by a crumpled Master Shaymmi Sylvan. They were all assembled. Treena looked around. It was an odd assortment of people and very rare to have two Elldean and three Dalinda in one area.

Elldean Stiann was thrilled to see Treena and greeted her with a warm hug.

"It is good to see you safe, and it appears your rescue mission went well and you brought back some extras."

Matthias smiled, Matteo scowled, and Sylvan nodded, a small smile on his cleanly shaven face. Treena returned their looks with smiles of her own, choosing to ignore the scowl of Matteo.

"A few unexpected things came up while in Cynsellam, and a very unusual one in Namurrn. We met Thedra's love, to begin with."

"You did?" Stiann was surprised. "And?"

"And he is the Deacon of Namurrn."

Cyrus was the first to react. "No, I find that impossible. She never trusted the Church."

Stiann gave a different response. "Well, that would explain why she was always so quick to change the subject when I asked about him."

"He is a kind man, who is disillusioned by the leadership of the One Church and how it allows its monks to behave. In my opinion, he would make a fine First Elder."

"Anyone would make a better one than the one we have," muttered Matteo.

"I couldn't agree more," added Sylvan. "He is using the artifacts we find to reverse his aging."

Stiann leaned forward. "Can you tell me more?"

"I watched him hold a beautiful helmet, clearly Dalinda in origin, that lost its color and then gradually turned to a fine ash in his hands while his face changed and gained youthfulness."

Everyone around the table shifted uncomfortably at that news.

Sylvan coughed and looked to Treena. "I am sorry to cause you pain when you have been nothing but kind and generous, but I must inform you that the same thing happened to Thedra."

There were gasps and denials as people tried to understand what Sylvan had just stated. He explained what he had seen in the dungeon.

While the Elldean discussed the revelation with Sylvan, Treena looked to Cyrus. He was staring at the table and looked to be struggling for breath.

"You want to tell them what you did or should I?" She spoke loud enough for everyone to stop talking and look at her. She sat there, glaring at him.

Cyrus looked up and went to speak.

Treena talked over the top of him. "And before you try to say I misunderstood, remember that Braith, Aven, and Sylvan all witnessed it too."

Cyrus swallowed hard and looked back to the table top. "I don't know why I did it. I usually go to confession and ramble off some nonsense to keep the father happy and leave. I don't know why I just blurted it out."

Stiann looked sternly at Cyrus. "What have you done?"

"I am the reason for Thedra's death, and why they know the Dalinda exist."

Treena spoke. "He went to confessional and told them to check the eyes of the traitor."

"That was you? Do you have any idea what you have done?"

Cyrus looked lost. "I am beginning to."

"I can understand why you helped hide Sylvan's body and created that whole mess, but to reveal our secret is beyond comprehension. You have put us all in danger, and Aven is not trained to handle it and there will be a young man discovering his abilities at some point over the next few years who will be in greater danger than ever before." Treena was angry.

Cyrus stood, knocking his chair backwards. This brought Braith to his feet. "You cannot speak to me like that."

Treena stood calmly, drawing herself up to her full height, which was a few inches taller than Cyrus. "I will speak to you however I wish. I think your title has gone to your head. Let me be clear; I carry the same title as you and so does Aven and you caused the death of your mentor." She pointed vehemently at him.

Cyrus sat down and crossed his arms like a sulky child. Braith and Treena also returned to their seats.

"The full Dalinda Council will need to be informed of this." Elldean Stignafson spoke up. "Your behavior, Lord Cyrus, cannot be ignored."

Cyrus continued to sulk.

"Well, I have some interesting information for our Master Shaymmi and his two Shaymmi-in-training." Stiann changed the topic. "Lady Katatreena and I had discussed the possibility of them being not who they think they are. I also went to Namurrn, but to speak to another Elldean and to discover what her collection of scrolls say on the subject." He turned to the three Shaymmi. "Gentlemen, you are not Shaymmi at all. I believe it to be a name that was created by the church. I am uncertain if today's First Elder is aware of your true nature and origins. I find it difficult to believe, after knowing his feelings about the Dalinda, that he would keep you around if he understood who you really are."

Elldean Ferron interrupted his musings. "Stop talking in riddles and get on with it."

"You are not Shaymmi, you are the lost Shomma. The beings capable of traveling the Elemental Planes and the Keepers of Oredmoor," he announced.

He was greeted with stunned silence.

"You think we are the fabled Shomma?" Sylvan was incredulous.

"That is ridiculous."

"It explains Aven's reaction to Matthias," Treena chimed in.

Braith looked confused. "How?"

Stiann explained. "The Dalinda and their Shomma work closely together with one Oredmoor."

"Their Shomma?"

"Yes, there is a connection between a Shomma and a Dalinda. The Shomma is always older and trained in the basics of Oredmoor care before the powers of the Dalinda usually surface. For each Dalinda there is a Shomma, but not the other way around." He looked at Aven and Matthias, who probably had unconsciously chosen to sit next to each other. "Matthias is Aven's Shomma. They are connected and that is why she is not frightened of him, when she is typically terrified of men."

Cyrus uncrossed his arms and stared and sat forward. "Shaymmi Hadrian was, *is*, my Shomma? I felt an instant connection to her when we met. I thought it was just sexual attraction."

"At your age, I can see why you might confuse it with that. But I am certain that Aven's connection to Matthias is far more pure and about respect and protection."

Treena pondered what Stiann had said. "Hang on, you said that each Dalinda has a Shomma, but not the other way around. What do you mean?"

"Sylvan, are any of your peers your age?" Stiann asked the former Shaymmi.

"No, I sit in the middle of two sets of Shaymmi or Shomma."

"And what about the Master Shaymmi before you?"

"I am not certain."

Mathias cleared his throat. "He also sat age wise between two sets of Shaymmi."

Everyone looked at him. Matthias shrugged. "I like the library."

"They are the Elldean's favorite places too," agreed Stignafson.

"If there were still Oredmoor, Sylvan would be the Master Shomma, capable of communicating on the Elemental Plane with all of the Oredmoor, not just his Dalinda's."

Treena noted for the first time that Matteo's face didn't look angry or annoyed—he looked hesitant.

"The male Dalinda, that is yet to come into his powers, will be Matteo's?" She asked the question she knew he wouldn't.

"Yes, exactly."

Curiosity got the better of Treena and she turned to Sylvan. "If Hadrian is Cyrus's Dalinda, then who is mine?"

"His name is Wout. Everyone was wary of Hadrian and her ambition and everyone warms to Wout immediately. It's like he cares for everyone he comes into contact with."

Stiann laughed. "Sounds perfect for Treena. She too cares for everyone that she comes in contact with."

Braith stood abruptly. "I need to get some fresh air," he announced and left the room.

Aven looked to Treena and smiled.

"Don't say it," Treena muttered.

Chapter 62

Treena

The meeting concluded not long after Braith had left to get some air. Cyrus had excused himself, probably before anyone could question him further about his choices and the three revealed Shomma began to ask more pointed questions of the Elldean. Treena picked up her now empty plate, and with the excuse of taking it to the kitchen she left the conversation. She quickly washed the plate and left it out on the sink to dry and then went out the back door in the hopes of finding Braith.

The heat of the mid morning sun was strong, and Treena removed the light shawl she had been wearing in the house, folded it neatly and left it on the railing of the steps that went down into the peach orchard. She looked amongst the fruiting peach trees to see a pair of trousered legs in the distance. Treena set off in the direction of the legs. It didn't take her long to ascertain that the legs belonged to Braith—he had boots she would recognize almost anywhere. As she approached, he had his back to her and he didn't turn, even though it was clear that someone was moving toward him.

"Hello?" she said softly.

"Hi." Braith tilted his head back and watched several birds circle lazily above them.

Treena refrained from rolling her eyes and made her way to stand in front of him. He refused to look at her. She looked up to the birds.

"Do you know what breed they are?" She attempted to make conversation.

"No."

"So, are we going to talk about it, or are you going to give me short answers for the rest of the day?" she asked.

"Talk about what?" Braith continued to gaze upward.

"Ah, great. You are going the childish route."

"Fine. Let's talk about it." He brought his head down to look at her.

They stood there for several moments. Now she had started the conversation, she wasn't sure what to say next.

Braith reached up and grazed the back of his hand along her cheekbone. "Can you take those glass things out without a mirror so I can see your proper eyes?"

Treena dug around in the pocket of her tunic, she had not put a kerchief square in. "I don't have anything to put them in."

Braith pulled out his own kerchief. "Will this do?"

"Yes, thank you. Just hold it in your palm for a moment." Carefully Treena took the colored glass lenses from her eyes, revealing the telltale golden eyes of a Dalinda underneath. She popped each lens into the kerchief and deftly folded it before delicately placing it in her pocket.

"I was jealous," Braith admitted as she returned to looking at him.

"Yes, I gathered that. Though, I don't understand why. I was curious about him, that is all."

"It is hard to explain. But it feels odd to know that somewhere in the monastery in Cynsellam is a man who is connected to you in a way I could never be. You heard Sylvan describe him. You match him."

"Even if for some reason I meet Wout, he will never have the trust and years of friendship I have with you. You must also hear Stiann when he said not all connections have a sexual component." Treena boldly reached out and took his hand. "You are the most precious friend I have."

"What would you say if I said I wanted to be more than friends?"

It was her turn to reach up and gently brush his hair away from his eyes. "I would say that even though I find that thought appealing, I don't know if it would be smart for us to start something. You need to go back to Hamlyn to run your business, check up on my kids, and make sure Aven's siblings and my parents are safe." She paused, not liking what she had to say next. "I don't know what we are going to do from here. Plans will have to be made, but we will need to keep moving as Sylvan and Cyrus as well as Aven will be hunted. We need to find a safe place to gather and make further decisions. I will not be returning to Hamlyn any time soon."

He leaned in and kissed her. She wound her fingers into his hair and returned the kiss, pouring her want and desire into it. His hands held her waist and pulled her against him, the tension between their bodies almost hummed. Somewhere, in a small corner of her mind she wondered if the feeling was normal or was it more pronounced because of her elemental powers. Sylvan had described them as vibrations before.

They pulled apart and Braith rested his forehead on Treena's. "You sure you don't want to start something?" He kissed her again before she could answer.

When they pulled apart Treena spoke first. "I never said I didn't want to start something, I said it wouldn't be smart."

He grinned at her. "So, what you are saying is...?"

This time she kissed him with all the passion she had, and when the kiss finally ended, both were breathing heavily. "I don't know what I am saying. Could we just kiss and figure out the rest later?"

Braith stared at her, longing clear on his face. "Your eyes are glorious. I wish you didn't have to hide them. They are the true you."

Treena had no reply for that, so she just smiled shyly at him. She never knew what to do when given a compliment.

His face changed expression and she tried to decipher what it meant.

"Though, those eyes are also the reason we have to be apart and that your life is not as simple as I thought it was."

"I can't change who I am. Not that I want to."

"And I would never ask you to. It was more an observation."

"Let's stop talking. It has been established that we can't change anything."

Braith raised an eyebrow at her. "What would you prefer we do?"

"Hush and just kiss me."

Chapter 63
Treena

Treena held her ground as the young man rushed at her. *Really?* she thought to herself as she stepped to the side, turning slightly, leaving one foot out for him to trip on as she put her hands on his back as he passed her, ending with a hefty shove. He landed with a heavy thud and groaned as he rolled onto his side and caught his breath.

"How do you keep doing that?" Matteo asked, his voice filled with awe.

"I am using your own momentum against you." She held out her hand to help him up. "And you have to stop rushing at me. Unless we are in a confined space, it won't work. You can use your bulk to tackle a person, but only if you can catch them."

He let her help him up and they both watched as Aven instructed Matthias in some very basic footwork, while he held a wooden dagger.

"This is all very odd," Matteo commented, almost to himself.

"Yes, I guess it is to someone who was on a very different trajectory a few days ago."

"I am not sure what I think about it all." Matteo watched as his twin joked with Aven.

"It will take some adjusting, but I think you will get there, as we all do when we are called." Treena felt philosophical.

"What makes you so sure?" The familiar scowl appeared on his face.

"The Elemental Gods choose us, so we must have faith that they know our true selves."

His dark brown eyebrows raised up in surprise. "Mmmm, you still think that, even though it appears that Cyrus revealed your secret and has put you all in danger? He seems to be a bit full of his own importance compared to you. And you say the Elemental Gods chose him?"

Treena couldn't help it, she began to laugh. It was good to laugh and she hadn't done it in so long.

"Well, when you put it like that."

Matteo managed to smile at her, but did not join in the laughter.

"The Dalinda, like anyone else, still have their foibles and own free will. I think the Elemental Gods pick people who will sacrifice for the greater good. But the Dalinda have been idle too long and some of us probably dream of what we could have been if born in a different time."

"Not you?"

"No, I was content with my flock. I liked the training and the little things that made my life easier. Yet, in the end, it was the fact that it afforded me the ability to look after the ones who couldn't look after themselves, and I would have been happy to do that in Hamlyn forever."

Matteo smirked. "And you could have married Braith."

Treena laughed again. "I don't know if Braith is really the settling down and marrying kind. You do know who he is in Hamlyn, don't you?"

Aven and Matthias had joined them.

"Now, I am curious. What does he do?" asked Matthias.

"He is the Master of the thieves," Aven announced cheerily.

This time Matteo laughed. "Oh, that is brilliant. A criminal and a Dalinda."

"Yes, yes, very funny." Treena tried to look stern, but the grin she fought to suppress didn't help her cause.

Sylvan stuck his head out the back door. "You lot about done? I would like to discuss a few things and get plans rolling. We can't hide here forever."

"Yes, we have finished for now. Matteo can try and beat me again tomorrow," Treena teased. She was pleased to see a look of determination cross his face rather than petulance.

They gathered their belongings and made their way through the kitchen and into the main living area of the farmhouse. Braith and Stignafson were sitting in a corner, chatting quietly, while Stiann quickly gathered up the scrolls he had been studying and stacked them neatly on a bookshelf. Ferron had laid out several pitchers of fresh water and bowls of assorted nuts and dried fruits. Cyrus was coming down the stairs to join them.

The group moved to sit around the table and were joined by the others already in the room. Braith sat next to Treena and took her hand under the table and gave it a gentle squeeze.

Stiann sat at the end of the table, with the other two Elldean on either side of him. Sylvan took the place on the other side of Treena, while the twins and Aven sat opposite. Cyrus sat at the other end of the table.

"I wanted to discuss with you what should be done next. Who needs to be informed formally of the current situation and what should be left to just filter through the Loyalists, as it always has. I am open for discussion on anything."

Sylvan cleared his throat. "Would it be worth our while trying to get word to the Shaymmi that they are being used by the First Elder and that their gifts are not for him to abuse for his own uses?"

"I'm not sure if there is any point at this time and it puts someone at risk. Would they believe just anybody if we sent someone to inform them?" mused Stiann.

"I hadn't thought of that," admitted Sylvan. "Probably not. They would probably only believe me."

"And to be perfectly blunt, I want to spend some time studying you and watching you instruct the boys about the Elemental Plane, so I don't believe there is any cause for you to go back to the monastery anytime soon." Stiann was honest.

The other two Elldean nodded their agreeance.

No one spoke for several moments. Treena broke the silence. "We need to call a full Dalinda Council meeting. They need to be informed of Cyrus's part in this current situation as well as meet the rediscovered Shomma."

"That hasn't been done in a century." Elldean Stignafson reminded her.

"And your point? I think it is time to stop hiding. We will deal with Cyrus, but we can't change what he has done." Treena felt that bluntness was perhaps the only way to get her point across to these people, who had become too comfortable hiding. Her discussions with Aven over the journey here had made her come to the harsh reality that they may have just been resting on their laurels, rather than doing something purposeful with their power. "The First Elder knows we exist. He will send people out to hunt us. We can no longer escape that fact. We can only be prepared."

No one looked at Cyrus, everyone just shifted in their seats uncomfortably.

Elldean Stiann looked at Treena like he was a proud father. "I take it you have been giving this some consideration?"

"Yes, we have been trained to lead and look after the people. I think it's time we did just that. Of course, it will have to be done with stealth and ingenuity, but I am certain between the Council, the Elldean, and now the Shomma, we can come up with ways to help our cause and hinder Albin's."

"And you have some thoughts on how?" Stiann urged.

"We need to change the narrative to one that suits us. The church teaches that there is One God and that the Dalinda were eliminated for their hubris. The word will spread that we are back, whether the church likes it or not. Let us help it make us look more appealing than the current ruler." She paused and noted they were all intently listening to her. This would have made her falter, now it gave her strength that what she said was worthwhile. "We have the Loyalists begin to surreptitiously start to talk to people about the old ways. Encourage lighting a candle on the festivals we aren't allowed to celebrate and have it showing in the front window. You can't get in trouble for having a candle burning and enjoying a song with your family over a nice meal. Have the bards amongst us start to sing the old songs, the ones about the heroics of the Oredmoor and Dalinda. They can change the lyrics so it is implied. The people are worn out and live in fear. The church keeps demanding and people are growing desperate. They need hope."

"Clever and passive ideas. All well thought out. Reza would be proud." Stignafson winked. "What about the Dalinda Council?"

"We meet at the Compound. I will head there now with the Shomma and Aven and keep their training up. It would be a bad idea if we all traveled there at once, as the place is supposed to be abandoned."

"Is it empty?" asked Mathias.

"No, there are always a few Elldean and Loyalists in residence, for just this reason. They rotate people through every year as it is so isolated," answered Elldean Ferron.

"I will be going with Treena," announced Stiann. "To help with the tutoring of the Shomma and Aven."

Cyrus sat a little taller in his chair. "I will go with them. As the Dalinda are being called to council, I will help make the Compound ready to receive them all."

Elldean Stiann nodded his agreement and turned to Braith. "What will you do, Braith?"

"I am heading back to Hamlyn. Lady Katatreena has left a flock of children that I will now see too, and her and Aven's families will need to be protected. I will meet with the Loyalist group there and put her plan into action. Someone will also need to be found to replace Ezekiel in the Hamlyn monastery. On the way, I will also stop at Namurrn and explain the situation to our friends."

Treena tried to ignore the lonely feeling that had settled in the pit of her stomach as she continued to grasp his hand under the table.

Stiann looked around the room. "Well, that is all settled then. Any final questions before we start sending out messages to call the Elemental Council to order for the first time in over a century?"

Aven looked to Treena as if she wanted to speak. "Go on, Aven. Do you have something to ask or add?"

The young girl who was healing and growing in confidence daily, especially now that she was not the only student since Matteo and Mathias had joined her in combat training as well as studies, spoke clearly. Most of her street accent was gone. "I don't know if it is a question or just something I don't understand."

"That doesn't matter. Just say it," encouraged Ferron, who had taken to mothering and fussing over Aven.

"I was just thinking that if the Dalinda and Shomma still exist, then wouldn't it stand to reason that the Oredmoor still exist too? Or what would be the point of the other two being born still?"

All the adults in the room sat staring at her, dumbfounded.

THE END

For Now

Water; Book 2, Sky Hunter Saga
Pre-order
Now

THE FIGHT FOR SURVIVAL HAS BEGUN

Glossary

Albin - The First Elder
Aleeya - Aven's sister
Amina - Shaymmi
Aria - Goddess of Air. Also, one of the Islands in the Elemental Archipelago
Arum - Sylvan's father
Astind - Town in Duthyne
Artious - Glass Blower in Cynsellam
Aveline - Member of the Elemental Council
Aven - Member of the Elemental Council
Basbrugge - A city in Duthyne
Blane - Member of the Elemental Council
Braith - Master of thieves in Hamlyn
Bree - Young girl in Hamlyn
Brohim - Town in Duthyne
Calantha - Member of the Elemental Council
Chalyx - God of Metal. Also, one of the Islands in the Elemental Archipelago
Chunky – Patron of Fion's brothel
Churlirenn - Town in Duthyne
Cynsellam - Capital of Duthyne
Cyrus - Member of the Elemental Council
Dacrow - Aven's brother
Dalinda - A member of the Elemental Council and a Sky Rider
Dasnee - Member of the Elemental Council
Den Keepers - Carers of the Oredmoor
Deek - Street kid in Hamlyn
Derkop – Bartender in Fion's Brothel

Dinaden - Member of the Elemental Council
Dinnant - City in Duthyne
Double Bay - North in Duthyne
Double Ridge Mountain Range - Simply known as Double
Ridge. It is the natural border between Duthyne and
Teongaras.
Dunelm - Town in Duthyne
Duthyne - A country on the Continent of Sota
Dyella - Aven's sister
East Teur Landing - Town in Duthyne
East Monns - Town in Duthyne
Elemental Archipelago - consists of 5 islands (Aria, Loam,
Pyre, Torrent and Chalyx)
Elldean - Lore Keepers for the Dalinda
Emilia - Florist in Hamlyn
Eteswan - City in Teongaras
Ferron - Elldean, married to Stignasson
Fion - Aven's father
Forewaay - City in Duthyne
Freya - Deek's older sister
Gannblers Gulch - A colossal ravine with a river at the
bottom used as the natural border of Yanf and Duthyne
Gryff - Arch Deacon of Ostville
Hadrian - Shaymmi
Hailey - Young street kid in Hamlyn
Hamlyn - Port City in Duthyne
Haselt - Small town in Duthyne
Illyius - Cardinal of the Monk Warriors
Inaya - Shaymmi
Inderbeck - Port City in Duthyne
Jarleth - Member of the Elemental Council
Jeska - Aven's sister
Jocastta - Arch Deacon of Dinnant

Jodan - Loyalist in Namurrn. Married to Nikolina
Jorge - Servant of Sylvan
Kassian - Master Goldsmith, lived a century before.
Katatreena - Member of the Elemental Council
Kauberr - Town in Duthyne
Kets Harbour - next to the City of Hamlyn in Duthyne
Lake Burloc - Large lake on the edge of the Oakshore
Forest in Duthyne
Lanae - Aven's sister
Landwin - Cardinal
Learah - Shaymmi
Leonora - Sylvan's eldest sister
Loam - God of Earth, also one of the Islands in the
Elemental Archipelago
Lowie - Shaymmi
Mathias - Trainee Shaymmi, Twin brother of Matteo
Matteo - Trainee Shaymmi, Twin brother of Mathias
Menura - Town in the Razor Ridge Mountain Range
Menuridae Falls - Massive waterfall system that begins next
to Menura and ends in Lake Burloc
Mignus - Master Silversmith, retired in Ostville
Milian - Arch Deacon of Basbrugge
Mirendabaen - Town of Duthyne
Namurrn - Large Town in Duthyne
Nels - Arch Deacon of Forewaay
Nikolina - Loyalist in Namurrn. Married to Jodan
No Man's Land - the border between Yanf and Duthyne
Norkdon - Town in Duthyne
Oakshore Forest - In the north of Duthyne
Obadiah - Arch Deacon of West Monns
Oberst - Aven's brother
Oredmoor - Sky Hunters
Ostville - Town in Duthyne

Ostville - Town in Duthyne
Otto - Sylvan's brother-in-law, married to Sanno
Parisa - Pastor that runs the servants at the monastery in Hamlyn.
Piress - Glassblower who makes contacts for Aven and glasses for Stiann.
Pyre - Goddess of Fire, also one of the Islands in the Elemental Archipelago
Rayan - Shaymmi
Reza - Member of the Elemental Council
Sanno - Sylvan's sister
Sarst Bay - sits between Teongaras and Duthyne
Seene - Shaymmi
Shaymmi - Specialised employees of The First Elder
Shomma - Custodians of a Dalinda and their Oredmoor
Sorenn - Arch Deacon of Inderbeck
Stiann - Part of the Elldean
Stignasfon - Elldean, married to Ferron
Sylvan - Master Shaymmi
Talitha - Sylvan's mother
Teik - Town in Eastern Duthyne
Teongaras - A country on the Continent of Sota
Thedra - Member of the Elemental Council
Thoreau - Master Silversmith
Tiago - Shaymmi.
Timmy - Young boy for poor quarter in Hamlyn
Titus - Deacon of Namurrn
Torrent - Goddess of Water, also one of the Islands in the Elemental Archipelago
Tristam - Member of the Elemental Council
Ulrik - Arch Deacon of Hamlyn
Vivia - Cardinal

To receive up-to-date information, news and exclusive offers
please sign up for M.M. Reynolds newsletter.

www.mmreynoldsauthor/subscribe.com

Follow M.M. Reynolds on your favorite platform

Website:

https://www.mmreynoldsauthor.com/

TikTok:

https://www.tiktok.com/@mmreynoldsauthor

Facebook:

https://www.facebook.com/mmreynoldsauthor

Instagram:

https://www.instagram.com/mmreynoldsauthor

Bookbub:

https://www.bookbub.com/profile/m-m-reynolds

Goodreads:

https://www.goodreads.com/author/show/35521922.M_M_
Reynolds

Acknowledgments

I would like to take a few moments
to say thank you.

To my children, thank you for
teaching me to let go of the small stuff. I am proud of you.

To my family, thank you for the
love and support you have shown me throughout the years.

To my friends, the ones that have
my back and are forever in my corner – I cherish you.

To my editor, Rochelle J. Simas – Fluffy Fox Publishing.
Thank you for the kind words that
always accompany the return of my fabulously edited manu-
scripts.

To my ARC, Street, Beta, and Proofreader Teams.
You are appreciated.

About M.M. Reynolds

M.M. Reynolds adores reading, traveling and dragons. Classic epic fantasy with grand adventures, harrowing quests, and fated destinies are her favorite things to read and write.

She has studied sci-fi and fantasy writing, and is a sucker for happy endings.

M.M. Reynolds is currently working on a six-book fantasy series, The Sky Hunters, while editing a sweeping epic fantasy trilogy, The Fractured Werld.
There may also be an Atlantis reimagining in the works.

If you like a little, okay, a lot of steam in your fantasy, she also writes steamy classic fantasy and paranormal romance under the pen name Taya Rune.
Taya Rune is a 2 times USA Today Bestseller and has hit #1 on Nook, Apple, and Amazon for her fairytale retellings.
For more information check out her website.

M.M
REYNOLDS
CLASSIC FANTASY AUTHOR